OUTSTAN

"Exhilarating . . . the constant twists will keep the readers hooked. This is a nonstop thrill ride."
—*Publishers Weekly*

"The propulsively paced plot has a definite Lifetime Movie Channel vibe, but Jackson effectively juices things up with plenty of sexy suspense and a generous amount of high-octane thrills."
—*Booklist*

PARANOID
"Jackson gradually builds up the layers of this tangled psychological thriller, leading to a stunning finale. Jackson knows how to keep readers guessing and glued to the page."
—*Publishers Weekly*

LIAR, LIAR
"The author's managing of the past and present separately is an effective method of clue dangling to keep readers in the dark until the huge OMG reveal. Fans of Lisa Gardner, Paula Hawkins, and J.T. Ellison will devour this one-sitting nail-biter."
—*Library Journal,* Starred Review

YOU WILL PAY
"This suspenseful thriller is packed with jaw-dropping twists."
–*InTouch Weekly*

NEVER DIE ALONE
"Jackson definitely knows how to keep readers riveted."
—*Mystery Scene*

TELL ME
"Absolutely tension filled . . . Jackson is on top of her game."
—*Suspense Magazine*

Published by Kensington Publishing Corp.

LISA JACKSON

YOU'LL FIND OUT

ZEBRA BOOKS
Kensington Publishing Corp.
kensingtonbooks.com

Contents

THE SHADOW OF TIME

To Nancy

Chapter 1

Shane Kennedy had been wrong. Dead wrong. He didn't make mistakes often. In fact, he very rarely made mistakes, and the realization that this morning was not only an error in judgment but also an exercise in frustration made him clench his teeth and jut his jaw against the early November morning air. He prided himself in his ability to think clearly, solve problems, handle any situation, *and* avoid costly or time-consuming errors. Yet here he was, doing exactly the opposite of what all of his instincts instructed him to do, caught up in the enticing but bitter nostalgia of the past, acting the part of a fool!

As he leaned against the moss-laden trunk of a barren oak tree, he wondered what had possessed him to come here—it wasn't as if he was welcome. He muttered a silent oath under his breath and watched the scene before him with fascination . . . and contempt. He must have been out of his mind, driving most of the night just to . . . what? he asked himself. To see her again? Talk to her . . . touch her? He snapped his mind closed at the thought with another oath. Damn! He closed his eyes as the cold, familiar sense of betrayal crept silently up his spine, and he hiked the collar of his coat up more closely to his throat as if to ward off the chill of the early winter morning.

Perhaps it was because four lonely years had passed, and time has a way of twisting memories to make them appear more captivating than they actually were. Or perhaps he had just forgotten how mysteriously beautiful she could be. Or, more likely, even in Shane's own estimation, he had secretly hoped that the years would have begun to take their toll on Mara's winsome features and that the signs of age would have started to weather the regal loveliness of her face, making him immune to her beauty. But he had been mistaken—and a fool to even believe that the passion she had once inspired would have died within him. It was a false hope on his part, nothing more. Even now, in the cold, misty morning, cloaked in an unflattering black coat, Mara appeared more serenely beautiful than he had remembered. And if age had caught up with her, it was only to add a determination and a maturity that increased the seductive quality of her elegant beauty. The memories that her presence evoked shattered Shane's resolve.

He had come to the lonely cemetery on impulse, and now he realized the gravity of his mistake. One look at Mara was not enough to satisfy him. His fists balled at his sides as he discovered, to his disgust, that despite the pain of the last four years, he still wanted Mara as desperately as he ever had. The thought made his black eyes spark with contempt. The feeble excuses that had propelled him to the well-manicured cemetery on the hillside were already fading. It was an inexcusable mistake; he should never have come, never have broken into her privacy. But, still, he lingered, unable to take his eyes off of the attractive new widow.

The cold, gray morning was clouded in mist, giving the ceremony an eerie, uneasy quality, and the light dusting of dry snow that covered the ground added to the ethereal feeling that captured Mara. A light breeze tossed the few remaining dry leaves into the air in frozen, swirling circles that spiraled heavenward.

Behind the flimsy protection of the black veil, Mara's cobalt-blue eyes stared down at the gravesite, unseeing. The usual sparkle that lighted her face was gone, replaced by a serious cloud that made her delicate features more tightly pinched than normal. Her skin was still flawless, and her high cheekbones were as regally sculpted as they ever had been, but there was a determined set to her jaw that stole the usual softness from her face. Unconsciously, she licked her arid lips and stared down at the brass casket with dry eyes. In one hand she clutched a single white rose to her black-draped breast, in the other, she clung firmly to the tiny fist of her dark-eyed daughter.

At the final words from the preacher, Mara dropped the snowy blossom onto the coffin and coaxed her reluctant child to do the same. The mourners began to disperse slowly, with only an occasional hoarse whisper of condolence cast in her direction. She smiled grimly behind the thin, black veil and nodded briefly at each of the sympathizers before making her way back to the black limousine that was idling quietly nearby.

Once inside the luxurious car, Angie looked at her mother in a childish imitation of concern. "Is Daddy gone forever, Mommy?"

"Yes, honey—I'm afraid so," Mara responded, and placed a comforting kiss on the child's forehead.

"Good!" Angie snorted.

Mara felt a dry tightness in her throat at the stinging

words of her daughter, although the outburst wasn't totally unexpected. She closed her eyes and in a soft, consoling voice replied, "No, Angie, it's not good . . . why would you say such a thing?"

"Because it's true! Daddy don't like me!" The little girl crossed her chubby arms over her chest in an attitude that dared her mother to argue with her.

"No . . . oh, no . . . that's not the way it was, honey. Not at all. Daddy loved you very much."

The child puckered her lips before shooting Mara a knowing look. Mara swallowed with difficulty and bit nervously at her thumbnail. She wondered how she was going to stave off the inevitable argument that was brewing. How could she lie to her own daughter? Although only three years old, Angie had a keen sense of perception—so like her father's. Once again, Mara tried to reason with the child. "I know that Daddy . . . was a little . . . gruff with you at times, Angie. And, maybe, he was overly grouchy. But honey, you have to remember that Daddy was very, very sick. Sometimes . . . the things that he said, well, he just didn't mean them. You have to believe that Daddy loved you very much."

"Why?" Angie demanded, imperiously.

Mara hazarded a quick glance at the chauffeur, whose bland expression told nothing about his thoughts on the difficult conversation between mother and daughter. "Because . . . oh, honey, Daddy's gone. Can't you just forget the times that you and he quarreled?"

"No!"

"Look, Angie—" Mara's voice became a hushed whisper "—there are going to be a lot of people at the house this afternoon. Please promise Mommy that you'll be good."

"Who?"

"Who?" Mara echoed, confused for an instant. "Oh, you want to know who will be at the house today?" The impish child nodded, tossing her blond curls. "Let's see," Mara began, placing a comforting arm around her wayward daughter's small shoulders. "I know that Grammie and Aunt Dena will be there. Maybe cousin Sarah and . . ." Mara's voice trailed on tonelessly while she listed all of the relatives who would attend the intimate gathering of those closest to Peter. She was relieved that she had managed to change the course of the conversation with Angie, and fervently hoped that the little girl wouldn't bring up the touchy subject of her father for the remainder of the day.

As Mara thought about the afternoon ahead of her, she mentally groaned. It would be trying, at best. The thought of all of Peter's friends and relatives trying to console her made Mara's weary mind whirl. Couldn't they just leave her alone and let her deal with her grief quietly and in solitude? No matter what kind of a marriage she and Peter had shared, being a widow was a new and frightening experience. She needed time alone.

When she thought about widowhood, Mara felt her throat become dry. Although she was relieved that Peter's suffering was over, she felt guilty at the thought. It all seemed so senseless—the malignancy that had forced him into an early grave. Now, after all of the tears had been shed and the suffering had ended, she wondered uneasily if it had been her fault that the marriage had been foundering. Why was it that the only thing that had held Peter to her in the end was the devastating news of his terminal illness? Peter had been kind to her, at least in the beginning, and she couldn't forget that kindness, even if in other ways he had failed. She sighed despondently to herself. What was the use of dredging up old, unwanted memories? Poor Peter was gone, and if it hadn't been for him, what would have happened to her and Angie? Mara looked anxiously at her bright-eyed daughter sitting on the velvet gray upholstery of the long, black car. Angie's eyelids drooped, and the tangled mass of golden ringlets sprang out discordantly from beneath her tiny black hat. It was a shame to dress such a lively child in black, Mara thought, but after all, this was Peter's funeral, a time for mourning, and if Peter hadn't married Mara four years ago, what would she have done? Mara closed her eyes and pushed the nagging question aside. It wouldn't do to dwell on the past. Not today, not ever. How many times had she given herself that very same advice—always for the same reasons.

The driver eased the sleek ebony car through the twisted road of the graveyard, and the motorcade followed his lead. A long, flexible line of cars wound its way past the cemetery gates and down the hill toward Asheville and the Wilcox Estate that bordered the western North Carolinian city.

If Mara hadn't been so distracted with her daughter, perhaps she would have noticed the one mourner who stood slightly apart from the crowd. She had been too busy with Angie to realize that the tall man with the brooding black eyes followed her every move. Even now, as the large limousine made its way toward the city, the man waited and watched. His eyes, dark as obsidian, held a quiet flame in them, and although he tried desperately to deny the urges within him, he knew that he would find a way to get close to Mara again. He would see her again—if only for a short while, he vowed to himself. It had been four long, agonizing years, but Peter Wilcox's untimely death had ended Shane's tormented vigil. Unfortunate for Wilcox, but quite the opposite for Kennedy, Shane thought grimly. His speculations were ruthless, and he felt a slight twinge of conscience but ignored it. He reminded himself that Mara had it coming; nothing could alter that fact and the quiet anger of betrayal smoldering in his mind.

The burning picture of the suffering widow stayed with him and played dangerous games with his mind. The heavy black coat and gracious veil that Mara had worn couldn't hide her serene beauty from him. He could still visualize the slender curve of her calf, the bend of her knee, the swell of her breasts, and the perfection of her face. It was an image that had tormented his nights for over four years. He had been patient—a gentleman in all respects—but now the waiting was over. A slight gleam of satisfaction stole across his angled features.

Shane stood watching the procession of cars, mesmerized. The wind, promising still more snow for the Blue Ridge Mountains, ruffled his thick raven hair, but still he stared into the breeze, mindless of the chill, until the last vehicle passed over the crest in the road and was no longer in view. Damning himself for his own impetuous desires, he strode to his car. It would be better to wait, and he knew it, but there was an urgency to his movements. Once inside the silver Audi he turned the ignition key, and the sporty car roared to life. He paused for a moment, his hands poised over the steering wheel, and uttered a curse at his hesitation, which seemed, somehow, to be a sign of weakness. It was a mistake, but to hell with it, he had to see Mara again, face to face, and find out why she had deceived him four years ago. But it was the day of her husband's funeral, his conscience argued with him—anyone would need a little time to adjust. He ignored the thought, and muttering a low, self-derisive oath, he cranked the wheel of the car to follow the funeral procession.

The limousine carrying Mara and Angie headed up the slight incline toward the gracious Wilcox Manor. Small by genteel southern standards, it was nonetheless impressive and stately. The circular drive was long and guarded by ancient white oak trees. Though the onset of winter had left the giant oaks stripped of their once lush leaves, the tall trees added a royal dignity to the estate.

The house was a white clapboard structure that seemed larger than its two stories due to the knoll on which it stood. With a backdrop of pine trees and gently rolling hills, the clean white exterior of the manor seemed to reflect the pristine brightness of the new fallen snow. Teal-blue shuttered windows and a broad front porch of polished red brick enhanced the gracious, colonial house. The grounds, now blanketed with the new snow, were only a portion of the original, vast country estate. Most of the acreage that had been used for farming and timber had been parceled off to neighboring farms as the cost of machinery and taxes had escalated over the past few years.

Even in the severity of winter, rhododendrons and azaleas peeked through the mantel of dry white snow, exposing their still green leaves. Tufted grass pierced through the icy drifts to remind Mara of warmer days, and Mara's words vaporized in the air as she whispered to her child. It was a bitterly cold day, and yet, even in the dead of winter, the Wilcox estate held the easy Southern country charm of North Carolina and welcomed the grieving family and friends of Peter Wilcox.

Fortunately for Mara, Angie had fallen asleep in the car. Lovingly, Mara carried the child into the house and headed directly up the sweeping staircase that flanked the elegant, marble-tiled foyer. Polished oak and rosewood gleamed as she cuddled Angie more closely to her. On this day, as she had often in the past, Mara felt a deep melancholy that made her cherish Angie as if she were the only child in the universe.

Although Peter's mother protested, Mara stood her ground and insisted that the tired child rest. Mara didn't want to chance another outburst from Angie about her late father, especially in front of the mourning guests. There was no need to add any further tension to the already gloomy and uneasy afternoon.

"Please explain to the others that I'll be upstairs with Angie for a few minutes," Mara pleaded with her mother-in-law.

June, usually agreeable, touched a nervous finger to the collar of her tidy, black silk dress. "But don't you think that Angie should stay down here and . . ."

"No, I really don't," Mara interrupted, as kindly as possible, as she began to mount the ancient, curved staircase. "I'll be down later, as soon as I'm sure that Angie is comfortable." With her final statement, Mara continued up the stairs, carrying her limp child to the bedroom.

As Mara laid the girl on the bed, Angie's eyes blinked open for just a moment, and once again Mara was reminded of how much her eyes were like her father's.

A hot pain seared her heart at the memory. Angie sighed deeply, her eyelids dropped reluctantly, and she snuggled contentedly into the blankets. Mara gently lifted the hat from Angie's head. Golden curls splayed in unruly ringlets around her face, and Mara thoughtfully brushed the blond hair away from Angie's cherublike cheeks. Despite her tension, Mara couldn't help but smile down on the sleeping child—her only physical link to the girl's father.

It took her nearly half an hour to descend the stairs and face the rest of the family, but Mara had taken time in preparing herself for the onslaught of condolences from bereaved family and friends. The funeral had been a draining ordeal, and Mara was beginning to feel the exhaustion of the day and the worry of the last six months wearing upon her. Her normally wholesome appearance paled, her color was washed away, and the skin over her high cheekbones was stretched tightly. Even the sparkle in her clear blue eyes had faded, and the smile, once quick and elegant, had seemed to disappear. The torment of Peter's illness had affected his wife deeply. No matter how difficult the marriage had been, Peter's painful death seemed brutal and senseless to Mara. So unfair! Now she wanted to be alone. She didn't have the strength to smile or speak to any of the guests, especially Peter's sister, Dena, whom she had been avoiding for the past few days. Dena had made it clear that she wanted to talk to Mara and discuss Peter's will, and Mara could feel the inevitable confrontation in the air. She only hoped that Dena would have the sense and common courtesy to bring up the subject another day, in more private surroundings.

As Mara descended the stairs she realized that some of the guests were already leaving. June was escorting a young man, whom Mara recognized as a business associate of Peter's, out of the broad front door when Mara joined her to smile politely at him and accept his condolences. Mara couldn't help but notice that June's nerves were tightly drawn and that the older woman's eyes, though dry, were slightly swollen and red rimmed. There was a dead look of weariness in her face and her normally full lips had pulled into a tight, thin line that was neither a smile nor a frown. June Wilcox was a very private person, but Mara knew how devastated the older lady was over her only son's death. Nervously, June fidgeted with the single strand of pearls at her throat.

The door closed as one of the last guests departed, and Mara and June were alone together for the first time that day. Mara gently touched her mother-in-law's frail shoulder. "Why don't you go upstairs and get some rest," she suggested. "It's been a long day."

"I'm fine," June insisted staunchly, dismissing Mara's advice with a wave of her finely boned hand.

Mara wasn't convinced. "No one will miss you. Most of the guests have already gone."

"I know, but . . ." June wavered for a moment and managed a stiff smile for Dr. Bernard, the family physician and old friend.

"You should take Mara's advice," the kindly old man stated authoritatively. "It's been difficult for you." His brown, knowing eyes traveled over the strained features on June's face. "And don't be afraid to take any of those pills I prescribed if you feel that you need them."

"I won't," June agreed hastily, but the doctor raised a suspicious gray eyebrow as he shrugged into his raincoat.

"Good day," Dr. Bernard said with a wave of his

broad hand, and once again Mara was alone with her mother-in-law.

"Pills?" Mara inquired.

"Oh, you know," June responded with a shake of her perfectly coifed gray hair. "Tranquilizers, or some such nonsense."

Mara pulled her eyebrows into a single line of concentration. "I didn't know you were on any medication."

"Don't be silly," June interrupted a little crossly. "It's not medication—not like you mean. They're just nerve pills. Doctor Bernard passes them out to half of the women in the county."

Mara was about to disagree but was forced to let the subject drop as several of the remaining guests filtered into the hall and extended their final condolences to the family. She acknowledged the sympathy before making her way as gracefully as was possible through the open doors and into the drawing room, where only a handful of guests remained. She spoke quietly to some of Peter's friends before they, too, excused themselves.

Fortunately, Angie, exhausted from the long ceremony earlier in the day, slept through most of the afternoon. By the time she did awaken, only the most immediate members of the Wilcox family were left in the house: Peter's mother, June, and his sister, Dena.

The argument was just beginning to boil when Angie, dragging her favorite tattered blanket behind her, crept unnoticed down the stairs.

"I don't even know what you're talking about, Dena," Mara was saying in a tight but controlled voice. *"What* man was here?"

"It was really nothing," June began, but was silenced by Dena's icy stare.

"Oh, so now you're pretending that you don't know him?" Peter's auburn-haired sister asked insolently.

"Don't know *whom?*" Mara repeated. Her slim hands were turned palms upward in a gesture of complete bewilderment.

"Look, Mara, if you think you can pull the wool over my eyes the way you have with the rest of the family, you're wrong. Wrong as hell!" Dena snapped, her green eyes glittering with an unspoken challenge.

"Dena!" June gasped. "Why must you be so crude?" she asked, before spotting a groggy Angie on the stairs. "Uh-oh . . . look who just woke up! Did you have a nice nap, precious?" June asked, turning all of her attention to her grandchild.

The blond girl rubbed her eyes with her small fists and then held out her arms expressively to her grandmother. June bent down and groaned slightly as she lifted the child into her arms. Mara wondered fleetingly to herself if her mother-in-law should overextend herself—Dr. Bernard had mentioned something about pills. But Mara's thoughts were interrupted as June smiled at Angie and continued talking to the girl as she carried the small, sleepy child out of the room. "Why don't you and I go outside for a while," she suggested, reaching for Angie's coat. "Mommy and Aunt Dee Dee have some . . . er, business to discuss."

Dena visibly cringed at the cutesy-pie name that Angie had bestowed upon her. After grandmother and child were safely out of earshot, on the opposite side of the French doors, Dena whirled back on Mara.

"I mean it, Mara!" Dena hissed. "I want to know all about that man!"

"Dena!" Mara's thin patience snapped and the tone of her voice chilled. "For the last time, *what* man?"

The redhead paused and let her clear green eyes

reappraise Mara. Her full lips pursed and the finely plucked brows drew together thoughtfully. As if finally understanding that Mara knew nothing of the stranger, she began to explain in a decidedly calmer voice. "There was a man here today—a tall fellow. Good-looking, but unconventional, if you know what I mean. He asked to see you, practically insisted!" Green eyes watched Mara closely, as if gauging her reaction. "Mother refused to let him in because she didn't know him, and he declined to introduce himself—said his business was with only you! You were with Angie at the time. I thought that perhaps he might have been your attorney," she suggested.

"You know that I use the family attorney! Are you sure that he wasn't a business associate of Peter's? I certainly don't know anyone—"

Dena cut in. "Well, he acted as if he knew *you!* He became demanding, insisting to see you. When mother refused he stormed off in a huff. Now, are you sure you don't know him?" Dena inquired, arching her eyebrows suspiciously as she studied Mara's pensive face.

"I really couldn't hazard a guess," Mara said evenly, but a puzzled expression crowded her features. "Must have been a friend of Peter's," she mused, half to herself.

"I doubt that," Dena disputed and walked lazily over to a table laden with uneaten appetizers. She regarded Mara with feigned innocence as she popped a shrimp canapé into her mouth. "This man, he wouldn't fit in with Pete's usual crowd, if you know what I mean."

"That's just the point," Mara sighed. "I don't know what you mean. As a matter of fact, I really haven't understood anything that you've been saying, *or* implying," she admitted, and touched her suddenly throbbing temple. Any discussion with Dena seemed to always end in a headache.

"Well," Dena said, fingering several different hors d'oeuvres and stalling for theatrical effect. "This man, he was different." She thought for a moment and a smile curved her full lips. "A little rough around the edges . . ."

"Coarse?"

"Hmmm . . . no," Dena shook her deep-red curls, absorbed in thought. "Just, how can I explain it? Tougher, I suppose. He looked as if he knew what he wanted in life and wouldn't let anything or anyone get in his way!"

"Nice guy," Mara murmured sarcastically.

"I wouldn't know," Dena rejoined, and shrugged her slim shoulders, "but he was definitely more interesting than the usual crowd that Peter hung out with." She let a polished fingernail linger on her lips as if savoring a very pleasant thought.

Mara was tired of the game playing, and Dena's interest in the stranger didn't concern her. "It doesn't matter, Dena. I've no idea who that man was or is. If he wants to see me so badly, then he'll certainly be back. If not—who cares? Honestly, I don't see why he should upset you so much."

"He's not the reason I'm upset, and you know it!" Dena shot back at Mara, her pensive smile dropping from her face.

"The will?" Mara surmised, and Dena's spine seemed to stiffen slightly.

"I mean it, Mara," Dena threatened. "Peter may have inherited the bulk of the company shares from Daddy, but I still have some say in what goes on!"

"And I'll bet that you'll say plenty," Mara returned ruefully.

"You can count on it! Imagination Toys is as much a part of my life as it was Peter's. And if you think I'm going to sit idly by while you turn a profitable toy empire into a . . . a . . ."

"A tax loss?" Mara prompted. "As Peter was doing?"

"Peter was sick!"

"Yes . . . that he was," Mara agreed in a controlled and unwavering voice. "But not in the beginning, when profits first began to fall off."

"That's not the point!"

"Then what exactly is the point, Dena? I'm tired, and I want to spend some time with Angie. So why don't you get right to the crux of the problem?"

"Angie! Angie! It's always that kid with you, isn't it? I really wonder why you married Peter in the first place. Oh, yes, now I recall. You were pregnant, weren't you? But why in the world did you have to marry Peter, for God's sake? It's not as if Angie was his child!"

"That's enough!" Mara felt her cheeks begin to stain with unwanted color at Dena's cruel supposition. "Let's leave Angie, and for that matter, Peter, out of this argument. I'm going to take a few days off—maybe even a week or two. I'm not really sure. But I'm going to spend that time alone with my daughter!" Mara's voice was stretched as tightly as a piano wire, but she tried to keep her rising temper under control. "It's been a long, hard day, and we've both said some things that we shouldn't have. When I get back to the office, you and I will talk about the company. We'll settle our differences then."

"And who will run the company while you're off vacationing with the kid?" was the insolent inquiry.

"Don't worry about it. It's all been decided. John Hammel is perfectly capable . . ."

"The accountant?" Dena was incredulous, but Mara firmly stood her ground.

"That's right."

Dena's eyes flashed emerald fire, but she let the words that were forming in the back of her throat die. She could see that it was of no use to try and talk to Mara now. Dena knew her sister-in-law well enough to realize that the determined line of Mara's jaw meant business, and she had to content herself with the fact that her barb concerning Angie's questionable paternity had wounded Mara. Dena smiled slightly at the thought. "All right, Mara, I'll wait until you get back. But if you step on my toes, you had better believe that I'll call my lawyer in an instant and contest Pete's will!" She snapped her long fingers to add emphasis to her warning.

"Oh, Dena," Mara sighed, suddenly weary. "Does it always have to be this way between us? Are you really threatening me?" Mara's large blue eyes looked beseechingly up at Dena's triumphant smile.

"Don't think of it as a threat, *dear,*" Dena suggested with a voice that dripped venom and a self-satisfied smile lighting the green depths of her eyes. "Consider it a promise!" With her final words, Dena didn't wait for Mara's response. The redhead whirled on her high leather heels and clicked out of the room, following the path whereby the grandmother had escaped earlier with her grandchild.

As the porch doors banged shut, rattling the glass panes, Mara felt herself slump into the nearest chair.

How was she going to cope with the Wilcox family? What could she possibly do about June's failing health and Dena's imperious demands? It was difficult enough making the adjustment into widowhood and single parenting, but to make matters worse, she had to fight Dena tooth and nail on every topic concerning the toy company. It crossed her mind that perhaps Mara should give in to Peter's older sister's demands. Then if Imagination continued to lose money, Dena would have no one to blame but herself. Maybe the best thing for all concerned would be for Mara to pack up Angie and leave her in-laws to squabble among themselves. But she wouldn't do it—couldn't. Too many other people depended upon her strength for her to just give up. Peter's mother, June, had been especially kind to her. And Mara was a fighter. It went against everything she believed in to give up without exhausting all possible alternatives. There had to be a reasonable solution to the problem with Dena.

The fatigue that had begun to creep up her spine finally overcame her and she shuddered. The last six months of watching Peter slowly wither away had been excruciating, and for the first time since his death Mara gave in to the bitter tears of exhaustion that burned at the back of her eyes.

The drive back to Atlanta was a blur in Shane's memory. So lost in thought was he that he didn't even notice when the sharp mountains melted into the plains and low hills of western Georgia. He was angry with himself for trying to see Mara and even angrier at the sophisticated gray-haired woman who had refused his admittance. It had crossed his mind to ignore the protests of the older woman and push past her to find

Mara, but his common sense and decency had changed his mind. His timing was all wrong, along with everything else he had done since he had read Peter Wilcox's obituary two days earlier.

He would bide his time, at least for the present. He knew that he had to see Mara again, and soon, and he damned himself for his weakness. But certainly with a little imagination he would be able to find a way to get close to her . . . for just a little while.

Chapter 2

A week in the Florida sun had brightened Mara's disposition and outlook on life. She and Angie had spent the time playing on the beach, making sand castles, and hunting for treasures cast upon the white sand by the relentless tide. They played keep-away from the waves and watched as tourists, dressed in gaudy colors, lapped up the sun's warm golden rays. It was a wonderful time for mother and daughter to become reacquainted, without the shroud of Peter's illness cloaking them in its black folds.

The sun had tanned their skins, and Mara looked robust and healthy once again. A sparkle had returned to her cornflower-blue eyes, and two rosy points of color enhanced the natural arch of her cheekbones. Angie's hair had bleached to a lighter hue, which seemed to imitate the long, golden tendrils of her mother, the brighter shade deepening the color of her near-black eyes. The little girl seemed healthy and happy, and it was with more than a trace of hesitation and dread that Mara returned home, back to the ancient clapboard-

and-brick house that she and Peter had shared, and back to the offices over the manufacturing plant of Imagination Toys, located in the heart of the industrial section of Asheville.

Months had passed since the funeral, and the mountains surrounding Asheville had warmed with the summer sun. The white oak trees lining the drive displayed their lush, green leaves, and the air was laden with the scent of pine. Already the large dogwood tree in the backyard had lost its petals, and only a few remaining flaming azaleas and purple rhododendron blossoms lingered on the branches.

Summer had come, and for the first time in several years Mara felt free. Free from the disease that had ravaged Peter but had bound her to him, and free from the hypocrisy of a loveless marriage. The days were long and warm. Although Mara spent many hours working at the office, she always managed to put aside a special time of the day to spend alone with Angie. During the day, while Mara was working, Peter's mother, June, watched carefully over her three-year-old granddaughter, but in the late afternoon and evenings, when the soft breeze of twilight whispered through the pine boughs, Mara and Angie were inseparable. It was this time of day that Mara found the most precious. She loved being with her curly-haired, slightly precocious daughter and found Angie's bright smile and eager young mind a continued source of contentment. And Angie, for her part, seemed to thrive on the love she received from her mother and grandmother.

Mara's days at the plant were more difficult than her quiet evenings at home. There was an almost unbearable undercurrent of tension between Mara and her sister-in-law. After returning from her vacation, Mara had agreed to let Dena run the advertising department. Mara had hoped that the added responsibility would satisfy the fiery Dena. She reasoned that if she gave Dena a fair chance to show her talents, perhaps Dena would work harder and pull with Mara instead of always against her. In the beginning Dena had seemed content, but as time passed she began getting bored with the job, realizing that it was little more than an empty title—a placebo to satisfy her ego. All of the major decisions concerning Imagination Toys were still handled by Mara. She had taken over the job slowly, as Peter's illness had forced him into inactivity.

Also, despite Mara's efforts to the contrary, the company was still losing money. Several larger corporations had expressed interest in buying out the controlling interest in Imagination, but Mara had steadfastly refused their offers. The last thing she would allow to happen was to prove Dena correct and be forced to sell the family business. The toy company had been started by Peter's great-grandfather, and each successive generation of Wilcox family members had lived comfortably from the profits. That was, until the company had begun losing money under Peter's mismanagement. Now the recession was complicating the problem, but no matter what, Mara wouldn't let the company fail, or so she promised herself.

One larger corporation based in Atlanta, Delta Electronics, was persistent in offering to buy out Imagination. Mara had never spoken to the owners directly, but each week she had received several inquiries from Delta's attorneys. Just last week Mara had spoken to Mr. Henderson, counselor for Delta, and hoped that he had understood her position about the sale—that there would be none. Henderson wasn't easily put off—in fact, he was persistent to the point of being bothersome—but this week was the first in several that Mara hadn't opened a formal-looking envelope from Atlanta. Mara congratulated herself; it seemed as if Mr. Henderson had finally gotten the message.

She stretched in the chair. It was late Friday afternoon and shadows had begun to lengthen across her tiny office. As she sat at her desk she cast a glance out the large window and at the sun lowering itself behind the wall of Appalachian mountains. Long, lavender shadows climbed over the colonial and modern rooftops of downtown Asheville. The familiar view of the skyline and the charcoal-blue mountains shrouded in wispy clouds was calming after what had been another hectic week at the office. Her eyes moved from the window to the interior of her office. She smiled lazily to herself and ignored the small pile of paperwork that sat unfinished on her desk. Slowly she let her hands reach behind her neck and lift the weight of her tawny hair from her shoulders. Still holding her hair away from her neck, she slowly rotated her head, hoping to relieve some of the tightness from her back and shoulders. It had been a long, tiring day, punctuated by arguments with Dena, but it would soon be over. The antique wooden clock on the wall indicated that it was nearly six o'clock, and Mara looked forward to going home and spending a long, quiet evening alone with Angie.

Mara let her eyes drop from the face of the clock to roam across the interior of the office. Although she was now legally president and general manager of Imagination Toys, the tiny room was somewhat austere. She had allowed it to be cut down in size from the immense room that it had been while Peter ran the company. The plant needed more work space and less administrative office, she had determined, and therefore allowed the room to be divided into workable office space. The same room that had housed only Peter before was now able to provide a work area for a secretary and two salespeople, and still allow Mara room to move. The only luxury that she insisted upon was that she keep the large window with the view of the mountains she loved.

Mara would have liked to have refurbished the office, but that was one extravagance that would have to wait, along with a list of more important and necessary items. As it was, the budget couldn't be stretched to cover the new three-needled sewing machines that were needed for the dolls, nor would it allow for a new shipment of higher grade plastic for colored building blocks . . . or fabric, or an upgraded puzzle saw—the list seemed to be endless. At the very bottom was interior design for Mara's office.

The velvety tones of her secretary's voice on the intercom scattered her thoughts. "Mrs. Wilcox?"

"Yes?" Mara inquired automatically, not letting her eyes waver from their silent appraisal of the office.

"There's a gentleman to see you . . . A Mr. Kennedy."

"But I don't have any appointments this afternoon." Mara began, before the weight of Lynda's surprise announcement settled upon her. In a voice that was barely audible, Mara spoke into the transmitter, her attention drawn to the little black box on the corner of her desk. "What did you say the gentleman's name was . . . Kennedy?" Mara's mind began to whirl backward in time. She sucked in her breath and then chided herself for her breathless anticipation. After four years of living with the truth, why did she still feel a rush of excitement run through her veins at the memory of Shane? A dryness settled in her throat.

Mara could hear a confused whisper of conversation coming from the other end of the intercom. Then Lynda's voice once again. "I'm sorry, Mrs. Wilcox, but Mr. Kennedy insists that he has an appointment with you. He's with . . . just a minute . . . Delta Electronics."

Kennedy . . . Kennedy . . . Kennedy, the name repeated itself in Mara's mind. It had been so long since she had allowed herself to remember Shane—his dark eyes, the deep resonate timbre of his laughter, the warmth of his touch . . .

"Mrs. Wilcox?" Lynda asked uneasily through the intercom. "He says it's urgent that he speak with you . . ." Lynda was becoming unnerved by Mara's hesitation and Mr. Kennedy's persistence. "Mrs. Wilcox?"

Mara tried to quiet her suddenly hammering heart and gather the air that had escaped from her lungs in a gust at the memory of Shane. "Delta Electronics?" Mara repeated. She didn't bother to mask the interest in her voice.

"That's correct," Lynda agreed quickly, relieved to hear the usual ring of authority back in Mara's voice.

"I've already responded to Delta's law office. Mr. Henderson understands exactly how I feel, but if it would make Mr. Kennedy feel any better, I'll be glad to see him. Please show him into my office." Mara's fine, dark, honey-colored brows drew together in concentration. Why was this Kennedy so insistent—hadn't Henderson conveyed her message properly? She tapped her fingernails nervously on her desk and then straightened the collar of her blouse.

The knowledge that one of the representatives for Delta Electronics was named Kennedy had shaken her poise. Not that Kennedy was an uncommon name, by any means. Yet each time she heard it, she became distracted by vivid visions of the past and long-dead emotions would try to recapture her.

Not knowing the reasons for her actions, Mara let her fingers sweep all traces of her personal life from her desk, the family portrait of Mara and Angie, a Lucite cube with snapshots of Angie as a baby, and a few scraps of construction paper that were Angie's first unsteady attempts at art. As Mara's nerves tightened, she pushed all the mementos of her life into her desk drawer and turned the lock, thinking at the time that her actions bordered on paranoia, all because of a common surname.

Satisfied that no tangible evidence of Angie was visible, she placed a friendly, though slightly strained, smile on her lips. She stood up to meet the man who had already shaken her poise and felt a queasy uneasiness in the pit of her stomach.

The door swung open and Mara managed to stifle the scream that threatened to erupt from her throat. Her eyes widened in disbelief, and she clasped an unsteady hand to her breast as her knees began to give way.

"Oh, God," she whispered hoarsely. "Oh, dear God . . ."

She found it impossible to breathe as Shane Kennedy, the man she thought dead, entered the room. In an instant, four years of Mara's life dissolved into thin air. Her heart began to clamor unreasonably in the confines of her rib cage, and she knew that she desperately needed some fresh air. Her eyelids fluttered closed for a woozy instant. Was it really Shane, or merely a mirage that her willing mind had created—a trap of her subconscious? Her legs were still rubbery, and she braced herself on the edge of the desk, letting the strong mahogany support her weight. Her face blanched with the shock of seeing him again, and though she tried heroically to pick up the pieces of her poise, she found it impossible. Her fingers dug into the polished veneer of the desk and her vision became distorted with tears that had been hidden away for four years.

Time hadn't been particularly kind to him. Although his strong masculine looks were still intact, he seemed hardened and weathered. A touch of gray lightened his otherwise jet-black hair, and there were deep lines of strain running across his forehead. Though dressed impeccably in a lightweight jute-colored business suit, the tanned texture of his skin suggested that he spent much of his time outdoors. His face was angular, as it had always been, but it seemed more proudly arrogant than she remembered. In that one breathless instant, when their eyes met, all time seemed to have stopped. And though he didn't smile, a quiet surge of recognition and remembrance lighted his eyes. Mara swallowed with difficulty and tried to quiet her thundering heart, hoping to God that when he extended his hand to hers, he wouldn't notice that her palms were damp.

"Dear God, Shane;" she murmured. "Is it really, you?"

"Mara," he began, walking more closely to her desk. The voice was the same deep-timbred tone that had haunted her nights. "It's been a long time—too long!" He reached for her outstretched hand and closed his over it warmly. Mara felt as if she might faint. She looked into his eyes. They were as black as she remembered, but different, somehow, as if they had witnessed sights that no man should see. In their ebony depths she visualized pain and agony.

"Shane?" Mara whispered, weakly, and her voice cracked with the dry emotion of four dead years. "But . . . your father told me . . . I thought that . . ."

"You thought that I was dead," he finished for her, and his voice held no hint of emotion.

Her face became ghostly white from the shock of seeing him, and her weak knees gave way. Pulling her fingers from the strength of his grasp, she braced herself on the desk and lowered herself onto the chair. Shaking her head in disbelief, she lifted her face to meet the power of his gaze. Dresden eyes reached out for his. She wanted to run to him, to let him fold her into the security of his strong arms. She longed to touch every inch of him, to let her trembling fingers confirm what her eyes were seeing—that he was alive and not just a part of a distant memory. She felt compelled to tell him her most intimate secret and cry the tears of yesterday. But she couldn't. Her voice remained still as the severity of his gaze held her pinioned silently to her seat.

Mara let her head rest heavily on the palm of her hand, and her golden blond hair fell over one shoulder as she tried to calm herself and deal with the fact that he was here, with her, after all of this time. Shane was alive! She looked up at him again, letting her eyes travel upward to meet his. Tears that had been pooling in her large eyes began to run unchecked down her cheeks.

An ache, deep and primitive, spread through Shane. What was it about Mara that made him want to cup her chin in his hand and whisper promises to her that he couldn't possibly keep? Why, still, did he feel an urge to protect her, even though she had wounded him once before?

"I didn't mean to startle you, Mara. As a matter of fact, I would have preferred that my attorney handle this entire affair," he said, knowing his words to be false. He avoided her probing gaze and straightened the cuff of his sleeve. A knife twisted in her heart as she realized that he hadn't even wanted to see her. He had only come because his attorney had been ineffective. "But you proved just as stubborn as I remembered," Shane continued. Then a quiet cough caught his attention, and he remembered the receptionist who had led him into Mara's office. The girl's face burned with embarrassment over witnessing the unusual and intimate reunion between the stranger and her employer.

Shane's chilling statement indicating that he would rather not have seen Mara personally helped her find a portion of her shattered composure. She managed to dismiss the receptionist, to the girl's obvious relief. "Thank you, Lynda, that will be all." Lynda nodded curtly and hurriedly left the room, carefully closing the door behind her.

Mara closed her eyes for a moment and tried to get a grip on her tattered emotions. He was here, after four long years. He'd been alive all the time, her mind reminded her, and a cool sense of betrayal mocked her. Where had he been these past four years? What had he done? Why had his father lied to her? And why had he supported that lie by not returning to her as he had promised? Why would he let her believe him dead, only to resurrect himself now?

The air in the small room was charged with electricity, and the unanswered questions loomed between them like an invisible barrier. For several seconds there was a heavy, uneasy silence, as if the questions about the past were insurmountable.

"Why?" she finally asked him, and somehow found the resolve to look directly into his frigid dark eyes. "Why did you let me think that you were dead . . . all of these years . . . all of these years?" her voice became a hoarse whisper. There was disbelief and anguish in her question, and she felt the strain of unwanted tears once again filling her eyes. Unashamed, she brushed the tears aside.

Her poignant question and tortured expression were too much for Shane to bear. Knowing it to be a mistake, he stalked over to the desk and leaned across it to bring his face only inches from hers. Without hesitation, he let his finger touch the curve of her cheek and cradled her delicate chin in his hand. She felt herself tremble at his familiar touch, and a tear slid down her cheek. His eyes were dark, cloudy, but when she looked more closely, she could swear that she noticed a tenderness and a yearning hidden in the ebony depths of his gaze. As he whispered her name, letting the warmth of his breath touch her face, she thought she could melt into him. "Mara . . . there's so much to say . . . so many questions that have to be answered"—a confused look stole across his features—"but I don't think that this is the right time, nor the right place. You and I we need time, alone together, to sort things out."

His words were soothing to her raw nerves, and his caress was enticingly familiar. She closed her eyes, tender memories returning in full force.

As the words came out of his mouth Shane mentally cursed himself. He should never have come back again. Never! But as the months had passed he had found it more difficult day by day to stay away from her. And so he had come, with the flimsy excuse of purchasing her toy company for bait. He had come back, and now he found himself caught in the web of her charms once again. Even now she was so innocently alluring, so sensitive, so perfect. His hand slid easily against the silken texture of her neck. His thumb found the erratic pulse in the hollow of her throat and lingered, and with his free hand he pushed aside the golden curtain of her hair that had partially hidden her face. Although he paused long enough to look into her eyes, Mara knew that he wanted to kiss her, and the knowledge warmed her. Perhaps the last four years weren't wasted. Her pulse began to quicken, and when his eager lips found hers, she felt a ripple of desire shake her entire body. His lips, warm and inviting, seemed to touch her soul and set her body on fire, just as they had always done. She knew that he wanted her still, even after hiding for the last four years.

When he dragged his lips from hers, disappointment shadowed her features, but as her blue eyes found his she recognized a raw and naked passion smoldering in his gaze. And there was something else, an incredible anger—deep and ugly.

"Why are you here?" she asked. Her senses were dazed, numbed by his touch, but she had to understand the resentment and wariness that seemed to control him.

"I wish I knew," he answered quickly. And then, as if denying the naked truth in his voice, he suddenly stood up and tugged at the hem of his suit coat. "Didn't my attorney get in touch with you? I thought that he had made my position clear. I want to buy Imagination Toys!" The intimacy of the moment before was shattered.

"You?"

"Let me rephrase that; Delta Electronics is interested in your company." His voice was still husky with passion, and as if to cool the intensity of the moment, he walked over to the window and stared at the mountains. One of his hands was plunged deeply into his pants pocket, pulling the expensive weave of his tailored suit away from his body. As the coat stretched backward his shirt tightened against his flat, taut stomach. Even though he was fully dressed, Mara was reminded of his slim, well-muscled build. Four years hadn't changed the masculine strength of his physique, nor the stirrings in her own body at the sight of him.

"And you own Delta Electronics?" Mara guessed, trying to keep her mind on the conversation while her thirsty eyes drank in every inch of him.

A curt nod was the only response as Shane continued to stare at the distant mountains. When Mara didn't immediately continue her questions, he paced back to the desk. His austere gaze prompted her.

"Oh, Shane," she murmured, but his face remained tense. She swallowed with difficulty, and said, with as much professional aplomb as possible, "I'm sorry. But as I told your counsel, Mr. Henderson, the company is not for sale." She tried to quell the anger that was beginning to boil within her. Anger that he had left her, anger that he had come back into her life without so much as an explanation or an apology, anger that the only thing he wanted from her was the Wilcox family business, and anger with herself for still loving him. She had dreamed about him, relived the violent nightmare of his death, but never had she realized how desperately she still loved him . . . a love that was just as it had always been—unreturned. And now the cold betrayal. He had left her without so much as a second glance, until now, when he wanted something.

"Isn't the price high enough?" he asked, breaking into her thoughts.

She shook her blond head and lowered her gaze to meet his directly. "It has nothing to do with money. The company is not for sale. Period! Now, if there's nothing more . . ." She left the sentence dangling between them and without words invited him to leave. Her throat tightened at the thought that he would walk away from her, but she knew she had no choice—she was much too vulnerable to him. And, after all, what he wanted from her was business—pure and simple. She needed time to think things out and get her tangled thoughts in order. As much as she feared being separated from him, she knew it was the wisest course of action. She had to find the courage to tell him those things that he would need to know, now that she knew that he was alive.

His dark eyes narrowed, he rubbed the back of his neck thoughtfully, and he paced restlessly before her. "You'd like that, wouldn't you?"

"Like what?" she asked, perplexed.

"You'd like to be able to just turn me down and send me packing," he accused. "Well, it won't work." A smile tugged at the corner of his mouth. "I want this company, and I intend to have it!"

"Just like that?"

"Just like that!"

"But I'm not selling . . . remember?" Mara's temper was barely under control. "I don't see how you think you'll be able to persuade me to change my mind!" Despite her strong words, she felt herself beginning to tremble.

"Maybe I won't have to," Shane mused, pulling thoughtfully on his lower lip. "As I understand it, you didn't inherit all of the stock of the company. You don't even have controlling interest. Perhaps some of the other members of the Wilcox family would be interested in my proposition . . ." he suggested.

A picture of a triumphant Dena entered Mara's mind. Unconsciously she pursed her full lips, and her eyes held steadily to Shane's. "Am I to assume that you're threatening me?" she asked in a voice that she hoped showed no strain of emotion. His dark head cocked with interest. "I really don't know what it is that you expect of me," she accused, tossing up her hands in exasperation. "First, you come marching in here, right from the grave, I might add, and nearly shock me to death. And, secondly, you try to intimidate me into selling something to you that is definitely *not* for sale! I don't know how I can make my position any more clear! The company is not for sale." Her eyes had turned to chips of blue ice. "I'm sorry if my response disappoints you!"

Shane laughed, and the familiar sound destroyed all of Mara's resolve. "You haven't disappointed me, Mara. I thought that maybe you had changed, but I was wrong. Thank God!" The severity of his gaze eroded, and for the first time that afternoon Mara saw kindness in his eyes—the kindness that she remembered.

He reached for her hand and held it lightly in his. "It's good to see you again," he whispered honestly.

"But Shane . . . why?" She tried to ignore the tingling of her fingertips where they touched his. "Why?"

"Shh . . ." He placed a sensitive finger over her lips to quiet the questions that were uppermost on her mind. "Have you had dinner yet?" Shane asked, still holding her fingers.

"At six o'clock in my office?" Mara inquired, feeling the tension begin to leave her body. "Not hardly."

"Then let's have it together."

"Now?"

"This evening."

Mara began to shake her head. Everything was happening too quickly and she was beginning to feel claustrophobic, caught in the same emotions that had trapped her four years ago. He was pushing, and she needed time to think. It was too easy to fall under his magic all over again. She ached to fall into the seduction of his onyx eyes, but she couldn't allow it. It was too late.

"Why not?" he asked smoothly. Too smoothly.

"I . . . I have plans tonight." It wasn't a lie. There was Angie to consider. Shane's hot hand closed more firmly over hers, and she felt as if she were beginning to melt. "And," she withdrew her hand shakily, "I don't think that it would be a very good idea . . ."

"Why not?" he interjected. His dark eyes deepened as they found the blue of hers.

"You sound like a broken record . . ."

"Well?"

"I'm . . . really . . . very busy," Mara stammered, and knew in an instant that it sounded very much like the lie it was.

"Trying to maintain the image of the suffering widow?" Mara's back stiffened, but a crooked smile slashed wickedly across Shane's tanned face. For a moment, Mara could see him as she remembered: younger, softer, and . . . warmer. That was it. Even when he grinned, she could sense a brooding coldness lying under the surface of his smile.

Unconsciously, Mara rubbed the warm spot in her palm that could still feel his touch. "It has nothing to do with images," she retorted. "I really am swamped."

"Oh?" his dark eyes moved over the top of her desk, which was barren except for a few shipping invoices.

"Yes," she replied hastily, feeling a compulsion to explain. "We're a little late with some of our shipments . . ."

"I know that!"

Mara's eyes met his in a clash of black and blue. Just how much did he know? She continued, a little breathlessly, "Then, of course, you understand that I've got a million and one things to do."

"Name one," he suggested laconically, and dropped himself into a chair opposite the desk. He propped his chin up with his folded hands and a slight glint of amusement touched his eyes.

Mara breathed deeply and wondered fleetingly why she was even participating in this absurd conversation. "Well, for one thing," she began, slightly goaded but refusing to back down on her lie, "it's almost the end of August, our busiest season. I've got Christmas orders that will have to be shipped, and very soon."

"Isn't that what the shipping department is for?" he suggested wryly.

"Everyone pitches in!"

"Including the president?" A black eyebrow cocked suspiciously.

"Including the president!" Mara's eyes snapped for an instant before she erected the cool facade on her face that suggested total authority. She straightened her shoulders and unconsciously inched the defiant tilt of her chin upward.

"Is that the way Peter ran the company?" Before Mara could think of a suitable response, Shane continued. "And just how is it going?"

"How is what going?" she asked, trying to keep up

with his twists in the conversation. The scent of familiar cologne wafted toward her, tantalizing her. Pleasant memories came thundering back, unwanted.

"The business! Now that dear old Peter is gone—by the way, my condolences—how is the business managing?" His tone was sarcastic, and once again angry fires blazed in his ebony gaze.

"Just fine!" she lied again. Why did she feel that she had to lie to him, to defend her position? The thought continued to nag at her and she vainly tried to push it aside.

"Is that so?" He looked at her skeptically as if to say "convince me."

"Of course it is!" Mara emphasized, a trifle irritably. Just who did he think he was, waltzing into the office without an appointment, shocking the living daylights out of her, dredging up old memories, and making her feel a burning need to explain her life to him? Shane's eyes dropped to her hands, and she realized that she was twisting the wedding ring that she still wore on her right hand. Scarlet crept up her neck as she let her fingers drop beneath the desk top and out of his line of vision. Once again, his gaze hardened.

"Well, then, if everything is going so smoothly, there's no reason that you can't have dinner with me, is there?"

Trapped! He had tricked her, and they both knew it. She had let him corner her all too easily. Mara breathed more deeply and tried once again to dissuade him. Her most winning smile neatly in place, she responded. "Look, Shane, just because the company is doing well doesn't mean that there isn't any work to be done. Quite the contrary. The busier the toy company is, the busier I am." She stretched her palms upward in a ges-

ture that said more clearly than words, "any fool can
understand that simple logic." "Besides which, I told
you that I'm busy tonight."

"And you can't fit me into your busy schedule?"

"Exactly."

Shane's eyes seemed to darken to the color of midnight. "Then I take it you're not interested in my
proposition?"

Mara pushed her hair away from her face and looked
away for a minute. What did he mean? "Proposition?"
she repeated. "What proposition? I already told you
that the company is not for sale!" She tried to keep the
interest in her voice at a minimum. She could sense
that he had another offer, and she hadn't spent the last
four years learning the business from the ground up to
blow it at this point. Perhaps he was willing to invest
some capital in the company, for a minority interest. In
any event, she had to find out what his proposition was.
Obviously, Shane Kennedy wanted something from
her, and very badly. Her heart stopped at the thought
that perhaps he wanted her, but she quickly banished
the traitorous idea. She wasn't a fool, and she realized
that he hadn't waited four years to pick up what he had
once thrown away so ruthlessly. No, this was only
business, she reminded herself, but a part of her longed
for more. She would have to try and maintain her cool
disinterest until she heard all of the facts.

In answer to her question he replied, "The proposition that I'm going to make to you over dinner." His
voice had deepened an octave, and Mara had to stifle
an urge to let herself remember a younger time when
they had shared a smile, a kiss, a caress . . .

"I thought the question of dinner was settled," she
heard herself retort.

"Not until you agree to have it with me."

Mara was becoming exasperated. Even though the man seated across from her was devastating her senses, she knew that she had enough complications in her life at the moment and that she didn't need to add Shane Kennedy to the list. It was he who had left her. Mara knew herself well, and she realized that she was still just as vulnerable as the day that they had said their farewells. Four years hadn't muted her senses or her imagination; her racing pulse gave witness to that fact. Several years may have come and gone, but no man had ever touched her the way that Shane Kennedy had. No man, including Peter. Mara turned crimson at the thought, feeling guilty and apprehensive. Why was Shane back? Did he know about Angie? The thought frightened her. Why did she feel that there was more than just his interest in the toy business that had prompted Shane to return to Asheville—and to the mountains where they had first made love?

As she looked pensively over to the man that had once been her closest friend and most intimate lover, she wondered if he could read her thoughts. Could he ever realize just how desperately she had loved him and how many nights she had found herself dreaming of him? Ever since Peter's death, Shane's image had become more clearly defined on her tired mind. Unconsciously, she wetted her suddenly dry lips with the tip of her tongue.

Shane maintained his composure, though Mara's unintentional provocation had bothered him. A thin smile played over his lips as he rose from the chair and took her hand in his. "Please have dinner with me, Mara," he whispered, and at the moment he breathed her name, she knew it was useless to argue. More than anything in the world at this moment, Mrs. Mara Jane Stevens Wilcox, recently widowed wife of Peter Wilcox, wanted to spend time with the only man she had ever truly loved: the father of her child.

"All right, Shane," she agreed, with the first sincere smile of the day. "I'd love to have dinner with you . . . and to listen to your proposal."

"Proposition," he corrected with a mirthless smile, and Mara found herself wondering if she had made a bitter mistake. *He's changed,* she decided. *He's changed very much.*

Chapter 3

The meeting with Shane had left Mara drained and bewildered. As she watched him leave her office she sat motionless; her eyes following the strong, swift strides of his straight-backed exit. He didn't turn around.

A part of Mara, still young and incurably romantic, urged her to run after him and hold onto him for fear that he would once again vanish in the night and this time be gone forever. She wanted and needed to throw her arms around him and cradle his head close to her breast. She could almost feel the pounding of his heartbeat echoing against hers.

She wanted to cry out *"I had your daughter— I couldn't give her up, she was my only link to you. I loved you; God, Shane, but I loved you and I love you still!"* But she remained at her desk, silent. Restraint and common sense held her tongue. His name, which had been forming in her throat, died before reaching her lips, and she watched quietly as the door closed behind him. He was gone.

Mara reached for the wheat-colored linen jacket that was draped over the back of her chair and paused for one last calming look through the window to the mountains. Dusk was painting a purple shadow against the gentle hills, and the line of the distant horizon was melting into darkness with the coming nightfall. As her fingers rubbed idly against the cool windowsill, Mara tried to think rationally about Shane and the past. An increasing anger burned quietly within her as the shock of seeing him ebbed and she came face to face with the fact that for four long years he had allowed himself to hide from her—hidden in a feigned death. Why? Her thoughts nagged her, and she idly rubbed her temple in concentration. *Why,* after all of those tender and loving months together, would he suddenly reject her and conceal himself in the lie of his death? Her thoughts were ragged and scattered, but no matter how much she tried to ignore the obvious, it remained as the only possible solution. Four years ago Shane hadn't wanted her. Had he found out about her pregnancy? Was the love she imagined that they had shared together only a simple girlish dream, dashed when he had somehow learned of her pregnancy?

Her honey-colored brows knit together in concentration as she tried to remember the past. The memory was elusive, kept in the corner of her mind that she had tried to ignore for years.

"Working late?" A cool female voice broke into Mara's thoughts, and she visibly shrank from the sound.

Recovering herself, she turned to face her sister-in-law, who was leaning casually in the doorway. Mara glanced quickly at the clock, and then back to Dena. "What are you doing here? It's after six!"

"Dedication to the job?" Dena asked coyly, and laughed at her own sarcastic sense of humor. Mara could feel the cold tightness of apprehension. There was a long, tense pause as her gaze locked with Dena's.

"Was there any reason in particular that you wanted to see me?" Mara asked while she fished in her purse for her keys.

"I thought that you wanted to go over the advertising budget," Dena explained.

"Oh, that's right!" Mara agreed, and shook her head as if to clear out the cobwebs. "I'm sorry, Dena. I forgot all about it."

"Your mind on other things?" Dena suggested, with a twisted smile curving her full, glossy lips and one gracious eyebrow cocked.

"I guess so . . ." Mara replied evasively as she walked back to her desk, flipped open her appointment book, and scribbled a note on one of the blank sheets. "There!" she said with finality. "I've jotted a reminder to myself to meet with you early Monday morning." Mara looked up from the desk and gave Dena a warm, ingratiating smile. She hoped that Dena would take the hint and leave, but she was mistaken.

The redhead remained in the doorway. It was obvious that something was on her mind.

"Isn't Monday all right with you?" Mara asked, and crossed to the front of the desk.

"Monday's fine," Dena agreed with an indifferent shrug.

"Good!" Mara exclaimed with more enthusiasm than she felt. "Then . . . I'd better be going. I'm late as it is. Was there anything else?"

"Not really," Dena returned while seeming to be distracted by a flaw in her cuticle. When she looked up from her fingernail, she smiled. "Who was the man that came to see you this afternoon?"

Mara wasn't surprised that Dena knew about Shane. No doubt Lynda, the receptionist, had mentioned the unusual reunion to Dena.

"Have you been lurking around here for the past forty minutes just to find out about Shane?" The thought amused Mara, and she couldn't hide the twinkle in her eyes.

"He's the same man that came to the house on the day of Peter's funeral," Dena announced, and let her eyes watch Mara's reaction. It was Dena's turn to be amused as she noticed the color draining from Mara's face and the look of surprise that was reflected in the cool, blue depths of her eyes.

"Shane? He was the stranger?"

"If Shane is the name of the man who came to see you this afternoon, then none other. I don't suppose that he told you about his confrontation with Mother?" Mara had difficulty in finding words, but Dena read her face. "I didn't think so," she said aloud, obviously pleased with herself.

"You know him?" Mara asked, still sifting through the information that Dena had given her. Shane had been to see her on the day of the funeral? Why? Surely not with his business proposal. He wouldn't bother the grieving family just for the sake of business—or would he? She couldn't help but remember the frigid look of Shane's black eyes. And, realistically, why else would he try and reach her? But then, what about the last ten months? Why had he waited?

"No, I don't know him," Dena replied, watching the play of emotions on Mara's face. "At least, not yet."

"But you intend to?" Mara guessed, and a sinking feeling swept over her.

"I didn't say that," Dena responded coyly. "But I would like to know what it is that makes him appear and disappear so suddenly. What did he want from you?"

Mara sighed and leaned heavily against her desk in pensive concentration. She wanted to tell Dena that it was none of her business and leave it at that, but she couldn't. Actually, Shane's purpose did include Dena, and every other member of the Wilcox family. And since Dena had already heard about the peculiar meeting this afternoon, it would be better for all concerned for Mara to be honest with her sister-in-law. Mara crossed her ankles in front of her and let her hands and hips support her weight against the desk top.

"Shane's an old friend of mine," Mara began, leaving the intimacy of the relationship out of the discussion. "I haven't seen him in quite some time. As a matter of fact, I thought that he was dead." A gleam of interest sparked in Dena's eyes, but faded when Mara continued in the same, even, businesslike tone that had commanded the conversation. "I didn't know that he was alive, and so naturally it came as quite a shock when he walked in here, robust and as healthy as a horse. The reason that he came here is that he's interested in purchasing Imagination Toys."

If she thought that she would shock Dena with her announcement that Shane was interested in purchasing the toy company, Mara was disappointed. Dena listened to Mara intently and pursed her lips thoughtfully.

"And you're considering his offer?" Dena surmised.

"No. I told him, from the beginning, that Imagination wasn't for sale!"

"He doesn't look like a man who would be easily discouraged," Dena mused, and let her green eyes follow the hallway to the outer office, where she had seen Shane pass on his way out of the building. "Maybe you should hear him out," she suggested, and tossed an errant copper lock back into place behind her ear.

"About selling Imagination? You must be kidding!"

"Well," Dena began, shrugging her slim shoulders, "why not? If the price is right . . ."

"Dena! Listen to you! Imagination was your great-grandfather's lifeblood. We can't just sell it to the first man who's interested . . ."

"Of course we can. Stop living in the glory of the past and face facts, Mara! The company's losing money, and it has been for quite some time. Unless you can come up with another inspiration like those ridiculous reincarnations of space creatures from the last hit space movie—"

"You mean the plastic action figures from *Interplanetary Connection?*"

"The same. Since we lost the contract for the movie's sequel and we haven't come up with any other block-buster toys to fill the gap, Imagination's profits have plunged! A man like—"

"Shane Kennedy," Mara supplied, with a touch of reluctance. Aside from her personal feelings, Mara knew that Dena was close to the truth.

"He might just be the godsend that we're looking for!" Dena touched her lips absently and Mara could almost hear the wheels turning in her mind. To herself, Mara begrudgingly admitted that Dena was making a valid point. "Come on, Mara, what do you need this company for, anyway? You know as well as I do that you'd rather be spending more time with Angie—she needs you . . ." Dena's words hit a raw nerve with Mara, guilty that she left her daughter with June every day so that she could work full-time. Dena pressed her advantage. "And, after all, what do you know about running a toy company?"

Mara's back stiffened. "I think I know as much as Peter did. At least I should," she sighed. "My degree in business administration should count for something, don't you think? And I worked in several offices before I married Peter and came to work here . . ."

Dena didn't seem convinced, and Mara felt tired and drained from the ordeal of meeting Shane again. Suddenly she gave into the pressure. "All right, Dena, you know that I'm opposed to the idea, but if it makes you feel any better, I'll talk with him and try to keep an open mind. I'm supposed to meet with him tonight—to discuss an alternate proposition rather than a complete buy-out."

"Tonight?" A light of interest brightened Dena's face, and then she quickly sobered. "Just give him a chance, Mara. Hear him out. What have you got to lose?"

"The company," Mara murmured, but wisely Dena didn't comment. With a flourish, Mara locked the door of her office and headed out of the building. She wondered about Dena's concern. It seemed almost too genuine. Wearily, Mara thought that perhaps she had judged Dena too harshly at times. And yet, whether it was intuition or mental wounds from past experience, Mara still didn't feel that she could completely trust the svelt-figured redhead. Was it possible that she was overly suspicious of Peter's older sister?

It was later than usual for Mara to leave the office. She pulled out of the parking lot under the building and carefully merged her car into the traffic of the business district of Asheville. The small sidestreets of town were relatively free from traffic at this time of evening. The air was thick and hazy as Mara drove through the colonial town with its splashes of modern architecture and onto the highway that would eventually take her to the countryside and the Wilcox estate. Fortunately the Friday night traffic had thinned to the point that allowed Mara to wheel her imported car home in record time. The lemon-colored Renault darted up the prestigious tree-lined drive and ground to a halt near the garage at the back of the house. Mara slipped from behind the wheel of the car and half ran up the brick walk. She was too preoccupied to notice the bloom of the late azaleas or the hint of honeysuckle that perfumed the air as she opened the kitchen door and called out her familiar greeting.

"Angie! June, I'm home . . ."

June appeared promptly from the den near the back of the house, and a wave of relief washed over her pinched features. "I was just about to call the office," the older woman chastised as she removed her reading glasses. "I was beginning to get worried about you. It's late . . ."

"Nothing to worry about," Mara replied with a wan smile. June's piercing eyes looked questioningly at Mara. To avoid her direct gaze, Mara reached for a glass and turned on the faucet. The cool water slid deliciously down her parched throat. After a lengthy drink she dried her hands on a nearby dish towel and faced her mother-in-law. June's features were drawn, and Mara couldn't help but wonder about the older woman's health.

"I had an unexpected appointment at the last minute," Mara explained. "That's why I'm late." She gave her mother-in-law a warm smile and tried to brush June's fears aside, but the anxious expression on June's face indicated that Mara had failed to reassure her. "I'm sorry," Mara sighed with genuine affection. "I should have called."

"It's all right, dear. I suppose I worry too much," June acquiesced, and then with more vehemence than Mara thought possible, June continued. "It's just that

you're so wrapped up with that damned toy company!"
Mara stiffened at her mother-in-law's change in attitude, and June chuckled softly. "Forgive me, Mara, I shouldn't use such foul language."

Mara looked seriously at the little old woman. "Do you think that I'm neglecting Angie?" she asked, mentally bracing herself for June's reply. Once again the guilt for the hours away from her child weighed heavily on her conscience.

"Oh, goodness, no, Mara!" June murmured and touched a fond hand to Mara's shoulder. "Angie's just fine. If anything, I'd say that she's a little spoiled."

"Then?"

"I don't think that you take enough time for yourself. If you're neglecting anyone, it's *you*."

Mara let the pent-up air escape from her lungs, but June hadn't finished. "It's unnatural the way you spend all of your time at home or the office. You're young, you should be around young people . . ."

June's lecture was interrupted by the sound of the back screen door slamming and light, running footsteps hurrying to the kitchen. Angie let up a shriek of delight and gales of childish laughter when she caught sight of her mother. "Mommy! Mommy!" Angie shouted, and scurried over to Mara's outstretched arms.

Mara scooped her daughter up off the floor. "How's Momma's big girl?" she asked, and placed a kiss on Angie's smudgy cheek.

Angie giggled with joy and tightened her arms around Mara's neck. "Southpaw got kitties!" Angie declared, crossing her chubby arms importantly over her chest.

"She does?" Mara asked, and Angie wriggled out of her arms. Before the tiny feet hit the floor, they were in motion, and the little blond girl ran out the back door as quickly as she had entered. "Hurry, Mommy . . . I show you the kitties!" she called from somewhere in the vicinity of the back porch.

"So the big day has finally arrived?" Mara asked June.

"Oh, yes, I guess so. Angie's found the spot where Southpaw has hidden her kittens," June explained with a chuckle. "I haven't been able to pull her out from under that porch all afternoon!" Mara laughed aloud at the thought of her daughter and her fascination for Southpaw's proud new family.

Mara reached into the refrigerator and gathered some vegetables for Angie's dinner. She glanced at her mother-in-law and noticed that June seemed preoccupied while staring out the window at Angie. "June, are you feeling well?" Mara asked carefully.

"Of course, dear," June replied spritely, and Mara wondered if she had imagined the strain on the older woman's face.

"You're sure?" Mara prodded.

"Of course, Mara. Why do you ask?"

"Well, I was hoping that you would be able to stay with Angie tonight," Mara mentioned, and hastily added, "but if you have other plans . . . or if you would like to rest . . ."

"Nonsense! I'd love it!"

"Good. I really do hate to bother you, but the man that came to see me late this afternoon insists that I hear him out—tonight!" Mara's thoughts lingered for a moment on Shane.

"That's perfect!" June responded, and her tired eyes brightened at the prospect of having Angie for the evening. It was a luxury that she hadn't experienced much. Since Peter's death, Mara hardly ever went out. "She can stay at my place with me! I've been meaning to take her on one of those miniature train rides in the park, but it's been impossible. The train only runs on the weekends."

"Great," Mara whispered.

June knew her daughter-in-law well, and she regarded Mara's oval face thoughtfully for a moment. There seemed to be a trace of disturbance in her wide-set blue eyes. "Mara . . ."

"Yes?" Mara looked up from the potato that she was peeling.

"Is everything all right?" Gentle concern forced June's graying eyebrows together.

"Sure." Mara laughed, but she heard the hollow sound of her voice. How could she explain to her mother-in-law, the woman who showered so much love on Angie, that Mara was going out with her old lover—the father of her child, the man that she would have married if it had been possible? How would June react to the knowledge that Angie wasn't Peter's daughter, and that the man who fathered the little girl whom June cherished was a total stranger to his child? How could Mara wash away the deception that she had committed for the last four years, under the false belief that Angie's father was dead?

"If you say so," June agreed, absently, as she studied Mara. June had been raised with Southern manners, and she never was a woman to pry, not even into the private lives of her own family. She watched Mara's slim and graceful figure anxiously as Mara headed out to the back porch in search of Angie. In June's opinion, Mara took life much too seriously.

"Angie," Mara called as she opened the screen door and searched the back yard for her spritely young daughter. "Angie! Where are you?"

"Right here," was the muffled reply from somewhere nearby. Mara looked down the porch steps in the direction of the sound. Two dusty tennis shoes were the only evidence that Angie was close at hand. Mara hurried down the steps and balanced on one slender knee as she grabbed Angie's exposed ankles. A muted squeal of surprise and anticipation erupted from somewhere under the porch.

"Angie Wilcox! Just look at you!" Mara exclaimed, with a good-natured laugh. She extracted the little girl from beneath the lattice work that supported the back porch, and she brushed the cobwebs from Angie's golden curls. "You're a first-class mess!" Mara teased as she surveyed the dirty child.

"Kitties! Kitties! Southpaw got kitties in there!" Angie jabbered excitedly and pointed a knowing finger at the porch. Against Angie's better judgment, Mara picked up her daughter and carried her up the steps toward the house.

"Let's go up and have some dinner," Mara suggested, hoping to deter Angie's interest in the newborns. Angie looked longingly back to the porch until Mara whispered in her ear. "Guess what, dumpling?" Mara asked in a secretive voice.

Angie's eyes widened expectantly. "What?" the little girl whispered back, in a show of affectionate collusion with her mother.

"You get to stay overnight with Grammie tonight. What do you think about that?" Mara asked, and poked a loving finger at the exposed belly button in the gap between Angie's shirt and pants.

"Are you coming, too?" Angie asked eagerly, and Angie's cherubic face, aglow with anticipation, tugged at Mara's heartstrings.

"Not this time, sweetheart," Mara admitted, and Angie's animated face lost its smile. Mara hurried on.

"But you'll have to tell me all about it tomorrow. Grammie's going to take you on a train ride in the park."

"A train with a whistle?"

"I think so . . ."

Once again Angie's impish face illuminated with expectation, and Mara gave the child a bear hug as she carried the little girl into the kitchen for dinner.

The grandfather clock in the living room chimed eight o'clock, and Mara could feel herself stiffen with each vibrating note. She thought about pouring herself a drink but discarded the idea, seeing it as a show of weakness. The big, old house was dark and cold ever since June had left with Angie, and the tightness in Mara's stomach seemed to knot and twist with each passing minute.

It had been impossible not to think about Shane in the last half hour, and each time his image assailed her, Mara sensed the same old feelings that he had aroused in her in the past: intrigue, joy, contentment, and finally despair. Now, new and ugly sensations marred the beauty of the past as she felt the chill of betrayal and the heat of anger.

It had been over four years since Mara had called Shane's father on the telephone and learned the devastating news that Shane had been killed in a terrorists' attack in Northern Ireland. Mara had realized that as a television cameraman, Shane's occupation could at times be dangerous. She knew that this particular assignment in Belfast would be difficult and risky. But when confronted with Mara's fears for his safety, Shane had waved them off, emphasizing that the film, a frank documentary on the political battle in Northern Ireland, was important, not only for his personal career advancement but also for public awareness. It was his hope that the film would demonstrate the political unrest of a society torn by religious and economic strife.

Shane had downplayed the hazards and dangers of the assignment, and Mara had reluctantly accepted his careful explanations and ultimate decision to make the trip to the tiny island. Later she realized that it had been her own foolish attempt to hide behind a curtain of half-truths, because the knowledge of the bloodshed and risks that Shane might have had to encounter were too much for her to bear.

Mara hadn't known that she was pregnant when Shane had left her alone in the airport terminal. Perhaps if she had realized that she was carrying a child, she could have convinced him to stay with her and the baby, and they could have been married, as she had hoped. But as it was, she never saw him again—until he walked into her office over four years later.

It was in the telephone call to Shane's father that Mara had hoped to get in touch with the father of her child and let him in on the glad news. Shane had been gone for over six weeks, and in that long, lonely time, she had received only one badly connected telephone call and a hastily written card. Then, abruptly, nothing.

But the raspy voice of Shane's father, and the heavy pause as she asked about Shane, heightened the dread that had been mounting. Before the old man could whisper the news to her, she understood that Shane was gone—forever. She managed to quell the scream of disbelief and bereavement in her throat and murmur her sympathies to the stranger on the other end of the line. She tried to hang up the phone, but didn't, and the receiver dangled awkwardly in midair for the rest of the evening as she sat in stunned silence. She cried herself to sleep that night, and when slumber did finally come, it was fitful and shattered by the truth: Shane was dead.

For the rest of the week she cried intermittently, unable to piece together the fragments of her broken life. Her appetite disappeared with fatigue and nausea. When Peter Wilcox, an old high school friend, had dropped by to visit her, he had found Mara lying on the couch, disheveled, crying bitter tears and battling unsuccessfully with morning sickness. He had helped her to the bathroom, and the sight of her thin body, torn with uncontrollable retching as she hung her head over the basin, didn't stop him from attempting to comfort and console her.

With strong and commanding movements, he had helped her get dressed and had listened compassionately when she had explained, through convulsive sobs, about Shane. And the child.

Peter had the strength to make the decisions that Mara couldn't. He understood her grief for Shane, and then forced her admission into a local hospital insisting that it was necessary for her health and that of the baby. The one consoling thought throughout Mara's turbulent period of anguish was the knowledge that she was carrying Shane's child.

Slowly she regained her strength, and though never nonexistent, the pain of her grief eased. Peter helped her through her deepest depression. His words were comforting, his arms were strong, and above all else, he was kind to Mara rather than critical or judgmental. It was as if he had taken it upon himself to see that she was cared for. And as the days passed, Mara could sense that Peter was falling in love with her. Although she never returned the depth of his feelings, it seemed only reasonable that she should marry him. She had a child to care for and Shane was dead—or so she believed.

The first arguments in the marriage didn't begin until after Angie was born. It seemed to Mara that once the baby arrived, and the physical evidence of Mara's passion for another man existed, Peter and she became alienated. Although Angie bore the Wilcox name and the secret of her parentage was never discussed, all of the attention that Mara lavished upon the child seemed to annoy Peter and add to his resentment of the blond little girl.

Mara and Peter would quarrel, bitterly at times. Then he would leave her, sometimes for days. She had heard the gossip about his supposed affairs, but she ignored it and refused to forget the kindness he had shown her when she needed it most. And then came the sudden shock of his illness and the steady deterioration of a young and once healthy man.

The grandfather clock struck the quarter hour, and Mara was jarred back to reality. Headlights flashed through the windows and a car engine died in the driveway. It had to be Shane. Mara felt a shiver of anticipation—or was it dread—as the doorbell announced Shane's arrival.

When Mara opened the door, she braced herself and tried to cool the race of her pulse that gave evidence to her tangled emotions. But as the doorway widened and the warm interior lights spilled into the night, Mara suddenly realized how vain her attempts at composure were. Shane was too much the same as he was when she had been so mindlessly in love with him. She could sense the return of familiar seductive feelings, and she wanted to be propelled backward in time to a familiar setting that was carefree and loving.

A smile touched the corners of the hard line of Shane's mouth, and his eyes seemed to come alive as he looked down at her. His gaze poured over her, and even fully dressed in a rose-colored crepe gown, she felt naked. Shane loosened his tie and raked his fingers through his ebony hair in a gesture of indecision. "You . . . look . . . gorgeous," he murmured with a frown, as if the thought were a traitorous admission. "But then, you always manage to look elegant, don't you?"

His voice was a seductive potion to her, and she felt a need to break his disarming spell. "Shane . . . I—"

He interrupted. "Aren't you going to invite me into your home?" A black, somewhat disdainful eyebrow cocked.

"I thought we were going out."

"We are. But we have to talk a few things over first. Don't you agree?" There was an urgency to his words, as if four years was too long a time to bridge the widening abyss that separated them.

Mara drew in a long, unsteady breath as she realized that she hadn't moved out of the doorway, as if her small body would somehow discourage him from entering her home. She didn't know quite why, but she understood that she couldn't let him into the house, into her privacy, into her heart. Not again.

"Can't we talk in the restaurant?" she asked, still forming a weak barrier to her home.

"Would you feel safer in a crowd?"

"No . . . yes . . . oh, Shane so much has happened in the last four years. Perhaps we're making a big mistake. I'm not really sure that I want to—"

"Of course you do," he coaxed. "As much as I do." His dark eyes held hers for an instant, and without consciously thinking about it she stepped away from the door. By her movements she invited him inside.

In a scarcely audible voice she managed to pull together her poise and her graciousness. "Excuse my manners, please come in," she whispered. "Could I get you a drink?"

The tightness of his jawline seemed to slacken a little. "Yes—thanks. Bourbon, if you have it."

"I remember," Mara murmured, and led him through the tiled foyer and into the drawing room. As she walked she sensed his eyes roving over the interior of the house, probing into the most intimate reaches of her life. Although he said nothing, there was an air of disapproval in his stance. His dark eyes skimmed the elegant drawing room with its expensive furnishings. He missed nothing: the gracious mint-green brocade of the draperies, the peach-colored linen and velvet that highlighted the Chippendale chairs, the ornate and lavish antique tables that had been part of the Wilcox home for generations, the walls covered in linen and proudly displaying past members of the Wilcox family, even the plush pile of the authentic Persian carpet. Nothing escaped his gaze, from the French doors near the garden to the hand-sculpted Italian marble fireplace, Shane stood with one hand in the pocket of his chocolate-colored slacks, his tweed jacket pushed away from his body, and Mara could tell that he was tense, tightly coiled. When she handed him his drink, she was careful not to let her fingers brush against his, for fear that the passion that had smoldered within her for so long would suddenly be ignited.

Shane's studious gaze traveled to the fireplace, and Mara froze. The glass of wine that she held in her hand remained motionless in the air, suspended halfway to her lips. Upon the Italian marble of the mantel stood a picture of Angie as an innocent two-year-old. The portrait captured Shane's attention, and he strode meaningfully over to the fireplace for a closer look at the child. Mara's breath constricted in her throat as she watched him. Dear God, would he know? Could he guess? Should she tell him—could she? *"She's your daughter, Shane! Your own flesh and blood."* Mara wanted to shout the words but was unable. She raised the trembling glass of wine to her lips and let the cool liquid slide down her suddenly parched throat.

"Is this your little girl?" Shane asked, studying the portrait carefully.

"Yes . . . yes it is. It . . . I mean, the picture was taken almost two years ago . . ." Mara whispered. Again she swallowed the wine. *Tell him! Tell him!* her insistent mind commanded. *No matter what has happened in the past, he has the right to know about his child! No pain or anguish that you have suffered at his hand gives you the right to withhold the fact that he fathered Angie. It's his right! Tell him the truth! Tell him NOW!*

"She's very pretty," Shane observed, "just like her mother." He fingered the portrait as if drawn to the beguiling child's face, and Mara knew that if she didn't steady herself, she would faint. If only she had the courage to tell him the truth. A faint shadow hardened Shane's features. *He must know,* Mara thought.

"Are you all right? Mara?" Shane asked the question, suddenly aware that Mara's face had blanched. His voice seemed distant. "Is something wrong?" Concern flooded his features, and he let his hand drop from the picture frame as he half-ran across the room to Mara's side. His arm captured her waist just as she felt her knees give way and the glass in her fingers slid to the carpet.

"There's so much to explain," she whispered against his jacket.

"I know, I know, baby," he murmured, and kissed the top of her head as he persuaded her to sit on the stiff Victorian sofa. "Don't try to explain anything now. Are you all right, or do you need a doctor? Where are the servants tonight?" His dark eyes darted to the hallway. He started to get up, but Mara placed a staying hand on his sleeve.

"I don't have any servants," she said softly. The faint feeling had passed and color returned to her cheeks.

"No servants? In a house this size?"

"No live-ins. I . . . do have a woman who comes in once a week to help me with the cleaning. The same for the gardener. But that's it. I cook my own meals, and June watches over Angie."

"June? A governess? Where is she?"

Mara's throat tightened again. "No, June's not a governess. Actually, she's Angie's gr- . . . Peter's mother. Angie's with her this evening."

"I see," he retorted, and took a long swallow of his drink. He pulled uncomfortably at his tie and gave Mara a reassessing look. "She must have been the woman who threw me out of here on the day of the funeral!"

"So you were the stranger! Dena guessed as much!" Mara gasped. "Why were you here that day?" Her large, liquid eyes looked directly at him, and he remembered a younger, more innocent time. He found it impossible to fight the urge any longer. An unsteady finger reached out and traced the delicate outline of Mara's refined jaw. Tenderly he persuaded a wisp of tawny hair back into place behind her ear. She felt herself shudder at his touch. He sighed deeply and shook his head.

"I was there that day simply because I couldn't stay away from you any longer. Peter's death was an easy excuse; I wanted to see you. But for some reason your mother-in-law balked, wouldn't let me near you. It was as if she suspected me of something . . . sinister. I could read it in her eyes. I explained that I was an old friend, gave her my card, but she absolutely refused . . ." His voice trailed off, and Mara could sense the restraint that he forced upon himself. The finger stopped its seductive motion. With a scowl he pulled his hand away from her face.

"Then it wasn't business," she whispered.

"Not at all." He walked away from her and buried his fists into his pockets. Satisfied that the distance between them was sufficient, he leaned against the fireplace and surveyed her. Involuntarily, his jaw tightened.

"And now, Shane?" she demanded, hoping that her voice wouldn't give her ragged emotions away. "What about now? Is it business that brings you back here?"

"Yes and no." The expression on his face was as enigmatic as his words. There was a kindness in his features, and yet a different, steely hardness stormed in his eyes. For a moment he hesitated, and Mara was aware of a breakdown in his reserve, but it was quickly reconstructed.

"Did you say that you gave June your card?" Mara inquired, puzzled.

"Yes—but she wouldn't have anything to do with me. Did she give it to you?" he asked, and read the negative answer in her eyes. "I didn't think so. I know it sounds absurd, but that woman holds something against me."

"That's impossible. She doesn't even know you."

Shane shrugged his broad shoulders. "That's the impression that she left with me. But it really doesn't matter."

"She was just upset—it was the day of Peter's funeral, you know."

"Like I said, it doesn't matter. I think we should get going," he suggested, curtly. "We're already late for our reservation."

"I thought you wanted to talk . . ."

"I do and we will. But you look like you could use a good meal, and so could I. We have lots of catching up to do."

Mara regarded him with interest. "What about the proposition about Imagination?"

"That, too."

The evening was dark and still, and the silence was a thick, heavy cloud that separated Mara from Shane as they rode together in the sports car. Neither spoke, afraid to shatter the tranquility of the evening. Each was surrounded by the cloak of his own private thoughts. As Mara cast a surreptitious glance at Shane, she noted the thick black hair blowing softly in the wind, the slightly arrogant straight nose, and the deep-set darkness of his eyes. In the car, with only inches separating their bodies, she was acutely aware of him and his brooding masculinity, just as she had been on the first night that they had met. It had been nearly five years ago, but she could remember that night as clearly as if it were yesterday.

Mara hadn't wanted to attend the surprise birthday party that one of the girls in the office was throwing for the boss. But the hostess had been insistent, and Mara succumbed to the pressure. She didn't want to be the only employee who couldn't make it to Mr. Black's fiftieth birthday party. Against her better judgment she agreed to attend.

That night Mara toyed with the drink in her hand, already forming a plausible excuse to leave the festivities early. The music was loud, the guests even louder, and she seemed distinctly out of place. She looked around the room to find Sandy, the hostess, in order to excuse herself and make a hasty exit.

The dark-eyed stranger must have arrived late because Mara hadn't noticed him earlier. But when she finally did see him, she found him staring intently at her from across the room. His black eyes were friendly, beguiling, and although there must have been over twenty people in the room, in the one suspended instant, when her eyes touched his, Mara felt that she was alone with him. Her breath caught in her throat as he advanced toward her, but she was unable to tear her eyes away from his face.

His was an interesting profile, contoured in smooth angles and planes. His eyes were deepset and very black, the color of midnight. His jaw was strong and square, with the slight trace of a dimple cleaving it, and his nose was extra straight. There was the beginning of laugh lines around his eyes and lips, and an amused twinkle in his eye sparkled as he sauntered over to Mara.

For a hushed moment there was an awkward silence between them, and finally, out of embarrassment, Mara dragged her eyes away from his. She swirled the untouched drink in her hand and gazed at the small whirlpool she created, hoping that she didn't appear as nervous and out of place as she felt.

The man leaned against the counter that separated kitchen from family room and startled Mara by uttering a curse under his breath. "God, I hate these kinds of parties, don't you?" he asked, studying her and taking a long swallow from his drink.

"Birthday parties?" she repeated, thinking the question strange. She shrugged dismissively. "No . . . they're all right, I guess."

His lips formed a grim sort of smile and his eyes reached out for hers. "No, you don't understand. I don't have anything against a birthday celebration—usually."

Mara was clearly confused, and her bewilderment showed on her delicate face. She shook her head negatively, and her blond hair brushed against her neck. "You're right, I don't understand."

"You really don't, do you?" he inquired, obviously amazed. Her subtle innocence intrigued him.

"If you would just tell me what you're talking about," she suggested, a bit sarcastically, and feeling as if he was playing some sort of private game with her.

"Don't you get it? Look around you. Do you notice anything different about us?" He waved his hand expansively, including the rest of the guests in the room.

"About *us?*" she echoed as her eyes glanced toward the other people in the room. Suddenly it dawned on her, and she felt herself blush. "Oh, I see," she mumbled, and discovered that she couldn't meet his dark, probing gaze.

"Damn that Bob Brandon and his wife! They're always trying to get me matched up with somebody!" His jaw clenched and Mara felt an uncontrollable urge to run. She could see as plainly as he that she had been set up as the only single woman to naturally balance the one odd man out. That explained why Sandra Brandon had been so insistent that she attend the party. When Mara had attempted to make excuses yesterday at the office, Sandra had become positively demanding that Mara attend. It was evident now why Sandra had been so insistent. Sandra liked everything in life even, and in her mind there was no such thing as an unattached male.

Shane finished his drink with a flourish and placed the empty glass on the counter. Mara could see that he was trying to control his irritation with the uncomfortable situation. At first she imagined that he was disappointed that she was his date, but his next statement changed her opinion.

"Well, if Bob and Sandy think that I need their assistance in my love life, who am I to argue?" He smiled mockingly. "How about a dance?"

Mara was embarrassed, uncomfortable, and angry with Sandra. She didn't need any man thinking that he *had* to keep her entertained for the evening. She tried vainly to get out of the dance. "You don't have to . . . I mean I . . ."

"You mean 'yes,' don't you?" His dark eyes brooked no argument and he pushed her carefully into the center of the room. The music was soft, barely discernable over the din of the party, and Mara felt stupidly self-conscious, as if she were trying to draw attention to herself. But the moment that the tall man with the strangely appealing eyes wrapped his arms over her and held her intimately against him, she forgot the rest of the guests. It was as if all of her senses were immediately electrified, and the soft, sultry music filtered over the slightly boisterous noise of the crowd to encompass her and the powerful man who held her.

At first her movements were stiff, but as Shane pressed more closely to her, she felt herself begin to relax and mold to the warmth of his long, lean body. His hand at the small of her back guided her. Her head rested lightly against the soft fabric of his shirt, and she closed her eyes to listen to the beating of his heart. She heard a controlled, rhythmic beat, unlike the pulsating drumming in her rib cage.

When her eyes fluttered open for an instant, she noticed Sandy Brandon smiling smugly at the sight of her wrapped in Shane's strong arms. Color darkened Mara's cheeks, but she couldn't help but feel totally at ease with the stranger. They danced together, their bodies swaying with the music, for what seemed both an instant and an eternity. When the tempo of the songs quickened, Shane pulled Mara by the wrist toward the door.

"Let's find a spot that's not so crowded," he decided with a husky voice.

"What do you mean?" she inquired cautiously, and her breath seemed too tight for her throat.

A smile blazed across his tanned face. "I'm suggesting that we leave."

"Together?" she blurted incredulously.

"Of course together," he whispered. "Otherwise our plan wouldn't work, would it?"

"What plan?"

"Well," he drawled, eyeing the crowd with apparent disdain, "I don't know about you, but I'm tired of Sandy Brandon playing the role of matchmaker in my life."

"I don't see how you can hope to change her. She's an incurable romantic who adores fixing people up."

"Doesn't she, though," he observed dryly. "Maybe we can change all that, at least in our case."

"How?" Mara asked, bewildered.

"You'll see," he stated enigmatically. "Do you have a coat?"

Mara couldn't resist the intrigue of the moment. And the look on Sandy Brandon's surprised face as she spied Mara leaving with Shane was worth the gamble of leaving with a complete stranger.

Shane and Mara left together in the flash and roar of his sports car. At the time Mara told herself that she was being careless and throwing caution to the wind—acting completely out of her usually shy and reserved character. All for the sake of a practical joke, or so she tried to convince herself. If she had been honest with herself, she would have had to confess to falling prey to an attraction that she had never before experienced. The dark-eyed stranger was bewitching.

They drove for over an hour in the convertible, at first quietly, as if each might have suddenly regretted the impulsive dash away from the party. But as the black night sped by, and the minutes ticked forward, Shane began to talk and draw Mara out of her silence. Mara was entranced by the romance of it all—riding into the night with a virile, handsome stranger and casting aside all consideration for time or reality. She felt as free as the wind that caught her honeyed hair and brushed it in tangled waves away from her face. His words were serious and kind, and when he favored her with a smile that touched his eyes, the sound of her laughter was caught in the night wind and left in the darkness.

It was nearly midnight when Shane stopped the car. They were far from the city—light-years away from the real world—parked in the solitude by a wooded river. The moon cast a rippling slash of silver on the water and the stars dotted the sky. A light, midsummer breeze played with her hair and the faint fragrance of honeysuckle hung in the air.

Shane held her hand as they walked along the shore of the river. She leaned on him often as the heel of her sandals would slip against the rocks at the river's edge.

They spoke hesitantly and softly, as if the silence of the night were a fragile spell that they dare not break. He paused underneath the protective, needled limbs of a large pine tree, and in the darkness his hand pulled her more intimately to him. In the night, with eyes wide and searching, Mara read the silent passion in Shane's features. His lips found hers in a tentative, gentle kiss, and she felt herself respond to the warm, enticing pressure of his mouth. The faint taste of brandy wet her lips, and she let herself lean against him as the hot burst of womanhood exploded in her body. The kiss, which started so tenderly, deepened in passion, and a dizzying, unreal sensation swept over her. Mara sighed deeply against Shane's lips, yielding to the warm, liquid mouth that was enveloping her.

Suddenly he froze, and as he dragged his lips from her, he swore at himself under his breath. He rotated his head from hers, as if by gazing out into the distance, he could assuage the hunger of desire that ripped through his body.

Mara listened to her own ragged breathing, and she could almost see his body stiffen as she noted with a welling sense of disappointment that he was trying to escape from her and the yearnings of his body by putting a distance between them.

"Oh, God," Shane groaned to himself and looked heavenward. "What am I doing?"

He glanced at her with eyes full of smoldering passion and put a protective arm across her slim shoulders. Tenderly he led her to the base of the pine tree, on a bed of soft boughs, and helped her into a sitting position against the trunk. He sat with his back braced by the tree. She sat, half-laid, in the warm cradle of his strong arms. Her pulse was running wild with surging heat through her body, and she leaned against him. Her heart pounded loudly in the silent, starry evening, destroying the peace of the night.

Time and rational thought had ceased. Mara was mesmerized by the soft night and the warm touch of the man who held her so intimately. His breath fanned her hair, and a musky scent invaded her nostrils. The whisper-soft kisses that he rained against the back of her neck teased her skin and heated her blood. Her pulse, already on fire, blazed through her veins.

"Mara," his throaty voice murmured against her hair. "I want you . . ." It was an unnecessary admission, a fact as true as the night itself.

"I know" was the only response that would pass her lips. His hands on her shoulders were enticing, inviting. The evening was warm and seductive, and the pine tree hung over them, guarding them in its heavy, needled branches. Only a slight breeze disturbed the serenity of the nightfall by mildly moving the boughs.

"You're beautiful," Shane coaxed, and his fingers tickled her neck. "I know this is crazy—I don't know how to describe it—but I need you, Mara. Not because you're a woman, but because you're unique . . . special . . . captivating. You're you, and I want the most intimate part of you."

"You don't even know me," she protested feebly, knowing that she was succumbing to the magic of the seductive night.

"But I do," he whispered hoarsely, and she believed him. She believed the persuasive touch of his fingers against her skin. She believed the warm enticement of the night. And she believed the ragged sound of longing in his voice as it was torn from his throat in an admission of surrender.

His fingers found the buttons of her blouse, and she didn't stop the tender exploration of his lips against her burning skin. She knew only that she wanted him and needed him, and she let him guide her into a new feeling of awareness. He taught her of a need so great that it was a consuming, unquenched ache that burned within her. They discovered each other, and Mara found for the first time in her twenty-four years the bittersweet yearnings and fulfillment of love. She found a satisfaction so strong that it dissolved the pain and replaced the ache with rapture. It was a night lost in the stars. The quiet lights of Asheville winked in the far-off distance while Mara experienced a night ridden with flaming desire and warm, molten surrender.

Dawn awakened her with its rosy warming rays, and Mara realized in the filtered sunlight that she could never love another man. Shane Kennedy, a virtual stranger, but most intimate lover, possessed her body and soul. The memory of the passion that they shared beneath the pine tree overpowered her with its intensity.

When she stirred, Shane opened a lazy eye and squinted against the filtered glare of the morning as it passed through the soft curtain of pine needles. A pleasant, enticing grin stole over his features as he watched with unashamed interest when Mara tried to conceal and cover her nudity. Embarrassment welled within her and she held the scanty protection of her blue chiffon blouse over her exposed breasts.

His dark eyes became serious. "Don't!" he commanded.

"Don't what?" she asked, feigning innocence.

"Don't ever hide from me." He tugged at the blouse and slowly pulled it out of her fingers. His eyes slid restlessly over her breasts and the directness of his gaze mingled with the cool morning air forced her nipples to harden into taut rosy buttons.

"I'm not . . . trying to hide," she murmured, but her voice cracked with emotion and she lowered her head, letting the gilded curtain of her hair shelter her face.

With a groan, he hauled himself up to sit beside her. His face was close to hers, and his fingers cupped her chin in order that she meet his inquiring gaze. "What's wrong?" he asked and she could feel his black probing eyes.

"I'm not used . . . to being . . . naked with a man," she admitted huskily before closing her eyes and letting the flush of scarlet that burned on her cheeks speak for her.

"Well," he mused, encircling her with his arms and giving her a bear hug. "I think that you should get used to it . . ."

She shook her head and feared that the tears gathering in her eyes would spill. "I can't," she whispered.

"Sure you can. You have a beautiful body, and you should be proud of it. You're not ashamed, are you?"

She answered mutely with only her eyes, and bit her lip in order to choke back the sobs that were threatening to explode within her. Her head was rested on her knees for support, as she tried to fight back the storm of tears that threatened to overcome her.

"Mara." His voice was firm. "Please look at me. Don't push me away from you. Not now. Not ever! You mean too much to me."

"You . . . don't have to say . . ."

"Shh. I'm only saying what I mean," he admitted solemnly.

Her eyes found his and she could feel herself begin to drown in the warmth and kindness that she saw in his face, a face that was virile and masculine yet softened with the innocence of recent sleep. His words were spoken slowly and deliberately, as if he had weighed their importance all night.

"I want you to come and live with me."

Mara felt a frown distort her features, and the tears that were promising to fall began to slide unchecked down her cheeks. "Live with you?" she repeated hoarsely, and turned her face away from him. "I . . . I don't know if I can live with you—or any man for that matter, without being married."

"Don't you think that we should get to know each other a little better before we talk about marriage?" he asked realistically, and gave her an affectionate shake.

"I don't know what to think," she admitted.

"Then just trust me, Mara. Trust me . . ."

And she did.

Chapter 4

That period in her life, when she lived so naively and happily with Shane, was long over, she reminded herself as the sleek silver car raced through the busy streets of Asheville. The sports car ground to a halt before an expensive restaurant and inn. The large, three-storied structure stood out in gleaming relief against the darkness of the night. Established just after the Civil War, the inn was painted white, with traditional green shutters on each of the bay windows. Shimmering lanterns, reflecting against the paned windows, poured out a Southern welcome to Mara, beckoning her to enter the well-known establishment.

Mara was propelled unwillingly back to the present and the betraying fact that Shane had a purpose in seeing her. She moistened her lips and couldn't help but wonder if he, too, had been absorbed in memories of the past that they had shared together. The thought was intriguing, but traitorous. If he had wanted to see her, if he had needed her as desperately as she had needed him, he would never have left her to think that he was dead for all of these years.

The shimmering lanterns and the warmth of the night reminded her of the romance and passion that she had shared with Shane. How many times in the past four years had she fantasized about just such an evening with the only man she had ever truly loved? And how many times had she ruthlessly destroyed those conjured imaginings because of what she had thought was the truth—that Shane was dead, gone forever?

Once again the creeping sense of betrayal cooled her blood. Shane must have felt the change in her mood, because as he helped her from the car, he trapped her with a dark, questioning look.

She walked gracefully toward the colonial restaurant, Shane's commanding fingers guiding her with a light but persuasive pressure on her elbow. She tried to ignore the enticement of his touch and concentrate on the elaborate restaurant. The cheerful decor of gleaming wainscoting and blue, floral-print wallpaper helped to lighten her mood. And the staff of the inn, dressed in colonial attire, made her forget momentarily her dilemma with the man she still so feverishly loved.

Shane declined the waiter's invitation that he and Mara join some of the other guests along a long, linen-clad table for family-style dining, where the "down-home" feeling grows as you sit down at the large table with the other patrons and pass the chef's specialties around the table. He preferred more intimate dining arrangements, and the amiable waiter led them to a corner of the inn near a large window, where they could enjoy privacy and a view of a private duck pond. Amber-colored lamps reflected on the water, and a few water birds skimmed quietly on the surface of the pond near the shoreline.

The waiter began to hold Mara's chair for her, but

Shane smiled at the man and assisted Mara into her seat himself. Once she was comfortable, he took his place directly across from her and stared deeply into her eyes, as if trying to delve into the farthest reaches of her mind. Without asking her indulgence, he ordered for the both of them, and for the moment Mara forgot the nagging feeling of deception that had converged upon her. A smile teased her lips, lessening the crackle of the tension in the air, as she noticed that still, after all of the years apart from him, Shane remembered all of her favorite dishes, even down to pecan pie.

After a vintage bottle of Cabernet Sauvignon had been poured and Shane had tasted the wine, he broke through the pretense of small talk that had enveloped them since entering the restaurant. His dark brows drew together and he rubbed the back of his neck with his fingers. Mara sipped her wine patiently, waiting to hear explanations, reasons, alibis, excuses, ANYTHING that would help her understand why he had lied to her four years ago and what he wanted from her now.

"I told you that I was interested in purchasing Imagination Toys," he stated, and watched for her reaction.

Mara nodded slightly and ran a polished fingernail over the rim of her wine glass. "And I told you that Imagination wasn't for sale." A muscle worked in his jaw and a scowl creased his forehead. His entire body became rigid.

"That you did. But I was hoping that you might have altered your position."

In answer she puckered her lips thoughtfully, but shook her head. To Shane, her pensive motion and concentrated brow were the most alluring provocations that he could imagine. Her tawny hair moved wistfully against her cheek as she thought.

"I'm sorry, but I can't sell. It's not that your offer isn't tempting . . ." Her deep blue eyes met his in total honesty. "It's just that I feel . . . responsible . . . not only for the company, but also to Peter's family."

Something akin to anger swept his face, and his eyes, once darkly enticing, became stony. "Responsible to the Wilcox family?" he echoed, incredulous. "Your loyalty surprises me!"

"My loyalty surprises *you?"* she repeated in disbelief.

"That's right," he snapped. "I really don't think that devotion is your long suit!"

"Why not? I've always been faithful to . . ." she tried to explain, but the last word, which should have been Shane's name, stuck in her throat. It was the truth. In her mind she had never loved another man, and she had remained faithful to Shane until she had thought him dead and Peter had convinced her to marry him. But even during the marriage, she had never loved her husband—not with the same burning intensity that she had tasted with the man who was seated angrily opposite her in the quaint Southern restaurant. She tried tactfully to change the subject. After clearing her throat, she spoke in a voice that was devoid of the feelings that were raging within her.

"You said earlier that you had an alternative proposition? I'd like to hear it. I'd also like to know why you're so interested in Imagination. There must be a dozen toy companies that would do just as well."

"You're probably right. But I chose Imagination because of you. No other reason."

"Not exactly sound business practice," she deduced,

but she couldn't help but lift her eyebrows to indicate that she hadn't missed his comment or any of its poignant implications. Her heart turned over, and for a moment she thought that he might elaborate, but the waiter came to remove the dishes and serve the dessert. Shane's intimate mood seemed to have vanished.

When he spoke again, it was in a tightly controlled, businesslike voice. "Do you know anything about Delta Electronics?" he asked.

"Your company?" She shrugged her slim shoulders and touched her napkin to her lips. "Not much, other than the fact that you manufacture computers—"

"Micro-computers," he corrected. Her brows pulled together, and he sighed. "I guess I'd better start at the beginning."

"It might help!" She leaned back against the chair in a totally attentive pose.

"When I got back from Northern Ireland," he began, but her face froze in disbelief at his words, and all of the tension of the last few hours destroyed her facade of Southern civility.

"When you got back from Northern Ireland?" she whispered with a distinct catch in her voice. "Just like that?" She snapped her fingers. "You haven't even explained to me what happened to you in that horrible war, and why you let me think that you were dead!" Her eyes showed the anguish that she had lived four years ago and her breath was ragged and torn from her throat. "You were just going to start a lecture on microcomputers with a phrase like 'when I got back from Northern Ireland'? For God's sake, Shane, what happened over there? Why did your father tell me that you were dead? For so many years you let me think . . ." Her voice broke with emotion and tears began running down her face and onto the table. She reached for her napkin to cover her eyes, but her small clenched fist continued to pound against the table, rattling the silver and the wine glasses. "Why? Why?" she murmured, only vaguely aware that people at nearby tables were beginning to stare at the spectacle she was creating. Her shoulders drooped, and she couldn't stem the uneven drops that ran in darkened smudges from her eyes.

Shane listened to her tirade, his large hand half covering his face, as if to shield him from her torment. He couldn't bear to see her so ravaged, and yet he knew that he was the source of her anguish. Aware that he had to get her out of the restaurant, he fumbled in his pocket for some bills and stuffed them into the open palm of the waiter as he helped Mara to her feet and ushered her out of the building past the disapproving eyes and gaping mouths of several of the well-to-do patrons.

The drive home was silent, and with extreme difficulty Mara regained her poise. She stared into the night and felt the brooding silence of the man seated so closely to her. Mara was drained and exhausted, and Shane was driving the small car as if the devil himself were chasing them. The tires screeched against the pavement, the gears were ripped savagely, and Mara wondered vaguely if Shane was going to kill them both. It didn't matter, she thought wearily, but an image of Angie's laughing face broke into her lonely thoughts, and she realized that everything mattered. It mattered very much. Her life, Shane's life, and most especially their daughter's welfare.

When the headlights flashed against the oak trees that guarded the circular drive and the large front porch of the house loomed into Mara's view, she felt a wave of relief wash over her. The strain of the day had taken its toll on her, and she was thankful to be home.

Shane walked her to the door, and she didn't object when he asked to come in. She fumbled with the key, and he helped her unlock the door. Their hands touched in the darkness, and a warm possessive heat leaped in Mara's veins. She tried to calm herself and tell herself that all of her reminiscent memories were to blame for her reaction to him, but she couldn't ignore the pounding of her heart at his touch. Shane pushed open the door, and once inside, locked it. Mara didn't protest— it was impossible to do so, because it felt so natural that he was home with her again after nearly five long, lonely, years.

Still silent, he poured himself a drink from the decanter at the bar. He lifted the glass to her in a silent offering, but she shook her head negatively. The last thing she wanted was a drink to cloud her tired mind.

After slumping onto the couch, Mara kicked off her shoes and tucked her feet beneath her on the soft cushions. She waited. Shane finished his quick drink and poured himself another. She watched. Was it her imagination, or did Shane's hands tremble slightly as he poured the drink? He poured yet another glass of brandy and handed it to her over her whispered protests.

"You want to know about what happened in Belfast, don't you?" he asked curtly.

She took a deep breath and nodded. Her blue eyes reached out for his as she nodded her head.

"All right, but here." He gave her the brandy.

"I didn't want a drink, remember."

"You might change your mind," he responded gravely, and without further question she accepted the drink.

Shane sat beside her, but didn't look at her. Instead, he concentrated on the clear amber fluid in his snifter and pulled at his tie, which he finally discarded angrily. When he began to speak, his voice was hushed, disturbingly distant.

"You know that several of us went over there?" She nodded. "Well, everything was going just fine—most of the work had been completed. The rest of the crew had already taken off back for the States, leaving just Frank and me to finish the last few finishing touches. There wasn't much work left—Frank and I just had to retake a couple of feet of film that hadn't worked out quite right the first time. If everything had gone as planned, we would have been home within the week.

"It was uncanny how well everything went together." He paused for a long drink, and his eyes darkened in memory. Mara felt her stomach tighten. "The last day that we were shooting, it wasn't even anything controversial, just a shot of parents and kids in the park, that sort of stuff. There was this cathedral, a huge stone building, and the parishioners were just arriving for services. It was an absolutely gorgeous Sunday morning . . ."

"And?" Mara prodded, as his voice trailed off.

"And . . . Frank and I stopped for a quick shot. We left everything in the van, other than the shoulder camera and the portable microphone.

"There were a lot of people there, all ages. Parents, children, babies, grandmas, all talking and climbing the steps. The children were playing, laughing, but suddenly I—" he searched for the right words, and his voice was tight, as if it was an effort to speak "—sensed . . . felt that something wasn't right. I had been filming the gardens, near the steps of the church, but I pulled my camera away from the church just as a horrible noise came from a parked car. The car exploded, metal flew everywhere, people screamed and ran, the timbers of the church rocked, the stone steps cracked . . . there was blood, bodies . . . cars smashed into parked vehicles to avoid running over the people who had been knocked into the street by the explosion. And then I felt something painful on the side of my head—I heard a baby cry just as I passed out. When I came to, I was in a hospital bed, and a nurse was shining a light into my eye. Two weeks had passed." Shane's voice sounded as dead as Mara felt. Tears glistened in her eyes and she took a sip of the brandy.

"And the children that you saw playing?"

Shane drew a whispering breath and shook his head. "That's the worst of it. Several entire families were killed. All of them." Shane turned to face Mara and she saw the rage and guilt that contorted his features. "Those people died because of me, Mara."

"What? How can you blame yourself? That's crazy . . ."

"Why do you think that particular church was bombed—at that time? It was common knowledge that we were filming a piece on terrorism at the time—"

"No!"

"It wouldn't be too difficult to have figured out the general area where we would be—"

"I don't believe it. How could they have known?" His eyes held the sincerity and the pain of the guilt that he had borne for four years. "You can't be sure . . ." she whispered, but knew that her protests were only the ghost of hope that he would absolve himself of his blame.

Pain twisted his features. "I know, damn it! I know.

It was our story that brought attention to that area of the city. We'd been friendly with several of the local residents, and they must have been on the opposing side, you see, and somehow, we weren't careful enough. The word got out, and we created an opportunity for the terrorists to strike again!"

Mara closed her eyes, as if by force she could destroy the painful picture that Shane was painting.

"You can't blame yourself!"

"Then who is to blame Mara? Who?"

"The system . . . the economics of the country . . . the Protestants . . . the Catholics . . . I don't know."

"Well, I do!" With his final damning admission, Shane swallowed the remainder of his drink. He looked to the bar, as if he intended to pour himself another, but put the empty snifter down in disgust. "Don't you think that I've tried to convince myself that there was nothing I could have done to prevent this—that we were all just victims of fate? But late at night, when I have to face myself alone, I see those young eager faces, and I know that somehow I was a part of that tragedy!"

"Oh, Shane," Mara murmured, hoping to somehow heal the wounds that had been festering within him. She reached out her hand and gently stroked his chin. Her fingers became moist from the tiny beads of sweat that had accumulated over his upper lip. He swallowed before continuing.

"And so . . . there was a mix-up of some sort. Everyone at the hospital thought I was Frank—and that Frank was me." His voice was low. "We didn't carry our identification on us—it was locked in the van, and the van was totaled as a truck braked to avoid colliding with some of the injured on the street. Our I.D., camera gear . . . film . . . clothing . . . everything was in the van. And somehow, at least for a while, in all of the confusion and aftermath of the explosion, the mix-up in our identities remained."

Mara guessed the rest of the grisly story. "And Frank was killed?"

"He died before the ambulance could get him to the hospital."

"Oh, God," Mara breathed, and felt a nauseous rumbling in her stomach.

"That's right, Mara. Dad didn't lie to you. He actually thought that I was dead."

"Oh, no . . ." Mara murmured, her fingers still caressing the firm line of his jaw. "So much has happened to us . . ."

"I know, Mara, I know." His lips touched hers and she felt a yearning that she hadn't known for years. His tongue outlined her lips and tasted the salt of her tears that had passed over her mouth. With a shudder, he groaned as he pulled her more closely to him. When he parted her lips and their tongues met, she felt a rush of molten desire well up from the deepest part of her and spread through her blood in thundering currents of fiery passion. His hands touched her hair, at first tentatively, and finally in heated desire as he wound the blond curls through his fingers and let his face nuzzle the length of her neck, exploring her throat, the shell of her ear, the supple muscles of her shoulders.

His fingers moved from her hair and down her neck in down-soft touches of intimate persuasion. She gasped for air as his thumb found the pulse at the base of her throat and outlined the delicate bone structure in warm circles of desire. The seductive movements created a whirlpool of heat, to churn desperately within her. She sighed against him and felt his own labored moan as he searched for and discovered the top button of her dress. He took the pearl button in his mouth and with ease forced it through the buttonhole. As he did so, his tongue touched deliciously against the rounded swell of her bosom, and her breast ached with need. His head dipped lower—to the next button. Once again the warm, wet tongue lapped enticingly at her breast, only to draw away in agonizing suspense. His fingers slowly opened the dress, parting it only enough to let him caress the ivory cleavage with his face.

"Oh, Shane," Mara sighed, the warmth of ecstasy overtaking her. A nagging thought told her that she should stop him, but she found it impossible to deny that which she had wanted for four years. She wanted to enjoy the sweet surrender of her body to his, and forget, at least for the next few hours, all of the sadness and sorrow that had separated them over the past four years. She wanted to reach out to him and help salve some of the guilt that he had borne.

He sighed against her and pushed the clean angles of his face into the folds of her skirt. The same words that she remembered from their first night together echoed in her ears. "Mara, God, but I want you. I've ached for you for over four years," he admitted in hot breaths that scorched through the silk fabric of her dress and caressed her legs in hot whispers. "Let me love you again."

His hand reached under the hem of her skirt to embrace her thigh, and she groaned softly as her legs parted. "Let me love you, Mara," he pleaded, and her answer was a breathless moan of yearning hunger. He stroked her thigh, and involuntarily she arched. He pulled at her panty hose and discarded them into a heap on the floor. And then, ever so gently, he petted her—letting his warm fingers brush against the length of her calves and thighs. "I want you, Mara, I want you as no man has ever wanted a woman."

"Oh, God . . . Shane, I want you, too."

With her soul shaking admission, he scooped her into his arms and lithely carried her out of the drawing room and up the expansive sweep of the staircase. She clung to him and placed liquid kisses against his neck, but at the top of the stairs he hesitated, and she nodded in the direction of her room. He carried her into the expansive bedroom and stopped near the door. He eyed the darkened room speculatively, and for an indeterminate minute he hesitated.

"Is this the bed you shared with Peter?" he asked harshly.

Her eyes, glazed with drugged passion, instantly cleared. "No," she whispered. "I moved into this room . . . before he got sick."

"Humph!" His dark eyes found hers, and after a flicker of doubt he carried her over to the bed. The down comforter sagged beneath their combined weight, and the cool satin felt smooth and welcome against her bare legs.

"You don't know how much I've missed you," Shane conceded, his breath dew-soft against her earlobe.

Her own breath, a prisoner in her lungs, escaped with the question that had been searing her mind for the past twelve hours. "Then why, Shane? Why didn't you come back to me?"

Her blue eyes pleaded with him, and the picture she made—a lovely full-grown woman, still innocent in her own blushing manner—was too much for him to bear. The golden hair, tousled carelessly against the cool blue comforter, the flush of pink under the surface of her creamy complexion, and those eyes—blue as the morning sky and innocently mature. "It doesn't matter—not anymore—I'm here now," he whispered before pressing his lips, moist with hunger, against hers.

She let her lashes fall over her eyes, and let her body react to the exquisite rapture that he was evoking within her. Too many years had passed, and too many unanswered questions still lingered. An ugly corner of her mind nagged at her, but she ignored the thought and abandoned herself to him. Her hands caught in the thick black silkiness of his hair, and her fingers moved against his scalp, as if by their touch she could erase the pain of four desolate years.

His hands slid beneath the dress and let it slip silently to the floor. Warm palms pressed urgently against the contour of her spine and the supple roundness of her hips. He pulled her urgently to him, and she could feel his virile need and hunger burning in his loins. "Oh, Mara," he whispered as he unclasped her bra and let her breasts, snowy white, fall unbound against him. "You're more beautiful than I remembered." Tentatively, he reached forward and circled one rounded swell with his finger, enticing a sweet ache in Mara that aroused her to even higher pinnacles of yearning.

His tongue, warm and soft, touched delicately against her breast and teased her nipple until she felt a swelling ache of torment. His hands and fingers massaged her, and finally, just as she thought she could endure no more of his teasing, the warm, moist cavern of his mouth closed over her waiting taut nipple, and a bursting wave of desire engulfed her. She shuddered with the force of her emotions.

Quickly, he discarded what was left of their clothing, destroying the flimsy barriers that kept her from him. She sucked in her breath as she looked upon him, long and lean and virile—exactly as she had remembered him and precisely as she had fantasized about him a hundred times over in her mind. Her fingers outlined the strong muscles of his back and abdomen, which glistened with a salty film of perspiration.

His voice broke through the night, in pure animal pleasure. "Oh, God, Mara ... I can't wait any longer ..."

His head lowered and he kissed her abdomen and belly button, letting his tongue slide urgently over her skin. His hands pulled against her hips, until his face was covered with the warm creamy complexion of her abdomen. Soft purring noises escaped from her throat as he murmured her name over and over against her warm flesh.

Just as she thought she could endure no more of the tormented ecstasy, he pushed her legs apart with his knees and settled comfortably in the saddle of her soft hips. "I'm sorry, Mara, but I can't wait any longer," he groaned, as his face came up to hers and his lips sought the warmth of her mouth.

"Neither can I," she whispered, and in one hushed instant, he came to her, moving against her with the desire that had tortured him for years. She felt molten hot explosions ripping through her body, his cataclysmic, shuddering surrender, and a burst of passion as their bodies came hungrily together in complete, rekindled union.

Shane cradled her against him, and she felt younger than she had in years. She gave into the yearnings of her body, and fell asleep nestled in the warm strength of his arms. She knew that she had to tell him about

Angie, and she wanted desperately to understand everything that he had experienced in Northern Ireland, but she couldn't bring herself to shatter the peace that they had found and shared together.

Late in the night, when Shane awakened her with his own returning passion, she thought about the absurdity of the situation, but kept her thoughts to herself. In the morning, she promised a guilty corner of her mind— I'll get everything straight with him . . . in the morning.

Chapter 5

When morning dawned, sending forth warm rays of summer sunshine, and Mara awakened sleepily, she felt a tranquility and a peace that she hadn't experienced in years. Curling up comfortably against Shane's strong body in a dreamless sleep had created a warm, delicious feeling that wrapped her in a rosy cloak of good humor as she stretched languidly on the bed.

She watched Shane, still sleeping soundly next to her. The lavender sheet, which she clutched to her naked breast, was draped casually over his dark-skinned body. All tension seemed to be drained away from him, and the rock-hard muscles were relaxed in slumber. Even with the evidence of a beard against his chin, he looked younger and softer than he had the night before. He lay on his side, an arm stretched over his head, his bronzed skin deepened by the pale color of the bedding.

The morning sun was to Mara's back, and through the window it cast warm rays past the thin slats of the blinds, causing an uneven striping of shadows over his body. He stirred after a few moments, the sun in his eyes and Mara's intense gaze awakening him.

A sleepy eye cracked open and a smile, crooked but becoming, spread across his features as he let his eyes wander caressingly over her body. He stretched, and in one lithe movement pulled the sheet away from her breasts. His dark eyes reached for her, and she could sense the flames of passion sparking in their ebony-colored depths.

"Do you know," he inquired lazily, as a finger came up to outline the swell of her breast, "that you're more beautiful in the morning than I had remembered?" His finger stopped its warm, seductive movement. "I didn't think that was possible."

She reached for his finger and halted its further exploration by holding it to her lips. "And do you know," she countered, suggestively, "that you and I have an incredible mountain of things that have to be sorted out today?"

"But we've got all morning," he assured her, and brushed a golden curl away from her face.

"No . . . no, Shane, we don't."

The firm quality of her answer surprised him. "What do you mean?" he asked, and suddenly became serious. Noting the pained look that had crossed her face, he pulled away from her, but couldn't help but touch her forehead, as if to wipe away the lines of concentration that furrowed her brow.

"There are things that we have to discuss . . ."

"Nothing so earth shattering that it won't wait," he argued seductively, and pulled her down to lie next to him before covering her lips with his. The weight of his chest, crushing against her breasts, made her heart race in anticipation. His magic was working on her again.

Reluctantly, she pulled her mouth from his, determined to explain about Angie. "Shane . . . there's so much to say," she began, trying to ignore the passion that was heating within her. "Some things have to be discussed."

"So . . let's discuss them right now," he suggested. His smile was satisfied, almost evil, as he let his fingers circle her lips in rapturous swirls.

"Shane! Be serious . . . *please,*" she implored breathlessly.

His weight shifted and he eyed her studiously. Something was weighing heavily on her mind—that much was obvious. "All right," he agreed, pulling apart from her. The few inches on the bed that separated them seemed an incredible distance to Mara. He levered himself on one elbow, partially supported by a pillow, and watched her, waiting to hear whatever confession she thought was necessary. He thought fleetingly of Peter Wilcox, and a sour, uneasy feeling formed in the pit of his stomach.

His stare was intense, and his partially covered body compelling. Mara had trouble finding the words that should have come easily to her—how could she begin?

"Let's go downstairs," she suggested, biting her lip.

"I thought you wanted to talk."

"I do. But I would rather do it . . somewhere else . . . where I can think more clearly . . ."

His dark eyebrow quirked in interest and he shrugged his shoulders. "If it would be easier for you." He reached for his clothing, cast in a wrinkled pile on the floor, and wondered about the upcoming discussion. There was a confrontation in the air—he could almost taste it.

Knowing that if she didn't explain to Shane about Angie as soon as possible, she would lose her frail nerve, she wondered how he would take the news that he had a nearly four-year-old daughter. Would he believe it? How would he react? Mara slid off of the bed and walked quickly to the closet to grab her apricot-colored terry robe that was hanging on a peg. She didn't turn around, but she could feel Shane's dark eyes roving over her naked backside as she shrugged into the robe. "A pity," she heard him mutter to himself, but she didn't respond to the passion she visualized was on his face. She knotted the belt of the robe angrily, forcing herself to keep the promise of the night before—that she would tell him about Angie. It was his right! She meant to keep that promise to herself, no matter how difficult it proved to be. Also, before anything else happened, she *had* to know why he had waited so long to come back to her, and the reason for his sudden desire for her after four quiet, lonely years.

The seductive mood of the bedroom was broken by the airy cheerfulness of the kitchen. The clean hard surfaces of bright rust-colored tile and warm butcher-block countertops brought Mara back to reality. As she sat across from Shane at the small breakfast table, Mara wondered if she had the nerve to ask all of the questions that plagued her. She swirled cream into her coffee and watched her cup studiously as the dark brown liquid absorbed the milky cream.

Steeling herself, she raised her eyes to meet his. The pungent aroma of coffee filled her nostrils as she looked deeply into his black gaze. As if anticipating the worth of her question, Shane's face became completely sober, his stare penetrating. Mara felt as if he were looking into the deepest corners of her mind.

"You wanted to talk," he coaxed gently.

She licked her lips, a movement he found devastatingly distracting. Her voice was low and direct. "That's right," she agreed hesitantly. Oh, God, why was this so difficult? "There are things that we have to discuss. Things I need to know . . . things that you *have* to know."

A dark eyebrow cocked. "Go on . . ."

Mara sighed deeply, took an experimental sip of the scalding brew, and glanced out the windows, past the broad expanse of green lawn, past the now empty stables to the backdrop of the imperial mountains. How could she begin? How could she explain that he had a daughter? Turning back to face him, the silence beginning to gnaw at her, she found Shane still glaring at her, and this time she found the strength to meet his unwavering black gaze. Her voice, though breathless, was firm, and she controlled her hands that had begun to tremble by gripping the coffee cup tightly.

"Shane, I need to know why you didn't come back to me. I just don't understand why it took you four years to show up."

A flicker of doubt and confusion flashed over his face. He seemed almost suspicious, and his voice was harsh, brittle. "I thought that I explained all of that last night."

Mara closed her eyes and bit her lower lip. This was going to be more difficult than she had imagined. "I understand about the hospital and the identity mix-up. And I realize that your father didn't lie to me—he thought you were dead at the time that I spoke with him." She gulped a drink of hot coffee to steady herself and strengthen her determination. "But," she continued, "what I don't understand is why, when you finally got out of the hospital . . . why you didn't . . . you wouldn't . . ." her voice trailed off.

"I didn't come back for you," he finished for her. "You don't understand that?" he snapped, fury and incredulity twisting his features. A storm of emotion passed over his face, and his eyes had turned to stone. His voice was vehement with the anger that he had repressed for the last four years. "I *did* come back for you, Mara, after spending nearly two months in a London hospital! And when I got back here, what did I find? Were you waiting for me as I had expected you to be? No! Of course not—that was much too much to ask, wasn't it?" he challenged from across the table.

The words that were forming in Mara's throat died as he blasted on.

"You know, I wondered why you never answered my letters. And I thought it strange that your phone had been disconnected, with no forwarding number. But I found out, didn't I? The hard way. I found that the woman I loved and who I thought loved me was married to another man. Within three months, Mara . . . three lousy months!" His lips curled in contempt as he looked at her and the fury that he had hidden away surfaced.

A feeble protest formed in her mouth, but he continued to speak harshly, as if the dam of silence that had held his torment at bay was suddenly washed away. All Mara could do was listen, unbelieving.

"Not only that, Mara dear," he sneered, "but you were pregnant, weren't you? I wonder just how long you had planned to keep me on the string? My trip to Northern Ireland was very convenient for you, wasn't it?" he blasted.

She shook her head in confusion and frustration, tears sprouted in her eyes and blurred her vision, but still he continued. His tirade wasn't over.

"I don't know how I could have been so blind," he admitted, his voice heavy with self-contempt. "You must have been seeing Wilcox while I was still here— or very soon after. All the time that I was away, I thought—no, make that I *expected*—you to be faithful, but I guess that was too much to ask, wasn't it? The minute my airplane took off, you conveniently found yourself another lover, didn't you? Tell me—" his voice broke with the emotion that he had hoped to keep hidden within him "—just how long did you think you could keep up the charade with me? Were you seeing Wilcox while I was still in Asheville? What was it—his money that attracted you to him?" Bright fires of anger and disgust burned in his eyes.

"No!" she screamed, finding her voice. He grabbed her wrist menacingly.

"Liar!"

"No, no!" She shook her head in shame and disbelief. Was this the same man who had been so gentle, so thoughtful in bed only minutes before? "Peter was never my lover!"

Shane yanked on her wrist, and she was forced closer to him, leaning across the table. The coffee cup clattered to the floor, breaking and splashing the murky liquid against her robe. Shane's tormented face was only inches from hers, and his hot, angry breath scorched her cheeks.

"Don't lie to me!" he commanded.

Blue eyes snapped in indignation. Without thinking, she felt her free hand arc and she slapped him with all of the force that she could find, while she pulled her head regally high, over the taunts of his degrading insults.

"You bastard! How dare you accuse me of being unfaithful!" she shot back at him. "I never looked at another man, much less slept with one!"

"How can you expect me to believe that?"

"It's the truth!" Her lips thinned, and her eyes glittered like ice. "If you would let go of me and just listen for a minute, you could stop these ridiculous insinuations."

Shane's eyes narrowed. He knew that he should be

suspicious, but the honesty of her eyes and the haughty disdain with which she looked upon him shook his resolve. His grip on her wrist slackened. She withdrew her hand and rubbed the wrist, never letting her eyes leave his face.

"Then . . . what about Wilcox?" he accused, harshly. "Why did you marry him?"

"I thought you were dead, for God's sake!" She slumped back into her chair and rubbed her tired eyes. "Shane, if you would just calm down and listen, I'll try to explain." A tremor in her voice belied her commanding words.

Shane crossed the kitchen and raked his long fingers through his black hair. Leaning against the cherrywood cupboards, he folded his arms over his chest and eyed her warily. His muscles were tight, tense, as he watched her. She wasn't lying, he knew that much instinctively, and the sting of her contempt still burned against his cheek. "All right," he conceded impatiently, his voice barely audible. "I'm listening."

"It's true," she began, her blue eyes never leaving his. "I was pregnant when I got married."

His lips thinned menacingly, but he remained silent, his stony gaze daring her to continue.

"But . . . it's not what you think. You see . . . I . . . I was pregnant when you left—only I hadn't realized it at the time. And then—" her voice trembled and she began shredding a paper napkin from the table "—and . . . then, when you didn't call . . . or write, I became worried. I called your father, because I needed to get in touch with you, and that's when I found out that you were dead . . ."

"You wanted to get in touch with me?" Shane was incredulous and darkly angry. "Why? Did you want my address in order to send me a wedding invitation?"

he asked, his lips curling with sarcasm. "Why, damn it!" A fist crashed against the countertop.

"You're not listening—I wanted to get in touch with you—needed to tell you about the baby . . ."

"As if I would want to know!"

". . . our baby, Shane—don't you understand? I was pregnant with *your* child!"

"Oh, God," he groaned, and shook his head. "No . . . it's too farfetched . . ." he began, but the anger in his eyes died as he came to terms with the truth. A quiet uncertainty lingered in his gaze, and his tanned face drained of color. "What are you trying to say, Mara?" he demanded, his lips barely moving and a look of incredulous disbelief crossing his face. His fingers gripped the edge of the counter as if for support.

"For God's sake, Shane," Mara cried, her breath torn from her lungs. "I'm trying to explain to you that Angie's your daughter, that I only married Peter because it was the best thing that I could do for *our* child!"

"You can't expect me to believe . . . all of this," he retorted, but his midnight gaze wavered.

"It's true," Mara breathed. "Why would I lie?"

"I don't know . . ."

"Then why can't you believe me?"

Shane pushed a wayward lock of hair angrily aside, and Mara noticed that his hands trembled. "You can't really expect me to believe that you were pregnant with my child, and yet the minute you thought I was dead, you were able to find a replacement father. It's all too incredible."

"Incredible or not—that's the way it happened, all because I thought that you were dead!" Her blue eyes, clouded with disappointment at his reaction, pierced his. "Angie is your daughter!"

"Why . . . why didn't you tell all of this to me last night?"

A grim smile captured her lips. "Yesterday was confusing and shocking—I hadn't expected to ever see you again. And when I did, I wanted to be sure that the timing was right, I guess." Her honeyed brows drew together thoughtfully. "I needed time to work things out . . ."

"You mean, that it occurred to you not to tell me," he accused.

"Never!"

"Oh, God," Shane moaned in painful prayer as the realization of the worth of her words caught hold of him. Mara wasn't lying. As incredible as it seemed, Angie was his daughter. Knowing what he did now, the resemblance in the portrait he had fingered just last night startled him. Peter Wilcox had raised his child in the four years that he had been away. "And how," he asked raggedly, stunned by the weight of her announcement, "did you think that marrying someone else would be good for her?" His question slashed through the air like a gilded saber.

"What else could I do?" she implored, her eyes filling with tears of despair as she witnessed an impenetrable mask closing over his angled features.

"You could have been honest and strong enough to have kept the baby yourself and not be pressured by Asheville society's morals. You could have given *my* child *my* name, if indeed she is mine!"

"You saw the picture on the mantle—she's your daughter, Shane, whether you want to believe it or not! And I won't stand for your giving me the advantage of your hindsight and telling me what I should have done with my life!" She stood up and faced him with an arctic gaze. "I thought you were dead, Shane—DEAD!

Not missing. Not even hiding from me, but dead! I *never* expected to see you again. You could have prevented that, you know, by coming home to me. I don't think I owe you any apologies, none whatsoever. Peter wanted to marry me, and I agreed. I wanted our child to grow up in a normal lifestyle, with loving parents. Everything that I did was with Angie's welfare uppermost in my mind! Can't you see that?"

"What I see is that you schemed for Wilcox to marry you, and I call that tantamount to prostitution—passing off another man's child as his!"

Mara slapped the table in frustration with her small, curled fist. "Don't even suggest anything so absolutely preposterous!" she warned him. "I didn't pass Angie off as anything but your child—to Peter. And he had the kindness and the decency to marry me and accept Angie, nonetheless. He knew that she was your child, but for the sake of practicality we let everyone else think that she was his."

For a moment there was a long silence. Shane looked out the window, seemingly mesmerized by the view of the gracious lawn, the gleaming white fence, the empty paddock. He rubbed the back of his neck furiously with his hand as if trying to wipe away some of the anger that was raging within him, before turning once again to face Mara.

"Shane," she said evenly, "if I had had even the slightest idea that you were alive—"

"What about my letters?" he demanded.

"I never got any letters from you and the mail from my old apartment was forwarded here . . ."

"Well, someone got them, you can be sure of that. They were never returned to me!" He paused for a moment, his black gaze clouded as he thought. "And what would you have done, Mara, if you had known that I was alive? Would you have waited for me? Is that what you were beginning to say?"

"Of course."

He waved his hand angrily in the air and cut her off in mid-sentence. Closing his eyes and shaking his head, he walked past her and out the kitchen door. As the screen door banged shut Mara sighed deeply. Her own anger and indignation burned within her, and she knew it was best to let him be, give him time alone to accept the fact that he had a child. What had she expected anyway? That he would be thrilled with the fact . . . that he would love the child instantly, that he would fall in love with her all over again?

As she reached down and began to pick up the pieces of the shattered coffee cup, she wondered to herself, what was it that they always said—you can never go back? Well, they were right.

Mara took the time to wipe up the floor and straighten the kitchen before following Shane outside. Once again in control of her ragged emotions, she knew that she had to finish the discussion about Angie. Whether Shane liked the fact or not, he had a daughter to consider.

Her resolve wobbled a little as she saw him sitting, his head in his hands, on the top step of the long, shaded back porch. The morning sun was high in the sky, and only a few wisps of white clouds lingered near the mountain peaks. The air was flavored with the scent of pine and honeysuckle, and aside from the deep anger that kept Shane and Mara apart, the day promised to be perfect.

If Shane had noticed her entrance into his privacy, he didn't acknowledge her presence. He continued to hold his head in his hands and stare, almost unseeing, at the glorious Carolina day.

Mara dusted a spot on the steps and sat next to him. "Perhaps I shouldn't have told you," she whispered, half to herself as she smoothed the apricot robe over her legs.

"Don't be ridiculous. I wanted to know," he muttered in a voice devoid of emotion. "Besides which, you can't run from the truth, Mara, as you did when you married Wilcox."

Mara sighed heavily. "I told you that I married Peter for Angie's sake."

"Is that right?" he shot back vehemently. "And what about you? Didn't you do it for yourself?" His dark eyes swept over the large colonial house, the expansive back porch, the elegant gardens, and the rest of the well-tended grounds. "This isn't such a bad way to live, is it? Lots easier than raising a child on your own. I don't suppose that it took you very long to get accustomed to this kind of lifestyle, now, did it?"

"You don't understand . . ."

"You bet I don't! How could you marry another man, Mara, knowing that you were carrying my child? And what about all the nights after you were married? Do you expect me to believe that you and Wilcox never made love? You can't possibly take me for such a fool!"

The tears that she had pressed back began to tumble unwanted down her cheeks, but she managed to level her gaze at Shane. "No, Shane, I don't expect for you to believe anything of the kind. If I did, it would be a lie. I did make love to Peter, over and over again in the three years that we were married." Shane winced at the words, his dark eyes glowering in bitterness. "But you have to remember," she cautioned, noting the twisted look of rage on his face, "that I believed you were dead. Otherwise, I swear that I would never have let

Peter, or for that matter any other man, lay a finger on me! You have to believe that!"

Shane's face was rigid, his severe jawline clenched as he watched her. The clear honesty in her eyes, the regal tilt of her defiant chin, the stain of tears that ran down her cheeks, everything about her posture convinced him that she was baring her soul to him.

He groaned to himself and then reached for her hand, which he pressed to his lips. "Oh, baby," he sighed, letting his broad shoulders droop. "What's happened to us? Why can't we trust each other?" He pulled her gently onto his lap and buried his face against her breasts. "I believe you, Mara—I believe you."

Mara shuddered in relief and clutched him as if she thought he might disappear. Her choked words came out between breathless sobs. "I can't pretend that Peter and I didn't sleep together . . . nor do I expect that you have remained faithful to me . . ." He began to interrupt but she quieted him with a finger to his lips. "Let's just not talk about it . . . or think about it. I don't want to hear about any of the women in your life, and Peter is dead. It's just us now—the past doesn't matter."

"And Angie," he reminded her as he crushed her to his body. She could hear the pounding of his heart echoing deep within the cavern of his chest. Tears slid silently down her cheeks in long-denied happiness.

"Come on, Mara . . . let's go upstairs and get dressed. There's a young lady I can't wait to meet, and you and I have a lot to do."

"Such as?" she asked quietly.

He regarded her silently for a moment, and then a sad smile crept over his face. "Such as pick up our daughter and get married as quickly as possible."

Against all of the urges of her body, she slowly extracted herself from his embrace. "It's just not that easy, Shane," she whispered. "We can't get married."

His hand, which still caught hers, tightened around her fingers and the muscles in his face hardened. "Of course it's that easy, Mara. We can get married immediately. What's to stop us?"

"There are things . . ."

"What things?" he demanded, deep furrows edging over his brow.

Her voice was soft and low, but decisive. "It's not just us, you know. We have other people and their feelings to consider."

"What kind of a game are you playing, Mara? I don't give a damn about other people!" He stood up, and pulled her up beside him—forcing her to gaze into his eyes. His hands clutched the terry robe at her shoulders, and his strong arms held her away from him. His fingers, once gentle, held her tightly, roughly pinching her arms, and his face was twisted in suspicion. "For God's sake, Mara," he implored. "What do we care about other people. We have a daughter to think of— don't we?" Doubt was beginning to creep into his eyes.

"Of course we do, Shane, but you can't expect a three-year-old child to just accept you as the natural father that she didn't know existed. She thought that Peter was her dad—and he was! Angie needs time to adjust—and . . . and so do I!" Her admission was torn from her, and the words surprised even herself, but the firm resolve in her cold, blue eyes never slackened for a moment.

"What are you suggesting?"

"Give it time, Shane . . ."

"You've had time."

"Angie hasn't! Think of her!"

"I am thinking of her, damn it, but I don't know if, after all of these years, I can wait any longer . . . knowing that she's mine."

"You have to! We all need a little breathing room— we've all had some rather extensive shocks, wouldn't you say? You and I . . . we have both come over some incredible, almost insurmountable hurdles in finding each other again. And time has a way of sorting out all of the unnecessary things in life and healing old wounds. We need time, and we need it now."

"You're stalling!"

"I'm not! Just think about it, Shane."

Shane reluctantly released Mara, and she stepped backward. His eyes, two black diamonds, glittered with mistrust and confusion. "All of this is hard for me to accept," he admitted. "First you tell me that I have a three-year-old daughter that I've never met, and then you tell me that I can't have her with me."

"This isn't any more difficult for you than it is for me," Mara reminded him. "Less than twenty-four hours ago, I still thought that you were dead, and now I find out that for four years you deliberately hid away from me. Four years!"

"Not intentionally," he clarified, again taking solace in the view of the mountains from the back porch. "Remember, I thought that you had betrayed me."

"There's just so much that we have to work out, don't you see?" Mara asked, reaching out and touching his cheek.

"I don't know if I can wait," he admitted moodily, and rubbed his forearms in frustration. "I want to see Angie now, this very minute, and I want to change her name to Kennedy. If I have a child, I want that child to bear my name and live with me. Enough of this pretense about her being Wilcox's child!"

Mara let her hand slide from his cheek to his shoulder, but if he noticed her gesture of consolation, he didn't respond. "I'm not asking for you to give up anything that is rightfully yours. I wouldn't. I'm only asking for a little bit of patience. Maybe after you meet with Angie, actually see her, touch her, talk to her, you'll understand. She's a little precocious—perhaps spoiled, and she's only three. She needs to get to know you before we try and explain that you're her 'real' father."

Shane's face was captured in a storm of emotions. He wanted desperately to believe and trust Mara, and he couldn't fault her reasoning. But there was a deep, primeval urge that controlled him and argued that he should immediately claim what was rightfully his.

"There are other people to consider, too," Mara suggested.

"Who?" Anger and frustration were boiling just beneath the surface of his visibly calm exterior.

"June, for one, and—"

Shane interrupted viciously. "June?" he sneered in contempt. "Peter's mother? You're concerned about her welfare?"

"Of course I am. She's not particularly well, and the shock of finding out that Angie isn't her grandchild . . . well, I don't think that it would be particularly good for her health. I don't want to do anything that might worsen her condition."

"Condition? Are we talking about the same woman who wouldn't let me in to see you on the day of the funeral?" he demanded in disgust. "You're concerned about her welfare, when she has had every opportunity to know and love my daughter as her own grandchild? Stop the theatrics, Mara—June Wilcox has already gotten more than she deserves!"

"She's not well," Mara attempted to explain, but Shane silenced her with a rueful stare.

"Neither is my father," he said through clenched teeth. "As a matter of fact, he's in a nursing home, and he hasn't even suspected that he has a granddaughter, much less one that is going on four years old. Would you deny him the joy of knowing Angie in order to promote the charade of your life as the faithful wife of Peter Wilcox?"

"No . . . but . . ." Shane was seething. He dusted off his hands and leaned against one of the heavy white posts that supported the porch roof. He crossed his arms over his chest and watched Mara, mutely inviting her to continue her denial and explanation. She could tell that he was tired of the conversation, and that his anger was simmering just under the surface of his self-control. Barely concealed rage fired his ebony eyes, and Mara found herself desperately attempting to control the conversation that was rapidly deteriorating into another battle.

"But what?" Shane prodded as her voice trailed off. He came up with his own assumptions. "But Peter's mother's state of mind is more important than Angie's real grandfather? The man that's lying in an Atlanta nursing home, barely able to feed himself. The man that doesn't even *know* about his grandchild. Is that what you were beginning to say?"

Mara shook her head violently, and the golden curls of her hair moved in soft waves against the light peach color of her robe. "Of course your father has to know," she said quietly.

"When, Mara? Today? Next week? Six months from now? Ever? When will you think the time is right?" Shane asked, his fists clenching and relaxing against his body.

"Just how long would you be willing to wait, gambling on my father's health?"

Suddenly Shane looked old. His hastily donned clothing was wrinkled, and the shadow of a beard that darkened the lower half of his face seemed to age him. The barely controlled fury that had taken hold of him when he understood Mara's position emphasized the deep lines that etched his arrogant forehead. His eyes, dark and distrustful, never left Mara's face. They silently challenged her, dared her to deny him.

Mara couldn't answer. Her emotions had tangled up within her to the point that she couldn't speak. How could she expect him to understand? How could she ask him to wait? And yet, what else could she do? It had taken four years to get where they were today; could it all be undone in just a few minutes?

Shane's voice challenged her pensive thoughts. "Are you sure that your only concern is for Angie, and for Peter's mother?"

"You have to understand that—"

"What, Mara?" he demanded. "That you're afraid to give up what little hold and control you have on the Wilcox estate? The role of Peter's widow gives you control of the corporation, doesn't it?"

"Peter's will has nothing to do with us!"

"Doesn't it?"

"Of course not! If I were concerned about my ownership of the stock, I wouldn't be foolish enough to tell you about Angie, would I?" she tossed angrily to him. "Honestly, Shane, I don't think I know you anymore. How could you think so little of me—after all we shared together?"

"Then why the wait?" he demanded. "I've met June Wilcox, and I doubt that she really is sick. And as for Angie, I think she probably will adjust to me without too much trouble. This entire argument is about the Wilcox fortune, unless I miss my guess. Aren't you afraid that when Angie's true identity is announced, the rest of Peter's family will contest his will and try and take back whatever inheritance Peter left you and Angie? After all, how does anyone know that Peter knew the secret of Angie's paternity—they have only your word, don't they? And that won't count for much, believe me. As far as the Wilcox family is concerned, June included, you're a traitor, Mara, and I doubt that they would tolerate you running Imagination Toys . . . or—" his gaze swept the vast estate, bathed in early morning sunlight "—allow you to be mistress of this house . . ."

"No!" Mara cried, leaning against the polished white railing for support. "It wouldn't be like that!"

"Prove it!"

"What? I . . . I don't understand."

"Sure you do." His rough voice was flavored with honey. "All you have to do is give me the right to claim my child!"

"I will, you know that," she said, letting her forehead drop to her hands. "I just need a little time . . ."

"You've had four years!" he snapped.

"And you gave them to me, didn't you?" His arms, crossed rigidly over his chest, as if to ward off her words, dropped to his sides. His gaze softened slightly, and he pinched his lower lip between his fingers as he regarded her thoughtfully.

"All right, Mara. You win. I'll give you a little more time to let everyone adjust to me . . . but not much!"

"I . . . we . . . don't need much . . ."

"Good. How about one week, is that enough?"

"Two would be better . . ."

"Fine! Two it is." His smile was nearly genuine. "But that's it—no more stalling!" His dark eyes gleamed with satisfaction, as if a particularly savory thought had occurred to him. "Now," he suggested, "why don't you get dressed and we'll get going. I'd like to meet Angie as soon as possible."

The elation that Mara should have felt escaped her. There was something almost too pleasant about Shane's change of mood—something too practiced and smooth, and it continued to bother her as she hastily took a shower and pulled on her clothes.

Chapter 6

The drive toward Asheville was quiet and fast. Shane seemed to concentrate on his driving, his brooding thoughts keeping him silent, while Mara feigned interest in the view from the car as it sped through the mountains and toward the city. The countryside of deep rolling hills, ancient wooden fences, and bright splashes of wildflowers passed quickly out of Mara's range of vision as the sleek sports car hurried northward on Interstate 26, across the clear waters of the French Broad River and into the city limits of Asheville.

Mara felt the usual rush of pride that always captured her as she entered the city. Nestled in the heart of a million acres of natural mountain wilderness and the tallest mountains in the eastern United States, the Asheville plateau and the city that bore its name seemed to reach out to her. Tall, stately modern office complexes stood proudly against older, more finely detailed turn-of-the-century buildings, and the entire city was graced with tall mountain trees—pine, oak, chestnut . . . Mara took in the familiar scenery that never failed to awe her. The clear mountain air and the bright morning sunlight only added a deepening intensity to the grandeur of the busy town.

Shane pulled the car into the parking lot of one of the older, nineteenth century inns near the center of the city and helped Mara out of the car. With his arm hooking persuasively under her elbow, he gently pushed her into the elevator and tapped impatiently on the paneled walls as it ascended to the fourth floor. Mara sat mutely, somewhat amused, as Shane raced around his hotel room, changed, and shaved, as if every second was being wasted. Secretly she was pleased with his anxiety and nervousness at the prospect of meeting Angie, and yet, she still couldn't shake a feeling of wariness and tension about the meeting. How would Angie react to Shane? And what about June? Why did Mara feel that there were serious undercurrents of tension that seemed to take hold of Shane at the mention of her mother-in-law's name? Was it jealousy of the woman's relationship with his child, or was it deeper than that?

"Come on. Let's go," Shane called to her, interrupting her thoughts. He was racing to the door, fumbling with his tie, and reaching for his keys all in one movement.

"Slow down," Mara cautioned good-naturedly. She got up from the bed, where she had been sitting, and reached up to help him with the knot on his tie. "We've got the rest of the morning . . ."

"Can't you see that I'm in a hurry, damn it!" Shane muttered, jerking on the tie impatiently.

"Too much of one," she said chuckling and touched his cheek, where he had obviously nicked himself with the razor.

A crooked, lazy smile stole over his lips as he noticed the amused twinkle in her eye. "You're enjoying all of this aren't you? You're actually taking pleasure in watching me fall all over myself as I try to hurry to meet my daughter."

Mara couldn't help but blush. "I guess you're right," she conceded, avoiding his gaze. "It's heartwarming to see your more human side surfacing. And—" her eyes locked with his "—it's an incredible relief to realize how important Angie is to you." Her voice caught for a moment. "I . . . I was afraid that maybe, when you found out about her, you wouldn't want her . . ."

A pained expression crossed his features. "How could you think anything of the kind?"

"It's been a long time, Shane."

"Too long," he agreed and wrapped his arms around her. He brushed a kiss across the top of her forehead. "You know that I'd love to stay here and make love to you all morning," he murmured, his eyes sweeping over to the large, comfortable wooden-framed bed, "but I really do want to meet my child. I've waited much too long, already."

No one answered Shane's impatient knock, and so after several awkward moments, Mara let herself into June's apartment with her own key. She called out to her daughter and mother-in-law, but there was no answer, only a dull echo from the empty rooms.

Shane followed Mara through the entry and into the living quarters of the tidy, modern apartment. Other than a few pieces of Angie's clothing draped unceremoniously over the back of a floral couch, there was no sign that the child was about. Without Angie or June inhabiting it, the apartment seemed cold and sterile, the cool blue tones of the carpet and furniture austerely precise and impractical.

Shane eyed the living room with obvious contempt, his dark eyes only softening when he observed Angie's tattered blanket tossed carelessly on the floor. He stooped to pick it up, and smiled to himself as the worn pink blanket unfolded to reveal a nearly naked and slightly dirty doll. "Can't you afford something a little bit . . . cleaner?" he asked, eyeing the doll's tousled frizzy hair and lazy blue eye.

"I've tried, believe me," Mara laughed. "But she prefers Lolly."

"Lolly?" Shane repeated uncomfortably. "But . . . you manufacture toys. Isn't there something you could find to replace . . . Lolly?"

Mara's lips curled into a grim smile. "I would hope so," she muttered, shaking her head pensively, "but it seems that our Angie, like the rest of the toddlers in America, prefer the products of the competition."

"Lolly isn't manufactured by Imagination?"

Mara shook her head again. "Ironic, isn't it?"

Shane looked upon the doll quizzically. "A damned shame," he whispered, straightening himself to his full height. Still holding the doll tentatively, his eyes swept the apartment to rest on the wall behind the couch. His frown deepened as he recognized portrait after portrait of Angie and Peter adorning the smooth white surface. "Your husband?" he guessed, with a bitter edge to his voice.

Ignoring the sarcasm, Mara walked to the wall laden with family portraits. She rested with one knee on the couch and pointed to several of the pictures, her voice taking on the quality of a teacher. "Yes, this is Peter— with Angie, when she was about six months old. And this one, next to it, is a picture of June, her husband, Peter, and his older sister, Dena. The next picture is of Peter, Angie and me . . . Angie was about two at the time; it was just before we learned of his illness—June insisted that we have it taken. And this large portrait, here on the left, is of the entire family, including the cousins and aunts of Peter and his family. The lower, smaller shot is . . ."

Mara had been pointing to each of the photographs in turn. The fact that Shane was obviously angry spurred her onward. No matter what else happened, Shane would have to learn to accept the fact that she had been married to Peter. Nothing could change the past.

"That's enough," Shane nearly shouted, reaching out and capturing Mara's arm. "I've seen enough of the Wilcox family history for one morning. Let's go and find Angie. Where do you think she would be?"

Mara retrieved her hand from Shane's grasp. "June mentioned something about taking her to the park for a miniature train ride. It's just across the street . . ."

"Good. Let's go."

"Don't you think we should wait? June was really looking forward to spending the morning with her."

"We're going, Mara, and now. You really can't expect me to sit here—in this shrine to your husband— and wait for his mother to bring back my child, can you?"

"No, I suppose not . . ."

"Then stop dragging your feet, and let's go."

Shane grabbed the few belongings that he recognized as being Angie's and followed Mara out of the apartment and across the street to one of the well-manicured parks of Asheville. It was nearly noon, and although the day was warm the mountain breezes that cooled the city made the late August morning feel crisp and invigorating. The trains were on the far side of the park, near a small depot, and although the track wound through the lush vegetation all along the perimeter of the gardens, Mara reasoned that the most likely spot to find June and Angie was near the miniature station.

Mara heard her daughter before she actually caught a glimpse of her. Over the clacking of the wheels on the small track and the occasional blow of a whistle, Mara could hear Angie's laughter and shouts. Both Shane and Mara stopped in their tracks when they rounded a bend in the path and could view grandmother and child. Angie was digging in a sandbox of sorts, and June was watching her over the top of a magazine as she sat on a bench in the sunshine. Angie was obviously having the time of her life, and June seemed to be enjoying the peaceful, warm morning. Mara smiled, but couldn't help but feel a lingering sadness steal over her as she thought about June and her frail health. June so obviously enjoyed and loved Angie, and Shane didn't hide his dislike for Peter's mother. Mara felt her heart go out to the elderly woman who had been so kind to her. With Shane's preoccupation with his child, and insistence that Angie become his legal daughter, June would lose that fragile link that she felt she had to her dead son. She had always thought that Angie was Peter's daughter, and Mara knew that when the truth came out, June would be devastated to learn that Angie was Shane's child. Would she feel betrayed, lied to? Suddenly Mara's life seemed a complicated labyrinth of deception.

Shane's hand tightened over hers, and after a momentary pause he walked directly toward the unsuspecting grandmother and child. Mara found her throat tightening with each step she took. After all the years of yearning for the chance to be with Shane again, she found herself dreading what she had dreamed about. When it came time for Shane to claim Angie, how would it affect June . . . Dena . . . and Angie herself? How could Mara anticipate that final confrontation with such sublime happiness and increasing dread?

June looked up from her magazine and then used it as a shield over her eyes to ward off the late summer glare from the sun. She watched Mara and Shane approach her bench, and the broad smile that had lighted her face when she recognized Mara faded as she identified the strange man walking briskly and determinedly toward her,

"Good morning, Mara," June beckoned, noticing the lines of worry crowding Mara's normally clear forehead.

At the mention of her mother's name, Angie looked up from her digging and squealed with delight at the sight of Mara. "Mommy!" she chirped, running over to Mara and leaping into her arms. She clung, monkeylike, to her mother and began chattering wildly. "Grammie take me on train rides-just like the big ones in the book, and they have whistles and real smoke and . . ." her voice trailed off as she observed Shane for the first time. Her black eyes collided with her father's and although Shane smiled, there was distrust in Angie's stare. "Who he?" she asked pointedly, sticking out her lower lip. "Why he got Lolly and my blankie?"

One chubby arm held onto Mara's neck, while the other reached out impatiently to claim her things. Shane handed the doll, draped in the tattered blanket, to his daughter. Importantly, Angie clutched them to her chest, all the while eyeing Shane with suspicion.

Mara had trouble finding her voice but finally managed the introduction. "Angie . . . June . . . this is Shane Kennedy, a friend of mine, and someone who's interested in the toy company."

"We've met," June replied, taking Shane's proffered hand with obvious disinterest.

"That we did—on the day of the funeral," Shane agreed amiably. June's blue eyes narrowed icily.

"I don't like you," Angie said, glaring at her father.

Mara gasped and turned several shades of crimson. "Angie! That's not nice! We don't say things like that. You apologize to Mr. Kennedy."

The child folded her arms defiantly over her chest and stared up at Shane with obvious mistrust. "No!"

"Angie," Mara cajoled, her patience beginning to thin. She set the girl down on the bench next to her grandmother. "Now you be nice. Mr. Kennedy is Mamma's friend . . ."

Silence. Awkward, warm, embarrassing, uncomfortable silence. Angie turned her head so as to avoid direct eye contact with her mother, and a small smile tugged at the corners of June's mouth. She seemed to be extracting a small sense of satisfaction at Angie's behavior and ill manners.

Shane ignored Angie's rejection altogether. "There's no need for an apology, Angie," he said, and Mara shot him an uncompromising glance. "I've met a lot of people that I didn't like in my life; I just wasn't honest enough to admit it."

"But she shouldn't—" Mara began, but Shane waved off her arguments.

"You're right, she probably shouldn't be so . . . forthright. But it doesn't matter—not with me."

Angie looked as if she didn't quite know what to make of the conversation. Fully expecting further protests from her mother, she was surprised when none came about. After casting a confused and furtive glance at her mother's friend, she sat down on the bench and began playing with the doll and blanket, telling Lolly about her morning in the park on the trains.

"Excuse me, Mr. Kennedy," June said, meeting Shane's dark gaze. "Did Mara say that you were interested in purchasing Imagination?"

"That's correct."

"Well, I hope she explained to you that the company is absolutely, without condition, not for sale!" June retorted. Mara was surprised. June never took an interest in the family business, much less interjected an opinion of company policy.

"That she did," Shane agreed, leaning against an oak tree and watching Angie play with her doll.

"Then . . . I guess . . . I don't understand why you're still here . . ." June evaded.

"As Mara stated earlier, she and I are old friends," Shane replied smoothly, almost intimately. Mara felt a wave of color once again stain her cheeks.

"Oh, then you're here in Asheville for the weekend?"

"At least," he drawled, a slow smile spreading over his arrogant features.

June's lips pursed slightly. "I see you were at the apartment. Did you get all of Angie's things? Her nightgown was in the spare bedroom."

"No, we only picked up the blanket and the doll. But I thought you could bring her other things over when you come to stay with her on Monday."

"Well," June began crisply, a hint of exasperation flavoring her words. "In that case, I'll be running along." She picked up her magazine, tossed it into her basket, and rose from the bench. At the effort, her skin seemed to pale.

"Wouldn't you like to spend the rest of the afternoon with us—perhaps go to lunch?" Mara offered.

"I don't think so" was the stiff reply, aimed directly

at Shane. "Dena's coming over later in the day—for the life of me I don't know why—I can't remember the last time she came to visit me."

"Thanks so much for looking after Angie," Mara whispered, giving June a kiss on the cheek. "I'm sure she had a wonderful time."

June's face relaxed a bit as she looked at Angie, busy again in the sandbox. "Yes, I think she did. It was my pleasure." June's long, bony hand clasped firmly over Mara's. "I'll see you Monday morning."

"All right."

"Good-bye, Angie," June called out to the little girl, who looked up from her play long enough to flash June her most ebullient smile and wave her hand and blanket at her grandmother.

When June was out of earshot, Shane turned his attention back to Mara. "I'd say she doesn't like me much, wouldn't you?" He cocked his head in the direction that June had taken.

"She probably just didn't like the fact that you attempted to see me on the day of Peter's funeral. She was pretty upset. Peter was her only son."

Shane shrugged indifferently, but Mara couldn't help but think about her mother-in-law. The chilling undercurrent of tension that had developed when Mara had introduced Shane to June couldn't be ignored, and the withering look of haughty disdain in the older woman's eyes—a look so atypical of June—spoke of a deep-seated mistrust or hatred. Why did June instantly dislike Shane? Was it, as Mara had suggested, because he had broken through unspoken bonds of civility and tried to see Mara on the day of the funeral? Did June overreact because she was emotionally drained at the time, or could there be another, deeper, angrier cause for June's personality reversal?

"I think your suggestion earlier was great," Shane said, breaking into Mara's distracted thoughts.

"What . . . what was that?"

"Lunch. I'm starved. One cup of coffee wasn't quite enough this morning." Shane dropped a protective arm over Mara's slim shoulders. "Quit worrying about June. It's her right not to like me."

"It's just that I don't understand it. It's all so out of character for her. She's usually a warm, open person."

"Somehow I find that hard to believe."

Further conjecture was cut short as Angie came up dragging her blanket behind her. Mara smiled at her child. "Are you hungry, Angie? How about some lunch?"

"Hot dogs?" Angie asked, her eyes lighting.

"Hot dogs?" Mara repeated. "Is that what you want?"

Angie shook her blond curls vigorously and pointed in the direction of a local vendor pushing a metal cart with large bicycle wheels and a bright green umbrella.

"Hot dogs it is," Shane agreed with an amused smile.

"Are you sure?" Mara asked, eyeing the mustached vendor and his steaming wares dubiously.

"Whatever the young lady wants," Shane laughed, and Angie began running off in the direction of the vendor.

"Don't you think you're pouring it on a little strong?" Mara asked. "Angie's already spoiled. The last thing she needs is an overindulgent father."

"We'll see," Shane said enigmatically, his dark eyes following the path of the escaping child.

The rest of the afternoon was spent in the park with Angie. Though shy at first, Angie finally accepted Shane and even let him have the privilege of holding her blanket as they walked through the city. The Summerfest Arts and Crafts Show was being held at the Civic

Center, and Shane insisted upon looking over the various arts and crafts made by local mountain craftsmen and the Cherokee Indians. At the show, Shane purchased Angie a beaded bracelet, which she proudly wore around her wrist. By the time the afternoon shadows had lengthened, Shane carried a tired Angie against his shoulder, back to the car parked near June's apartment.

The drive back to the house was as quiet as the drive into the city. Dusk was beginning to take hold of the countryside and a deep red sunset formed a backdrop for the purple-hued mountains. Angie slept quietly in the back seat, with only a deep, contented sigh escaping from her lips disturbing the quiet hum of the sports car. Shane was thoughtfully, broodingly silent during the journey home, and Mara could almost feel his dark thoughts begin to take hold of him. They were almost back at the Wilcox estate before he broke the silence that had captured them.

"I don't know if I can hold up my end of the bargain," he admitted.

"The bargain? What bargain?"

"Our deal, that I give you two weeks to sort things out before we tell Angie that I'm her father."

"You promised," she reminded him, gently touching his coat sleeve.

"I know . . . I know. But—" he paused, trying to find the right words as he shifted down and turned up the long, circular drive "—that was before I knew her. She needs me."

"And?"

A sarcastic grin curved his lips. "You were waiting for this one, weren't you? Well, you're right. I need her. That's what you've been waiting to hear, isn't it?"

Tears began to pool in Mara's eyes, and her voice deepened. "I'd be a liar to deny it. You see, well . . . Peter and Angie never did get along . . ."

"What do you mean?"

Shane stopped the car, and pulled the key from the ignition. Angie stirred but settled back into a comfortable sleep.

"Peter resented Angie."

Shane touched Mara's shoulder, and she could feel the heat of his fingertips through the light cotton of the blouse she was wearing. "He resented her?" Shane whispered. "But I thought that you married him in order to have a normal family life. Isn't that what you told me?"

Mara nodded mutely. "I did, and I thought it would work. But I was wrong. After she was born, everything changed. And he was never close to her. Not as a baby or a toddler . . ."

Shane rested one arm on the steering wheel, and supported his head with his hand. His voice was level, and quiet, but filled with rage. "He didn't do anything to her, did he?"

Mara gasped. "Oh, no. Peter was never violent or cruel. "No . . . no . . . but he was impatient with her, or he would ignore her altogether. He wanted more children . . . his children. But after seeing his lack of interest in Angie . . ." She shrugged her shoulders.

"So that was your 'perfect marriage,' was it?"

"I didn't say it was perfect. I don't think that there is such a thing."

"No?"

She stuck her chin out determinedly and looked him in the eye. "No."

"You've changed a lot in the last four years, Mara."

"I don't think so. I've just become more realistic. Life has a way of forcing you to give up your dreams."

"Don't ever give up your dreams, Mara."

"Haven't you?"

He cupped her chin in his hand and watched while his finger outlined the soft hill of her cheek. "Never," he whispered and let his lips touch hers.

"Are we home?" Angie asked from the back seat, rubbing her eyes and only catching a glimpse of the intimate kiss.

"Yes, honey," Mara said, hurriedly opening the car door and reaching for Angie. "Come on in the house and I'll fix us a quick dinner."

"Can I play with the kitties—Southpaw's kitties?" Angie asked, her gaze running around the foundation of the house, looking for the mother cat.

"For a few minutes, honey. Until dinner is ready."

A smile spread over Angie's face, and she immediately took off in the direction of the back porch.

It was nearly nine o'clock by the time dinner was over, Angie was bathed, the dishes were done, and the little girl was asleep in her bed. She had found the kittens and talked Shane into crawling under the back porch to get them. Against Southpaw's soft protests, Shane extracted the kittens and helped Angie make a bed for them in the screened-in portion of the porch. Southpaw didn't seem too pleased with the new arrangement, but Angie was delighted with a bird's-eye view of the four chubby gray-and-white cats. "You can help me name them," she had announced to Shane, who was more than thrilled at the prospect, supplying names of his favorite football players.

"I don't think O.J. is a very good name for a kitty," Angie confided in Mara as she was being tucked into bed.

"Neither do I," Mara laughed. "But if Shane likes it, maybe we had better use it."

"Don't like it," Angie repeated with a yawn, and Mara kissed her lightly on the forehead. Angie snuggled against the pillow, and before Mara could turn out the light, the little girl was breathing deeply and evenly. Shane stood in the doorway, watching the intimate scene between mother and daughter, and wondered how he had found himself so tangled up with Mara all over again. It wasn't what he had planned, and he mentally chastised himself for his weakness where Mara was concerned. All the years of bitterness and deception were beginning to wash away, and he knew that if he allowed himself, he could fall in love with her, just as easily as he had the first time, nearly four years ago. An uneasy feeling that he had never really stopped loving her crept over him, and he wondered if there was ever a time when he hadn't cared for her, as he had forced himself to believe. But now, as she bent down to kiss his child, and the moonglow caught the golden highlights of her hair, a warm feeling of protectiveness stole over him. Was it Mara that he cared for, or was he just succumbing to latent feelings of fatherhood for the child he had never met until late this morning? Now that he knew about Angie, was he mixing up his feelings for Mara with his newfound emotions for the little blond girl with the slightly upturned nose and the mischievous twinkle in her dark eyes?

"She doesn't think much of the names that you gave the kittens," Mara whispered as she closed the door quietly and started down the long carpeted hallway toward the stairs.

"I heard," Shane chuckled, walking at Mara's side. "Can you blame her? Who ever heard of naming new-born kittens after football heroes? No wonder she thinks the names are ill-fitting."

"'Crummy,' I think, was the word she used," Shane replied, and noticed Mara's wistful smile. "She's not exactly afraid to speak her mind, is she?"

"Not that one," Mara agreed.

Shane apparently found the thought amusing and chuckled at the image of the outspoken child.

"Oh, you think it's funny, do you?" Mara baited. "Well, just you wait. You'll get yours. Let me tell you, her outbursts can be embarrassing—damned embarrassing!"

Shane touched Mara's arm just as they stepped off the staircase and headed toward the back of the house. "You know what they say, 'From the mouths of babes—'"

"I know," Mara agreed, waving off the rest of his quote and snapping on the kitchen lights. "And I suppose you're right," she admitted reluctantly. "Anyway, I wouldn't change one thing about her."

"I would," Shane countered, and clicked the light back off. Once again, the kitchen was dark, except for the pale, filtered moonglow.

"What?" Mara asked, breathlessly. The light mood and banter of a moment before had changed when darkness had covered the room. It was as if she could *feel* Shane standing next to her, not touching her, and yet reaching out to her. "What would you change about Angie?" Mara was slightly taken aback. All afternoon she had been led to believe that Shane was absolutely enchanted with his headstrong young daughter.

"I want them back, Mara," Shane whispered, and his fingers brushed invitingly against her upper arm. "The three years that I haven't known her . . . haven't been around her . . . I want them back."

She paused a moment before answering. The silence was burdensome and painful, and it was with difficulty that she found her voice. Her fingers touched his and pressed his hand more tightly against her arm. "Those years are gone, Shane . . . if they were so important to you, you should have taken them when you had the chance."

"Damn it, Mara! I didn't have a chance!"

"Oh, Shane," Mara sighed, rotating to face him and looking deeply into his eyes that were almost ebony in the darkness of the room. "We can't change the past. It's difficult, I know—and we've both made mistakes. But we have no choice but to live with them."

"I suppose you're right," he admitted thoughtfully, though the tone of his voice lacked conviction. His fingertip reached up and touched her eyelid, and the thick brush of her eyelashes.

Mara closed her eyes and leaned against him. "For the rest of the weekend, let's try to forget all of our problems and the past. Can't we just concentrate on the present and the future?" she asked, leaning against his chest.

He hesitated, and reached for her right hand. After taking in a long breath and letting his fingers entwine through hers, he continued: "That depends."

"On what?"

"A couple of things. The first being that you tell me just how you think another two weeks will give you the courage you need to face June Wilcox and tell her that Angie is my child." His fingers tightened over her hand.

"I told you before, June's not well." Mara's eyes flew open, and even in the shadowy night, she could tell that Shane was becoming angry again. But why?

His grip on her fingers was severe, nearly crushing, and her eyes flew down to their hands, suspended and tangled between them in the darkness.

"The second thing I would like to know is why you still insist on wearing your wedding ring, even though your husband is dead? Does it hold some special significance? Or is it just that you don't want to give up that last little piece of evidence that you were married to Peter Wilcox? Was your love that lingering that you can't bear the thought of taking off his ring?" Shane's words were ice cold and they shattered the intimacy of the moment. Mara fought to withdraw her hand, which he reluctantly released.

For a moment she was unsure, and then slowly, with careful and theatrical precision, she slid the wide gold band off of her finger and placed it on the windowsill, where it winked in the moonlight.

"Satisfied?" she asked him, and once again snapped on the lights. Instantly the room transformed into the warm kitchen with rust accents. "Why do you constantly want to battle with me, Shane? Why is it, just when I think we're making some concrete headway toward working things out, you find another excuse to bring up the past?" Her eyes glittered with the provocation she felt. "The reason that I wear the ring is obvious, at least to most people. It discourages unwanted male attention." She turned and placed the teapot on the stove to heat some water. She was angry and was having trouble reining in her temper. Why did she still love him so desperately? He was so unpredictable, so moody, so prone to swings in temperament, and still she loved him.

The whistle on the teapot caught her attention, and she carefully poured two cups of scalding water, before steeping in them a rare blend of pekoe. With barely controlled indignation, she handed Shane a mug of the hot liquid.

"You have a lot of admirers, do you, now that dear old Peter is gone?" He observed her over the rim of his cup, and his black eyebrows quirked in dubious interest.

"That's not the point . . ."

"Then, please—" he turned up a disbelieving palm, encouraging her to continue her explanation "—enlighten me."

Mara nervously tapped her fingers on the edge of her cup, feeling somehow as if she was being cornered and manipulated. Still, she couldn't help but take the well-placed morsel of bait, although she eyed Shane suspiciously before accepting his suggestion. She sighed wearily into the tea leaves. "I suppose that it's no secret that since Peter's death, when I became the woman in charge of Imagination, there have been a few persistent gentlemen—and I use the term loosely—who seem to think, in their lofty opinions of themselves, that I, a mere woman in charge of a large corporation, need their expert advice—or at the very least, their bodies—to help me deal with my loss of Peter and the awesome responsibility of running the company. It's apparent that most men can't understand how I can cope without a husband and father for my child, not to mention managing the business, to boot." As Mara began talking, warming to her subject, all of her secret thoughts came tumbling out. "I've become some sort of target, Shane, and I don't like it." Her proud chin inched upward in defiance. "I'm not the kind of woman who *needs* just any man who happens along." Her cheeks had become flushed, and she paused for a moment, to stop the angry quivering of her lips. "I don't under-

stand why some of the men around here don't think a
woman can run Imagination Toys . . ."

"Perhaps they've read the financial statements and
realize that the company has been losing money ever
since you took over the reins."

"Not fair, Shane," Mara admonished, suddenly willing to do verbal battle with him. "The company has
been losing money for quite some time, long before I
took over. It all started sometime before Peter's illness
was diagnosed, and although I haven't been able yet to
turn things around and operate in the black again, I
refuse to take full responsibility. I'm not accepting the
blame for the recession!"

"You're hedging! The recession is just a convenient
excuse! You can look over the earnings reports of most
of the companies in this region—and they're still making it. Why is it that Imagination can't face up to the
competition, anyway?"

"We've had a few bad breaks . . ."

"It comes with the territory, Mara. Every company
has 'bad breaks,' but some seem to rise above them
and find a way to make a profit."

"I guess I don't really understand where this conversation is heading," Mara snapped, and put her teacup
down with a clatter against the butcher-block countertop. "Are you criticizing the way I'm handling the company?"

"Not yet."

"But you intend to?" she asked indignantly.

"Perhaps, if it's necessary," he promised.

"Then, why, now, all of the arguments?"

"I only asked you about your wedding ring."

"And I was only trying to explain to you that the
only reason that I wear the ring is to discourage certain
businessmen from coming on too strong with me. Is

that so hard to understand?" Blue fire danced in Mara's eyes as she stood before him, silently challenging him to pursue the argument. When he didn't immediately accept the dare, she prodded him. "And really, admit it, isn't that what you thought, along with everyone else, that there was no way that I would be able to run the toy company effectively?"

An unsuppressed smile lighted his near-black eyes.

"I thought so!" she stated, shaking her head and pursing her lips until they whitened. Blond curls rubbed angrily against her shoulders. "Well, just because I'm a woman doesn't mean that I can't handle the job. Nor does it mean that I need *any* male help!"

Shane's lips thinned, and he set his cup down next to hers on the counter. "I think that we should get something straight between us, once and for all," he replied with quiet determination. "I didn't come up here to Asheville with any intention of helping you."

"But I thought . . ."

"It doesn't matter what you thought. I came here with the express purpose of buying out the company. You know that. Because you refused to sell, I've had to alter my position."

"What are you getting at?"

"I just want you to know that my personal life, including the fact that I've found out that I'm Angie's father, doesn't necessarily alter my position with regard to Imagination. If anything, it probably strengthens it!"

"I don't understand," she admitted flatly.

"Don't you? Come on, Mara, you're a bright woman. Don't play games with me."

"I'm not playing games with you, Shane. I'm only trying to understand you."

"Then understand this—I don't like the idea that you and I made love in this house last night."

"What?" Mara was stunned. "What are you talking about?" she asked, clearly perplexed by the twists in the conversation and wounded that he hadn't shared the same supreme ecstasy and bliss that she had experienced during their lovemaking.

"I'm talking about playing second best to the memory of a dead husband," Shane ground out, his eyes darkening. "Do you know how hard it was for me to make love to you last night, in his house, his bed, his sheets? Everything around me, including you, was owned by Peter Wilcox! Do you have any idea how I feel each time that I hear his name or see his picture? Don't you realize that every time I see Angie, I wonder just how much influence Peter had over her? How did she feel about him? Did she love him? Was he kind to her? Did he hurt her, or mentally abuse her?" He paused for a moment, but before Mara could find her tongue and refute his insinuations, he continued with his tirade. "And the same goes for the toy company. I don't want to live, or work, in the shadow of another man's memory. I can't accept that."

"For God's sake, Shane, can't you, for just a moment, forget about Peter?"

"How?" He grabbed her by her thin shoulders and with a shake, forced her to look squarely into his tortured eyes. "How, Mara?" he repeated, through clenched teeth. "Everything that I should have had, he took . . ."

"He didn't take anything that you weren't willing to give, Shane. And besides, what's the point? Peter's dead!"

"But he was alive once, wasn't he?" Again the involuntary shake. "And he made love to you, didn't he? How many times was he invited into your bedroom, like I was last night? How many times did you moan your surrender to him, just as you did to me?" Shane asked, his grim face showing the strain of his pent-up emotion. His rage was so out of control that Mara could feel his hands trembling where they gripped her upper arms.

"I . . . I thought that we had decided to put all of that . . . behind us," she said, reaching up and smoothing a lock of black hair away from his forehead.

"It's difficult," Shane admitted, his grip relaxing slightly. "And . . . I'm not really sure that I even want to try to forget. Not as long as we're trapped in this house—*his* house."

There was a silence, long and charged with electricity that hung between them. Finally, Shane's arms dropped to his sides and he cleared his throat. Still visible, his anger was a tangible force.

"I'm going back to the hotel, Mara," he stated thoughtfully. "I'll call you in the morning."

"But you could stay here tonight," she invited, suddenly afraid that he might leave and, once again, be lost to her.

"No, I couldn't."

"But last night . . ."

"Last night was different. There's too much here to remind me of the things that I would rather not remember." His black eyes traveled over her body, and she could see the sparks of passion rekindling in their ebony depths. "I want you, Mara, as much as I ever have," he admitted, his dark eyes reflecting the intensity of his words. "But I want you on my terms—not yours, nor Peter Wilcox's. So I'll wait—as you've suggested for two weeks—to claim what is rightfully mine. But, then," he warned quietly, "things will be my way!"

As he turned to leave, Mara found her voice and called out to him. "But what about Angie? Are you just going to walk out of her life for the next two weeks?" she cried. What was he doing? Why, dear God, was he leaving, just as he had once before?

"Of course not. Don't you know that I'll be back?" The fear in her eyes was unmasked, and he felt an uncompromising urge to run to her, to wrap his arms around her thin shoulders, to whisper promises to her that he couldn't possibly keep. But somehow he found the strength to stand his ground. "I'll see you in the morning," he promised. "And we'll go out, just the three of us. But," his voice deepened again, "I don't want to spend any more time than I have to being reminded of your husband."

Mara took a step toward him and opened her mouth to protest, but his next words halted her.

"Remember, Mara, this was all your idea. You're the one that needed the extra time to adjust. For the next two weeks, we're playing by your rules!"

Mara followed him to the door, intent on changing his mind, but somehow lacking the resolve to argue with him. She stood in the doorway as he stepped into his Audi, flicked on the ignition, and roared down the driveway. The headlights faded into the darkness, and the silver car and the man she loved were swallowed in the night.

Shane never looked over his shoulder, but Mara's image, a dark silhouette backed by the warm lights of the house, lingered in the rear-view mirror and burned in Shane's tormented memory.

Chapter 7

The weekend passed quickly for Mara . . . too quickly. Sunday had dawned hot and humid, and Mara had packed a picnic basket filled with fruit, wine, cheese, sourdough rolls, and ham. Shane had arrived promptly at ten and, after a friendly reunion with Angie and the four kittens, hurried Mara out the door and into the car. They had driven to Chimney Rock Park, southeast of Asheville, where they had hiked along the terraced trails to view Hickory Nut Gorge and Hickory Nut Falls, one of the highest waterfalls in eastern America. The clean, cascading water, the steep cliffs, and the lush, dense foliage seemed to take the heat off of the above average temperature. Although Shane had to carry Angie part of the way up to Chimney Rock, he hadn't complained, and the awe on the little girl's face as she gazed thousands of feet down the hazy, spectacular, seventy-five-mile view of the canyon and Lake Lure was worth the hot climb.

But when dusk had stolen over the Blue Ridge, Shane had taken Mara and Angie back home, and once

again left for his hotel. After a long, hot day of enjoying his company, Mara felt strangely empty inside as
she watched his car disappear down the driveway. Would
it ever be possible for Shane to love her? Would they
ever have a chance to build a normal family life, or
would there always be a reminder of the past to haunt
them and keep them apart? Was the love of a child
great enough to conquer the barriers that had separated
them? Where would they go from here? The questions,
nagging and whirling in her weary mind, kept her
awake for most of the night. When June came to the
house the next morning to watch Angie, Mara could almost feel the cold, piercing blue gaze of her mother-in-
law knifing through her thin layer of makeup and fresh
blue, jersey print dress to see the effects of Mara's turbulent emotions for Shane.

"Hi, Grammie," Angie called from the kitchen table,
where she was studiously attacking a stack of three
pancakes and unknown gallons of blackberry syrup.

June's drawn face broke into a smile at the sight of
the little girl, who was nearly covered head to toe in
purple smudges of syrup. "Goodness, Angie! Look at
you. You'll certainly need a bath this morning—" the
older woman chuckled "—unless, of course, you plan
on hiding under the porch all day with those kittens."

Angie set her fork down and looked quizzically at
her grandmother. The syrup on her face and hair made
her look almost comical. "Oh, no. The kitties is not
under the porch anymore," she tried to explain. "Come
on, Grammie. I show you." Angie bounced out of her
chair and hurried out the back door, which slammed
behind her.

Mara cringed at the sound. "Just a minute," she
called to her daughter through the screen. "Why don't

you finish your breakfast, and then Grammie can go with you to see Southpaw?"

"I all done!" Angie asserted, her voice sounding more distant than just the back porch. She was obviously too distracted with the kittens to eat any more breakfast.

"Are you sure?" Mara asked, almost to herself, as she surveyed the barely touched breakfast. "You haven't eaten much . . ."

Angie poked her head through the narrow opening of the screen door and hurried back into the kitchen. "I said I all done!" she reasserted.

"But you barely touched the pancakes."

Angie puckered her lips in thought and then decided to ignore her mother. She took a swipe at her mouth with her napkin, as if, once and for all, to close the subject on breakfast, and then raced out the back door, leaving the half-eaten stack of pancakes to soak up the remainder of the syrup.

Mara didn't feel up to battling with Angie so early in the morning after a restless night. Knowing that she was probably making a maternal error, she ignored Angie's disobedience and ill manners and tried to still the throbbing near her temples. Her early morning headache seemed to be pounding more harshly against her skull.

"Would you like a cup of coffee?" Mara asked stiffly, seeing the worried expression in June's eyes. Mara held the coffeepot in midair and avoided June's direct gaze. Was it Mara's imagination, or did June seem older and appear more troubled today than usual?

"I'll get some later," the older woman replied, and cast a furtive glance to the back porch. Angie was quiet, and June decided that the little girl was unlikely to interrupt, at least not during the next few minutes. She touched her neck hesitantly and nervously before she broke the silence that had been building between herself and her daughter-in-law.

"I saw Dena Saturday afternoon. She came and visited me," June began, gauging Mara's reaction.

"And how was she?" Mara asked, sipping her coffee and reaching for Angie's dirty dishes.

"Concerned."

Mara's throat tightened convulsively, and she unconsciously bit at her lower lip as she deposited the dishes into the sink and turned on the water. "Concerned? About what?"

"You for one," June replied, cautiously.

"Anything else?"

"The company." June's graying eyebrows drew together, and she hesitated for a moment, as if what she was about to say might be unpleasant. "She seems to think that you're being bullheaded about selling Imagination Toys."

Mara smiled grimly to herself as she placed the few dishes into the dishwasher. "I know that," she admitted, drying her hands on a nearby cotton towel and turning to face her mother-in-law. "But you have to understand that I want the company to make it, and I think that it can. Selling now would be a mistake, I'm sure of it," she stated, with more conviction than she actually felt. "Right now, with the company losing money, we couldn't get a decent price for Imagination, even if we did want to sell. But if we could just turn the company around, to at the very least a breakeven point, the price we could ask would be substantially higher."

June seemed to relax a little as she pulled her ivory knit sweater more closely over her thin shoulders.

"Chilly in here, isn't it?" she observed in a distracted voice, and then, as if suddenly remembering the train of the conversation, she snapped back to the subject at hand. "Well, Mara, I'm glad to hear that you're not anxious to sell Imagination," she offered. "I know it's a big job, running an unprofitable business in the middle of a recession, and sometimes I worry that you're working too hard, but the toy company is part of the Wilcox heritage. From my husband Curtis's grandfather down to Angie . . ." Mara felt her heart stop at the mention of Angie's link in Peter's family. June hesitated only slightly. "I know that Dena would like to sell the company lock, stock, and barrel," June stated through thinned lips.

After readjusting her sweater, the older woman sat down at the table and didn't argue when Mara placed a cup of black coffee and the sugar bowl on the table within arm's reach. After taking an experimental sip of the scalding brew, June smiled faintly and continued.

"It's really not Dena's fault, you know?"

"What isn't?"

"Her attitude toward you."

Mara tried to shrug off the insinuations, but June would have none of it.

"Don't try to hide it from me, Mara. I know my own daughter, and I realize that she has never been fond of you . . . not since the beginning." Mara drew in a steadying breath. The subject of the bitterness that existed between herself and Dena had never been brought out into the open. It was as if under the cover of Southern civility, the unacknowledged problem would somehow disappear. As close as Mara was to June, she never expected that June would ever admit she knew of the animosity that existed between Peter's sister and his wife.

"She's always felt a little inferior, you know," June conceded, "and I suppose she has every right to feel that way. Curtis made no bones about the fact that he wanted a son to carry on the family business, and Curtis could never quite hide his disappointment that Dena wasn't a boy. Not that he didn't love her, you understand. But, well, it's different between a father and daughter than it is with a son." June smiled sadly into her coffee cup. When she lifted her faded blue eyes to meet Mara's interested gaze, Mara noticed a genuine pain and empathy in the older woman's eyes.

"I guess that I should have tried to patch things up between father and daughter, but I thought that as Dena grew up the situation might change. I should have known better, you know. Curtis and Dena were so much alike, from their red hair to their hot tempers! Anyway, when Peter came along, five years later, Curtis was delirious that he finally had his 'son.' Dena couldn't help but feel left out, and slighted." June sighed. "I realize that now, with women's liberation and everything else, things have changed, and that today it's not so important to have that first-born son. But then, Curtis never really accepted his daughter as anything but the second child, although she was his first. And even if she did have the temperament to manage the business, he would never have given her the chance!"

June seemed tired and weary. "You don't have to explain all of this to me," Mara whispered, touching the frail woman's shoulder.

"Oh, but I do!" June responded viciously, and inadvertently spilled some of the coffee, sloshing it onto the saucer. "I know that Dena, well, she comes across a little catty sometimes, but I want you to know that it's really not a personal vendetta against you."

"I know that," Mara admitted. "Don't worry about it."

"I can't help it. She's caused a lot of trouble for you in the past, but I think it's because she's felt left out. First from her father's attention, and now from what she sees as her rightful inheritance. It didn't help, you know, when Bruce broke off the engagement after learning that she wouldn't inherit the bulk of Imagination Toys."

Mara felt herself cringe as she remembered how upset Dena had been when her flaky lawyer fiancé had jilted her only months before the wedding had been planned.

"What do you think I should do about Dena?" Mara asked, feeling that June had recounted the painful memories with a purpose in mind.

"I don't know. I've never really understood Dena, or her reasons. But she seems to think that it would be best for all concerned to sell Imagination to that Kennedy man." Mara noticed June's jawline tighten at the mention of Shane.

"And you?" Mara asked quietly. "What do you want?"

June hesitated a minute. "This was the Wilcox family's lifeblood. Their way of life and their heritage. I . . . I would hate to see it sold to a stranger." June's voice had taken a firm, almost hateful tone that surprised Mara.

"Any decisions regarding the sale of Imagination will be put to the stockholders in the company, all of the members of the family. You know that, don't you? Just because Angie and I own the largest block of stock doesn't mean . . ."

The screen door banged shut, announcing Angie's return to the kitchen. "Mommy! Grammie! Namath's eyes are open!" the little girl squealed breathlessly. "Come see! Hurry!"

Mara laughed nervously as she dried her hands on a nearby towel. She was relieved to have a break in the intense conversation with her mother-in-law. She followed Angie and June out the door and onto the screened-in back porch that housed the more delicate hanging plants. It was already warm in the small enclosure, and aside from a slight breeze off of the mountains, the morning promised another hot day, despite June's comments to the contrary. Just as Angie had announced, the largest of the gray kittens' eyes were beginning to crack open.

"See, I told you," Angie whispered in obvious delight as she held up the fat fluff of fur.

"That you did," June agreed with a smile. "Now, tell me, what was that kitten's name?"

"Namath," Angie responded with a frown. "Mr. Kennedy gave him *that* name."

At the mention of Shane's name, June visibly paled. For a moment Mara wondered if the older woman would collapse, but just as Mara placed a supporting hand under June's elbow, the color came back into her cheeks.

"He . . . named the cats after football players?" June guessed with obvious distaste.

Mara nodded mutely while Angie chattered on about the kittens, pointing out O.J., Franco, and Bradshaw in turn. June was appalled, but didn't attempt to cool Angie's enthusiasm.

"Do you like O.J.?" Angie asked innocently.

"It's . . . fine," June managed, feebly, and Angie appeared satisfied with her grandmother's approval.

"I liked Whiskers better," the child mused, and June nodded her silent agreement.

"I have to get going to work now, honey . . . you be a good girl for Grammie, won't you?"

Angie turned her attention away from the kittens long enough to give her mother a kiss on her cheek. Mara's eyes caught June's distracted gaze. "Are you up to handling her today?"

"Of course."

"You're sure?"

"Don't worry," June said with a sad smile. "We'll get along just fine." A genuine fondness lighted her tired, blue eyes.

The sadness that had stolen over her mother-in-law hung with Mara during the drive into Asheville, and although she mentally tried to shake off the depression, she failed. The warm morning sunshine, the smell of wildflowers, the pastoral view of horses grazing on the high plateau, nothing discouraged the feeling of melancholy that converged upon her. The only thoughts that touched her were worries about June's health, Shane's impatience, and Angie's welfare. How in the world was she going to solve her dilemma and tell June that Shane was Angie's father? And how would the little girl take the news? Would she understand? Could she?

The day was just beginning, and Mara found herself sighing as she opened the door to her office.

"Mrs. Wilcox!" a young female voice declared as Lynda came running up behind her. "I'm sorry, but I couldn't stop him!"

"What? Lynda, what are you talking about?"

"Mr. Kennedy—the man who was in here Friday night . . ." The receptionist blushed with the memory of Friday afternoon and the reunion of her employer and the stranger.

Mara smiled with only a trace of impatience. "Yes?"

"He . . . well, he absolutely insisted . . ."

"Insisted upon what?"

"I told him it was irregular, that no one was allowed in your office—other than you—but he just started ordering me around, and . . . well . . ."

Mara pushed open the door to her office and saw the object of Lynda's dismay seated regally behind Mara's desk, pen in hand, running through a stack of ledgers.

"It's all right," Mara stated stiffly to the confused receptionist. "Mr. Kennedy has my permission to be in my office . . . and . . . er . . . see any documents that he wishes."

Relief flooded the girl's features. "Thank goodness," she murmured as she hustled down the hallway back to her desk.

Mara felt her temper heating and braced herself against the closed door to the office before she confronted Shane.

"Just what do you think you're doing?" she inquired, eyeing him suspiciously. "You have Lynda half out of her mind with worry that she's done something wrong."

Shane tossed the ledger he had been studying onto the desk top. "What?" His attention was finally focused on Mara.

"I said that Lynda has strict orders not to allow anyone in here without my permission. I'm surprised that you got away with it—much less bribed the accounting department out of the bookkeeping ledgers."

"I like to get to work early. I didn't know when you would get in, and I didn't want to wait." Once again he looked down at the stack of manila-colored ledger cards. A scowl creased his dark brows.

"So you just decided to take over my office . . ."

"For the time being."

Mara was becoming exasperated and found it difficult to hide the fact. She crossed the room, tossed her purse into a nearby closet, and marched over to the desk. "Why don't you tell me what you're doing," Mara suggested, and stood near him.

Perhaps it was her condescending tone of voice that galled him, but whatever it was, he picked up a stack of ledgers and waved them in the air arrogantly. "How can you possibly expect to run a company this way?" he charged, his black eyes igniting.

"What do you mean—what are you talking about?" Mara asked, stunned.

"I mean that I don't know how you can expect to compete effectively in the marketplace when you're working under such burdensome and antiquated systems in the office. It's no wonder that Imagination is in the red!"

"I guess I'm just a little overwhelmed by all of this," Mara stated, motioning to the stacks of records that covered her desk, "but I don't understand a word you're saying." She couldn't hide the hint of sarcasm and anger that tinged her words.

"What I'm saying is that you're trying to dig a well with a teaspoon . . ." The confusion and smoldering indignation in her gaze begged him to continue. "What I'm trying to say is this—Toys are a big business, and in a recessive economy any toy company, Imagination included, has to be not only innovative but also technologically advanced. You can't be so bogged down with paperwork that you're ineffective."

"You're saying that Imagination needs to modernize?" she guessed.

"Right."

"And . . . I suppose you think that the first step would be to purchase a computer?"

"You need the accuracy and speed that only a computer will give you . . ."

"What I don't need is someone, especially an owner of a computer company, to tell me how to spend money that I don't have!"

"You can't afford not to invest."

"Spoken like a true salesman," she quipped curtly.

"I'm serious, Mara. How many people do you have working in your accounting department, aside from Hammel?"

"Three."

"And the combined salaries and benefits total over thirty thousand dollars annually?" he guessed.

Mara nodded thoughtfully.

"A good microcomputer would cost you less than a third of that and would supply you with reports on inventory, financial statements, product costs . . ."

"Save your breath." She fell into a nearby chair. "I've heard it all before. It's just that I haven't had the time or money to convert to a computer. No matter what you say, it's an expensive investment."

"I don't see that you have much of a choice."

"Why not?"

"Because if you want my assistance, I'm going to insist upon it. There's no way that I'll invest in a company that doesn't have an effective way of keeping track of inventory and product costs or effectiveness of advertising and sales promotion. This is the age of computer technology, Mara, and you can't expect to run a competitive company the way it was run ninety years ago—"

"Wait a minute," Mara said, interrupting him. She held her palms outward, as if to push aside any more of his arguments. "You're getting the cart before the horse.

Before you make any further decisions about the company, don't you think it would be a good idea to tell me exactly what you have in mind, in terms of investing in Imagination?"

A grim smile cracked his features. "Fair enough."

"Well?" she asked anxiously, and pushed aside the impulse to bite at her lower lip. Instead she studied the sharp planes of his rugged face, his thick black eyebrows, his brooding lower lip that protruded slightly, and the thin shadow of a beard that appeared even in the morning. In a dark blue business suit, striking burgundy tie, and crisp, white shirt, he bore an arrogant but somehow intriguingly masculine presence. He tapped his lips thoughtfully with a pencil as he spoke.

"I told you before, that I had no intention of giving Imagination the benefit of my assistance without something in return. And since you refuse to sell out to me, I'm willing to invest in the company."

"How?"

"I've done some research. You don't own a majority interest."

Mara's stomach tightened. "That's true," she admitted.

"However, I know that it's impossible to buy up enough shares of the company to take over. For one reason, June Wilcox would never sell her interest to me."

"That's probably true, too."

"So I've decided to buy up as many shares as the family is willing to sell to me—and then I'll offer to loan the toy company some money, at prime interest rates, for the purchase of some necessary pieces of equipment."

"Such as a computer from Delta Electronics?"

"For starters, yes." Mara stiffened. "Along with some equipment to start converting the factory."

"Into what?"

"An assembly line for computer components. The reason I want a part of Imagination so badly is that I want to start a new line of video games that would, for the most part, be built in Atlanta. The components, partially assembled, would be sent up here to be used for the inner workings of video games and small learning devices for educational toys."

"Can't you do all of that from Atlanta?" Mara asked, wondering aloud. "Do you really need Imagination?"

"Let's face it. Other than what I've read, I know very little about toy manufacturing and sales. On the other hand, Imagination has a sizable list of sales outlets; it has, for the most part, a reputation for making durable, reliable products and a fair amount of name recognition. Besides which," he added in a more ominous tone of voice, "you need me more than I need you."

"You're that sure of yourself?"

Shane leaned back in the desk chair and cradled his head in his palms, rumpling his black hair. "I know that you've had your share of bad luck, whether it was deserved or not."

"Deserved?"

"Face it, Mara. Much of Imagination's problems stem from the fact that for the past ten years, ever since Peter took over the company, profits have plummeted—aside from the one shining spot in the past few years—those funny-looking plastic dolls from that hit space movie."

"*Interplanetary Connection*," Mara said with a sigh, knowing that although she hated to admit it, Shane was right.

Shane seemed to sense her change in mood, and the look of defeat that paled her intense blue eyes made him feel inwardly guilty, as if he had been the cause of all of her problems.

"I understand that the movie production company has decided upon another manufacturer to handle the toy products for the movie sequel."

"That's right," Mara said, avoiding his gaze and looking out the large window at the towering Blue Ridge mountains in the distance.

"Why?"

Mara tightened her lips and swiveled to meet his inquiring gaze. "Several reasons," she began. "First of all, the production company didn't like the packaging, which I told them we would change, at our expense. Then they were unhappy with the advertising campaign, and I agreed that we would use an independent firm of their choosing."

"Then what was the problem?"

"It has something to do with a few of the more exotic extraterrestrial beings from the sequel. It seems they're much more intricate than the aliens in *Interplanetary Connection,* and the production company feels that a more malleable plastic for the action figures would make them appear more lifelike.' '

"And you disagree?"

Mara shook her head and pursed her lips pensively as her dark, honey-colored brows drew inward over her eyes. Thoughtfully, she clasped her hands together and tapped her chin. "No, I'm willing to go along with just about anything Solar Productions wants, but unfortunately the competition seems to have cornered the market on soft plastic; at least they can produce the action figures much more cheaply than we can."

"And just who is the competition?"

"It's all confidential, of course, and Solar Productions won't tell us, but my guess is it's San Franciscan

Toys, a rather new company from California. They seem to have a budget that NASA would envy, and the right marketing skills to sell even the cheapest, most shoddily made toys, such as . . . that Lolly doll that Angie is so fond of."

Shane's face relaxed at the mention of his child. "And how is she this morning?"

"Just fine and still enthralled with the kittens."

There was a pause in the conversation, and the smile left Shane's eyes. "Did you see June this morning?" he asked, almost under his breath.

"Yes."

"And were you able to tell her that I'm Angie's real father?"

"I thought about it," Mara admitted, "but I just couldn't. She looked so . . . tired this morning, I didn't want to risk it."

"If the woman is so damned unwell, why do you let her stay with Angie? There could be an accident of some kind. Aren't you afraid for her?"

Mara rubbed her temples furiously. "Of course I'm concerned," she snapped back.

"Well?"

"Have you considered the alternatives? With my irregular hours, a preschool is out of the question. And as for a private sitter, I've never been able to find one that would give Angie the same care and love that June gives her. There are no alternatives. June is the best choice. Besides which, being with Angie is good for her."

As Shane rolled his dark eyes expressively toward the ceiling, the door to the office swung open and Dena slid into the room. She began talking before noticing Shane behind the desk. "I waited for ten minutes, and then I realized that you had probably forgotten our . . ." she stopped in midsentence, her green eyes taking in the tall man sitting behind Mara's desk and the crackle of tension in the air. It didn't take a genius to guess that she had walked smack-dab into the middle of an argument . . . and from the looks of it, a personal one. Dena stopped short of the desk and adjusted the bulging folder under her left arm.

"Oh, Dena," Mara cried, slapping her palm against her forehead. "I forgot all about our meeting . . ." And then, shaking her head at her own stupidity, she added, "Excuse me . . . I don't believe you've met Shane Kennedy," Mara apologized as Shane rose from his chair and offered his hand to Dena.

"Pleased to meet you," Dena drawled in her sweetest southern accent, placing her small palm in Shane's.

"The pleasure is all mine," Shane countered, his dark eyes twinkling to add reinforcement to his words.

Mara watched the exchange between Shane and Dena with curiosity. What kind of game were they playing with each other? Dena smiled demurely, and let her hand slide out of Shane's grasp.

"Would you like to postpone our meeting again?" Dena asked Mara. The smile never left her voice, nor her glittering green eyes. Her burnished hair was coiffed attractively to fall in curly tangles to her shoulders and her sleek Halston original knit suit hugged her body possessively. Dena looked every bit the professional advertising executive.

"What meeting?" Shane asked. "I hope I didn't interrupt any of your plans . . ." The phrase sounded innocent and natural enough, but Mara found it hard to ignore the intensity of his words or his gaze.

"Mara and I were supposed to go over the advertising budget," Dena quipped, sitting down on the couch opposite the large, glass window and crossing her slim legs with practiced elegance.

"Perhaps we should talk about the budget later . . ." Mara proposed anxiously. Why did she feel it much better to keep Dena and Shane apart? The two of them together, for some unfathomable reason, seemed entirely too threatening.

Dena ignored Mara. "Shane Kennedy," she mused aloud, pursing her petulant wet lips. "You're the man interested in purchasing the toy company?"

"I was."

"No longer?" Dena pouted, tossing Mara a barely concealed look of disappointment.

Shane slid down in his chair and settled on his lower spine. "Mrs. Wilcox refuses to sell."

Dena's eyes narrowed just a fraction, and for a moment, her well-placed smile faltered. But gathering all of her professional aplomb, she begrudgingly said nothing about Mara's decision.

Shane answered the questions in Dena's eyes. "Mara has persuaded me to take an alternative position with the company . . . that is, if the board of directors approves."

"Alternative position?" Dena repeated innocently. Only Mara noticed the hardening of her sister-in-law's determined chin.

"I'm considering purchasing shares of the company and making a loan that would enable Imagination to continue its operation."

"Kind of you," Dena murmured, a bit sarcastically. She was reappraising Shane—sizing him up. There was something about him that was more disturbing than his evident male virility . . . an uneasy haunting familiarity . . . that kept nagging at her. What was it about him that bothered her so? Nervously she toyed with her pen as she watched him. "What's in this for you, Mr. Kennedy?" she asked, and Mara felt herself stiffen. Up until this point, Dena had held onto the pretense of being a competent, interested shareholder. But there was a relentless persistence in the redhead's eyes that unnerved Mara.

"Call me Shane," he responded with a pleasant smile. "Don't worry . . . Dena—" he used her first name cautiously, but she nodded politely as he did so "—this isn't a one-sided endeavor. Delta Electronics will profit admirably from the venture."

"Hmm . . ." was her unsure response.

"Now, if you'll excuse me, I've got to get busy," Shane admitted. "Mara, first I'll need an office with a telephone. Then, I want all of these ledgers transferred to that office. Oh, and I'll need space for the terminal . . ." He ran his finger thoughtfully along his jawline.

"Anything else?" Mara asked sarcastically.

"Yes." His fingers snapped decisively. "Arrange for a board meeting sometime this week, if possible, and I'll have a written proposal for all of the members of the board."

Mara felt the muscles in her back stiffen. He was so efficient, so damned efficient. There was an unquestionable air of authority and businesslike demand to all of his movements.

"You can use Stewart Callison's office," Mara stated, reaching for a stack of the ledgers and holding the door open with her foot. "He's on vacation and won't be back until the middle of September. If you're still here when he returns, we'll rearrange everything, I suppose."

Shane reached for a pile of his paperwork and his briefcase, and followed Mara down a long, white hallway to the small cubicle that was Stewart's office. If he thought the accommodations confining, he didn't complain, but stacked his work neatly on a corner of the desk.

It took several trips to carry all of the ledgers to Shane's office. When at last Mara's office was once again her own, she was surprised to find Dena still sitting, half-draped across the small leather divan.

"Let's go over the budget right now," Mara suggested, finally dropping into her rightful chair behind the desk. She pulled a file from her drawer and spread it on the desktop.

"Can it wait?" Dena asked, distractedly.

"But I thought . . ."

Dena made a dismissive gesture. "The budget can wait. What I want to know is why you insist on being bullheaded about Kennedy's offer to buy out Imagination?"

"I explained all of that before."

"Wasn't his offer high enough?"

"We never even got down to dollar signs."

"Then you didn't give the man a chance!" Dena accused viciously.

"Listen, Dena. I told you before, I'm not interested in selling. At least, not now. Shane's made a very interesting counterproposal that he intends to present to the shareholders. If the majority accepts his terms, then perhaps Imagination will still be able to pull out of this slump."

"And if not? What then, Mara?" Dena cut in, her temper rising angrily. "Then we'll be in debt to Kennedy, along with a list of other creditors as long as my arm. What good will he have done us?"

Mara listened patiently, the only evidence of her anger being the silent drumming of her fingers against the empty coffee cup on her desk.

"Why don't you just give up, for God's sake? You were never cut out to run this company, and by now, even you should be able to see it. Ever since you took over, the losses have increased to the point of no return. Take your chance while it's offered; sell the whole damned company and be rid of it! Parceling off a few shares to Kennedy and having him loan us some more funds is only forestalling the inevitable."

"You're suggesting that I take the money and run?"

"In so many words, I guess so."

"Why? Why are you so anxious to get out of the company? If you don't like being a part of it, why don't you just sell your shares to Shane and be done with it?"

"You'd like that, wouldn't you?" Dena countered.

"What do you mean?"

"You'd like to be rid of me. I know that I've been a thorn in your side, and really, I haven't meant to be," Dena persisted. "But it galls me to no end that you . . . someone who really isn't related to anyone in the family . . . is running Imagination."

"Dena," Mara began, choosing her words carefully. "I understand why you resent me. And I know that you feel that you should have inherited the bulk of the company stock, as you were your father's first born, but—"

"Stop the theatrics, Mara," Dena commanded, rising from her insolent position on the couch. "And don't bother to try and convince me that you're doing the 'right thing' for either me, my mother, or your kid by carrying out Peter's wishes. The whole thing doesn't wash with me, not one little bit," Dena announced, bitterly.

"Dena—"

"Don't start with me, Mara," Dena persisted, rising up from the couch to look down her nose at her sister-in-law. "As far as I'm concerned, it's all or nothing with this company."

She turned on her heel to go, but Mara's voice arrested her. "Just give it a chance," Mara suggested wearily.

"Not on your life!" With her final retort, Dena marched regally out of the office and quietly closed the door behind her.

Mara gritted her teeth and quietly attempted to calm herself. The next two weeks were not going to be easy by any means.

Chapter 8

The first week of Shane's visit flew by at an exhausting pace. Personnel were shuffled, the microcomputer, "Delta's finest," was shipped and assembled, and truckloads of information, anything from payroll records to scrapped ideas about products, were fed into the large keyboard with the video screen. Shane insisted that everyone in the office be able to run the machine, at least to some degree. The more private files concerning personnel or secret new designs were specially coded so that only a few of the more trusted employees had access to them.

Mara was reluctant to sit at the keyboard and hesitant to work with the imposing piece of new machinery, but she couldn't hide the smile of satisfaction when she had mastered a few of the more basic programs. Within weeks, Shane assured her, she would be an expert concerning the Delta 830-G.

At home, where Mara should have had time to relax and unwind, the situation remained tense. June's health was a very real concern for Mara, as the older woman seemed far too distracted at times, and the grayish pallor of June's face couldn't be hidden by even the most expensive cosmetics. Angie was as exuberant as ever, and Mara wondered if the vivacious child was too much of a burden on June. But every time that Mara broached the subject of June's health, the older woman found a way of avoiding the issue. Mara even suggested that June make an appointment with Dr. Bernard, but the advice was conveniently ignored.

Angie was busy discovering the world. The four plump kittens were one of her most time-consuming infatuations, and her idolization of Shane was apparent to everyone, including June. Several times in the past few days, June had made excuses to stay late with Angie, at least until Shane's sleek silver Audi pulled into the driveway. Mara caught June observing Shane and Angie, and the older woman's mouth drew into a fine line of pain when she noticed the easy familiarity that Shane lavished upon the child. And Angie's innocent and loving response wasn't lost on June. Whatever love that Angie harbored for Peter was forgotten when the child was with Shane; that much was certain.

Mara was torn. She cared for her mother-in-law, she cherished her child, and she loved Shane with a passion that at times burned wildly through her body. The past week of watching him at work, while he was absorbed in some minor problem, made her body ache with longing for him. He hadn't stayed with her since the first night together, and somehow she felt betrayed. She knew that it was his own way of saying that until she told June about Angie, he wouldn't have any physical contact with her.

Mara was wise enough to realize that he still wanted her, perhaps more desperately than ever. She would catch him gazing at her, his eyes touching her, caressing her, and she knew in the black intensity of his gaze that he was burning for her. And yet he controlled himself, silently waiting for her to tell the world about Angie. Mara flirted with the idea of attempting to seduce him, hoping to break down his ironwilled control, but she hesitated, foreseeing more problems than the three of them already faced.

It was the day of the board meeting that the simmering tension between them snapped.

It didn't help that the day dawned hot, and that the cool mountain breezes that usually favored the high plateau of Asheville hadn't appeared. Instead, the dull, sultry heat was unnervingly oppressive, even in the early morning. The dust and bothersome insects that Mara rarely noticed seemed to be everywhere, inside the house as well as out. And Angie, usually happy to spend the day at home, clung fitfully to Mara's legs, whining and crying, begging Mara to stay with her.

Mara was standing at the mirror, trying to apply a light sheen of plum lipstick to her lips while Angie complained loudly beside her. Angie's face was red from the heat and passion of her outburst. Mara dropped the lipstick tube on the counter and bent on one knee so that she could face her child on her level. As she did so, she felt the tickle of a run climb up her knee in her panty hose. Ignoring the fact that she was already late and doubted she had another clean pair of panty hose in the house, she cradled Angie's curly head in her hands.

"What's wrong, Angie?" Mara asked, wiping a tear from the child's flushed cheek and reaching for a tissue to wipe Angie's nose.

"I don't want you to go," Angie sobbed.

"But, honey, you know Momma has to go to work . . ."

"No!"

"Tell me what's bothering you," Mara suggested. "I

can't make things any better unless you tell me what's troubling you. Don't cry, just talk to me."

"I . . . I don't want to stay with Mrs. Reardon . . . I want Grammie!" Angie demanded, stamping her bare foot imperiously.

"But, honey, Grammie will be here later. You know that she has to be at the board meeting today."

"No, she don't!"

"Angie," Mara said authoritatively. "Mrs. Reardon is a very nice lady. She comes here every Friday to help Momma . . ."

"But she don't play with me."

"Honey, she's very busy. She has to clean the house, but I just bet, if you ask her nicely, she would read a book to you."

"I don't like her!"

"Sure you do." Mara was having difficulty hiding the exasperation in her voice. The last thing she wanted this morning was a full blown battle with her child. The guilt about leaving Angie was beginning to get to her. Did all mothers who worked full-time at a career they enjoyed feel the welling sense of guilt that Mara was experiencing? "Come here, Momma's got to find a new pair of panty hose," Mara called to the child as she stepped back into the bedroom and rummaged in her top bureau drawer. The digital clock on the nightstand reminded Mara that she was already twenty minutes late. Somehow, she had to placate Angie. If she left the child and Angie was unhappy, Mara knew that she would have trouble concentrating on the board meeting. And today, more than ever, she needed every drop of concentration she could muster.

"Hey, I've got an idea," Mara hinted in a secretive voice that Angie loved.

Instantly, the child was intrigued. She lowered her

small, blond head between her shoulder blades and her dark eyes danced. "What?" Angie asked, in a collusive whisper.

"Why don't you help Mrs. Reardon clean the house?"

Angie's face fell and she eyed her mother suspiciously. Mara ignored Angie's restraint and continued with her idea.

"Here—" she reached into the top drawer again "—is one of Mamma's old hankies. You can use it to wash the windows and polish the furniture, and look," Mara retreated into the bathroom, still tugging at the new panty hose. Quickly, she fished under the bathroom sink to retrieve a blue bottle. "This is a bottle of glass spray . . . you can spray the cleaner on the windows and wipe it off with the hanky . . . like this." Mara sprayed the cleaner onto the mirror and watched her image become distorted in a froth of bubbles. Then she folded the cloth and wiped the mirror clean.

Angie suspected that she was being conned out of her bad mood by her mother. And although she wanted to continue to whine, she was impressed with her mother's attempts to entertain her. Never had her mother let her touch any of the cleaning supplies. Her enthusiasm was slightly subdued, but she reached a chubby hand out toward the clear glass bottle half-filled with blue liquid. "Will Mrs. Reardon really let me?" Angie asked as she dashed into the bedroom, and after a quick sneaking look at her mother, sprayed a healthy spot of foam on the expensive satin quilt. The look on the child's face was one of expectant defiance.

"Angie Wilcox! What do you think you're doing?" Mara sputtered as she attempted to wipe up the mess on the quilt. "You can't play with this, unless you play with it the right way, with Mrs. Reardon's help! And,

never, never spray the furniture or the bedspread again!"
Mara admonished her daughter as she furiously wiped
at the stain on the quilt. Giving up, she pulled the bedspread from the bed and threw it in a crumpled heap
near the laundry hamper.

"You know better!" Mara reprimanded through tight
lips, as she guided Angie out of the room and toward
the staircase.

Angie paused under a solemn portrait of Peter's
grandfather and looked into her room. Mara nearly ran
over her. "I think I stay up here," the child mused.
"Lolly needs a bath and I give her one."

"Oh, no, you don't," Mara retorted quickly after following the train of the little girl's thoughts. Mara's thin
patience was fraying, and she was barely able to hold
onto her anger. "If you intend to play with that glass
spray, you do it with Mrs. Reardon."

Angie puckered her lips for a moment, seeming to
hesitate, but decided against arguing with her mother
any further. Clutching the dear bottle of spray as if she
were afraid someone might take it from her, she
grabbed her tattered blanket and followed Mara down
the stairs.

Mrs. Reardon had the vacuum cleaner roaring in the
den. The machine went quiet when Mara popped her
head into one of her favorite rooms in the house. It was
large and comfortable with an informal brick fireplace
and knotty pine walls. The varnish had yellowed and
aged to give the room a warm, homey look, and the
plaid sofa and leather recliner were a welcome relief
from the other, more formal furnishings of the house.
Large, leafy green plants grew well in this room with
its paned windows and view of the gardens to the rear
of the grounds. When Mara came home from work to
relax and unwind, it was always in this room. It was al-

ways casual and warm, and some of her fondest memories included reading to Angie in the den, or sitting on the couch with her child and building with blocks.

"I've got to go now," Mara called to the plump, middle-aged woman with the broad smile and crisp, floral apron. Mrs. Reardon looked up from plumping the pillows on the couch as Mara continued. "Angie's already bathed and had breakfast. And, oh, I gave her a bottle of glass cleaner. She wanted to help you clean the house," Mara lied a little sheepishly.

"So I see!" Mrs. Reardon laughed, exposing gold crowns over her molars. Mara spun around to see Angie studiously spraying an antique silver coffee service.

"Please, Angie, be careful," Mara pleaded, and kissed the chubby child on the forehead. Turning to Mrs. Reardon, she hoisted the strap of her purse over her shoulder and picked up her briefcase. "I should be in the office all day, if you need me. And June will be back here by early . . . or at the very latest . . . mid-afternoon."

"Fine . . . fine . . . I'm going to be here all day," Mrs. Reardon agreed distractedly as she wrapped the cord from the vacuum cleaner neatly around her broad forearm. "Don't you worry about a thing."

Mara felt as tightly coiled as a spring as she opened the back door and hurried past the flowering shrubs to her car. Was it her too vivid imagination, or did she hear the shatter of broken glass just as she was stepping into the car? After waiting a couple of extra minutes, knowing that Mrs. Reardon would come out of the house if indeed a calamity had ensued, she started the car. Thankfully, Mrs. Reardon had handled whatever catastrophe had occurred. With a sigh of relief, Mara wound her way past the dozen or so oak trees that were giving merciful shade to the driveway and inched the car onto the highway. Trying to make up for lost time, she pushed the throttle to the floor and began speeding toward the city limits of Asheville. The drive was hot and dusty, and by the time Mara parked in her favorite spot under the building, she felt drained. Why did she dread this board meeting so? An uneasy feeling akin to dread had steadily knotted her stomach.

"You're late," Shane snapped as Mara entered her office. He was leaning against the windowsill, his hands supporting him by propping his long frame against the sill. He looked starched and fresh in his lightweight tan suit and ivory linen shirt. A navy tie, just a shade lighter than his eyes, was staunchly in place. In comparison to Shane's crisp, unruffled look, Mara felt completely wilted.

"I know I'm late."

"The meeting starts in less than ten minutes!"

"I know . . . I'm sorry."

"Is that all you can say?"

Mara tossed her purse into the closet and put her briefcase down with a thud. "Don't start with me, okay?"

He stood up and straightened his suit. His dark eyes observed her and noted that her usually impeccable appearance was more than a little disheveled. Shane preferred her this way; she seemed so much more vulnerable, so much younger, more as he remembered her, but still he was disturbed. It wasn't like her.

"Bad morning?" he guessed, his dark brows furrowing as he walked toward her.

"It could have been better." She straightened the neatly typed pages of the proposal and counted to make sure that there were enough copies. She avoided his gaze.

"What's wrong?" he asked, echoing the question she had asked of Angie only a half hour before.

"Nothing . . . everything . . . I'm not sure."

"It's Angie, isn't it? I think you should tell me about it."

"Let's just forget it until the meeting is over, okay?"

He pulled the reports out of her hands and forced her head upward in order that she meet his gaze squarely. "What's bothering you?" he asked crisply, and his fingers strayed across her arms and throat.

"Shane, don't."

The soft blue silk of her dress brushed against her skin, and through the light fabric, Mara could feel the inviting warmth of Shane's large hands, coaxing her . . . massaging her . . . caressing her . . .

"Look, Mara, if something's wrong with Angie, I think I have a right to know—"

The door flew open. Startled and embarrassed, Mara shrank from Shane's tempting embrace. She felt her face begin to burn guiltily.

"Oh," Dena said, her curious eyebrows arching. Had she just stumbled onto something important? "I . . . I didn't mean to disturb you . . ." she began, stepping backward while her green eyes took in the intimate scene.

"You didn't," Shane replied curtly with a polite, but slightly irritated smile. "We were just on our way to the boardroom. Is everything ready?"

"Yes . . . that's what I came to tell you. Other than Cousin Arnie . . . everyone is waiting." The look of confusion and incomprehension never left her perfect face, and her dark, almond-shaped eyes puzzled over Shane's features.

For one heart-stopping instant Mara read the expression on Dena's face. *She knows,* Mara thought. *Dear God, Dena knows that Shane is Angie's father!* Surprisingly fast, Mara's composure and common sense took over. If Dena knew about Angie's paternity, she would have already made good use of it, unless she intended to use the information to embarrass Mara at the board meeting! Mara felt her insides churn. Never had she dreaded a board meeting more, but she managed a feeble grin.

"Good." If only she could hide the blush that still burned on her cheeks. "Let's go!" Armed with Shane's proposal, all fifteen copies, and as much confidence as she was able to muster, Mara led Shane and Dena down the stark white hallways into the elegant and slightly overstated boardroom.

Already the captain's chairs around the shining walnut table were, for the most part, occupied. Although a paddle fan circulated lazily over the crowd, a thin cloud of hazy cigarette smoke hung heavily in the air, and the whispered chatter that had buzzed only minutes before stopped as Mara entered the room and took her place at the head of the table. Her stomach lurched perceptively as she placed a strained smile on her face and looked into the eyes of all of the relatives of her late husband, most of whom she hadn't seen since the day of the funeral.

As Mara's eyes swept the interested but cautious faces lining the table, they locked with June's pale blue gaze. Dressed in burdensome black, which had become her only public attire since Peter's death, the older woman smiled tightly at her daughter-in-law and fidgeted with the single strand of natural pearls at her neck. Dena slid into a chair next to her mother, and the contrast between mother and daughter was shocking. Dena seemed devastatingly youthful and glowing with health. Her thick red hair, secured against the nape of her neck, curled softly at her neckline, the understated but elegant ivory silk dress enhanced her slim figure, and the discreet but expensive jewelry sparkled against her flawless skin. It all seemed to give Dena just the right touch of class that made her appear more beautiful than usual.

After informal introductions were made and coffee was offered to all of the board members, Mara called the meeting to order. Somehow she was able to speak, although she felt a painful constriction in her chest. The nervous glances and grim smiles on the faces of Peter's family didn't ease any of her discomfort. Did they all know? Was it possible that they could tell that Shane was Angie's father? Did they think her an impostor—a pretender to the crown? She knew that her restless thoughts bordered on paranoia, but still they plagued her. How in God's name was she going to get out of this? Sooner or later all of the family, June and Dena included, would know that Shane was the father of Peter's child. What would happen? And why, when everything appeared so useless, did she try so vainly to hold Imagination together? It seemed inevitable that, when the truth was learned, the family would contest Peter's will and a horrible, ugly lawsuit would ensue.

Mara wasn't really worried for herself; she knew that she could be as strong as she had to be. But what about Angie, and June? The press would have a field day with the story. How could Mara protect her child and her frail mother-in-law? Was it possible?

A few of the essentials for the board meeting, such as a treasurer's report and a lengthy reading of the minutes of the previous meeting, were accomplished as quickly as possible. Finally, her composure outwardly calm, Mara announced the purpose of the meeting, explaining in detail the financial woes of the toy company, and passed out the typewritten reports to each of the board members.

Shane rose to confront the members of the Wilcox

family. He looked exactly like what he was: young, tough, and confident. His smile, slightly crooked, seemed genuine, and his dark eyes took in every person in the room at once. He spoke distinctly, cross-referencing his speech with notes from the typewritten pages. After explaining the reasons that Delta Electronics was interested in Imagination and summarizing the contents of his proposal, he smiled confidently at the nervous pairs of eyes that watched him. The fan turned quietly overhead, soft strains of piped-in music melted in the background, the pages rustled as they were turned, and only an occasional cough or click of a lighter disturbed Shane's even monologue.

Mara noticed that the jute-colored open-weave draperies swayed with the movement of air, and that a few of Peter's relatives shifted uncomfortably in their chairs. But for the most part the board seemed to be uniformly concentrating on Shane; he had everyone's attention.

Mara listened and watched the effect of Shane's speech on the members sitting at the table. Some seemed absolutely convinced that Shane knew exactly what he was doing, to the extent that Cousin Arnie even nodded his bald head in agreement with Shane's more elaborate points. A few others were dubious, and the caution in their eyes was an open invitation to questions. And several, at least it seemed from their blank expressions, didn't know quite what to think.

Shane's speech was short and concise. When finished, he tapped the report loudly on the table, closed it, and sat down. "Now," he concluded, taking a long drink from the coffee cup that had been sitting, untouched, in front of him, "does anyone have any questions?"

For a stagnant second there was only silence, and

then it seemed as if everyone began to talk at once. Shane smiled to himself in amusement, but Mara's stomach quivered in worried anticipation. Finally, the boardroom quieted.

"Are you trying to tell me . . . I mean, us," Peter's cousin, Sarah, began after crushing out her cigarette, "that unless we take you, er, Delta Electronics up on their offer, Imagination Toys will . . . will go bankrupt?" Fear showed in Sarah's ice-blue eyes and her voice was strained with her feelings of incredulity. Never in her thirty-four years had she considered herself being anything but wealthy.

"That's being a little overdramatic," Shane observed with a good-natured smile that was meant to ease Sarah. "But it's obvious from the last financial statements Imagination Toys has provided me that the company is in trouble—serious trouble."

"Hogwash!" Peter's aunt Mimi declared, opening her gloved palms in a gracious gesture of explanation. "Imagination is just suffering a little because of the economy, you know, the recession or whatever those buffoons in Washington want to call it." She smiled sweetly, as if she had solved all of the problems, and her third husband patted her knowingly on her arm.

Sarah ignored Aunt Mimi. "But how can that be— that Imagination is in trouble? I thought that the company was worth . . . several million!" Sarah nervously played with her lighter, rotating it end on end as she asked her worried questions.

Mara's tightly controlled voice interrupted Shane's response. "Of course the company is worth quite a bit, Sarah. But for the past several years, the profits have been falling off, and in order to keep Imagination on its feet, we need an input of more capital into the treasury."

"Excuse me, Mr. Kennedy," Sarah's brother Rich argued, "but I really don't like the idea of someone other than the family putting up more funds for Imagination. This has been a Wilcox family venture for generations, and I think we should try and work out our problems among ourselves . . . no offense, you understand."

Once again the room buzzed with whispered chatter, all seeming to agree with Rich's impassioned speech. It was Mara's turn to speak. "I couldn't agree with you more, Rich," she said with a genuine smile. Rich positively beamed; he was so proud of himself. "Now," Mara continued graciously, "who would like to make the investment? Delta Electronics is willing to put up half a million dollars . . ." Mara's cobalt eyes skimmed the faces, and most of the eyes upon her avoided her gaze.

The room became hushed, and Mara felt that her point had been driven home. No one in the family was willing to put that much money into the failing toy company. Reluctantly, the family was coming to grips with the uncomfortable financial situation and the fact that Shane's offer was nearly a last-ditch effort.

It was Dena's slow, sultry speech that caught Mara's attention and started the creeping sense of dread that began crawling up her spine. Throughout the meeting, Dena's eyes had been narrowing on Shane, reassessing him, scrutinizing him, and now it was the redhead's move.

"Mara's right, of course," Dena patronized sweetly as she looked from one to the other of the tense faces that lined the table. "Not one of us can afford to put up that kind of money for Imagination, can we? And it's my guess that even combined, the coffers of the Wilcox family couldn't scramble together half a million dollars." Her smile melted to a determined frown. "And why is that?" Dena asked rhetorically. Silence. Shane's eyes had blackened and Mara felt the rush of color to her face, but other than the nervous click of Sarah's lighter, there was no noise. Dena answered her own question. "The answer is simple—for the last three quarters, ever since Peter's death, Imagination Toys hasn't paid any of us one thin dime in dividends! And whose fault is that?"

"You know the reasons for that, Dena. We discussed them last year, and the board approved my decision to withhold the dividends," Mara retorted through clenched teeth. She was conscious of the eyes of Peter's family looking at her, some with empathy, others with accusation. "We all agreed that it would be better to try and turn the company around, rather than bleed it dry with dividends."

"A lot of good it did," Dena snorted, and Cousin Rich smiled in agreement.

Dena tossed her auburn curls, unconvinced by Mara's argument, using the board room as center stage for her simmering dispute with her sister-in-law. Shane's black eyes never left the redhead's arrogantly beautiful face. Dena voiced her opinion. "I guess I just don't understand: if the company is such a burden, why don't we just sell it . . . all of it." She shrugged her thin shoulders theatrically. "From what I understand, Mr. Kennedy offered to buy it out, completely."

An audible gasp escaped from around the table. "Why weren't we notified?" "I never heard that!" "What's going on here, anyway?" Little catch phrases echoed and ricocheted around the small, enclosed room, and several pairs of eyes looked at Mara with unconcealed disbelief.

Mara felt Shane stiffen beside her, but she put a restraining hand on his coat sleeve. An act, she was sure, that everyone in the room noticed and questioned.

"Just a minute!" June's cold voice cracked through the air. She gripped the table severely, her knuckles white, and rose with difficulty. "Don't all of you go blaming Mara . . . and Dena, you should be ashamed of yourself!" She cut her daughter down with an icy gaze. "The reason that Mara didn't consider Mr. Kennedy's original proposal to buy out the company is that *I* suggested otherwise."

June's proud chin rose a regal inch. "Imagination Toys has been a tradition with the Wilcox family for generations, as Rich so magnanimously pointed out earlier." The color in Rich's round face drained. "Just because things aren't going exactly our way doesn't mean that we should throw in the towel." June's piercing blue eyes moved from one of her husband's relatives to the next in cool, commanding appraisal. There was no question as to who was the matriarch of the family.

"Actually, I do agree with Rich." Her eyes, now more kind, rested upon her nephew. "I wish that there was some way that we could avoid asking for outside help to save the company . . . but . . . it appears that we don't have much of a choice. Either we accept Mr. Kennedy's proposal, and I believe it is fair to both parties, or we scale down Imagination from a national toy company to a purely Southeastern endeavor."

Again, the hushed, excited whispers.

June lowered herself into her chair, clearly drained from the ordeal. Dena pursed her lips together petulantly and refused to look in Mara's direction. The rest of the family mumbled and grumbled among themselves. Aunt Mimi appeared positively flabbergasted, Cousin Sarah, appalled and nervous, and Cousin Rich, deflated.

After a few more direct questions about the proposal, the family was satisfied and voted, albeit somewhat reluctantly, to sell treasury shares in the corporation to Shane and accept a loan from Delta Electronics. It was a long, stifling affair, and nearly two o'clock in the afternoon by the time all of the details were ironed out.

Much later, when all of the board members had gone, having taken a little time to talk with Shane and voice their opinions, doubts, and hopes for the future of the toy company, Mara felt completely drained and worn out. If the morning with Angie had gone poorly, the board meeting was a total, unnerving free-for-all. It was over, and the battle had turned in her favor, but she couldn't help but wonder if it was all worth the effort.

"Let's go to lunch," Shane suggested, once they were alone in Mara's office.

"I'm not hungry," Mara declined, running her fingers through the thick tangle of her blond hair. "I've got a million things to do anyway."

"You should eat something."

She waved her hand in the air dismissively and placed a tight smile on her face. "No, thanks, I'll just have a cup of coffee—really, my stomach's too tied in knots to think about food."

Shane ignored her protests and reached in the closet for her purse. "Well, I'm going out for lunch, and the least you could do is keep me company . . . come on, it'll do you good."

"But I've got a ton of work to do."

"We all do, but nothing much gets accomplished on an empty stomach."

"All right," she agreed wearily, too tired of battling board members to argue any further.

Shane had been right, of course, and the fresh seafood salad that she had ordered had brightened her mood incredibly. He had been considerate, almost loving, and insisted that they talk about anything other than the company. Mara actually found herself relaxing for the first time that day, and though usually not her custom during a working day, she had indulged herself in a glass of cold Chablis.

The headiness of the wine on her tired body had just begun to tingle her spine when Shane's light mood vanished. He finished his drink, ordered a cup of coffee, and stared into the dark depths of the liquid, as if seeking answers for his life. His frown was commanding, and for a moment he uncharacteristically avoided Mara's gaze.

"I'm going to Atlanta tonight, for the weekend," he began, swirling the coffee in the cup before taking a sip. "I'd like you and Angie to come with me."

Mara ignored the direct invitation. "But I thought you would be here for another week."

Shane smiled grimly at his own black thoughts. "I will, but unfortunately there's some business in Atlanta that can't wait. I'll be there until Monday afternoon."

The invitation lay open between them, if only Mara had the strength and trust to accept it. "I . . . I don't know . . ."

"I take it that you haven't told June about my relationship with Angie?" Black eyes delved into her.

"No . . . not yet . . ."

Shane's fist thudded down on the table, scattering the silverware and spilling the water glasses.

"Why the hell not?" he demanded.

"You know why not."

"I've heard all your reasons, Mara, and they are nothing more than overblown excuses!"

"But Angie . . ."

"She would be better off knowing that I'm her real father and that I love her!"

"But . . . June . . ."

"This may surprise you, Mara, but I don't give a damn about June, or any other member of that circus you call a family. I saw them all this afternoon. Any one of them would be glad to sell if they thought they could make a dime out of it."

"No!"

"Open your eyes, Mara. The longer you wait, the more difficult it is going to be." He drew his head closer to hers and whispered hoarsely across the table. "And if you have any ridiculous notions that I might not insist that Angie become legally mine, you can guess again."

Mara felt her fingers shaking, but fortunately her voice was strong and didn't betray her turbulent inner emotions.

"You know that I have no intention of betraying you, and I have tried to talk to June, I *really* have."

"But?" he snorted, prompting her.

"It's been difficult."

"You're making it difficult!"

"You know that June hasn't been well . . . certainly you could see in the meeting today what a strain she's been under."

"That, Mara, was a show of strength, not weakness."

"I'm not talking about control of the company, Shane, I'm talking about physical well-being. You don't have to be a doctor to see that the woman is ill!" Mara stated emphatically, her blue eyes flashing with anger.

"In my opinion, June Wilcox is as strong as she wants to be. The way she handled that meeting today is proof enough for me. If she's ill, it's probably psychosomatic!"

"You're blinded by your own selfish interests!" Mara charged.

"Is it selfish to want what is rightfully mine?"

"You'll get it, Shane, I promise you."

"When, Mara? When?"

Mara let her head fall into the heel of her hand, and she rubbed her throbbing temples to ease the headache that had badgered her all day. "I don't know," she said quietly. "I honestly don't know. Can't you please be patient, just a little while longer?" Her blue eyes regarded him through the thick sheen of her lashes. They pleaded with him, and begged him to understand. "It won't be long," she whispered.

Thinking it was one of the most difficult things he had ever done, Shane forced himself to ignore the heartbreaking look of promise in her Dresden eyes. "You've got one more week," he replied in a clipped, well-modulated voice. Was he always in control, Mara wondered, was he always so intense? Was she wrong in denying him his child, if only for another week?

"You're being selfish," she murmured.

A hollow laugh was her answer. "No, sweetheart, if

I've made a mistake, it's that I haven't been selfish enough! But, believe me, all that has changed. I only want what is rightfully mine. Angie is my daughter, Mara, and I intend to have her! Soon!"

"And you will."

A grim smile played over his face as he called for the check and paid the bill. They walked in silence back to the building, both wrapped in their own desperate thoughts. Why must it be so difficult, Mara asked herself. Wasn't there an easy solution to the happiness that they both wanted?

Shane left that evening with only a crisp good-bye. He was polite but formal, and although Mara felt a need to reach out to him, to touch him, she remained stoic behind her desk, wondering how they would ever be able to solve their dilemma and become a family. Even the smile that she tried to flash at him failed and fell into a flat, tremblingly dismal line that barely curved upward at the corners.

She waited, and listened to his retreating footsteps as they echoed down the long corridor outside her office. Never had she felt more alone, and never had she felt so hollow and empty.

The drive home in the car was hot and dusty. Even the summer wildflowers seemed to droop along the roadside in the oppressive humidity, and by the time she got home, Mara was damp with perspiration. The giant oaks lining the drive, with their shimmering silver-green leaves reflecting the late summer sun, were a welcome relief to Mara's tired eyes. After a long day at the office, the aggravating board meeting, and the fight with Shane, it was all Mara could do to concentrate on her driving while squinting at the relentless afternoon sun. Now, as she slid the Renault into its usual spot near the garage, she lifted her sunglasses from her nose and wiped away the beads of perspiration that had collected on her cheeks. She paused for one more soul-searching minute in the hot car, her hands still lightly gripping the steering wheel. Was Shane right? Had she avoided the subject of Angie with June in a subconscious attempt to avoid the pain that she might cause Peter's mother? Was she only making excuses, not only to Shane, but also to herself? And was it even possible to tell June about Shane right now and get the truth off her chest? How would her mother-in-law take the news, especially now when Shane had just become a partial owner in Imagination?

The hot sun finally forced Mara to get out of the car and face her mother-in-law. Seeing no alternative to coming right out and telling June the truth, Mara steeled herself for what she knew would be a mental ordeal. Opening the door from the back porch, a cool blast of air from the central air-conditioning revived her and evaporated the clinging dampness from her dress.

"Mommy?" a high-pitched voice called. "That you?" Excited feet hurried toward Mara, and Angie rounded the corner, nearly colliding with her mother.

"Hi, sweetheart. How was your day?" Mara asked, her tired face breaking into a grin at the sight of her child.

Angie lifted her small shoulders in a childish imitation of adult indifference.

"Did Grammie let you go swimming in the wading pool?" Mara asked, bending down to lift the child and noticing that beneath the light pink T-shirt, Angie was wearing her bathing suit.

"That's right . . . and the kitties, too!" Angie agreed, with a wide, mischievous grin.

"Oh, no," Mara groaned as June, chuckling, hurried into the kitchen to allay any of Mara's fears.

"They're all right now. Don't you worry."

"But the kittens," Mara gasped, envisioning the entire scene vividly in her mind, "they're so small . . .I don't think they even have all of their eyes open."

"Believe it or not, they can swim . . . at least for a few minutes," June laughed. "However," she stated on a more sober note, "Southpaw was absolutely beside herself, and against her better judgment she jumped into the pool and dragged the bedraggled things to safety."

"Oh, Angie," Mara sighed, "we never . . . never, ever put the kitties in the water. They don't like it." Mara's voice was grave.

"They need a bath," Angie explained, innocence lighting up her round face.

"Southpaw will take care of that . . ." and then noticing that Angie did, for the first time, understand that she had made a terrible mistake, and that tears began to well in the child's eyes, Mara abruptly changed the subject. "What's this?" she asked, poking at a brownish smudge on Angie's cheek.

"Grammie and me made brownies today," Angie announced importantly.

"Did you?" Mara smiled fondly at her child and kissed Angie's tousled blond curls. "And are they any good?"

"Better'n you make!"

"That's because Grammie has a special recipe," Mara replied with a laugh as she set the child back onto the floor. Suddenly Mara felt that all of her cares and worries had melted. She was in her home, with her adorable child, and the problems of the office seemed distant and unnecessary. Angie, wily child that she was, instinctively knew from her mother's expression that the crisis concerning the cats was over, so she contented herself in the den off of the kitchen and played with her plastic building blocks.

"That's a switch," June observed, looking over the top of her reading glasses to watch her granddaughter.

"What is?" Mara opened the refrigerator door and extracted a pitcher.

"For once Angie is playing with a toy from Imagination. That doesn't happen often," the older woman mused thoughtfully.

"No, it doesn't," Mara agreed, pouring herself a tall glass of iced tea and offering one to her mother-in-law. "Unfortunately, Angie is a shining example of the kids in America today, when it comes to choosing toys. Why is that? What's wrong with our line?" Mara asked herself, furrows once again creasing her brow.

"I'm sorry. I didn't mean to bring up all of the worries of the office again," June apologized. She took off the orange apron that she had been wearing over her black knit suit and folded it neatly before placing it back into a drawer. It occurred to Mara, as she studied her mother-in-law over the rim of her glass, that June looked much better than she had earlier in the day. None of the strain or physical weakness that had been so evident at the board meeting was apparent. And, other than the light wrinkles around her eyes, a slightly pale complexion, and a whiteness around her lips, the older woman appeared healthier than she had in months. For just a few short hours to have passed, the transformation was almost impossible. Could Shane possibly be right? Was her mother-in-law's health only a convenient excuse, a psychosomatic act, a weapon that June could turn off and on, to use when she needed it?

Mara had known June for over four years. Although

it was evident that the woman wielded her power over her family like a brandished sword, Mara found it impossible to believe that June would knowingly try to deceive anyone, family included.

"How did it go—with Angie?" Mara asked in what she hoped would sound like an off-the-cuff manner.

"Oh, fine. Just fine," June replied. She took a seat at one of the café chairs near the kitchen table and an irritated look settled on her face. "If I were only able to handle the rest of my family as easily as I can Angie, life would be a lot simpler, let me tell you!" The corners of her mouth pulled into a disgusted frown.

"You're referring to the board meeting?" Mara surmised as she settled into a chair opposite June, near the broad bay window of the kitchen nook.

June smiled wistfully. "You know me so well," she whispered. Do I, Mara wondered, do I know you at all? Once again June's agitation lit her face, and she played her fingers over the rim of her tea glass.

"Honestly," June sputtered angrily. "That Rich, what a spoiled cur he's become . . . and pompous to boot! Where does he get such a 'holier than thou' attitude? Certainly not from Mimi, his mother!" June rolled her eyes heavenward in a supplicating gesture. "And then there's Dena. What can I say about her? She's my own daughter, but I swear, she doesn't have a lick of sense in that gorgeous head of hers!" Pale, watery eyes accosted Mara. "I hope the meeting wasn't too rough on you. The family can be vicious if they all decide to band together."

"The meeting went just fine," Mara lied, and wondered if June could see through her plastic smile.

"Good! Now, let's just hope we can bring the toy company out of its slump!"

"June," Mara began, looking into the den and noticing that Angie was playing with the doll house, out of earshot. Mara anxiously fingered a spot on the tablecloth and her insides began to knot in dread. "There's something I've been meaning to talk to you about."

"Oh?" June's spine stiffened, or was it Mara's imagination?

"It's . . . it's about Shane . . ."

June clamped her mouth shut, and in the same tone of voice that had effectively controlled the board meeting, she cut Mara off. "I think we've discussed Mr. Kennedy and his proposal to buy a portion of Imagination long enough, don't you?" June rose from the table with regal grace, as if to add physical emphasis to her words.

"It's not about the company." The words were spoken quietly, but they seemed to sizzle, hanging in the air.

June set her lips in a tight line and reached for her purse. "I have to go, and it's not that I'm not interested in what you have to say about Mr. Kennedy, but, well"— her slender shoulders drooped with the weight of her words—"I'm just not that fond of the man." June noted the pained expression in Mara's eyes, and two points of color stained her cheeks. In all truth, June loved the young woman sitting at the maple table with the checkered cloth as if she were her own daughter. "Perhaps I'm not being fair," June sighed. "But ever since that day that he came bursting in here . . . *demanding* to see you . . . I don't know." Her voice caught for a moment, and it was a hoarse whisper, barely controlled when she continued. "You know the day I mean, the day that Peter was buried."

Mara nodded and swallowed her tears of grief for the older woman's pain.

"I've had trouble accepting him," June explained.

"He's trying to help Imagination."

"I know that . . . and, well, I suppose that when I don't resent it, I do appreciate it. Really I do, in my own way." She took a deep breath, hesitating. "But there's something about him, I don't exactly know how to put my finger on it, but I just don't trust the man."

"Then why did you give your consent to let him invest in Imagination?" Mara asked, stupefied. June's pale blue eyes hardened to ice, and she seemed to talk in circles—never confronting the real crux of the problem.

"Oh," June continued determinedly, "don't get me wrong! I don't think he's fool enough to try and manipulate the company for his own interests entirely. He's too smart for that. But," she waved a suspicious finger in the air knowingly, "I've seen his kind before, and his ruthlessness is something that I don't like, and I can't trust."

"I don't know what you mean," Mara said simply.

"Oh, child." June's eyes closed for a second. "I'm just asking that you be careful with him. It's not hard for me, or anyone else, to see that you're falling in love with him. And I'm giving you my unrequested, and probably unwanted, advice. That man . . . he's dangerous. Treacherous to women." June's blue eyes, from her imperial position standing over Mara, impaled Mara to the back of the kitchen chair. "Don't let him hurt you . . . or Angie. That's all I'm asking."

Mara was stunned. June's theatric performance seemed to be exactly that—an act. Yet she played the part with all the vitality of a woman who's experienced the pain and anger of betrayal.

Mara had fully intended to confide in June that Shane was indeed Angie's natural father, but the contempt and disdain that June bore against him stilled Mara's tongue. Without being forthright, June had let Mara know in no uncertain terms that she disliked Shane Kennedy and considered him a threat to everything that she loved, including Angie!

As Mara watched June's sky-blue Lincoln Continental purr down the driveway, she wondered how she would ever be able to summon enough courage to tell the older woman that Angie was Shane's daughter.

Chapter 9

Shane didn't return. After a long, lonely weekend of soul-searching, Mara was disappointed when he called late Monday afternoon and informed her that his business would keep him in Atlanta until Wednesday or Thursday. The conversation was stilted and the unasked question hung between them on the telephone wires, spreading the distance between them into impossible miles. Shane didn't have to ask. Mara could *feel* the tension and knew that he hoped for her to tell him that she had made the break with Peter's family and told them about Angie. Mara couldn't.

The week stretched before her. At home she would find herself thinking of Shane, wondering where he was and what he was doing. It didn't help that Angie chattered nonstop about him and asked when he would be back—or had he gone forever, like Daddy.

For some reason Mara felt as if her relationship with her mother-in-law was deteriorating. The strain of their conversation about Shane seemed to have pushed the two women further apart. Although June was still enchanted with Angie, Mara sensed that the easy familiarity that she had shared with her mother-in-law was gone, most likely forever.

Then why was it that Mara found it impossible to summon the strength to quietly tell June that Shane was Angie's natural father and to explain the delicate situation to the older woman. Surely she would understand. The awkward set of circumstances in which they all found themselves entrapped wasn't Mara's fault, was it? Why, then, the guilt? Why did Mara still carry the burden of June's happiness and health upon her shoulders? The questions besieged her nights and disrupted her days.

It was Thursday when Mara noticed how on edge she had become. When Shane hadn't arrived in Asheville the day before, Mara was more than disappointed, she was downright scared. Vivid memories of the past assailed her; pictures of his jet winging into the night across the Atlantic to a troubled and strife-filled nation, the dull ache that had converged upon her when she had learned from his father of Shane's brutal death, the nausea of morning sickness combined with the pain in knowing that she would never see the father of her unborn child, and finally the joy and suspicion of betrayal that had assailed her upon his return. If he didn't come back to her, she wondered if she would have the mental tenacity to continue living. Fortunately, she had Angie. If Shane chose to turn his back on her again, there was always her child . . . his child to warm her days.

"You're being maudlin," she chastised herself aloud. "It's the heat that has finally got you down." She rummaged in her top drawer for her favorite pen and mentally cursed herself when she noticed that her fingers were trembling. "Damn! If those repairmen don't get here soon to fix the air-conditioning . . ."

"You'll what?" Dena asked, walking uninvited into Mara's office.

"Oh, I don't know, but they've promised to be here all week . . ." Mara looked up from her desk drawer and met the redhead's gaze. A dark prickle of apprehension darted up her spine as she noticed the catty smile on Dena's features. "Didn't you leave earlier today?" Mara asked, straightening and leveling her gaze at Dena.

The smile broadened. "That's right," Dena acquiesced and dropped herself onto the couch.

"And you're back?" Mara prodded, noticing that the clock on the wall indicated that it was nearly seven. "Why?"

"I called at the house. Mother said that you were working late, so I thought I'd drop by for a chat." Again the slightly vulgar smile.

"A chat?" Unlikely, Mara thought, and twirled the pen nervously. "What about?"

"Angie!"

Mara froze. The pen stopped twirling and dropped to the desktop.

"What about Angie?" Mara asked hoarsely. Was Angie hurt . . . or worse? What had happened? Mara's throat went dry before she realized that not even Dena would derive satisfaction from the child's pain. And that was the feeling that was written all over Dena's fine-boned features: satisfaction.

"Well," Dena mused, looking at the ceiling as if lost in thought. Idly she rubbed a corner of her mouth, drawing out the suspense. Dena loved theatrics and she was playing her role well. "It's really not just about Angie . . . actually it involves Shane as well."

Mara swallowed back the apprehension that threatened to overtake her. "What about Shane?" she asked calmly.

"I've been noticing the way that he acts when he's around the child."

"And?"

"*Possessive* is the word that seems to describe his actions." Dena nodded to herself before her dark green eyes flashed to Mara. "Yes, he's very possessive, I'd say."

"He thinks a great deal of Angie."

"I'll just bet he does!" Dena said sarcastically. Her polished lips curled into a self-satisfied smile.

"Dena," Mara said, her breath catching in her throat. She knew what was coming from the fiery woman, but Mara tried to stem some of the vehemence by appearing in command and in control of the situation. She drew herself up to her full height and, despite the heat, smoothed her dress and hoped to appear cool as she crossed round to the front of the desk and leaned against it. "Why don't you stop beating around the bush and tell me what you wanted to tell me. Then we can both go home."

"Why does Shane seem so possessive about *Peter's* kid?"

"I told you. He loves Angie."

"Hmph! Shane Kennedy doesn't strike me as the kind of man that would be fascinated by children."

It was Mara's turn to smile. "I think you're wrong on that one. Despite his hard business tactics, Shane's a very caring man."

"You should know."

"What's that supposed to mean?"

"Oh, don't play naive with me, Mara. I know you better than that! The dumb virgin routine seems to work on my mother, but it doesn't wash with me! As a matter of fact, it makes me sick!" Her last words were spoken with such a vehemence that Mara was slightly taken aback. Did Dena actually hate her that much? Why?

Mara's face tightened. She thought about telling Dena the flat-out, no-holds-barred truth, but she hesitated slightly. It would be better to tell June first. Her voice seemed frail, and she knew that drops of perspiration were beading on her forehead, but she forced herself to tell Dena a portion of the truth. Dena deserved that much. No matter how much Dena disliked Mara, she was Peter's sister and entitled to the truth.

"It's true. Shane cares for Angie very much—"

"And you, too," Dena snapped. "I'd be a fool if I couldn't see the way that he looks at you." A sadness seemed to sweep over Dena's features for a minute, and her voice lowered. "He . . . he looks at you as if he doesn't ever want to stop." She bit at her lip and some of the satisfaction and spunk seemed to have drained out of her.

"He's asked me to marry him. He wants to adopt Angie."

Mara's surprise announcement seemed to startle her.

"Sudden, isn't it?" Dena asked, her eyes calculating.

"A little . . . I guess . . ."

"I wonder what all the board members would think about this. First you coerce them into approving sale of stock to Shane Kennedy, and then, quick as a bunny, you marry the guy, giving you, Shane, and Angie's trust control of Imagination. Convenient, wouldn't you say . . . too convenient!" Dena's green eyes blazed with accusation.

"Oh, no, Dena that's not the way it is . . ."

"Then what way is it? I'm only telling you what it

looks like—a hasty marriage of convenience to get control of Imagination!"

"I've known Shane for years . . ." Mara attempted to explain, feeling her weight sag a little against the desk. Dena sensed her advantage and unfolded her long, jean-clad legs to stand up and face her sister-in-law.

"I just bet you did . . . I'll also bet that you've been seeing him on the side for years."

"What do you mean?" Mara said quietly, the meaning of Dena's words all too clear.

"I mean that I think you and Shane are having an affair, and . . ." Mara began to protest, but Dena shook her red curls and with a look that could turn flesh to stone, continued with her accusations. "I think you've been with him for years, long before Peter died."

Dena had come up to face Mara . . . so close that Mara could taste the heady scent of Dena's cologne as she licked her lips.

"You think I was unfaithful to Peter?" Mara said, shocked at the cold sound of the words as they stung the air.

"Weren't you?" As far as Dena was concerned, the question, spit with such passion, was purely rhetorical.

"Of course not!" Mara argued, her small fists clenched in frustration. "I . . . I thought that Shane was dead!"

"So you say," Dena goaded.

"You don't believe me?"

"Not for a minute!"

Mara took the time to close her eyes for just a second, long enough to steady herself and get control of her tattered emotions. She shook her palms and her head in the same dismissive gesture.

"Look, Dena. It doesn't matter if you believe me or

not. While Peter was alive, I was faithful to him. I know it and Peter knew it. What you thought then, or think now, doesn't matter." Mara could feel the hot stain of color on her cheeks, but she swore to herself that no matter how catty Dena became, Mara would control the situation and confrontation. If they were going to spar verbally, Mara was not going to lose her dignity nor her self-esteem.

Dena stepped back to put some room between herself and her sister-in-law. She knew the determined glint in Mara's cold, blue eyes was a sign that Mara's back was up against the wall. She only hoped that she hadn't pushed Peter's wife too far. Her purpose was to glean information, not to anger Mara. Dena knew her sister-in-law well enough to realize that if pushed too far, Mara would end this conversation and Dena would never again have the chance to find out if her suspicions were correct.

"All right, all right," Dena murmured, falling into a nearby chair and idly chewing on her fingernail. She averted her green eyes away from Mara's direct gaze and seemed to concentrate on the hem of her mint green plaid blouse. "I'm sorry . . . I had forgotten that you thought Shane was dead." Her eyes, when they lifted, were shining with pooled tears. Suddenly she looked older than her thirty-seven years.

Mara felt the play of emotions pull at her heartstrings, but she stood, unmoving, behind the desk. If she knew anything at all about Dena, it was that her sister-in-law knew well the art of drama. Were the tears a real sign of distress, or merely a prop in Dena's theatrical show?

"Perhaps . . . perhaps I'm wrong. But when I see Shane with Angie . . . the way that he seems to adore her," Dena stopped for a minute. "And it goes both ways. Angie seems to love him, a feeling that she never had for Peter."

"That's not true—"

"Don't lie to me, Mara! I can see it!"

Mara felt herself wavering with pity for Dena, and she damned herself for her own soft-hearted weakness. Dena had turned on Mara so many times in the past that Mara shouldn't ever trust her, and she knew it. But the way that her sister-in-law was slumped in the chair, swayed Mara's resolve, and against her better judgment, she decided to give Dena one more chance.

As the words were out of her mouth, Mara knew that she was making a mistake. "Okay, Dena . . . what is it, exactly, that you're trying to say?" Mara asked quietly.

Dena dabbed at her eyes with a tissue from the desk. "Oh, Mara," she sighed with genuine despair. "I know that I've been just awful to you sometimes. And I know it's not your fault that Dad left most of Imagination to Peter. But it all seems so unfair sometimes!"

"I know."

"No, no, you don't. No one could!" Dena asserted, her anger and frustration mounting. "Maybe all this . . . it wouldn't have been all so important, but it seems wrong to me!"

"What does?"

"The way things turned out! First you had Peter, and whether you were smart enough to know it or not, my brother worshipped the ground that you walked on!"

A lump in Mara's throat began to swell.

"And," Dena continued, "I was foolish enough to think, to hope, that Bruce would feel the same way about me." Her voice quivered. "Or at least that *some-one* would."

"Oh, Dena . . ."

"No, don't interrupt!" Dena cried, gathering strength. The heat in the room seemed to rise a few degrees. "And now, now Shane Kennedy comes along, on the pretense of investing in the company, and falls compliantly into your open arms! And not only that, but he *loves* you, Mara. God, how he loves you!" Dena pointed out, her small face twisting with the pain of thirty-seven unfulfilled, unloved, vanished years. "And . . . and he even wants Angie." Dena sighed. "Do you know how incredible that is?" She looked up at Mara and let the torture in her face go unsuppressed. "It all seems so incredible . . . such a storybook romance. It's almost as if . . ." her voice faded.

"As if what?" Mara asked, sucking in her breath.

"As if Angie were *his* child, for God's sake," Dena whispered.

The silence was electrifying, and the heat in the small, enclosed room pounded relentlessly against Mara's temples. Several times she attempted to respond to Dena's insinuation, and several times she failed, choking on a denial of the truth. Dena slumped in the chair, her face flushed, and her expectant green eyes the only sign that she wanted a response from Mara. The gaze silently pleaded with Mara for the truth.

Mara reached for her purse and tucked the small, leather bag under her arm. Finally, when the shock of the question had worn thin, Mara looked at Dena and smiled sadly. "You're right, Dena. Angie is Shane's child. I was pregnant with her and before I could reach him to tell him the news, I found out that he was dead. It's . . . it's a long story, and in the long run the only thing that matters to you is that I married your brother."

"But Peter? Did he know?"

"That the child belonged to another man?" Mara closed her eyes tightly and fought back the tears that began to well every time she remembered those long, desperate days and the feeling of despair that caught hold of her when she thought Shane was gone. It was Peter, young, supple, and strong, who had helped her get over her loss and find a reason for living in the fact that she was carrying Shane's child. "Yes," Mara whispered huskily. "Peter knew, and I believe that in his own way, he cared for and loved Angie."

"But . . . how could you? How could he . . ."

Mara shook her head and silenced her sister-in-law. Unwilling tears began to slide down her cheeks. "You have to remember that we, both Peter and I, thought that Shane was dead."

After a thoughtful silence, Dena asked the question that was uppermost on her mind. "What about Mother? Are you going to tell her?" It was more of a demand than a question.

"Of course." Once again Mara was apprehensive.

"When?" Dena demanded.

"I don't know . . . soon, I hope."

"Would you ever have told her if I hadn't put two and two together and realized that Angie was Shane's kid?" Dena asked, her usual air of sarcasm falling neatly back into place. She got up from the chair, reached in the pocket of her jeans for her keys, and stood, waiting insolently, leaning against the door.

Mara's tone was icy. The very least she expected from Dena was a little compassion after hearing the truth. "I planned on telling her by the end of the week."

"Give me a break!" Dena said with a mirthless laugh. "I bet you planned on marrying Shane before you told Mother the whole sorry story, and then I doubt you would have had the backbone to be honest."

Mara winced at Dena's sharp words. "You're right,"

she allowed calmly, "I was hesitant to tell June about Angie." Dena smiled wickedly. "But not for the reasons you think. Have you ever taken the time or consideration to talk to your mother and ask her about her health? She's ill."

"Oh, come off it, Mara. Don't give me any of your feeble excuses! You didn't tell mother because you're afraid of her and what she can do to you. Without the Wilcox wealth, honey, you and that kid are practically paupers!" Dena sneered.

Mara rose above the taunts of Dena's insults. "Your mother isn't well, Dena. I've tried to convince her to make an appointment with Dr. Bernard, but so far I'm sure she hasn't seen him."

"Don't change the subject," Dena exploded. "What you and I are talking about is the fact that you have lied to my entire family by passing off your kid as an heir to the Wilcox fortune!" Dena accused viciously. She pointed a long, bejeweled finger at Mara and shook the keys that she had wrapped in her palm to add emphasis to her belabored point. A thin smile of victory curled her lips, and unconsciously her tongue wet her lips. Never in her wildest imaginings had she expected Mara to give her an out-and-out full-blown confession. Green eyes glinted with triumph at the thought!

"No. I never intended to—"

"Oh, yeah, I know," Dena interrupted icily. "Your intentions were honorable. Well, just try and explain all that to the board. All of the family is involved here, and we've all been deceived. The board is going to be in an uproar, and you can bet that they will find some legal loophole to contest Peter's will! What you've done is considered fraud!"

Mara's initial shock at Dena's impassioned speech

had faded and boiling anger and indignation took over. Her thin, worn patience gave way. "Are you threatening me?" she challenged.

"You bet I am!"

"Why?"

"Because I want it, Mara. I want it all! It's my birthright. Imagination Toys is in my blood—"

"In your blood?" Mara managed with a laugh. "Are you kidding? You were willing to sell the entire company to the first interested buyer. Don't try to convince me of your loyalty."

Dena's grin spread slowly over her face. "Oh, but that was before I was sure that Angie wasn't Peter's child. Before, it was only conjecture—now, I know the facts!"

"And you plan on using 'the facts' against me, is that it?"

Dena's face froze in an overdramatized affront. She looked positively stricken, but just for the moment. "Against you—heavens, no." Once again the evil grin. "For me—yes!"

"How?" Mara asked, wondering why she was even listening to her sister-in-law. Clearly, Dena was obsessed with gaining control of Imagination.

"Do you know how long I've waited for this?" Dena asked, her eyes narrowing. "Years! All the time that we were growing up, I lived with the obvious fact that Peter was Father's favorite child. And then, when Dad died, his will was another slap in my face! He gave me less than a quarter of the estate, while Peter got it all! That wasn't bad enough, though. The topper came when Peter died young and his wife, a woman not even related to the family, inherited the bulk of the company along with the house. Do you know how angry I was?

How unfair it all was? Of course not! No one could." Dena's lips drew back tightly, white against the even row of her teeth.

For the first time in over four years, Mara saw her sister-in-law clearly. And despite Dena's threats and power plays, Mara felt a rush of pity for the obsessed woman. "Dena," she suggested gently, "have you ever talked this over with someone professionally?"

"What do you mean?" Dena asked, but she guessed Mara's unspoken thoughts.

"I mean . . . I think that you should talk your feelings over with a psychiatrist."

"Wouldn't you just love that, though?" Dena sneered, as if the idea was totally absurd. She shook her head in disgust. "I can't believe how transparent you can be sometimes. *I* don't need psychiatric help, and Mother doesn't need a doctor, so you can just quit dreaming up excuses to have us both committed, because it won't work!"

"I never—" Mara gasped.

"Oh, sure you did, Mara. You're just like me, only you won't admit it. You and I have been locking horns over the control of Imagination for years, and now I have the upper hand because, unless you give up all of your interest in Imagination and step down as president, I'm going to let this sordid little story of Angie's dubious paternity leak out to the papers. I think the social editor and maybe the financial editor would find it incredibly amusing."

"You wouldn't."

"Try me!" Dena cocked her head and looked at the ceiling as if lost in thought. "How does this headline grab you," she mused, " 'Local socialite uses child for control of toy company, or better yet, Imagination toys in shambles: Paternity of child heir in question.' "

"I know that you might find this hard to believe," Mara replied, her chin inching upward defiantly, "but I'm not really concerned what the newspapers might make of the story."

"But, think of your social standing in Asheville."

"I told you, I really don't care about anything like that," Mara repeated. She had heard enough of Dena's threats and accusations. She clutched her purse tightly in the well of her arm and moved closer to Dena and the doorway. "I'm leaving, now, Dena," Mara stated calmly. "If you want to stay here any longer, it's fine with me, but I'm not going to stay and argue uselessly with you. We're getting nowhere, and I'm tired of wasting my time. You've heard my side of the story, and you can do with it what you want. Obviously, I can't stop you. But I really do think that you should take your mother's feelings into consideration. I . . . I wasn't joking when I told you that I think she's seriously ill, and I'm worried about her."

"Why do you care so much about Mother?" Dena asked with renewed suspicion.

Mara sighed. "Because June has been very good to me and she loves Angie very much."

"Oh, yeah?" Dena inquired with a smirk of disbelief cast on her face. "Then the least you could have done, once Peter was gone, was be honest with her and let her know that the child she has prized as her only grandchild was fathered by another man! Instead you hid behind a lie, Mara!"

"That may be," Mara granted wistfully. She sighed to herself and somehow managed a feeble smile. "But I never expected to see Shane again."

"So what? The kid was his, whether he was alive or dead!"

"Look, Dena, I'm not denying any of that. What I'm

asking from you is that you please don't say or do anything that might upset your mother. I'm going to try and persuade her to see Dr. Bernard, and once I know that she's not seriously ill, then I promise, I'll tell her all of the truth."

Mara didn't wait for Dena's response. She started walking down the long corridor to the elevator shaft and snapped off the lights to the offices of Imagination. As the darkness closed in on her she heard Dena's well-modulated Southern drawl echoing in the hallway behind her. "You're copping out, dear sister-in-law," it accused, and then, just as the elevator door opened and Mara stepped into its gaping interior, she heard Dena's high-pitched, pleased laughter. An involuntary shudder skittered down Mara's spine at the sound. Just how desperate, how obsessed, how neurotic was the scheming redhead?

The parking lot under the building was peacefully quiet and was succumbing to darkness in the ever-lengthening shadows of the early evening. Blissfully cool air greeted Mara as she made a hasty exit from the elevator and headed toward her reserved parking space near the entrance to the building. She slid her tired body into the soft vinyl seat of the Renault and let out a nearly inaudible sigh. For a moment, allowing herself a few seconds of precious time to calm down, she rested her head on the steering wheel, and let her tawny hair fall forward around her face.

How did it all get so crazy, she wondered silently to herself as she attempted to shake off the feelings of apprehension and anger that still hung cloyingly around her. She found no answer to the enigma that had become her life.

"Damn," she muttered to herself, as she switched on the ignition of the car and started worrying about what action Dena might take after hearing Mara's confession. "Damn, damn, damn." How could everything in her life have gotten so suddenly complicated? All because of one little lie.

"Oh, don't worry about me," June had replied to Mara's request that she check in with Dr. Bernard. "You have enough problems of your own without bothering yourself about my health. I'm fine. *Really.* You worry too much."

It had taken a considerable amount of gentle persuasion, and Mara wasn't entirely convinced that the older woman would do as she promised, but June had finally, though reluctantly, agreed to have a checkup. When pressed for a date, June was uncharacteristically vague, but Mara left well enough alone. At least June had promised to visit the local medical clinic. Even that small victory was more than Mara could have hoped for.

It was late by the time Angie had taken her bath. But the sight of the young child with her fresh scrubbed face, laughing dark eyes, and halo of wet, golden ringlets made Mara forget, at least momentarily, about the pressures of her job and problems with Dena. There was something about Angie, dressed head to toe in animal-print pajamas, that made everything else in the world seem insignificant. Mara had taken time to put a rather complicated puzzle together for Angie, and the child laughed delightedly when she recognized that the picture was taking the shape of two adorable kittens.

The doorbell rang, and Angie scrambled off of her chair, nearly slipping on the tile in the kitchen and calling importantly over her shoulder, "I get it, Mommy."

Mara hurried from the kitchen just as Angie was

tugging at the brass handle of one of the twin front doors. With a grunt, she was able to open it and there, on the darkened porch, was Shane, and Mara felt her heart leap at the sight of him. He looked tired, worn out. His black hair was disheveled, and the light touch of silver near his temples stood out in the darkness of the night. At the sight of his daughter the fatigue seemed to leave his face, and he bent down on one knee to scoop up the youngster and hold her against his chest as if he would never let go.

Angie clung to Shane, just as desperately as he held her, and Shane's face, buried against the tiny neck of his child, was a tortured display of emotions. His love was so open and honest that Mara discovered she had to turn away from the poignant scene to avoid bursting into tears of frustration and self-reproach. How could she deny Shane the small but inherent right of a father to claim his child?

Shane set Angie back on the floor reluctantly, and answered every one of the child's endless questions.

"We doing a puzzle of kitties," Angie jabbered excitedly. "Do you want to see them?"

"Of course," Shane replied seriously. "Maybe I can help."

"I don't know," Angie said, her brows puckering in thought. "Even Momma has trouble . . ."

Shane shot Mara a glance full of amusement and delight with his child. "All the more reason for me to try," he bantered back at Angie, who was racing down the hall, back toward the kitchen.

"She missed you," Mara whispered quietly.

"Not half as much as I missed her," Shane muttered, and deep pangs of guilt twisted Mara's heart.

Angie, perched precariously on the edge of one of the chairs around the cozy kitchen table, had already managed to scramble several of the pieces of the puzzle by the time that Mara and Shane had reached the kitchen. Shane laughed good-naturedly, picked up the mischievous little imp, and plopped her squarely down on his lap. She giggled with mirth, and father and daughter began working on the puzzle, interlocking the intricate cardboard shapes.

While Shane and Angie huddled together under the Tiffany lamp, Mara put on a pot of fresh coffee, and the rich scent of java eventually permeated the kitchen and small dining nook where Shane and Angie were studiously arranging the puzzle. Mara watched with envy and pride as father and daughter became caught up in a world uniquely their own: Shane's muscular shoulders—Angie's small, busy hands; Shane's thick, rumpled, raven-black hair—Angie's tousled, slightly damp, blond curls; Shane's rough, deep-timbred laughter—Angie's musical, tinkling imitation; and both of them with their deep, black, knowing eyes.

Just as Mara was pouring the coffee into cups, they finished with their project. Within minutes, the jagged pieces of the simple jigsaw had, to Angie's amazement and pleasure, been rejoined and the two playful kittens in the picture once again stared back at Angie.

"Does Imagination have much of a market for these things?" Shane asked, eyeing the puzzle box.

Mara handed him a cup of steaming coffee. "Some . . ."

"Don't tell me, let me guess—the competition does much better than we do?"

A self-derisive smile curved over Mara's lips. "I wish I could disagree with you, but unfortunately, once again, you're right. San Franciscan has outdone Imagination three to one in puzzle sales, along with dolls, clay, balls . . . you name it."

"Not computer games for children?"

"I don't know," Mara sighed. "Until you came into the company, we weren't even in the electronics market."

Angie interrupted as a sudden, important thought struck her. "Mommy—is Snoopy on tonight?"

"Oh, honey, I'm sorry. I forgot all about it!" Mara glanced at her watch. "You're still in luck; if you hurry, you can see the last twenty minutes."

Angie darted into the den and snapped on the TV while her parents joined her at a slower pace. Angie insisted that Shane sit on the couch, and after racing through the house to find her blanket and Lolly doll, she hurried back to the den to scramble onto Shane's lap and reclaim her important position.

It had been a long, fatiguing day, filled with unsettling and turbulent emotions that had torn at Mara for hours. The outburst with Dena had been the worst, and Mara wanted to tell Shane about it, but the unspoken tension in the air stopped her. Although Mara was already emotionally drained and exhausted, she could feel the threat of another confrontation with Shane in the air. It wasn't so much what he said, as what he didn't say, and the dark, impenetrable looks that he passed in her direction. Deep lines of concern knotted his brow and indicated to Mara that he was ready for a showdown. Only Angie's presence had kept him from demanding answers to the questions that were hovering in the black depths of his eyes.

The Snoopy special was long over. While sitting near Shane on the couch, pretending interest in a dull variety show, Mara could feel the tension between them building, minute by minute. She wanted to close her eyes and transform the cozy den, with its paneled walls and shelves of books, into her favorite room with the two people that she loved most in the world filling it. But, although both Angie and Shane were only inches from her, she felt isolated and cold with dread; she knew that soon Shane would demand to know why she hadn't come out and told June the truth about Angie. Nervously, Mara played with her coffee cup, an action not lost on Shane. Only the softness and innocence of the heavy-lidded blond child cuddled in Shane's lap kept the imminent argument at bay.

Within a few silent, uncomfortable minutes, Angie had fallen into a deep, dreamless sleep. Mara reached for the tired child, intent upon taking her upstairs to bed, but Shane shook his head and pushed Mara's arm gently aside as he rose from the couch still clutching Angie. When he walked out of the den, Mara could see the top of Angie's curly head nestled securely against Shane's chest. Mara had to restrain herself from following them, but she knew intuitively that Shane wanted to spend a few quiet moments alone with his child.

Mara took the coffee cups and placed them in the sink in the kitchen. Shane was still with Angie; rather than disturb the long-denied intimacy between father and daughter, Mara stuck her hands into the pockets of her jeans and walked out past the back porch, into the darkness of the night. Although the temperature had dropped considerably since late afternoon, the air was still cloyingly warm, unusually thick, heavy with humidity. The dark sky was hazy, with only a few winking stars lighting the black expanse overhead; a hot, sultry, late-summer night. The promise of rain hung heavy in the air.

The only relief from a night that stole the breath

from her was a slight, pine-scented breeze, which lifted
Mara's hair away from her face and neck, cooling the
small, dewy beads of perspiration that had gathered on
her skin. Silently, wrapped in her own, private thoughts,
she strode down the garden path, not noticing the heady
scent of the late-blooming flowers or the murmuring
buzz of the evening's insects. Finally, after crossing a
broad expanse of slightly dry lawn, she reached the
white fence that separated the manicured grounds from
the paddock. She stood, her arms folded over the top
wooden plank of the fence, her left foot poised against
the bottom rail. In the meadow beyond, she saw the
shadow of a cat stalking field mice. In the distance,
Mara heard the soft call of a night owl, and the rumble
of an eighteen-wheeler on a remote highway. It was a
hot, restless summer night.

Mara felt Shane's presence before she heard the familiar creak of the screen door as it scraped over the
floor of the porch, and before he coughed quietly.
Looking upward, to the imposing second story of the
house, she noticed that the light in Angie's bedroom
was out, and surmised that the child was sleeping
soundly in her bed.

Mara's image, a dark womanly form, thrown in relief by the white fence, reminded Shane of a younger,
more carefree period of his life—an existence that they
had shared happily together. There was a childlike quality in the way that Mara hung against the fence, as if
she were still an adolescent school girl daydreaming in
the darkness. It was her form, a silhouette of innocent
womanhood, that played dangerous games with his
mind and beckoned him to walk closer to her.

He stopped short of her, his hands pushed to the

back pockets of his jeans, and watched as she turned to face him in the shifting moonlight. Soft strands of golden hair were lifted by the breeze and shimmered to silver in the hazy moonglow. In the quiet solitude of that summer night, their gazes locked, dusky blue with darkest ebony. In the distance, thunder growled.

His hand, as if in slow motion, reached out and outlined the curve of her jaw, the length of her throat, the swell of her breast to drop in frustration at his side. Mara felt the hardening of her nipples straining for release against the soft imprisonment of her clothes. Her breath became constricted in her throat, and when she attempted to speak, to try and bridge the abysmal gap that she knew was growing between them, she was unable to. The words of love failed her. The apology that she felt straining inside her—to amend for the fact that she had denied him his right to claim his daughter—was lost in the darkness. She needed him . . . wanted him . . . ached for his touch, and yet the words that would help heal the wounds and bind the two of them together were lost somewhere in the deepest part of her.

"Mara . . . oh, baby," he moaned, his hands on her shoulders, holding her at a distance from him and yet teasing her with their warm promise. A shudder ripped through her, a shudder of a need so deep that it inflamed all parts of her as she felt his fingers enticing warm circles of passion against her skin. Even through the light fabric of her blouse, his touch aroused her to the depth of his longing.

His lips descended hungrily to the welcome invitation of her open mouth. In an explosive, long-withheld union of flesh, Shane's tongue rimmed her anxious lips and delved into the sweet, moist cavern of her mouth. Softly she moaned and slumped against him, letting the heat of the summer night scorch her body by his passionate, hungry touch. Spiraling circles of desire wound upward through her veins from the most womanly core of her body. Her fingers touched and wound themselves in his thick, wavy black hair, communicating without words how desperately she wanted him . . . how much she needed him.

"Why do you make me ache so badly?" Shane asked, forcing her against him with a fierce power born of denial. Her supple body molded willingly to the throbbing contours of his. "Why do you torture me?" he whispered against the skin of her cheek. His lips roved seductively to the shell of her ear. "And why, why do I *need* you?" He buried his face in her soft, honey-touched tresses, and his hot breath caressed the very center of her being. "I *want* you, Mara," he murmured in hot, desperate longing. "God, how I want you!" His voice and hands seemed to embrace every part of her, and Mara could feel the insistent tips of his fingertips rubbing the taut muscles of her back, kneading them with urgent persuasion.

Far off, lightning paled the late summer sky, and for one breathless instant, Mara saw Shane's face as clearly as if it were early dawn. The muscles in his face were set and hard. The look in his shadowed eyes was that of a man plagued by his own traitorous thoughts.

"I . . . I don't mean to play games with you," she asserted, reading the anger and frustration on his features. "Surely you must know that." Her light eyes were probing, delving deeply into his black gaze. Once again, his lips sought and found the supple curve of her mouth, and any words that may have been forming in his mind were instantly forgotten with the fever of his embrace.

Mara found herself clinging to him, clutching him, holding on to him as if she thought he might, once more, disappear into the night and be lost to her. *Don't leave me,* she thought desperately. *Please, Shane, don't leave me ever again,* but the words were lost in the passion of the night. The tears that had been threatening to spill all day came at last, unwanted. Her eyes filled, and although she fought to push them back, the salty droplets slid down the soft hills of her cheeks to moisten her lips and give the heated kiss the tangy flavor of her despair.

His body stiffened as he recognized that she was quietly crying. After a pause, as if he was trying to restrain himself, he moaned, and then softly, gently, never allowing their bodies to drift apart, he folded his knees against hers and drew her down to the dry, soft carpet of grass. Far away, a pale, craggy streak of lightning flashed against the mountains and the dull, echoing sound of thunder reverberated through the surrounding hills.

"What's wrong?" Shane asked, his eyes guarded while his hands, with gentle strokes, smoothed the hair away from her face. With a wistful smile, he captured a tear from her eye on his finger and touched it to his lips.

She returned his smile with a wan imitation, and lay on her back, her crossed arms cradling her head. Shane lay, half sat next to her, his face bent over hers so closely that she could feel the warmth of his breath ruffling her hair and taste his heady, masculine scent that laced the air and lingered against her lips. His dark eyes showed nothing but genuine, intense concern, and all at once she saw the younger man that she had always loved so desperately. Did he know, *could he feel,* just how desperately she had loved him and agonized over him for the past few days . . . how much she had wanted him for the last four years?

"What isn't wrong?" she countered, finally able to answer his probing question.

"Nothing is," he corrected her and pressed a finger to her mouth, at first to silence her. But finally he surrendered to the longings in his body, and enticed her to open her lips and let him touch the inside of her. Slowly she complied, opening her mouth and accepting the exploring finger, letting the wild, suggestive impulses spark her blood. He touched her teeth, her gums, her tongue, and she reveled in the salty, bittersweet masculine taste.

His groan of surrender was primeval in intensity, and Mara felt him tremble with repressed passion. As the space of minutes lapsed he levered himself up on one elbow and with his free hand, opened the buttons of her blouse. The sheer fabric fluttered in the breeze to gape open in the filtered moonlight, an open invitation. He was entranced, filled with a need only she could fill, and while thunder rolled against the Blue Ridge, Shane moved over Mara and pressed his face into the dusky hollow of her breasts. "Oh, God, Mara," he moaned, letting his weight press against her, "you're beautiful!" With hands that trembled, he lifted the blouse away from her breasts and looked with naked yearning at the uneven pattern of her ragged breathing. Even through the flimsy fabric of her bra, the dark circles of her nipples pushed tautly upward, an anxious invitation to his hands and mouth.

Before touching either of the warm, supple peaks, he placed the palm of his hand over Mara's trip-hammering heart, and felt the rush of desire coursing through her veins in its erratic, pulsating beat.

Gradually Shane's hand moved. And while his eyes held hers, his hand slid over the lace of Mara's bra, and brushed against the tip of her straining nipple. A long, low sigh escaped from Mara's lips. And when through the soft fabric she felt his hot breath and warm, coaxing lips tease and brush her breast, she could stand no more of the bittersweet yearning. She arched her body up to meet his and let her fingers push his head more tightly to her breast, drowning in the sweet, warm, melting sensations that were oozing throughout her body.

"Oh, Shane," she murmured, calling his name over and over into the furious night. His answering groan and shudder of surrender further added to the heightened feeling of desire that was making her lose all thoughts of anything other than fulfilling the burning need that was flaming within her.

And his lips, after suckling tentatively at each of her nipples, left wet shadows of passion against her bra, and made the heat of her need smolder to new summits of desire.

The power of her hunger was dizzying, and without thought she found the buttons of his shirt and began slipping them through the buttonholes to expose the taut muscles of his chest and the powerful shoulders. Her fingers slid even more boldly to the waistband of his jeans before he took a long, steadying breath and held both of her hands in his. "Oh, Mara," he breathed raggedly, "don't do this to me." His eyes closed in agony.

Confused and disappointed, she pulled her hands from his and turned away from his dark gaze. "I . . . I . . . guess I don't understand," she admitted, torn by the depth of her need for him and the pain of his rejection.

"Neither do I," he conceded, in one long, lingering breath. Disgusted with himself for the breakdown in his willpower and angry because of the pain he was causing her, he let himself fall back onto the grass to gaze, searchingly, at the few winking stars that could be seen in the restless, dark sky. "I'm sorry," he breathed, wondering why he always felt such a need to apologize. "I told you before—I can't have you on these terms—Peter Wilcox's terms."

"Peter has nothing to do with us . . ."

The unasked question burned in the air, and though unspoken, Mara could feel the question in Shane's gaze.

"You don't have to say anything, Mara," he whispered. "I know that you haven't told June about Angie." Shane's words sounded dead with disappointment.

"I tried," she offered, somewhat apologetically. A gray-green flash of jagged electricity sizzled across the sky, lighting the mountain tops, and thunder rumbled ominously near.

"That's not good enough," he accused. "She has to be told!"

"She's . . . she's going to the doctor, sometime next week, I think. Once I know that she's all right, I'll tell her . . . everything."

"Too late." Shane's voice was as distant as the approaching summer storm.

"Shane, be reasonable . . ."

"Reasonable?" he repeated incredulously, throwing the word back into her face. "Reasonable? I think *I've* been more than reasonable." In a quieter tone, "It was my mistake." He pulled himself up into a sitting posi-

tion, and his eyes traveled over the tortured expression on her face. His shirt gaped open, exposing the tense, rock hard muscles of his chest and the dark mat of hair that swirled roughly between his taut male nipples. The ripple of his muscles in the warm night was electrifying, and Mara felt the feminine urges of her body once again responding to his enticingly male physique.

"You're insinuating that I haven't been fair. . . ." she charged, though her voice sounded frail.

A dark eyebrow quirked attentively. "No, I'm not. What I'm telling you is that you can't expect to have it both ways." He silently let his eyes run down the length of her body. Her blouse was still parted, and the sculpted form of her breasts heaving in the moonlight made his ache for her increase. Reluctantly, he moved his eyes away from the soft curve of her abdomen . . .

"You're wrong—I don't expect anything to work both ways," she pouted.

"Sure you do! Admit it, Mara, you want everything—Angie, the toy company, the Wilcox fortune, social standing, this house, and me. And I hate being last on the list!" His dark eyes narrowed.

"You're wrong . . . you're not last. Oh, Shane, don't you know that much, at the very least?"

"I know that you're hedging."

"I'm not trying to . . ."

"Well, then, dear," he teased, his face moving to within inches of hers, "you have to be willing to pay the price, and it won't be easy."

"The price?" she asked. "What price are you talking about?" Even in the shadows of the night, under the black cloud-filled sky, Shane could see that she was honestly confused.

"Can't you see what is bound to happen?" he asked.

"Once you make your surprise announcement to your mother-in-law that Angie is my child, can't you see what is bound to come crashing down on you, on us? The whole damned roof will cave in! All of that Wilcox family will go running to their lawyers in an attempt to save what they consider to be rightfully theirs. There is going to be one helluva mess, darling, and you'll be right in the middle of it."

He stopped for a moment to note her reaction to his thoughts. She had propped herself up on her elbows and was hanging on his every word.

"And what about the press?" he continued. "The newspapers will have a field day with this one, don't you think?" he asked.

Dena's taunts, issued earlier in the evening, came thundering back. "Oh, God," Mara moaned with the impact of his statement.

"And that's not the worst of it. There will probably be charges of collusion between you and me, as if we had planned the entire stock takeover. And," his voice grew even more sober, "Angie will be the target of it all!"

"No!" Thunder, closer now, clapped threateningly.

"You won't be able to avoid it."

"But . . . if you knew all of this . . . why did you take such a chance and invest half a million dollars into Imagination?"

"It's a sound investment, believe it or not," he stated with a grim smile. "And Imagination Toys needs me much more than I need them."

"Oh, Shane," she murmured. "I don't know if I'm up to battling with the family anymore."

"Sure you are. And any story they might dream up about collusion won't wash with the courts. Don't worry about it, I've already done the groundwork."

"You don't know Dena . . ."

Shane's eyes narrowed wickedly in a brilliant flash of lightning. "I saw her in action last Friday at the board meeting, and don't worry about Dena, I'm sure I can handle her . . ."

The rain, thick droplets, began to fall in a late summer deluge. Quickly, Shane pulled Mara to her feet and together they dashed toward the house. Once in the safety of the screened portion of the porch, they stood close, not touching, but together watched the fury of the storm unleash.

Shane's thoughts, deep and troubled, were as ominous as the black night itself. The rain beat a steady rhythm against the roof of the porch, and the downpour, still dusty with summer grit, gurgled with the sound of running water. Mara's clothes clung to her, and tiny droplets of rain, reflecting in the light from the kitchen window, ran in jeweled rivulets down the tanned length of Shane's neck.

"I expect that you'll tell June tomorrow," Shane announced, wiping the moisture from his face with the back of his hand.

"I don't know if I can . . ."

"You don't have a choice." His tone was even more cutting than his words. He rested his hands on his hips and looked off into the mountains before turning to face Mara. When he did, he crossed his arms over his chest. His hooded gaze pinned Mara against the screen, and involuntarily, expecting the worst, she felt her spine become rigid with dread. What she didn't realize was how alluring she appeared, her hair and face freshly doused with rainwater and her clothes clinging to her slim figure.

Shane's words came out slowly, as if with measured

intent. "You should know that while I was in Atlanta, I spent a lot of time with Henderson . . . my attorney."

"Yes?" she returned stiffly. Apprehension tightened her features.

"We talked about a lot of things, such as the collusion and fraud that the Wilcox family will no doubt charge us with."

"Go on," she coaxed, steadying herself for the final blow that she was expecting.

"And besides all of that, I told him about Angie."

Genuine fear took hold of Mara. Her fingers tightened on the screen. "And?" she prodded, her breathing irregular and constricted. "What did he say?"

"Well," he began, rubbing the back of his neck. "What it all boils down to is this—either you marry me right away and I adopt Angie, changing the records to indicate that she is my natural, biological child, or I'll start custody proceedings against you."

Mara's knees began to buckle under the weight of his threat. "No! Oh, Shane, you . . . you wouldn't!" Mara cried, unbelieving. "You can't . . . take her away . . ."

"I don't want to. You know that, but—"

"Don't do this to me!" she wailed over the pitch of the storm.

"You don't really leave me much of a choice, do you? I've set up a trust fund for her, but that's not enough. Damn it, Mara, it's just not enough!" His fist crashed into the screen. "I want her, damn it, and I intend to have her!"

"I told you that I would marry you," Mara pleaded.

"When?" he demanded, and the lightning crackled in the air.

"After I know for certain that June is well."

"There are no certainties in this life, Mara. I gave you two weeks, and they're gone!"

"But, Shane—"

"There's no more room for argument!" His eyes glinted in the night like tempered obsidian. "This is what's going to happen—I'm going to fight you tooth and nail for custody of my child unless you marry me tomorrow. And if you think that you can handle a legal battle—fine, I'll see you in court. But just be aware that I'll spare no expense, and I'll leave no stone unturned in order that I get at least partial custody of *my* child!"

"Shane, please . . . don't do this to us. Please, don't threaten me," she pleaded, her frightened eyes beseeching him.

"It wasn't my decision, Mara. It was yours!"

"I'll tell June next week, I swear . . ." she began, half-sobbing, the tears glistening in her eyes. ". . . but please don't take my baby away from me!" Mara's face twisted in fear and agony—why did he demand so much and give so little? She loved him with a passion that wouldn't, even after four long years, subside, and yet she felt as if he had never loved her. Why couldn't he understand and wait, just a little longer?

Lightning cracked across the sky and the thunder pealed loudly enough to shake the timbers of the old Southern mansion. The wind had picked up, but above the clamor of the storm, Mara thought she heard the faint sound of a child screaming . . .

"Angie!" Mara gasped, realizing that the girl was probably terrified. She turned toward the kitchen, but Shane was ahead of her, running through the house and dashing up the stairs two at a time. The thunder roared again, and the little girl shrieked.

Shane reached Angie's room before a minute had passed, and by the time that Mara had made it, breathlessly running to the bedroom, Shane held the sobbing, frightened child in his arms. He was whispering soft words to her and fondly stroking her hair with his hands. "It's all right, precious," he murmured against her small head. "*Daddy* is here now, and he's never, never going to let you get scared again."

Mara froze in the doorway, and Shane's dark gaze defied her to deny the words of comfort and love that he, as Angie's father, was giving to his child.

Chapter 10

Shane's vigil didn't end until early morning. He refused to leave, even long after the wrath of the storm had passed and Angie had fallen to sleep, cradled in his arms. It was a sight that, under a different set of circumstances, would have warmed Mara's heart. As it was, Shane's powerful presence as he dozed restlessly with his child in his arms reminded Mara of his threats. She found it impossible to believe that the man she loved, with his rumpled black hair and dark beard, would go so far as to take her child from her unless she married him. Never once had he asked her to live with him for love. No, it was only to give him back what he considered rightfully his.

Although Mara loved him deeply, and she knew that people were married for far less noble reasons, the thought that he was coercing her . . . with her child as bait, began to anger her. And so, as he sat in the leather recliner near the fireplace with the sleepy Angie on his lap, Mara found herself resenting the fact that he would do anything to have his way. It was several hours before she finally dozed.

When the first few silent rays of dawn crept over the high plateau and the sun cast fresh shadows on the wet lawn, Shane roused himself, and with a pleased expression on his face, carried Angie up to her room. Assured that the tired little girl would sleep until late in the morning, he stretched and went back downstairs. Mara was where he had left her, curled up under a plaid blanket on the couch in the den. He knew that she hadn't slept much the night before, and he also knew that he was the cause of her sleeplessness. If he had thought that the reason for her restlessness was a simmering passion for him, he would have been pleased. But as it was, he knew that it was his threats that had kept her awake, and he briefly wondered if he had pushed her too far. Was he asking too much? As he watched her in the early morning light, sunbeams filtered through the paned windows and her tousled hair glistened with gilded highlights. The strain that had aged the contours of her face last night had lifted in the peaceful repose of slumber.

For the first time since he had read Peter Wilcox's obituary, Shane Kennedy was unsure. Was he making a vast, irreparable mistake with not only Mara but also his daughter? Was Mara right when she charged him with being selfish to the point that he was interested in only *his* happiness. For a moment, he wavered. And then the picture of Angie's terrified face, starkly illuminated in a flash of lightning, burned in his memory. His lips curled in a grim smile. No, he was right, damn it, he was right!

Shane was gone when Mara finally stirred. She squinted against the bright sun, and it took her a minute to realize that she was in her clothes in the den. It must have been after three o'clock when she had finally dozed off. She stretched and counted each of the chimes from the grandfather's clock . . . five, six, seven, eight. She got up with a start—June would be at the house within fifteen minutes!

Thoughts of the storm, Angie's terror, Shane's threats, and unfulfilled passion whirled in Mara's head as she straightened the den and began to put on a pot of coffee. Gravel crunched in the driveway, and Mara knew that she had to face her mother-in-law. The thought that Shane had issued her an ultimatum still bothered her, but, Mara promised herself, she owed it to June to tell her the truth. Today was the day.

However, her resolve shook a little as she saw the stoop of June's shoulders and the tight whiteness of June's lips.

"Good morning," she called with feigned cheerfulness to the older woman.

"Same to you," June replied. "Aren't you going to work today?" June's pale blue eyes traveled up Mara's body, noting the rumpled jeans and wrinkled blouse.

"Yes . . . it's . . . just that Angie didn't sleep well last night, and well, we sort of camped out in the den."

Relief relaxed June's face. "I know what you mean; that storm kept me awake for hours!"

"How . . . how are you feeling this morning?"

The question made June straighten her shoulders sharply and stare, unblinking, into Mara's concerned gaze. "I told you, I'm a little tired, but other than that I'm feeling just fine." The tone of June's voice indicated that the subject was closed. Mara wasn't convinced that lack of sleep caused June's pale complexion, nor curved her thin lips into a tight, uncomfortable frown. To Mara, it was obvious that June was in pain.

After handing June a cup of coffee, Mara went upstairs and checked on Angie, who was still sleeping soundly. Then, after a quick shower, she changed into a soft, lilac print dress, and went back downstairs to the kitchen, intent on telling June the truth. But, apparently Peter's mother hadn't heard the approaching footsteps, and when Mara reentered the kitchen, she found June sitting at the table, swallowing several brightly colored pills from a variety of vials.

June's features mirrored her guilt as she looked up and saw Mara standing in the doorway. Quickly, she recovered herself and, with an effort at dignity, recapped the bottles and put them back into her purse.

Mara's blue eyes took in the entire situation, and she found that she had difficulty swallowing. June's condition must be far worse than even Mara had realized.

"Are those the nerve pills that Dr. Bernard prescribed for you?" Mara asked. She poured herself a cup of coffee, and although she was already late, took the time to sit across from her mother-in-law, hoping to communicate with her.

"Yes," June admitted, dusting the lapel of her moss-green jacket nervously. "Among others."

Mara took a scalding sip of the dark liquid and observed June over the rim of her cup. Why did the older woman look so defeated? Just how ill was she? Mara scowled into the cup and then, in a soothing voice, tried to broach the painful subject again.

"June," she reproached, "you would tell me if you were seriously ill, wouldn't you?"

"Of course," the gray-haired woman snapped, but she couldn't find the strength to meet Mara's concerned, intense gaze.

"And you would let me know if watching Angie was too much of a burden?"

"Yes, Mara, I would." This time, watery blue eyes reached out to Mara and begged her to understand.

"But, this morning . . . because you didn't sleep well . . . don't you think Angie might be too much trouble for you?"

"Nonsense! She's never any trouble for me! And . . . and . . . well, if I do get tired, today, Sylvia Reardon comes in to clean, doesn't she . . . I'm sure she'd give me a hand."

"Of course she would," Mara agreed thoughtfully. June's eyes pleaded with her, and Mara couldn't find the heart to refuse. Putting her coffee cup down on the table, Mara rose and grabbed her purse. "You will call me, won't you, if you need help. Shane's in the office today. So, if you need me, I can run home . . ."

June's smile seemed frozen on her face at the mention of Shane, and fleetingly Mara wondered if Dena had told her mother the truth. All during the drive into Asheville and for most of the morning, Mara was wrapped in worried thoughts about her mother-in-law. She stayed close to the telephone and waited in case June should need her.

It was late in the afternoon when Shane walked into her office. Although he had been in the building since early in the morning, he had been busy making sure that the computer was functioning properly and that the conversion of space in the factory for assembly of the new line of video games he hoped to promote was complete.

"I'm leaving for Atlanta," he said after closing the door to her office and dropping into a chair opposite her desk. He folded his fingers under his chin and studied every emotion that traversed her face. "Are you coming with me?"

"For the weekend?" she asked, hedging. She had been writing on her memo pad, but she stopped doodling, and her blue eyes fastened on his.

"For the rest of your life."

Mara took a deep swallow of air, let it out wearily and dropped her pen, before leaning back in her chair.

"You know that I want to Shane," and she seemed as if she meant every word she breathed.

"Then what's stopping you?"

"I just can't . . . not yet."

Shane's jaw tightened, and his dark eyes promised that he would carry out his threats of the night before.

"I tried to talk to June this morning, but . . . I caught her taking some pills. And I'm very worried about her," Mara explained.

"How can I make you understand that June Wilcox's problems aren't yours?" he asked. "And as for popping a few pills . . . don't you ever read the papers. Drug addiction, whether it's Valium, uppers, downers, whatever, isn't confined to California. Lots of men and women, wealthy or not, use—"

"That's not the way it is!" Mara shouted, interrupting him. Her tired nerves were stretched as tautly as a bow string. "She's ill, for God's sake!"

"Then she should see a doctor!"

"She will!"

"And until then, whenever it may be, I should content myself in the thought that it will probably be soon?" he inquired, disbelieving.

"It's only a few more days . . ."

"You think! And what if your suspicions prove true? What if the doctors do find that there is something seriously wrong with June, what then? How long will you expect me to wait then?"

"I'm not asking for much," she pleaded quietly, inching her chin upward in a show of dignity.

"Too much, Mara," he hurled back at her as he rose from his position in front of her expansive desk. He whirled toward the door and began to leave, but Mara's soft voice stopped him.

"Shane, wait . . ." she commanded, rising from her chair and reaching for him.

He spun on his heel to face her, but refused to capture her extended hand. All of the anger and pent-up rage of four years of frustration showed on the bladed contours of his masculine face as he stood before her. His dark eyes narrowed, almost wicked in their arrogance, and he looked down at her with his lips curling in undisguised contempt "I've waited, Mara. God, how I've waited. And I won't, *I can't* wait any longer! It seems as if you've made your choice!"

He left her standing helpless in the middle of the room, and he didn't turn back to face her. No "goodbye," no "I'm sorry," no. "I'll understand," and no "I love you." Nothing but a helpless, empty feeling that crept into her heart.

"Mrs. Wilcox . . . Mrs. Wilcox?" Lynda was inquiring through the intercom on Mara's desk. "Did you want me to come in for that dictation now? Mrs. Wilcox?" Lynda's voice brought Mara crashing back to reality.

"Yes, Lynda . . . but, make it in about five minutes, okay?" Mara asked into the black receiver. She needed a few minutes to gather her poise.

"You're the boss," Lynda quipped back lightheartedly.

Mara lifted her finger from the intercom and let the hot, fresh tears run unrestricted down her face. She was tired, not only from lack of sleep, but with worry. And she was frustrated, caught in the middle of a situation she couldn't control, torn with concern for a woman whose own family cared little for her, and in love with a man she didn't entirely understand. Mara let the bitter tears run unchecked, if only for a moment. "I'm not going to lose, Shane," she murmured to herself as she dabbed at the corners of her eyes with the tissue. "I absolutely refuse to lose to you . . . or to June. Somehow, I swear, we're going to find our way out of this!"

"Pardon me?" Lynda asked, standing in the doorway. Color washed over her face as she noticed that her employer had been crying. "Oh . . . well . . . if you want to do this . . . later . . . I'll come back," Lynda stammered, backing out of the office. Mara took command of the situation.

"It's all right, Lynda. Come in. I've got quite a lot of correspondence to get out before we go home tonight." Mara smiled sincerely at the young girl as Lynda took a seat near the corner of the desk and poised her pencil in readiness over her stenographer's tablet. With as much authority and poise as she could pull together, Mara began the dictation, and was relieved to see that Lynda's embarrassment faded. Somehow, Mara promised herself, she would get through this day and straighten out the problems she faced. It couldn't be impossible, she reasoned, her spine stiffening at the thought of the challenge. It was going to work!

With her new confidence neatly in place, Mara finished work at the office for the weekend. It was the first Friday in many that she was able to leave by five o'clock. Although the traffic in downtown Asheville was snarled and the evening was slightly warm, Mara refused to have her spirits deflated. Rather than use the air-conditioning in the car, Mara rolled down her window and listened to the sounds of the busy city. A few horns blared impatiently, an occasional motorist mouthed a stream of invectives, but for the most part, even in the height of rush hour, the feeling in the air was of calm equanimity. It was as if, by finally deciding to somehow solve her own problems, Mara had begun to defeat them. When she finally maneuvered her car out of the city limits, and the tree-lined streets broke from suburbia into the quiet of the mountain countryside, Mara pushed her sandaled foot more heavily on the accelerator and let the sporty car race toward home. The wind whipped and twisted her hair, the radio played lighthearted, soothing music, and soon she would be able to spend a quiet, warm summer weekend with Angie. She smiled at the thought of a picnic near the river.

As for June, Mara had convinced herself that she could deal with the older woman gently and fairly. Her plan was simple: it was time that she took the bull by the horns and began handling her own life. Whether June agreed or not, Mara was going to call Dr. Bernard and request a complete physical for her mother-in-law. And then, if June was strong enough, Mara would tell her the truth of Angie's identity. If June's health prevented a forthright confession, Mara would find a gentler way to break the news.

With her spirits soaring higher than the tops of the ancient oaks that welcomed her home, she hurried into the house and called out her usual greeting. "Angie . . . June, I'm home."

But the house sounded incredibly empty. No running footsteps or laughing chatter warned of Angie's arrival. The television had been turned off, and there was no noise in the house except for the regular ticking of the great old clock and the smooth hum of the air conditioner. Mara's voice echoed back to her, and though she tried to ignore it, a small tremor of anxiety taunted her. The house didn't *feel* right. "Angie?" Mara called a little louder.

The house was immaculately clean, evidence that Mrs. Reardon had been working earlier in the day. And the grass was freshly cut, Mara noted, her eyes scanning the lawn. Mr. Staples, the gardener, had worked outdoors. June's sky-blue Lincoln was parked in its usual spot in the garage. But the house was empty. Mara checked all the rooms—Angie's bed was freshly made. Hadn't she napped? Still, no sign of grandmother and child.

Rather than panic, Mara went back downstairs to the kitchen. Perhaps June left a note. Maybe someone came and took them for a drive . . . or a walk. Unlikely. No note. The only evidence that anyone had been in the deserted house since Mrs. Reardon had been in was a tiny, neat pile of dishes in the sink.

Mara, with real dread beginning to take hold of her, walked out onto the porch, and noted, with a slight sense of relief, that Southpaw and her family were snoozing in the late afternoon sun. But there was no sight or sound of Angie.

"Mara, is that you?" June's familiar voice called out as the screen door scraped against the boards of the porch. Mara nearly jumped at the sound, but was relieved when she saw June propped up on the yellow chaise lounge in a shaded portion of the broad expanse of porch. Sunlight, filtered through the chestnut tree in the back yard, cast moving shadows over June's delicate features.

"Didn't you hear me calling you?" Mara asked with

a laugh as she approached the older woman and noted the open magazine that had dropped to the floor.

"Well, I must have dozed off," June apologized and attempted to stretch. She grimaced in pain as her cramped muscles refused to straighten. "I was reading this article on floral arrangements, and I guess my lack of sleep caught up with me," she admitted with a sheepish frown. She tugged the reading glasses off of her nose and tucked them into her purse.

"It's been a long day for everyone," Mara agreed, her eyes skimming the hedge where Angie sometimes hid. The sun was still bright, and she was forced to squint. "Where's Angie?"

June stiffened, and her eyes snapped with fear. "What?" she asked. "I thought she was with you . . ."

"But I've been at work," Mara reminded her, wondering if her mother-in-law's tired mind was beginning to play tricks on her. "I left her with you . . . this morning."

"I know, I know," June snapped almost hysterically as she looked from Mara to the back yard, and back to Mara. She wrung her thin hands nervously. Mara swallowed the dread that was rising in her throat as June began to speak. "But I thought . . . I mean, that man told me that the three of you were going out somewhere . . . to the park or something . . . for the afternoon."

"What?" Mara gasped, and then controlled herself when she saw her own fear reflected in June's pale eyes. "What man?" she tried not to look desperate as she grasped the older woman's arm.

"Shane Kennedy!"

"He was here?"

"That's what I'm trying to tell you!" June retorted. "He was here, earlier . . . around two-thirty, I think." Nervous, trembling fingers were toying with the strand of pearls at her neck. "It was just before Angie's nap." A fast calculation indicated to Mara that Shane must have come to the estate directly after the argument in the office. "And he told me that the three of you were going to take the afternoon off and go see some sort of jazz festival in the park . . . or something like that. I honestly don't remember," she sighed, filled with hatred for Shane and self-remorse that she hadn't stood up to him and kept the child. June's stern eyes impaled Mara. "He lied to me, didn't he? He deliberately tricked me into giving him the child!"

"I . . . I don't know," Mara answered as honestly as she could, hoping that the fear that was beginning to take hold of her wasn't being conveyed to her mother-in-law.

June slumped back onto the plump, yellow pillows of the chaise. "I didn't want to let her go, you know," she admitted in a tight voice. "I wanted to call you, but he insisted that you had already left the office and were probably waiting for him at the park. It was a lie, wasn't it?"

"I don't remember making any plans with Shane . . ."

"Damn that man!" June hissed, slamming her small, bony fist into the soft cushions. "Oh dear god, Mara. What have I done?" she whispered, and the fist unclasped to fall over her small breasts.

Mara was scared, but not for the safety of her child. She knew the power of Shane's love for the little girl, and she knew that he wouldn't allow anything or anyone to hurt Angie. As long as Angie was with Shane, the child was safe. But of course, June knew nothing of

Shane's devotion to his child, and coupled with that, Peter's mother disliked Shane intensely. Mara read the fears on June's worried face, and somehow, she knew that she had to calm the older woman.

"It's all right," Mara began, placing a comforting hand on June's thin shoulders. June averted her gaze.

"No, it's not . . . I should never have let her go!" Self-doubt tortured her. "If anything happens to Angie, I'll never forgive myself!"

"Nothing's going to happen, don't worry," Mara said with a thin smile, knowing that her words didn't ring true. "There's just been a mix-up of some kind. That's all!"

June's watery blue eyes impaled Mara with the lie.

"Come on, now," Mara insisted, ignoring June's rueful stare and helping the older woman to her feet. "Let's go into the kitchen and I'll make you some lemonade. I'm sure that Shane will call shortly, or bring Angie back very soon." She smiled confidently at her pale mother-in-law as they made their way back to the inside of the house, and she hoped that June wouldn't notice the nervous collection of moisture that had beaded in the palms of her hands. What was Shane doing with Angie? He was supposed to be on his way back to Atlanta! And what, if anything, was all this nonsense about a jazz festival in the park?

June sat rigidly on the couch in the den. Her forehead was creased with a worried scowl, and she watched, unseeing, through the paned windows, out past the gardens. Mara hurried back into the kitchen, obsessed with her worries for Angie and her mother-in-law. What kind of game was Shane playing? Was he hoping to force a confrontation between Mara and her mother-in-law by abducting his child for the afternoon? Did he just need some time alone with Angie? Why would he take her away from Mara? The words froze in her mind, and thoughtlessly she cut her finger on the can of lemonade she had been opening. Without realizing what she was doing, she took a paper napkin and wrapped it over the finger.

The shrill ring of the telephone startled her from her dark thoughts, and in her anxious attempt to pick up the receiver, she spilled some of the lemonade onto the counter. Ignoring the mess, she grabbed the phone and answered it breathlessly.

"Hello? Shane?" *Dear God, please let it be him,* she prayed, closing her eyes.

"Mara!" Shane's controlled voice came to her over the wires. Mara's weak knees buckled and she slumped against the counter, unconscious of the dripping lemonade.

"Shane," she whispered, after swallowing with difficulty. "I've been half out of my mind! Where are you? Where's Angie?" Her fingers tightened around the ivory-colored plastic receiver.

A thick pause. Mara felt the seconds creep by. "I'm home."

"In Atlanta?" she nearly shouted. Then, thinking about June in the next room, she hushed her voice. "And Angie?"

"She's with me." His voice sounded cold, indifferent.

"Why?" she asked. "Why would you do this to me?"

"Let's not go through all of that all over again."

"But, I don't understand . . ."

She heard his deep, resigned sigh. "Neither do I. Not really," he admitted. "But I felt that I had to do something to get your attention."

"Get my attention? By stealing my child?" she hissed vehemently, and glanced furtively toward the den. How much of the conversation could June hear, piece together? Surely the older woman had heard the telephone ring and might wonder if it was news of Angie. Another fear assailed Mara. Perhaps June was, at this moment, listening on the extension, but she pushed the thought aside. It was ludicrous. June was, above all else, a lady, and she wouldn't stoop to listening in on someone else's call.

"Bring her back, Shane," Mara demanded.

"No."

"What?"

"I said 'no,'" he repeated quietly. "If you want her, come and get her."

"If I want her?" Mara gasped. "Oh, Shane, don't do this. Don't play games with me, and please, please, don't use Angie ... don't put her between us. It's not fair to her!" Mara pleaded desperately.

"And living with one parent, and a lie, is?" he asked, his voice rough.

"That could all be changed, very soon."

"I've heard that one before!" His voice sounded dead, emotionless.

"Shane, for God's sake, what are you doing? Can't you see what you're asking of our child?"

"If you'll listen, I'll explain," Shane retorted. Mara clung with both hands to the phone. Her eyes were closed as she concentrated on what he was saying.

"I did lie to June," he admitted, "and I'm not proud of it. But I knew that she wouldn't let Angie go with me unless she thought I was meeting you.

"I really hadn't planned on taking her with me. I just stopped by to say goodbye, and there Angie was, so glad to see me. She was filthy, covered with dirt from head to foot from chasing those cats, and . . . and it was impossible for me to leave her . . . I just couldn't."

"I . . . I understand," Mara whispered, her eyes shining with pooled tears as she imagined the vivid, touching picture he was painting.

He continued. "And of course there was June Wilcox, standing guard over *my* child—standing in the way of what should be ours alone, Mara. *Our* family. *Our* happiness. She had *my* child, and I couldn't stand it, not one minute more."

There was a pause, thick with agony. Mara heard Shane draw in a long, deep breath before he continued.

"And so you have it. I took Angie on impulse, but during the drive home, while she was sleeping in the car, I had time to do a lot of thinking, and I've decided to keep her." Mara's breath stopped. "She's safe, and she's happy. If you want to see her, then you'll have to come to Atlanta."

"That's blackmail!"

"No, kidnapping," he retorted angrily. "I've talked with Henderson, my attorney, and instructed him to start custody proceedings for Angie."

"No," she interrupted as panic gripped her, but Shane continued.

"And unless you get down here as fast as you can, I'm going to call the local paper, along with a few syndicated gossip sheets, and tell them the whole story from the father's viewpoint, of course, including the fact that I had to kidnap my own child."

"Shane don't—"

"I just don't want you to be under any illusions, Mara. You know that I mean what I say, and I'm telling you that I'm going to fight you tooth and nail for cus-

tody of Angie, if that's the way you want it. I mean it, I
don't care what it costs to get the best attorney in the
country, I'm willing to take my chances in court! Are
you?" he asked, brashly. In the background, Mara
could hear Angie chattering away.

"It . . . it doesn't have to be this way . . ."

"The choice is yours. If you don't want the fight in
court, then prove it!"

"How?" she asked weakly.

She heard his naked sigh on the other end of the
line, somewhere deep in Atlanta. "Oh, Mara, baby," he
whispered, "it's all so simple, if you want it to be. If
you're really concerned with June's health, I understand that. But I think that the solution to the problem
is to tell her the truth, as soon as possible. She's stronger
than you think, and I'm sure she can handle the news.
The sooner you tell her, the better." His voice, raw with
emotion, became soothing, coaxing. "It would hurt the
least, coming from you . . ."

The click in her ear indicated that he had hung up,
but Mara still clung to the phone, unwilling to believe
that the fragile connection that had bound them tenu-
ously together, had been severed. "No," she whispered
into the receiver.

"No . . . no . . ."

Finally, realizing that she had to take some kind of
action, she numbly hung up the phone and turned back
toward the den. But June was in the doorway, grasping
the molding for support.

"That was Shane, wasn't it?" she accused, blue eyes
unblinking.

"Yes . . . and Angie's with him . . . safe," Mara tried
to sound cheerful, and in an effort to meet June's inquisitive gaze, she began pouring lemonade. If June's

sharp eyes noticed the mess on the counter that had dripped to the floor, she didn't comment.

"Why did he lie to me?" The question knifed Mara in the back.

"He didn't . . . I mean it seems that he and I had a slight misunderstanding. That's all." Mara shrugged, reaching for the tall, frosty glasses of lemonade and handing one to June. The glass was visibly shaking.

"You're not telling me all of it!"

Mara took a sip of the liquid. "Mmm . . . no, but I will," she said, moving toward the den and hoping to appear calm. Mara flopped down on the recliner, in a position she hoped looked worry-free and unconcerned. "Shane took Angie to Atlanta . . . and I had forgotten all about it."

June studied her daughter-in-law dubiously, and the ashen color of her complexion didn't improve. Mara didn't blame the older woman for seeming suspicious; her story sounded too much like the hastily contrived lie that it was. She tried to amend it.

"Shane had talked about it with me earlier in the week, but with all of the fuss at work, you know, the new computer, those formidable video games, quarterly reports . . . it slipped my mind. I really didn't think that we had anything fimily planned." She shrugged her shoulders, smiled at her mother-in-law, and took a long sip from her glass.

"Then why didn't he tell me about it when he was here. I would have packed Angie's bag . . ."

"Oh, well," Mara gulped, "he thought I was bringing her extra clothes, and I suppose . . . that he thought you already knew about the trip. It wasn't a lie—he did plan to meet me at the park. I guess he left a message with the receptionist or something, and I just didn't get it." Mara almost cringed visibly at her ridiculous excuses.

"Lynda seems more efficient than that," June commented dryly, but the fear in her eyes seemed to have lightened a little and her stiff, fragile shoulders relaxed slightly.

"It doesn't matter how the mix-up occurred," Mara answered with a wan smile. "The important thing is that Angie's safe!"

"You're right, of course," June agreed. "Perhaps I over-reacted, a little. It's just that I love Angie so much." Mara's heart began to bleed for the little old woman. "And . . . that Shane Kennedy, he has a way of unnerving me." June rose with difficulty, reaching for her purse. Mara swallowed, and before June could leave, tried once again to tell the older woman about her relationship with Shane.

"He's an . . . unsettling man," Mara observed, bracing herself. June's entire body tensed, but Mara continued. "I thought so when I first met him . . . nearly five years ago . . ."

"Some people are just like that, aren't they . . . always putting you on edge," June commented nervously as she started out of the den toward the back door. "I'll see you on Monday, if not before," she said, and then added, "Have a nice time in Atlanta."

"June, wait!" Mara nearly shouted. "I need to talk to you. There's something I've been meaning to tell you . . ."

June turned on her heel, her eyes cold as ice as she looked through Mara and donned her mantle of easy, Southern sophistication. "Can't it wait, dear?" she asked without waiting for a reply. "I'm really very late already, and I have a bridge game scheduled for seven." She looked pointedly at her watch, and Mara noticed the sharp edge of impatience in her eyes.

"It . . . it can keep," Mara whispered, and June gave her a smile that reminded Mara of the way a person looks when they pat a dog on the head after it had obeyed an order.

"Good," June called cheerily . . . too cheerily. "I'll see you Monday."

"Sure," Mara whispered to herself, and mentally kicked herself for her own lack of courage. She watched June walk slowly to the garage and noticed her uneven gait. And with the same well-measured stiff carriage, June got into her car, pressed the throttle so heavily that the Lincoln's large motor raced in the garage, and turned the wheel of the car until it rolled awkwardly down the drive.

Mara waved as she watched June's lumbering vehicle roll lazily down the drive. Once the car was out of sight, Mara propelled herself into a whirlwind of action. She raced through the house, throwing whatever she could think of for herself and Angie into a suitcase. She only paused when she came to her daughter's room and found the tattered blanket and bedraggled Lolly Doll. Clutching both to her chest, she looked around the frilly empty room with its green and white gingham accents, the chest full of forgotten, unused toys, and the large, comfortable bed where Angie slept. Shane couldn't take the child away from her, Mara thought desperately. He wouldn't! And yet his promise of just that was what she most feared.

A custody battle that she might have won a few years ago wouldn't necessarily be in her favor today, not with all of the national attention given to the father's rights. And the fact that she had lied and had hidden the paternity of her child, whatever the motivation, wouldn't look good to judge and jury, especially since she, as Angie's mother, had inherited the bulk of the Wilcox fortune. Of course there were Peter's relatives, all of them to consider. When they found out what deception she had planned, innocent or not, they would be more than willing to testify against her. Mara clutched the tattered piece of blanket as if it were her child. No matter how innocent her intentions, she would appear guilty by all who judged her!

The other option open to her was to marry Shane as he had suggested. God, if only she could! She would have to tell the truth and get it out—end the speculation and the misery. Soon, no doubt, Dena would make good her threats.

That she wanted to marry Shane, Mara had no doubt. How many years had she wished for just that? The thought of uniting their small family sounded perfect, if only for one, vital flaw. Never in the last few weeks had Shane whispered one word of love to her. She wouldn't deny the depth of his passion for her, it was never in question. But still she doubted his love.

Her marriage to Peter, by the time that he had fallen ill, had become a sham. Mara had married once for the sake of her child, and she had survived that one loveless marriage vowing never to enter another. Now she was confronted with the same problem. Mara knew that Shane loved Angie, just as much as she loved her child, but she also realized that love for a child wasn't enough to support a marriage. What about the relationship between husband and wife? Could a marriage with Shane possibly work after all of the battles they had suffered together, after all of the wounds they had inflicted upon one another?

Questions, doubts, and fears kept nagging at her all the while that she fed the cats, locked the house, and threw her baggage in the little yellow Renault. Shane's address was wadded up tightly in her clenched fist, but she had already committed it to memory.

Knowing that she was in for the most heart-wrenching battle of her life, Mara twisted the key in the ignition, eased off the parking brake, and after expelling a long, uneasy breath, raced down the driveway. The drive to Atlanta would take over three hours. Mara bit her lip and ripped through the gears with renewed determination. Somehow, no matter what, she had to have Angie back . . . forever!

Chapter 11

Despite the dread that threatened to overtake her, Mara tried to remain calm during the tiresome drive southwest toward Atlanta. Although she had left Asheville in broad daylight, as Mara continued toward her destination the sun settled behind the mountains, shadowing the rolling hills of the Piedmont Plateau in a rosy dusk. Central Georgia was just as beautiful as she had remembered it, and the heavy scent of Georgia pine trees filtered in through her open window. Mara tried to keep her mind on her driving and staying within the boundaries of the speed limits. But as the minutes stretched into hours, and evening began to gather, she involuntarily treaded more heavily on the throttle of the racing sports car.

As each road sign along the drive had passed, illuminated milestones of her journey and the towns and cities themselves had come and gone as if they were green flags urging her on toward Atlanta: Flat Rock, Tuxedo, Greenville, Lavonia . ... Mara had read them and forgotten them, knowing only that putting the towns behind her brought her closer to her child . . . and Shane.

Mara's stomach knotted at the thought of him. He was playing a dangerous game, and Angie was in a precarious position—the rope in a tug of war between mother and father. The anger that had overcome her after the initial shock of Shane's phone call had slowly given way to dread. How serious was he? How far would he go to claim Angie? And a deeper, more frightening question—how far would she go to stop him from taking her only child from her? If only the marriage could work, if only they could be reunited, if only this battle between them could be resolved. The night closed in on her and the questions and fears flashed through her mind as rapidly as the endless stream of approaching headlights.

Mara was more than nervous when she finally saw the winking lights of Atlanta. She was downright scared! In the past she had always thought of Atlanta fondly, remembering pleasant springs with warm sunshine, the scent of peach blossoms, and the beauty of the pink dogwoods in bloom. But tonight, as her car raced nearer to its destination, she felt only despair and loneliness. How could she ever make her life with Shane? How could it ever possibly work? The nearer she got to the glimmering lights, the more her dread mounted, and she looked upon the city as if it were a devious, well-lit leviathan, waiting for her in the surrounding darkness.

It wasn't difficult to find the section of town where Shane lived. Located just off of Tuxedo Road, the most prestigious area of Atlanta, Shane's home was an enormous, red-brick mansion that rose three stories into the night. The grounds around the estate, well-lit with lamp posts near the long drive, were immense and meticulously well-tended. Pine trees, ancient oaks, magnolias, and the ever-present dogwoods flanked the mansion, softening the straight lines of the massive brick structure.

Mara stopped the car and gazed quietly up at the immense mansion that Shane called home. Warm light from eight-foot windows melted into the darkness and was reflected in the large white columns of expansive front porch, Clean, black shutters lined the windows, and glowing sconces near the door seemed to invite her into the house. She hesitated only slightly before stepping into the night and marching proudly up the three brick steps to the massive front door. Narrow paned windows on each side of the white door tempted her to look inside, but she refused, preferring to meet Shane's gaze squarely.

It took all of her courage to ring the doorbell, but the knowledge that Angie was inside the stately manor encouraged her. After pressing a trembling finger to the bell, she listened, and over the quiet hum of slow traffic she heard the sound of chimes announcing her arrival. The sound of her own heartbeat pounded in her ears, and then another, louder noise interrupted the soft city sounds. It was the reverberating drum of running footsteps. Excited, small feet were hurrying to the door. Mara set down the suitcase and bent down on one knee expectantly. The lump that was forming in her throat began to swell as the door was pulled open, and in the crack of the interior lights, Angie's expectant black eyes reached out and found her mother's teary gaze.

"It *is* Mommy!" Angie called over her shoulder as she burst through the door and, in a scrambling pile of soft arms and legs, crawled into Mara's waiting arms. "Daddy said you were coming," Angie volunteered as she clung to her mother's neck.

"Did he?" Mara whispered thickly.

Angie paused, as if a sudden important thought struck her, and held Mara's chin in her chubby hands. Her concerned eyes probed Mara's. "You hurt Mommy?" she asked innocently. "You crying?"

"No, no, I'm fine," Mara sniffed and managed a trembling, and slightly feeble smile. "I'm . . . just glad to see you, that's all."

A frown crossed Angie's face. "Shane said I could call him Daddy," Angie said matter-of-factly.

Mara bit her lip and looked deeply into Angie's dark eyes. "And what do *you* think about that?" she asked. Shane's approaching footsteps forced Mara's gaze upward past his slightly worn jeans and casual T-shirt, past the rigid lines of his chest and neck to the powerful, determined set of his jaw. When her eyes touched his, she felt a shiver of ice slide down her back, for nowhere in his commanding gaze did she see even the slightest hint of compassion. His eyes were those of a stranger, and the slightest hope that she held for them, that they could learn to love again, flickered and died.

From Mara's position, kneeling on the cool bricks of the front porch, Shane appeared larger than his natural six feet. And his stony gaze watched the intimate reunion of mother and daughter as if from a distance.

"What *do* you think about calling me Daddy?" Shane asked Angie, a trace of kindness lighting his eyes as his daughter turned to rain a smile upon him.

Angie lifted her small shoulders indifferently. Her eyes, large, round, innocent black orbs scrutinized her father, and her small face drew into a studious frown. "I not like my daddy," she admitted.

Shane stiffened, and the child continued with a curt nod of her head. "He not nice at all. I'm glad he's gone!"

"Angie!" Mara whispered reproachfully.

"No, no!" Shane interrupted, waving off Mara's soft rebuke. "I'd like to hear this. Why are you glad?" he asked Angie.

"He don't like me," Angie pointed out without any trace of emotion.

"How did you know?" Shane questioned, and Mara felt her stomach tighten in anticipation.

"He yelled at me. All the time." Angie squirmed out of her mother's arms, as if struck by a sudden thought. She began to race down the hall, giggling. "Come on, Mommy. Look what we got here!" The small child, sliding on the patina of the warm oak floor in her footed pajamas, slipped out of view as she rounded a corner down the long hallway.

Mara stood up slowly and reached for her suitcase, but Shane's hand intervened. Long fingers coiled around the soft fabric of her rose-colored jersey sleeve.

"Is that right . . . what Angie said. Did your *husband* mistreat *my* child?" The fingers tightened their grip.

Mara found her breath constricted in her lungs. Shane gave her arm an impatient shake and his nostrils flared in the half-light of the porch. "Did he hurt her?" His voice was low, almost a growl. "Was he cruel?"

"Of course not," she shot back, trying to retrieve her arm from his manacling grip and failing. Her blue eyes sparked with the quiet rage she had tried to dispel for the last few hours. "You should know that I would never allow anyone to hurt her. Not Peter. Not even *you!*"

"But what Angie said . . ."

"He was cross with her, nothing more." She pulled her hand away in a desperate tug.

"Often?"

"Enough."

"How could you . . . let a situation like that endure?" he charged, reaching for the suitcase and pulling the bag upward in a jerking motion that flexed the muscles in his arms and showed, emphatically, the extent of his long-repressed anger.

"*I* did what *I* had to do. What I thought was right!"

"By allowing a man who obviously hated her to be her father?" he ridiculed, as his lips curled in disdain. "What kind of mother are you?"

"A damned sight better mother than you were a father!" she spat back at him. "Remember, you were the one who disappeared for four years, letting me think that you were dead. And now I know the real reason, don't I?"

"What's that . . . the *real* reason?" he asked sarcastically.

"It's obvious," she began, her gaze taking in all of the interior of the house at once—the expensive period pieces that lined the walls, the plush carpeting that covered warm hardwood, the crystal chandelier, the entire estate. "You were too busy finding your fortune to have time for your family!"

"My family was married to someone else!"

"Because you left me!"

"I called, damn it . . . and I wrote to you, but you chose to ignore my letters!"

"*I* never got your letters, if you really did write them!"

"Oh, I wrote them, all right. And you can bet that someone, maybe your dear husband, got them . . . or just maybe you got them but decided to gamble with Wilcox. Because at the time he was a damned sight wealthier than I."

"That's ludicrous!"

"I don't think so," he accused. "And what's more, I think that now you're a desperate woman caught in her own web of lies!"

"At least I would never stoop so low as to kidnap a baby!"

"My baby, Mara . . . *Mine!*" he bit out as he spun on his heel and walked back to the interior of the house, swinging the suitcase as if it weighed nothing.

Angie's voice broke into the heated discussion and halted the sarcastic retort that was forming on Mara's lips. "Come on, Mommy . . . look what we got!"

Mara walked stoically behind Shane, and tried to ignore the way that his jeans pulled against the back of his thighs and buttocks while he walked. She tried not to watch the move of his forearms and shoulders as he carried the suitcase and set it down near the base of the stairs. Why, she wondered to herself, when she was so incensed with him, when her wrath was at its highest fury, did he still assail all of her senses?

Mara passed from the immense entry hall to a large room near the back of the manor. It seemed to be both a family room and a study. The room was decorated in masculine accents of rust and brown, and the furniture, unlike the entry hall and the other rooms that Mara had glimpsed, was contemporary. Shane's desk of polished walnut stood in the recessed alcove of a bay window, and a modern, cherry-wood filing cabinet served as a small room divider, giving the desk a small bit of privacy. Despite the warmth of the surrounding temperature, there was an intimate fire glowing in the marble fireplace, and a worn, oxblood leather couch with an afghan, hand-knit in hues of gold and brown, tossed carelessly over the back. In the midst of the furniture, right before the fireplace, was an incredible pile of toys scattered all over the braided rug.

"What's this?" Mara asked, her hot temper fading to incredulity at the sight of her daughter entranced by the sight of the colorful toys.

"Look, Mommy, here's a new Lolly," Angie pointed out by holding up the latest version of the popular doll. "And here's an 'lectric train, and . . . and some talking horsies . . ." Angie began rummaging through the pile of toys, holding up those of particular interest to her. All of the toys were brand-new, and the one imposing factor that Mara noticed was that none, not one, held the trademark of Imagination.

"Did Christmas come early this year?" she asked as she turned to find Shane leaning against the doorway, surveying both her and child, and obviously enjoying the look of frustration in her eyes. "And if Santa did come, why didn't he bring home anything from the assembly lines of Imagination?"

"It's an experiment," Shane shrugged, seemingly amused at her confusion.

"In frustration?" she guessed. "You find a way to get me down here to show off your collection of toys from the competition?"

Shane's deep, rumbling laughter broke down the wall of misunderstanding that had grown between them. "Of course not," he said as he walked into the room and settled himself down in the midst of the mess. He tossed a foam rubber soccer ball into the air and watched distractedly as it bounced off the ceiling. "I bought all of these toys while I was down here last weekend. According to the figures I've run up in my computer, these things are the thirty most popular toys sold in America today . . . not one of them is from Imagination."

"I could have told you that much." Mara sighed, dropping down onto the couch and fingering a toy dump truck.

"But," he contended, his eyes locking with hers, "you couldn't have told me why *these* toys are popular." He pointed to the pile of toys.

"Heaven only knows," Mara murmured, looking wistfully at Angie, who was beside herself with the toys. The new Lolly was being dragged upside down as she examined each of the other toys.

"Well, I thought that if I brought some of the toys home and studied them, perhaps I could find out what makes them the leaders in sales."

"While lining the pockets of the competition," Mara whispered.

"Sour grapes, darling," he retorted with the hint of a smile. "Besides, you can see for yourself, Angie's fascinated with them."

"Oh, she likes just about any new toy," Mara countered, cynically, "as long as it isn't made by Imagination."

"Exactly my point," Shane agreed, raising himself from the rug and pushing his hands into the pockets of his jeans. The motion tightened the muscles of his forearms, and his eyes darkened. Mara felt the change in mood, and all at once the room began to close in on her. She felt his presence, his intensity, his physical magnetism drawing her toward him.

For a moment, as their gazes locked and the questions and doubts that separated them loomed between them again, Mara felt suspended in motion, breathless. The furrow between his brows deepened and the line of his jaw seemed to protrude. "Are you hungry?" he asked, breaking the uncomfortable, shifting silence. He, too, was aware of the subtle change in atmosphere.

"Angie and I were just about to sit down. Come on, Angie, let's fix Mommy some dinner." Angie's blond head bobbed expectantly.

The dinner only took a few moments to prepare. Shane's kitchen, with its airy country charm, tiled floor, hanging brass pots, and indoor barbecue, was easy to work in, and within minutes, the steaks were broiled, the salad was tossed, and the potatoes came steaming from the microwave. They sat in a formal dining room, and while Shane poured from a vintage bottle of Cabernet Savignon, Mara lit the five, white tallow candles in the candelabrum. Angie's dark eyes danced with the festivities, and Mara realized, as she watched her child over the rim of her wine glass, just how much the little girl adored Shane. It was so apparent that he reciprocated that adoration, and that he would do nothing but the best for her. The intimate surroundings, the love of father and daughter, the warm, stately old house—it all seemed so right to Mara. And the laughter. God, how long had it been since she had heard the sweet sounds of Angie's laughter, so free and uninhibited? Mara felt as if, at long last, she had come home.

After a dinner that her daughter seemed to dominate, Mara caught Angie yawning. "Come on, pumpkin," she said, picking up her child, "let's get you up to bed."

Above Angie's predictable but insincere protests, Mara picked up her daughter and headed up the stairs. Shane followed her and carried the suitcase up to a room at the head of the stairs.

The room was twice the size of Angie's room in Asheville, and Mara eyed Shane suspiciously as she entered it. The walls were newly papered in a delicate yellow rosebud print, and the matching canopy bed and dresser looked as if they had been delivered very recently. The room was complete, down to a writing desk in the same dark pine as the posters of the bed and a full length, free-standing mirror.

"It looks as if you were expecting her," Mara whispered.

"I was," he agreed, and pulled pensively on his lower lip.

Angie snuggled deep into the folds of the down comforter and closed her eyes against the soft, clean new sheets. Shane left the room after a few moments, but Mara stayed, waiting until she was assured by Angie's deep, rhythmic breathing that the child was soundly asleep. "Oh, Angie," she murmured to herself as she brushed an errant blond curl from her daughter's face. "What are we going to do?"

As Mara descended the polished oak staircase she noticed that most of the lights in the house had been extinguished. Only the glow from the fire in the den illuminated her way back to Shane. Now that Angie was peacefully asleep, it was time to iron out all of the problems that they faced and hope that some of the damage of the last lonely years could be bridged.

Shane was sitting on the couch, staring into the fire, holding a half-empty glass of Scotch in his hand. At Mara's entrance, he barely looked up but contented himself with reading the blood-red coals of the smoldering embers. He raised his glass in a gesture of invitation for her to join him. She declined by shaking her head and stood uncomfortably in the doorway.

"We . . . we can't live like this, you know," she admitted, slowly crossing the room to stand directly in his gaze, before the fire. Heat from its glow warmed the back of her calves. The house was already warm, and the fire only added to its simmering heat.

"You're damned right we can't," he agreed forcefully. His dark eyes traveled upward, from the toes peeking out of her sandals, up the length of her calf to the curve of her hips and the swell of her breasts, to rest on her face—the face that had haunted his nights and, more often than not, awakened him in the darkness with burning need and longing. God, how long had he waited to make her his again?

Mara felt as if, with the touch of his eyes, he was undressing her, and that not only was her heated skin in his view, but also the very soul of her. The farthest reaches of her mind were being explored by the intensity of his gaze, the rake of his eyes on her body. Gradually, he stood, taking one final swallow of his drink before coming over to within inches of her. Her face tilted upward to meet his probing gaze. An uneasy awkward silence fell upon them, and the flames threw shadowed patterns across Shane's proud face.

"You had no right to take her," Mara whispered, her eyes searching his.

"I had every right."

Again the heavy silence.

"You *used* her."

A self-derisive smile, hard and cold, curled his lips. "I didn't. What I did was tell her the truth."

"The truth that you were her real father?"

"That's right." He braced himself against the mantle with one strong hand and touched a lock of Mara's hair with the other.

"And how did she take the news?"

His face softened with a smile. "She seems to like the idea. She's too young to really understand."

Mara let out the breath she had been holding, and felt the subtle pressure of Shane's fingers as they traveled from her hair to her throat. Her heart began to clamor for his touch, and when his fingers brushed the hollow of her throat, moving in slow, seductive circles, he found her racing pulse. His fingers lingered for a second, and then dropped to toy with the neckline of her dress.

"I'm glad you came," he murmured thickly into the deep golden silk of her hair. "I've waited so long . . ." His lips, warm and sensitive, found hers and captured her entire being in a kiss that promised unrestrained passion and fulfillment.

"I . . . I'm glad to be here," she admitted, feeling the gentle pressure of his hands as they guided her to the floor. Willingly, she yielded. "Oh, God, Shane," Mara whispered. "I'm so glad to be here."

As they dropped to the floor, Shane managed to pull off his shirt, and the shadowed flames seemed to flicker and dance upon his rugged, masculine chest. Mara felt the tiny beads of anxious perspiration begin to moisten her skin, and her heart was pounding within the walls of her rib cage. His hands found the wrap-tie of her dress, and in one swift movement the rose dress opened, exposing the feverish rising and falling of her chest that was protected by only the thin fabric of her slip. "It's so hot in here," she murmured, the touch of his hands and the heat from the fire igniting molten flames of desire within her. "I . . . I feel as if I'm going to melt . . ."

"Let's hope so," he murmured, his voice husky with yearning. "I *need* you so badly," he moaned as his lips rained dew-soft kisses upon her, across the gentle hill of her cheeks, over her eyes, and lower, past her throat to whisper against the French lace of her slip. Her breasts strained within the confinement of the sheer garment. His hot breath, laced with the tingle of Scotch, heated the dewy drops of perspiration on her body and made her ache for him with a primeval urgency that took control of her mind and soul. "Oh, Mara, baby, let me make love to you here, in our home . . . away from all of our problems."

Her answering sigh of surrender, and the anxious fingers caressing his skin, heating his flesh, were all the encouragement that Shane needed. Slowly he slid the dress over her shoulders, and let one strap of her slip fall to expose her breast, proud and round in the firelight. He closed his eyes as if in agonized pain. "Why do I want you so badly . . . why?" he sighed, almost to himself. When he opened his eyes to gaze deeply into hers, the passion that he tried so hard to deny smoldered in his gaze.

With trembling hands, Mara reached up and put her palms on either side of his head, until the pressure of her fingertips drew him down, closer to her, until his lips brushed against and finally captured the ripe and aching tip of her breast. "Love me, Shane," she pleaded. "Please . . . love me . . ."

His weight shifted until he lay boldly over her. Her fingers found the zipper to his jeans, and she knew, in an instant, how strong his passion had become. Within minutes he had found the most intimate part of her. She felt herself yielding, melting, softening to his touch in warm liquid waves of fulfillment.

"Marry me, Shane," she demanded, and the naked pleading in her eyes found the black passion of his. "Marry me," she whispered over and over again as she felt herself blend into him.

When at last his passion had subsided, he held her quietly in his arms and stared into the few final coals that still glowed in the fire. His fingers still rubbed her shoulder and breast, but he seemed lost in thought . . . distant.

Finally, with a groan, he sat up and pulled her into a sitting position as well. She felt warm and glowing as she gazed silently into the fire and felt the security of Shane's powerful arms holding her.

"I want you to marry me," he sighed, and she felt the muscles in his arms flex.

"I will." The answer was honest. "I . . . want it, too."

"When?" The question stung the air and Mara paused, but for only a moment. No matter what else she had learned and understood tonight, she realized that she could never deny Shane the right to his child. And in time, she hoped, once that she had proven her love for him, he would love her.

"I'll tell June the entire story on Monday . . . and this time I'll force her to listen. We can be married next week."

His thumbs cupped her chin and forced her to look into his eyes. "You're sure?"

"I've never been more sure of anything in my life," she returned, contentedly snuggling closer to him.

"June and the Wilcox family . . . they might give us a battle for Imagination . . ."

"I know," she murmured, "but let's cross that bridge when we come to it."

"Would you be willing to live here, in Atlanta?" he asked.

"If that's where you're going to be . . ."

He smiled crookedly and placed a kiss on the top of her head. "All right . . . good. But you have to realize that we might lose the toy company, or at least your portion of it."

Mara sighed deeply. "I know that, and I know that

I've worked hard to keep that company afloat. But to be perfectly honest, I haven't done a good enough job to turn it around, and it *is* part of the Wilcox family estate. Perhaps it should belong to them . . ."

"We'll see," he murmured, but once again the strong lines of determination hardened his expression. "We'll see . . ."

The morning dawned bright with the promise of hot weather. After a quick breakfast Shane insisted upon showing Mara the sights and pleasures of Atlanta. The drive toward Peachtree Street took only a few minutes, and after Shane parked the car he insisted that Mara and Angie join him for a walking tour of the city. The walk included a tour of some of Atlanta's finest and newest hotels, the fabulous Peachtree Plaza with its array of shops and the Toy Museum of Atlanta. The cool interior of the museum was welcome relief from the bustle of the busy city and the warm Georgia sun.

Mara and Angie were fascinated with the museum and the incredible display of antique toys, some dating from early in the nineteenth century. There was a collection of toys from around the world that particularly fascinated Angie, who stated quite emphatically that some of the dolls, especially the dolls from Holland in their wooden shoes and painted faces, were even prettier than Lolly.

By early afternoon, Angie had to be carried, and then, while Shane held her, she fell asleep, exhausted. The child was disappointed when she learned that she was being taken back home for a nap, but Shane avoided hurting her feelings by offering to take her to the zoo the next day. The pout on the little girl's face disappeared, and she settled into the back seat of the car with only mild protest.

Mara, too, was exhausted, but the feeling of serenity that she had found with Shane the night before never left her. The drive home was quiet, with Angie snoozing in the back seat. Shane took a long way back, pointing out spots of interest to Mara as they passed, and for the first time in years, Mara felt completely at ease, and the problems facing her with the Wilcox family seemed remote and distant. All of her awareness was focused upon Shane and how deeply she loved him. He had been right all along, she admitted ruefully to herself. She should have told June the truth about Shane the minute she saw him again.

The phone was ringing when they got out of the car. Shane quickly made his way into the house, but by the time he picked up the receiver, the line was dead. For some reason, an uneasy feeling swept over Mara, and she had difficulty shaking it.

After cleaning the breakfast dishes, Mara, led by Angie, toured the grounds. They were gorgeously groomed, and even though it was early fall, Mara could visualize what the gardens of azaleas and rhododendron would look like in the spring, flanked by stately pink dogwood trees.

"I wonder who takes care of all this," Mara mused to herself.

"Don't look at me," Shane laughed, joining Mara and Angie. "I'm incredibly poor at this sort of thing— black thumb, or something like that."

"Then you have a gardener?"

"Yes. A retired groundskeeper for a golf course. He comes here twice, maybe three times a week, to keep up the grounds and his wife takes care of the inside of the house."

Mara's eyes traveled up the three stories to the roof top. In the daylight the house seemed more immense and grand than it had in the night. "One woman takes care of all that?"

"I'm not messy . . ."

"But still. The house is so *huge.*"

A smile cracked across his face, and he bent down to whisper into her ear. "We need a big house. We'll have to have enough room for all of Angie's brothers."

Mara giggled despite herself. "I think we can wait a little while on that one," she teased as she and Shane started back toward the house. "Angie," Mara called at the child attempting to climb a small tree. "Don't hurt yourself! We're going inside . . . are you coming?"

"I coming in just a minute."

As Mara walked back into the kitchen, Shane headed toward his study. "There .are a couple of things I want to finish up in my office," he explained, "and then we'll go out to dinner!"

Mara watched him stride down the hall with his easy, familiar gait. Yes, she thought to herself, I could be quite happy here. From her vantage point, near the center island in the kitchen, she could look out the window and see Angie playing outside, scampering near a shallow goldfish pond. Mara could see it coming. Angie was about to go wading and try to catch a fish!

The phone rang just as Mara got to the door and warned Angie about staying out of the pool. Just as she had contented herself that Angie would stay out of the water, she heard Shane's footsteps approaching.

"It's for you," he stated, curtly.

"What?"

"The phone . . . it's that sister-in-law of yours, what's her name, Dana?"

"Dena," Mara answered, and wondered why Dena would be tracking her down. Her stomach tightened as she thought of all of Dena's threats. "Oh, God," she moaned quietly to herself.

"Mara, for God's sake, is that you?" Dena shrieked over the wires when Mara answered the phone.

"Yes . . . yes . . . Dena?" Mara asked, hearing what she construed to be sobs on the other end of the connection. "What's wrong?" she asked, and swallowed with difficulty. "Dena?"

"It's . . . it's Mother," Dena blurted out.

"What about her?"

"She's . . . she's in the hospital . . . that's where I'm calling from. I've been trying to reach you all day!"

"Just calm down," Mara whispered, but felt her own heart thudding with dread. "Now, explain everything to me. What happened?"

"I . . . I don't know . . ." Dena admitted through her sobs. "She was at some bridge thing last night . . . and, well . . . she just collapsed. An ambulance brought her here."

"And has she seen Dr. Bernard?"

"Along with about five others."

"How ill is she?" Mara asked, not daring to take a breath.

"They say . . . that she'll be all right . . . apparently she's suffered a series of slight strokes . . . they've finished with most of the tests and Dr. Bernard is letting her go home, as long as we can find a nurse to take care of her." Dena's voice was calmer, and her sobbing had subsided slightly.

"Have you found one?"

"Dr. Bernard gave me a name . . . Anne Hamilton."

"Have you called her?"

"Not yet . . . I thought I should call you first."

"Okay, look," Mara commanded. Her voice was

firm as she took control of the situation. If the doctors were releasing June from the hospital, she certainly wasn't as ill as Dena thought. "Call the nurse and get her over to June's apartment as soon as they release your mother. I can be at the apartment in about four hours. Can you handle everything until I get there?"

"I . . . I think so."

"Good, I'll see you later." Mara hung up the phone with numb hands. She turned toward the hallway and noticed Shane standing near the stairs, her suitcase in his hands. His eyes were dark, unreadable.

"It's June, isn't it?" he asked, grimly.

"She's in the hospital . . . she suffered a series of slight strokes, or something . . ."

"Let's go," he commanded. "Angie, come on," he said more loudly through the open door.

"You don't have to come," Mara offered.

"Of course I do."

The drive to Asheville was hampered by Saturday afternoon tourists, leisurely plodding along and gazing at the quiet beauty of the Indian summer day. Mara thought that she would be torn to pieces by the concern she felt for her mother-in-law and the guilt that she was carrying. What could have set off the strokes? A gnawing thought chilled her to the bone as she concluded it must have been because of Mara's reaction to the fact that June had let Angie leave with Shane without asking for Mara's permission. Somehow, the dread that had overcome Mara must have passed to her mother-in-law, leading to the grave turn in her illness.

The quiet, tense hours passed with the miles, and when Mara saw the Asheville skyline, her stomach had knotted to the point that a sharp pain of dread and fear passed over her. Shane parked the car in front of June's town house and helped Mara out of the car.

"Are you going to be all right?" he asked, his concern reflected in his dark eyes.

"As soon as I see for myself that June is getting better."

"Do you want me to come in with you?"

Mara shook her head. "No . . . I don't think so, not at first anyway. She . . . is nervous around you, anyway, and I wouldn't want to shock her. Besides, I think it would be better if Angie doesn't see her . . . not until I know that June's all right."

"It's my bet that she's done this on purpose," Shane commented, helping Angie from the car. "I don't trust her or any of the rest of the family, either."

"How can you say anything of the sort. She's ill, Shane!" Mara retorted, her frayed emotions getting the better of her.

"Are we going to see Grammie?" Angie asked, heading up the stairs.

"In a few minutes," Shane replied, and squatted down to face his daughter. "Grammie's a little sick, and she needs a little time to recover . . . ." His dark gaze sent Mara a dubious, incomprehensible look. "So why don't you and I go over to the park for an ice-cream cone?"

Angie puzzled the question for a moment. "And then I can see Grammie?"

"Of course you can, sweetheart," Mara said with a wan smile, before quickly hurrying up the stairs.

"Mara?" Shane called, pushing his hands into his pockets.

"Yes?"

A pause. "Good luck."

Mara smiled before knocking softly on the door and entering June's home. Everything was just as she had left it, the cool blue hues of the interior, the overstuffed floral couch, and everywhere, pictures of the family.

A door whispered closed and Mara looked up to meet the questioning gaze of a professional-looking, robust woman of about fifty. "You're June's nurse," Mara guessed. "Ms. Hamilton?"

"That's right. Who are you?"

Strong forearms folded tightly over her bosom.

"I'm Mara Wilcox, June's daughter-in-law," Mara explained with a polite though stiff smile. "How is she?"

"She's much better," the nurse began, relaxing slightly. "Dena said that you would be coming."

"Is Dena here, now?" Mara asked.

"I asked her to go home. She was absolutely beside herself!" The nurse took a seat on the sofa. "You can call her if you like,"

"No . . . no, what I would really like to do is see my mother-in-law, and offer to help her any way I can. How serious is her condition?"

"Dr. Bernard thinks she'll be up and around in a few weeks."

"But I thought she had several strokes . . ."

"Yes, but, fortunately only minor ones, and if she's careful, with her diet and exercise, she'll be fine. She'll just have to slow down a bit, that's all." Mara listened while the nurse continued to describe June's condition, and a feeling of relief washed over her as she realized that June could, quite possibly, live a normal, healthy life. "She's awake, now. Would you like to see her."

"Yes," Mara said, walking after Anne Hamilton toward June's bedroom.

The woman in the bed was hardly recognizable to Mara. Thin, drawn, and frail, without a trace of color on her cheeks, June looked much worse than Mara had expected. Pale blue eyes focused on Mara as she entered the room.

"Mara . . . is that you?" June asked weakly.

"I . . . I came as quickly as I could. Oh, June, how are you?"

"Still kicking," June allowed with a thin smile. She turned her eyes toward the nurse. "Could you give us some time alone?" she requested. The nurse smiled her agreement, but in a guarded look that she passed to Mara, she said more clearly than words, Don't upset her.

"June," Mara began, trying to think of a gentle way to break the news of her forthcoming marriage. "There's something I want to tell you." She stepped more closely to the bed and June raised a bony hand to wave off the words that were suspended in Mara's throat.

"No, Mara, it's my turn," the elderly woman stated with a raspy breath. "I've spent the last day waiting for you to show up, because *I* have to tell you . . . something I should have done a long time ago." For a moment the tired eyes closed, and Mara felt stifled and confined. The smell of antiseptic, the vials of pills, the thinly draped figure on the bed—it all seemed so cloyingly and disturbingly unreal.

The old woman continued. "I know that Shane is Angie's father," June said with a sigh.

"What . . . but how . . ."

June ignored Mara's question and continued with her own confession. "I've known about it for several years. When Peter found out about his illness . . ." —her voice caught—". . . that it was terminal, and that he couldn't father any children of his own, he told me that another man, one presumed dead, was Angie's real father. And if he seemed harsh with Angie, it was because he knew that he couldn't have children of his own."

"Oh, June," Mara sighed, slumping into a chair near the bed.

"Don't worry, I had already guessed that Angie wasn't Peter's child. I took a few courses in genetics when I was in school, and I know the odds against two blue-eyed people having a dark-eyed child. Nearly impossible. And," she sighed wearily, "I . . . I intercepted some letters that were forwarded to the house four years ago . . . I just had the feeling that Angie's natural father was alive somewhere." Tears began to pool in June's aging blue eyes. "I . . . still have the letters, and I didn't open them . . . I wanted to, but I just couldn't . . ."

"It's all right," Mara said, touching June's arm.

"No . . . no, it's not. I'm just a foolish old woman looking out for my own best interests, fooling myself, telling myself that I was helping everyone else . . . but it's just not so. And when, on the day of Peter's funeral, Shane Kennedy appeared on the doorstep, I remembered the name on the return address of the envelopes, and knew that he was Angie's father. I . . . I hoped that he would go away, disappear again, but I knew he wouldn't . . . he was so damned insistent that he see you."

Mara's throat seemed to have swollen shut, and she found it difficult to blink back the tears of pain she felt for her mother-in-law.

"I did it because I love Angie so much," June sobbed. "I . . . couldn't bear the thought of losing her . . . and you. I was afraid of becoming one of those lonely old women that you see walking in the park . . . all alone." She breathed heavily. "Oh, Mara, I'm so sorry . . . I put my happiness before yours . . ."

Mara looked up to see Shane standing in the doorway, holding Angie. How much of June's confession had he heard? He set the little girl down, and she scampered over to her grandmother's bedside. "Grammie, you okay? Look, I brought you flowers!" she said excitedly and held up a bedraggled bunch of daisies and dandelions.

"Thank you, sweetheart," June mumbled.

Shane strode to her bedside and watched the older woman. "I heard what you said to Mara."

"I'm sorry," June admitted.

"I just want you to know that I will never interfere with your relationship with Angie. I realize how important she is to you, and how much she loves you. I don't condone what you did, but I do understand it."

"Go . . . Mara . . . in the desk in the living room," June commanded. "The letters are in the bottom drawer."

"I don't know . . ."

"Get them," June insisted, some of her color returning. "Angie can stay in here with me."

Unsteadily, Mara walked back into the living room toward the antique secretary that June used as a desk. She knew that her fingers were trembling, and it was with difficulty that she found the unopened letters, addressed to her in Shane's bold scrawl.

"Oh, dear God," she moaned, and opened the first of three. Tears stained her cheeks and dropped onto the sheets of paper that swept her back in time four long years: Words of love dominated the pages and in the last letter was a proposal of marriage, dated over four years in the past. "If only I had known," she sobbed, looking into Shane's eyes. "If only I had known. I loved you so much . . ."

Shane folded his arms around her and pressed his chin against her head.

"You know now," he murmured, and his arms tightened around her, securing her to him. "God, Mara, I loved you . . . and I still do . . . and nothing matters but that we're together again."

"What about June . . . and the toy company?"

"It doesn't matter. I've bought up some of the shares from family members, and I think, now that Dena and June have reexamined their lives, that they won't object to moving the company to Atlanta, as long as they retain part interest."

"Are you sure?"

"We'll cross that bridge when we come to it," he said with a knowing smile. "As for right now, let's go in and tell Angie and June that we're getting married . . . I have a feeling that neither will object."

GYPSY
WIND

To Chris

Chapter 1

The small dark room was airless and full of the familiar odors of saddle soap, well-oiled leather, and stale coffee. It began to sway eerily, as if the floorboards were buckling. Becca knew that her knees were beginning to give way, but she couldn't steady herself and she had to clutch the corner of the desk in order to stay on her unsteady feet. Her throat was desert dry, her heart pounding with dread as she stared in horror at the small television set across the room. The delft blue coffee cup slipped from her fingers to splinter into a dozen pieces. A pool of murky brown coffee began to stain the weathered floorboards, but Becca didn't notice.

"No!" she cried aloud, though no one else was in the room. Her free hand flew to the base of her throat. "Dear God, no," she moaned. Tears threatened to pool in her eyes and she leaned more heavily against the desk, brushing against a stack of paperwork that slid noiselessly to the floor. Becca's green eyes never left the black and white image on the television but fastened fearfully on the self-assured newscaster who was tonelessly recounting the untimely death of oil baron Jason Chambers.

Flashes of secret memories flitted through Becca's mind as she listened in numbed silence to the even-featured anchorman. Her oval face paled in fear and apprehension and she felt a very small, very vital part of her past begin to wither and die. As the reporter reconstructed the series of events that had led to the fatal crash, Becca vainly attempted to get a grip on herself. It was impossible. Dry wasted tears, full of the anguish of six lost years, burned at the back of her throat, and her breath became as shallow and rapid as her heartbeat. "*No!*" She groaned desperately. "It can't be!" Her small fist clenched with the turmoil of emotions and thudded hollowly against the top of the desk.

Hurried footsteps pounded on the wooden stairs, but Becca didn't notice. She couldn't take her eyes off the screen. The door to the tiny room was thrust open to bang heavily against the wall, and a man of medium height, his face twisted in concern, rushed into the office.

"What the hell?" he asked as he noticed the defeated slump of Becca's shoulders and the stricken, near-dead look in her round eyes. She didn't move. It was as if she hadn't heard his entrance. "Becca?" he called softly, and frowned with worry when she didn't immediately respond. He took in the scene before him and wondered about the broken cup and the brown coffee that was running over a scattered pile of legal documents on the floor. Still Becca's fearful eyes remained glued to the television set. "Becca," Dean repeated, more sharply. "What the hell's going on here? I was on my way up here when I heard you scream—"

Becca cut him off by raising her arm and opening her palm to silence him. Taken aback at his sister's strange behavior, Dean turned his attention to the television for the first time since entering the room. The small black-and-white set was tuned into the news; the story, which held his sister mutely transfixed, was about some light plane crash in the Southern Oregon Cascades. No big deal, Dean thought to himself. It happened all the time; a careless pilot got caught in bad weather and went down in the mountains. So what? Dean shifted from one foot to the other and searched Becca's stricken white face, searching for a clue to her odd actions. What was happening here? Becca wasn't one to overreact. If anything, Dean considered his younger sister too even-tempered for her own good. A real cool lady. Becca's poise rarely escaped her, but it sure as hell was gone today.

While still attempting to piece together Becca's strange reaction, Dean leaned over to pick up some of the forgotten legal documents. It was then that the weight of the news story struck him: Only one man could break his sister's cool, self-assured composure, and that man, if given the chance, could cruelly twist Becca's heart to the breaking point. It had happened once before. It could happen again, and this time it would be much worse; this time that man had the power to destroy everything Dean had worked toward for six long years.

Silently Dean's thin lips drew downward and his icy blue eyes slid to the screen to confirm his worst fears. He waited while the sweat collected on his palms. A faded photograph of Jason Chambers was flashed onto the screen and Dean's pulse began to jump. It was true! Jason Chambers, head of one of the largest oil companies in the western United States, was *dead*. Dean swallowed back the bile collecting in the back of his throat.

The news of Jason Chambers' death didn't fully explain Becca's outburst. Dean wiped his hands on his jeans before straightening and then listened to the conclusion of the report. He hoped that the reporter would answer the one burning question in his mind—perhaps there was still a way out of his own dilemma. He was disappointed; the question remained unanswered. Dean's jaw tightened anxiously. When the news turned to the political scene, Dean turned the set off.

Becca slumped into the worn couch near the desk and tears began to run down her soft cheeks. She wiped them hurriedly aside as the shock of the newscast began to wear off and the reality of the situation took hold of her. Her hand, which had been raised protectively over her breasts, slowly lowered.

"Are you all right?" Dean asked, his voice harsh despite his concern. He poured a fresh cup of coffee and handed her the mug.

"I . . . I think so . . ." Becca nodded slowly, but she had to catch her trembling lower lip between her teeth. She accepted the warm mug and let its heat radiate some warmth into her hands. Though the temperature in the stifling office had to be well over eighty degrees, Becca felt chilled to the bone.

The silence in the room was awkward. Dean shifted his weight uncomfortably. He was angry, but he didn't really know whom to blame. It was obvious that Becca was caught in the web of memories of her past, memories of Brig Chambers and his tragic horse. Dean's lips pursed into a thin line as he paced restlessly in front of the desk while Becca stared vacantly at the floor. A silent oath aimed at the man who had caused his sister so much pain entered his mind. Brig Chambers could ruin everything! Dean coughed when he leaned against the windowsill and looked across the spreading acres of Starlight Breeding Farm. Brig Chambers, if he was still alive, had the power to take it all away!

Dean asked the one question hanging between his sister and himself. "Was there anyone with Jason Chambers in that plane?"

Becca closed her eyes as if to shield herself from the doubts in her mind. "I don't know," she whispered raggedly.

Dean frowned and rubbed his hands over his bare forearms. He pushed his straw Stetson back on his head, and his reddish eyebrows drew together. His blue eyes seemed almost condemning. "What did the reporter say?"

"Nothing . . . the accident had only happened a couple of hours ago. No one seemed to be sure exactly what caused the crash . . . or who was in the plane. The reporter didn't seem to know too much." Becca moved her head slowly from side to side, as if to erase her steadily mounting fear.

"The station didn't know who was in the plane?" Dean was skeptical.

"Not yet," she replied grimly.

Dean ran a hand over his unshaven cheek and pressed on. "But surely someone at Chambers Oil would know."

Becca sagged even deeper into the cracked leather cushions and toyed with her single, honey-colored braid. It was difficult to keep her mind on her brother's questions when thoughts of Brig continued to assail her. "The reporter said that there was a rumor suggesting that Jason might have had a couple of passengers with him," Becca admitted in a rough whisper. Hadn't Dean heard the story? Why was he pressuring her?

"Who?" Dean demanded. His blue eyes gleamed in interest.

Becca shrugged and fought against the dread that was making her feel cold and strangely alone. "No one seems to know for sure; I told you it's only speculation that anyone was with Jason . . . no one at Chambers Oil is talking."

"I'll bet not," Dean muttered, unable to hide the edge of sarcasm in his words. His eyes turned frigid.

"Maybe they just don't know."

"Sure, Becca," he mocked. "You of all people know better than that. If Chambers Oil isn't talking, there's a good reason. You can count on it."

"What do you mean?"

Dean looked his sister squarely in the eyes and the bitterness she saw in his cold gaze made her shudder. His scowl deepened. "What I mean is that we, you and I don't know if Brig Chambers is alive or dead!"

Becca drew in a long, steadying breath as she met Dean's uncompromising stare. Her brother's harsh words had brought her deepest fear out into the open and she had to press her nails into her palms in order to face what might be the cruel truth. *He can't be dead,* she thought wildly, grasping at any glimmer of hope, but fear crawled steadily through her body, making her blood run cold and wrenching her heart so savagely that it seemed to skip a beat in desperation.

She wouldn't allow the small gleam of hope within her to die. "I think that if Brig had been on the plane, the television station would have known about it."

"How?"

"From the oil company, I guess."

"But they're not talking. Remember?"

"I . . . just don't think that Brig was on the plane."
Why didn't she sound convincing?

"But you're not sure, are you?"

"Oh, God, Dean," she whispered into her clasped
hands. "I'm not sure of anything right now!" As quickly
as her words came out, she regretted them. "I'm sorry . . .
I didn't mean to snap at you; it's not your fault," she
confessed wearily. "It's all so confusing." Silent tears
once again ran down the elegant slopes of her cheeks.

"What are we going to do?" Dean asked, not moving
from his haphazard position against the windowsill.
Anxious lines of worry creased his tanned brow.

"I don't know," Becca admitted as she faced a
tragedy she had never before considered. *Was it possible? Could Brig really be dead?* Her entire body was
shaking as she drew her booted feet onto the edge of
the couch and tucked her knees under her chin. As her
forehead lowered, she closed her eyes to comfort herself. No matter what had happened, she vowed silently
to herself that she would find a way to cope with it.

Dean watched his sister until the anger that had
been simmering within him began to boil. His fist
crashed onto the windowsill in his frustration. "I told
you that we should never have gone back to old man
Chambers," he rebuked scornfully. "It was a mistake
from the beginning to get involved with that family all
over again. Look what a mess we're in!"

"Not now, Dean," Becca said wearily. "Let's not
argue about this again."

"We have to talk about it, Becca."

"Why? Can't it wait?"

"No, it can't wait, especially now. I told you that

going back to Jason Chambers was a mistake, and I was certainly right, wasn't I?"

"I had no choice," Becca pointed out. *"We* had no choice."

"Anything would have been better than this mess you managed to get us into! What the hell are we going to do now?"

Trying futilely to rise above the argument, Becca attempted to pull the pieces of her patience and shattered poise into place. "For God's sake, Dean, Jason Chambers is dead! For all we know, other people might have died in that plane and all you can think about is the fact that we owe Jason Chambers some money."

"Some money?" Dean echoed with a brittle laugh. "I wouldn't call fifty thousand dollars 'some money.'"

Becca could feel herself trembling in suppressed fury. "The man is *dead,* Dean. I don't understand what you're worried about—"

"Well, then, I'll enlighten you, dear sister. If Jason Chambers is dead, we're in one helluva mess. I don't pretend to know much about estates and wills or anything that happens when a guy as rich as Jason Chambers kicks the bucket, but any idiot can figure out that all of his assets and liabilities will become part of his estate. You and I and the rest of Starlight Breeding Farm are part of those liabilities." Dean took off his hat and raked his fingers through the sweaty strands of his strawberry-blond hair. "There's only one man who is going to benefit by Jason Chambers' death: his only son, Brig. That is, *if* the bastard is still alive."

"Dean, don't . . ." Becca began. She was visibly trembling when she rose from the couch, but in her anger some of the color had returned to her face and a spark of life lightened her pale green eyes.

"Don't you dare come to the aid of Brig Chambers," Dean warned. "Any praises you might sing in his behalf would sound a little hollow, wouldn't you say?"

"Oh, Dean . . . all of that—"

"That what? Scandal?" Dean suggested ruthlessly.

"I don't want to talk about it."

"Why not? Does the truth hurt too much? Don't you remember what happened at Sequoia Park?"

"Stop it!" Becca shouted irritably. In a more controlled voice, she continued. "That was a long time ago."

"Give me a break, will ya, Becca? Brig Chambers nearly destroyed your reputation as a horse breeder, didn't he? And that doesn't begin to touch what he did to you personally. Even if your memory conveniently fails you, I've still got mine." Dean wiped a dusty layer of sweat from his brow with the back of his hand before striding to the small refrigerator and withdrawing a cold can of beer. He dropped into a chair, popped the tab of the can, and let the spray of cool white foam cascade down the frosty aluminum. After taking a lengthy swallow, he settled back into the chair and cradled the beer in his hands. His cold eyes impaled his sister, but he managed to control his temper. Calmly, he inquired, "You're still carrying a torch for that bastard, aren't you?"

"Of course not."

"I don't believe you." Another long swallow of beer cooled Dean's parched throat.

"Oh, Dean, let's not argue. It's so pointless. What happened between Brig and me is part of the past. He took care of that."

Dean noticed the wistful sigh that accompanied her argument. "Then why did you run back to Brig's father when you needed the loan?"

Becca's full lips pursed. "We've been through this a hundred times. I had no other choice. No bank in the country would loan me ten thousand dollars, much less fifty thousand."

"Exactly. Because Brig Chambers ruined your reputation as a horse breeder." His knowing eyes glittered.

Becca ignored Dean's snide comment. "Jason Chambers was my only chance . . . *our* only chance."

Dean drained his beer and crushed the can in his fist. He tossed it toward the wastebasket and missed. The can rolled noisily across the floor to stop near the worn couch. "Well, Becca, you had better wake up and face facts. Our 'only chance,' as you refer to old man Chambers, is *dead*. And now, for all we know, his son, or whoever's still alive, practically owns our Thoroughbred. The only thing we've got going in our favor is that no one knows about the loan or the horse. That is right, isn't it? Jason Chambers was the only person who knew about Gypsy Wind?"

"I think so. He's the only one at Chambers Oil who would have been interested."

"Good! I guess we can count ourselves lucky that the local press hasn't shown much interest in her. Maybe we'll get a break yet. If our luck holds, the attorneys for Chambers Oil will be too busy with the rest of the Chambers empire to worry about our note for the fifty grand. Maybe they won't even find it. The old man could have hidden it."

"I doubt that."

"Why? He wanted to avoid the publicity as much as we did."

"That was before he died. I don't know what you're suggesting, Dean, but I don't like it. There's no way we can hide that horse and I wouldn't want to try. The

Chambers family has to be advised that the collateral for that note is Gypsy Wind. That's only fair, Dean."

"That's not fair, Becca, it's damned near crazy! How can you even think about being fair with the likes of Chambers? What's going to happen is that we'll lose our horse! The last six years of work will go down the drain! Take my advice and keep quiet about the Gypsy."

"I can't! You know that. Keeping quiet would only make things worse in the long run. Sooner or later someone in the Chambers family is going to find the note and realize that we owe that money. And what about the horse? Even if I wanted to, I couldn't hide Gypsy. For one thing, she's insured. Soon she'll start racing. One way or another the Chambers family is going to find out about her."

Dean muttered an oath to himself. "Okay, Sis, so where does that leave us? Back at square one? Just like we were six years ago? What the hell are we going to do?"

The headache that had been building between Becca's temples pounded relentlessly against her eardrums. To relieve some of her tension, she tugged at the leather thong restraining her hair and pulled the thick golden strands free of their bond. Absently she rubbed her temples and ran her fingers through her long, sun-streaked tresses. "I wish I could answer you, Dean, but I can't. Not right now. Maybe later—"

Dean ground his teeth together. "We can't wait until you pull yourself together, damn it! We haven't got the time!"

"What do you mean?"

"I mean that we have to find out if Brig Chambers is still alive! You've got to call Chambers Oil—"

"No," Becca blurted. "I . . . can't."

Dean bit his lower lip and shook his hands in the air. "You have to, Becca. We've got to know if Brig was a passenger on that plane. We have to know if he went down with his father."

"*No!*" Becca's face once again drained of color. Caught in the storm of emotions raging within her, she dropped her forehead into her palm. "We'll find out soon enough," she murmured.

"What are you afraid of?"

Becca's green eyes, when she raised them, pleaded with her brother to understand. "I'm not ready, Dean. Not yet. I don't know if I'll ever be . . . able to face the fact that Brig might be dead," she admitted.

"So I was right. You are still in love with him." Dean's mouth pulled into a disgusted frown. "Damn it, Becca, when are you going to realize that Brig Chambers is the one man responsible for nearly ruining your life?"

The tears that Becca had been struggling against began once again to pool, but she held her head proudly as she faced her reproachful older brother. Why couldn't Dean understand the pain she was going through? How could he remain so bitter? Her voice was low when she replied. "I know better than anyone what Brig did to me, and it hurt for a very long time. But I cared for that man, more than anything in my life . . . and I can't forget that. It's been over for a long time, but once he was everything to me."

"You're dreaming," Dean said icily.

"Just because it's over doesn't mean it didn't happen."

"Why are you telling me all of this?" Dean demanded as he stretched and paced restlessly in the confining room.

"Because I want you to know how I feel. I was bitter once and it's probably true that I should hate Brig Chambers, but I don't. I've tried to and I can't. And now that he might be dead . . ." her voice broke under the strain of her churning emotions.

For a moment sorrow and regret flashed in Dean's opaque blue eyes. It was gone in an instant. "There's no way I can understand how you still feel anything for that louse, and I think you had better prepare yourself: Brig might already be dead. As for Gypsy Wind, I think we have ourselves one insurmountable problem." His face softened slightly and for a fleeting moment, through the shimmer of unshed tears, Becca once again saw her brother as he had been during her childhood, the adolescent whom she had adored. The callused and bitter man had faded slightly. His expression altered and she could feel him closing her out, just as he had for the past few years. Now, when she needed him most, he was withdrawing from her. "Come on, Sis," he said tonelessly. "Buck up, will you?"

He opened the door to the office, and as quickly as he had burst into the room over the stables, he was gone. Becca heard his boots echoing hollowly against the worn steps. Slowly she followed her brother outside. She stood on the weathered landing at the top of the stairs. Holding her hand over her eyebrows to shade her vision, Becca watched the retreating figure of her brother as he sauntered to his battered pickup, hopped into the cab, engaged the starter, and roared down the dry dirt road, leaving a dusty plume of soil in his wake.

The late afternoon sun was blinding for Northern California at this time of the year, and the wind, when it did come, was measured in arrid gusts blowing northward off Fool's Canyon. The charred odor of a distant forest fire added to the gritty feel of weariness that had settled heavily between Becca's shoulder blades.

He can't be dead, she thought to herself as she remembered the one man who had touched her soul. She could still feel the caress of his fingers as they outlined her cheek or pushed aside an errant lock of her hair. She closed her eyes when the hot wind lifted her hair away from her face, and she imagined Brig's special scent: clean, woodsy, provocatively male. Idly she wondered if he'd changed much in the last six years. Were his eyes still as erotic as they once were? It had been his eyes that had held her in the past and silently held her still. Eyes: stormy gray and omniscient. Eyes that could search out and reach the farthest corners of her mind. Eyes that understood her as no one ever had. Eyes that touched her, embraced her. Eyes that had betrayed her.

"He can't be dead," she whispered to herself as her palm slapped the railing. "If he wasn't alive, I would know it. Somehow I would know it. If he were dead, certainly a part of me would die with him."

Slowly she retraced her steps back into the stuffy office and reached down to pick up the remains of the coffee cup. Her movements were purely mechanical as she straightened the papers and placed them haphazardly on the corner of the desk. She wiped up the coffee, but her mind was elsewhere, lost in thoughts of a happier time, a younger time. Though she sat down at the desk and attempted to concentrate on the figures in the general ledger, she found that the mundane tasks of keeping Starlight Breeding Farm operational seemed vague and unimportant. Images of Brig kept lingering on her mind, vivid pictures of his tanned, angular face and brooding gray eyes. Becca recalled the dimple that accompanied his slightly off-center smile and she couldn't help but remember the way a soft Kentucky rain would curl his thick, chestnut hair.

Deeper images, strong and sensual, warmed her body when she thought of the graceful way he walked, fluid and arrogantly proud. Her cheeks burned when she imagined the way he would groan in contentment when he would first unbutton her blouse to touch her breasts.

"Stop it!" she screamed as she snapped the ledger book closed and pulled herself away from the bitter-sweet memories of a love that had blossomed only to die. "You're a fool," she muttered to herself as she pushed the chair backward and raced out of the confining room. She had to get away, find a place in the world where traces of Brig's memory wouldn't touch her.

Her boots ground into the gravel as she ran past the main stables, across the parking lot, and through a series of paddocks, far away from the central area of the ranch. She stopped at the final gate and her clear green eyes swept the large paddock, searching for the dark animal who could take her mind off everything else. In a far corner of the field, under the shade of a large sequoia tree, stood Gypsy Wind. Her proud head was turned in Becca's direction, and the flick of her pointed black ears indicated that she had seen the slender blond woman leaning against the fence.

"Come here, Gypsy," Becca called softly.

The horse snorted and stamped her black foreleg impatiently. Then, with a confident toss of her dark head, Gypsy Wind lifted her tail and ran the length of the back fence, turned sharply, and raced back to the tree, resuming her original position. Dark liquid eyes, full of life and challenge, regarded Becca expectantly.

A sad smile touched Becca's lips. "Showing off, are you?" she questioned the horse.

Footsteps crunched on the gravel behind Becca.

"I thought I might find you here," a rough male voice called as a greeting to her.

Becca looked over her shoulder to face the rugged, crowlike features of Ian O'Riley. He was shorter than she, and his leatherish skin hid nothing of his sixty-two years. Becca managed a thin smile for the ex-jockey, but nodded in the direction of the spirited horse. "How did the workout go this morning?"

The bit of straw that Ian had been holding between his teeth shifted to one side of his mouth. "'Bout the same, I'd say."

Becca sighed deeply and cast a rueful glance at the blood-bay filly. As if the horse knew she was the center of attention, she shook her dark head before tossing it menacingly into the air.

"There's no way to calm her down, is there?" Becca asked her trainer.

"It takes time," Ian replied cautiously, but his words were edged in concern. "It's hard to say," he admitted. "She's got the spirit, the 'look of eagles,' if you will . . . but . . ."

"It might be her undoing," Becca surmised grimly.

Ian shrugged his bowed shoulders. "Maybe not."

"But you're worried, aren't you?"

"Of course I'm worried. History sometimes has a way of repeating itself." He noticed the ashen pallor of Becca's skin and thought that he was the cause of her

distress. He could have kicked himself for so thoughtlessly bringing up the past. He wanted to caution
Becca about the Gypsy, but he had to be careful not to
disillusion her. In Ian's estimation, Becca Peters was
one of the finest horse breeders in the country, even if
her brother was worse than useless. Ian attempted to
ease Becca's mind. "Gypsy Wind just needs a little
more work, that's all."

Becca wasn't convinced. "She does have Sentimental Lady's temperament."

"The spirit of a winner."

"It was Lady's spirit that was her downfall."

Ian waved dismissively and his face wrinkled with
his comfortable smile. "Don't think that way, gal.
Leave the worrying to me; that's what you pay me for."

"If I paid you for all the worrying you do, I'd be
broke."

Laughter danced in Ian's faded blue eyes and his
grizzled face showed his appreciation for Becca's grim
sense of humor. "Just leave Gypsy to me. We'll be
ready, come next spring."

"Ready for what?"

"Whatever the competition can dish out. Surprise
them, we will. Even the colts."

"You think she can keep up with the colts?" Becca
was clearly dubious and a cold chill of apprehension
touched the back of her neck. The last time she had put
a filly against a colt, the result had been a nightmare.
Becca had vowed never to repeat her mistake.

"Of course she can. Not only that, she'll outclass the
lot of them. Just wait and see. Remember, we have the
element of surprise on our side."

"Not much longer. The first time she runs, the press

will be there, digging up everything on Sentimental Lady."

"Let them. This time will be different," he promised. Ian gave Becca a hefty pat on the shoulders before he sauntered back toward the broodmare barn.

Becca's gaze returned to the fiery horse. She wanted to be unbiased when she appraised the blood bay filly, but Becca couldn't help but compare Gypsy Wind with her full sister, Sentimental Lady. Gypsy was built similarly to Sentimental Lady, so much so that it was eerie at times. Though slightly shorter than Lady, Gypsy Wind was heavier and stronger. Fortunately, Gypsy's long, graceful legs were stouter than Sentimental Lady's, capable of standing additional weight and stress. Her coloring was identical except that the small, uneven star which Lady had worn so proudly was missing on her sister.

Doubts crowded Becca's tired mind. Maybe she had made a foolish mistake in the breeding of Gypsy Wind. The question haunted her nights. How was she supposed to know that the offspring of Night Dancer and Gypsy Lady would produce another filly, an uncanny likeness of the first?

As she watched the dark horse shy from a fluttering leaf, Becca wondered what Brig would think if he saw Gypsy Wind. She had asked herself the same question a thousand times over and the answer had always been the same. He would be stunned, and afterward, when the initial shock had worn thin, he would be furious to the point of violence. Still, Becca had hoped to someday proudly show off the Gypsy to Brig. New tears burned in Becca's throat as she watched the dark horse and realized that Brig might never see Gypsy Wind. Brig Chambers might already be dead.

Becca let loose of the emotional restraint she had placed upon herself and cried quietly, feeling small and alone. She lowered her head to the upper rail of the fence and let out the sobs of fear and grief that had been building within her. Why had she never swallowed her stubborn pride and told Brig Chambers just how desperately she still loved him? Why had she waited until it was too late?

Chapter 2

The first gray fingers of dawn found Becca still awake, lying restlessly on the crumpled bedclothes. She snapped off the radio that had been her companion throughout the long night. The endless hours had been torture. There had been no broadcasts during the night to relieve her dread. She was numb from the reality that the only man she had ever loved might be lost to her forever.

The night had seemed endless while she stared vacantly at the luminous numbers on the clock radio, listening above the soft static-ridden music to the sounds of the hot summer night. Even in the early hours before dawn, the mercurial temperature hadn't cooled noticeably, making the night drag on even longer. Though the windows of her room had been open, the lace curtains had remained still, unmoved by even the faintest breath of wind. Trapped in a clammy layer of sweat, Becca had tossed on the bed, impatiently waiting for the dawn. When she had finally dozed, it was only to be reawakened by nightmares of an inferno, a disemboweled Cessna, and the haunting image of Brig's tortured face.

It was nearly six o'clock when her silent vigil ended. The familiar sound of a throbbing engine pierced the solitude as it halted momentarily at the end of the drive. At the sound, Becca rolled out of bed and quickly slipped into a clean pair of jeans and a T-shirt. She pulled on her boots as she ran from her room, flew down the stairs, and raced like a wild-woman to the mailbox.

Her heart was thundering in her chest and her fingers were trembling as she opened the rolled newspaper. Anxiously her eyes swept the headlines, stopping on a blurred photograph of a ragged, weary-looking Brig Chambers. *He's alive,* her willing mind screamed at her while her eyes scanned the article to confirm her prayers. Slowly the fear and dread that had been mounting within her heart began to ebb. "Thank God," Becca whispered in the morning sunlight as she crumpled into a fragile mound at the side of the road and let the tears of joy run freely down her cheeks. "Thank God."

It was several minutes before she could collect herself. She stood up and hastily rubbed the back of her hand over her eyes to stem the uneven flow. A tremendous weight seemed to have been lifted from her shoulders as she half-ran back to the house. She reread the article several times before finally opening the kitchen door. A wistful smile crossed her lips. She still felt sadness at the death of Brig's father, but the relief in knowing that Brig was alive warmed her heart.

The newspaper article indicated that Chambers Oil was not, as yet, making a statement concerning the crash, although the rumor that there had been passengers on the plane was confirmed by a company spokesman. The names of the persons accompanying the oil baron on his tragic journey were being withheld until the next of kin had been notified.

Becca stared at the picture of Brig and wondered how he was. His relationship with his father had been close, if sometimes strained. No doubt Brig was immersed in grief, but she knew that he would survive. It was his way.

The aroma of fresh-perked coffee greeted Becca as she entered the roomy old-fashioned kitchen. "What are you doing up so early?" she asked Dean as she reached for a mug of the steaming black coffee.

"Couldn't sleep," Dean grumbled. He sat at the table, his forehead cradled in his palms. His sandy hair was uncombed and he had two days' worth of stubble on his chin. It looked as if he had slept in his dusty jeans and T-shirt.

"You got in late last night," Becca observed quietly. "I didn't expect to see you till midafternoon."

"I guess I've got things on my mind," he replied caustically. He raised his bloodshot eyes to stare at his sister, and in an instant he knew that Brig Chambers was still alive. It was written all over Becca's relieved face. "You got the paper?" he asked gruffly.

Becca nodded, taking a sip from her coffee as she sat down at the small table. Because Dean was being irritable, she purposely goaded him. "Do you want the sports section?"

Dean's eyes darkened. "Not this morning." He reached for the paper and began skimming the front page. Mockingly he added, "I'm glad to see you're back to normal."

"A pity you're not."

"All right, all right, I admit it. I've got one helluva

hangover . . . Jesus Christ, give me a break, will ya?" His eyes moved quickly across the newsprint. "So Brig wasn't in the plane with his father!"

Was Dean relieved or disappointed? Becca couldn't guess. Her brother was becoming more of an enigma with each passing day. "Thank goodness for that," she sighed.

Dean shook his head slowly from side to side, trying to quell the throbbing in his temples and attempting to concentrate. "Okay, so now we know exactly what we're up against, don't we?" His eyes narrowed as he ran his thumb over his chin. "The question is, what are we going to do about it."

"I haven't quite decided—"

Before she could continue, Dean interrupted with a shrug and an exaggerated frown. "Maybe we won't have to worry about it at all."

"What do you mean?"

"I mean that it might be out of our hands already. Once Brig finds out about Gypsy Wind *and* the fifty grand, he might make his own decision, regardless of what we want."

"You think so?"

"What's to prevent him from taking our horse? After all, his old man practically bought her."

"I doubt that Brig would want the filly . . . you know that he gave up anything to do with racing—"

"Because of Sentimental Lady?" Dean asked bluntly. "Don't tell me you're still suffering guilt over her, too."

"No . . ."

"Just because Brig blamed you for—"

"Stop it!" Becca got up from the table and went over to the counter. For something to do, she began cutting thick slices of homemade bread. She didn't want to remember anything about the guilt or the pain she had suffered at Brig's hand; not now, not while she was still bathing in the warmth of the knowledge that he was alive. Realizing that she couldn't duck Dean's probing questions, she addressed the issue in a calmer voice. "I think the best thing to do is to wait, until sometime after the funeral. Then we'll have to talk to the attorneys at Chambers Oil."

"They'll eat you alive."

Becca sighed inaudibly. It was impossible to get through to Dean when his mind was set. Sometimes she wondered why he was so defensive, especially whenever the conversation steered toward Brig. After all, it was she whom Brig had blamed, not Dean. She placed the bread on the table near an open jar of honey. "We can handle the attorneys . . . but if you would prefer to talk to Brig—"

"What? Are you out of your mind?" Dean's skin whitened under his deep California tan. "I have *nothing* to say to Chambers!"

Becca assumed that Dean's ashen color and his vehement speech were caused by his hangover and his concern for her. She dismissed his hatred of Brig as entirely her fault. Dean knew how deeply she had been wounded six years ago, and her brother held Brig Chambers solely responsible. Dean had never forgiven Brig for so cruelly and unjustly hurting his sister. But then, Dean never did know the whole story; Becca had shielded him from part of the truth. Patiently, she forced a smile she didn't feel upon her brother. "I'll go and talk to Brig myself."

"Becca!" Dean's voice shook angrily and it made her look up from the slice of bread she was buttering. "Don't do anything you might regret . . . take some time, think things over first."

"I have."

"No, you haven't! You haven't begun to consider all of the consequences of telling Brig about the loan or the horse! Don't you see that it will only dredge up the same problems all over again? Think about what a field day the press will have when they learn that *you* and the money you borrowed from Chambers Oil have bred another horse, not just any horse, mind you, but nearly an exact copy . . . a twin of Sentimental Lady! It may have been six years, Becca, but the press won't forget about the controversy at Sequoia Park!" Dean's pale blue eyes were calculating as they judged Becca's reaction.

"Gypsy Wind is going to race. We can't hide her or the note."

"I'm not asking you to," Dean hastily agreed as he noticed just a tremor of hesitation in Becca's voice. He tried another, more pointed tack. "Just give it time. Brig Chambers has a lot more problems—important problems—than he can handle right now. His father was killed just yesterday. If you bring up the subject of Gypsy Wind now, it will only burden him further."

"I don't know . . ."

Dean pressed his point home. "Just give it a little time, will ya? Of course we'll tell him about the filly, when the time is right. Once she's proved herself."

"She won't race for another five or six months."

"Well, maybe we'll have sold her by then."

"*Sold her?*" Becca repeated, as if she hadn't heard her brother correctly. "I'll never sell Gypsy Wind."

Dean's lips pressed into a severe frown. "You may not have a choice, Becca. Remember, when Brig Chambers finds that note, for all practical purposes, he owns that horse."

"Then how can you even suggest that we sell her?"

Becca asked, astounded by her brother's heartlessness
and dishonesty. Sometimes she didn't think she understood her brother at all. She hadn't in a long while.

"It might be that the horse is worth more now! For
God's sake, Becca, we can't take a chance that she'll
get hurt when she races. Think about Sentimental
Lady! Do you want us to run into the same problem
with Gypsy Wind?"

Becca was horror-struck at the thought. Her stomach lurched uneasily. Dean's chair scraped against the
plank floor. He raked his fingers through his hair impatiently. "I don't know what we should do," he admitted. "I just wish that for once you would think with
your head instead of your heart!"

Becca's green eyes snapped. "I think I've done well
enough for the both of us," she threw back at him. "As
for listening to my heart—"

"Save it!" Dean broke in irritably. "When it comes
to Brig Chambers, you never have thought straight!"

Before she could disagree, the screen door banged
against the porch, announcing Dean's departure.

Ten days had passed and the argument between Becca
and Dean was still simmering, unresolved, in the air.
Although they hadn't had another out-and-out confrontation, nothing had changed concerning the status of
Starlight Breeding Farm and its large outstanding debt
to Chambers Oil. In Dean's opinion, no news was good
news. To Becca, each day put her more on edge.

Becca had considered calling Brig and trying to explain the situation over the telephone, but just the
thought of the fragile connection linking her to him
made her palms sweat. What if he wouldn't accept the

call? Did he already know about the note? Could he guess about the horse? Was he just waiting patiently for her to make the first move so that he could once again reject her? Though the telephone number of Chambers Oil lingered in her memory, she never quite got up enough nerve to call.

Excuses filled her mind. They were frail, but they sustained her. Brig would be too busy to talk to her, now that he was running the huge conglomerate, or he would be attempting to sort out his own grief. Not only had he lost his father in the plane crash, but also a friend. One of the persons on board the ill-fated plane was Melanie DuBois, a raven-haired model who had often been photographed on the arm of Brig Chambers, heir to the Chambers Oil fortune. Her slightly seductive looks opposed everything about Becca. Melanie had been short for a model, but well proportioned, and her thick, straight ebony hair and dark unwavering eyes had given her a sensual provocative look that seemed to make the covers of slick magazines come to life. Now Melanie, too, was gone. Dead at twenty-six.

On this morning, while packing a few things into an overnight bag, Becca tried not to think of Melanie DuBois or the young woman's rumored romance with Brig. Instead, she attempted to mentally check all of the things she would need for a weekend in Denver. Knowing it might be impossible to get hold of Brig at the office, Becca had vowed to herself that she would go back to the Chambers mountain retreat and find Brig if she had to. She had visited it once before when she was forced to borrow the money for Gypsy Wind from Brig's father. Becca was willing to do anything necessary to keep Gypsy Wind. That was the reason she was packing as if she would have to stay for weeks in the enchanting retreat tucked in the slopes of the Colorado Rockies. Wasn't it?

"I don't suppose there is any way I can talk you out of this." Dean said as he leaned against the doorjamb of Becca's small room.

"No." She shook her head. "You may as well save your breath."

"Then you won't begin to listen to how foolish this is?"

Becca cast him a wistful smile that touched her eyes. "Save your brotherly advice."

"When will you be back?"

"Monday."

Dean's bushy eyebrows furrowed. "So long?"

"Maybe not," she replied evasively. She snapped the leather bag closed. "If I can get everything straightened out this afternoon, I'll be back in the morning."

"Uh-huh," Dean remarked dubiously. "But you might be gone for the entire weekend?"

"That depends."

"On what?"

"Brig's reaction, I suppose," Becca thought aloud. Her heart skipped a beat at the thought of the man whom she had loved so desperately, the man she had once vowed never to see again.

"Then you really are going to tell him about our horse, aren't you?"

"Dean, I *have* to."

"Or you *want* to?"

"Meaning what?"

Dean strode into the room, sat on the edge of the small bed, and eyed his younger sister speculatively. How long had it been since he had seen her look so beautiful? When was the last time she had bothered to wear a dress? Dean couldn't remember. The smart emerald jersey knit was as in vogue today as it had been when Becca had purchased it several years ago, and her sun-streaked dark-blond hair shone with a new radiance as she tossed it carelessly away from her face. Becca looked more alive than she had in months, Dean admitted to himself. "Examine your motive," he suggested with a severe smile. He started to say something else, changed his mind, and shook his head. Instead he murmured, "Whatever it is you're looking for in Denver, I hope you find it."

"You know why I'm going to see Brig," Becca replied calmly. She hoisted her purse over her shoulder, but avoided Dean's intense gaze. Unfortunately, she couldn't hide the incriminating burn on her cheeks.

"Yeah, *I* know," Dean responded cynically, while picking up Becca's bag, "but do *you*?"

The cedar house seemed strangely quiet without the presence of his father to fill the rooms. Though it was still fastidiously clean and the only scent to reach Brig's nostrils was his father's favorite blend of pipe tobacco, the atmosphere in the room seemed . . . dead.

It's only your imagination, he chastised himself as he tried to take his solemn thoughts away from his father. It had been nearly two weeks since the company plane had gone down, and it was time to bury his grief along with the old man.

In the past twelve days Brig had come to feel that his life was on a runaway roller coaster, destined to collide with any number of unknown, intangible obstacles. There had been the funeral arrangements, the will, the stuffy lawyers, the stuffier insurance adjusters, the incredibly tasteless press, and now, unexpectedly, a wildcat strike in the oil fields of Wyoming. It appeared that everyone who remotely knew Jason Chambers had a problem, a problem Brig was supposed to handle.

Damn! Brig ran his fingers under the hair at the base of his head and rubbed the knot of tension that had settled between his shoulder blades. In the last week he hadn't had more than two or three hours sleep at a stretch and he was dog-tired. The last thing in the world he had expected was for his robust father to die and leave him in charge of the corporation.

Brig had worked solely for Chambers Oil for the last six years, and in that time his father had trained him well. Brig had become the best troubleshooter ever on the payroll of Chambers Oil. No problem had seemed insurmountable in the past, and usually Brig flourished with only a few hours of sleep. But not now—not tonight. In the past the problems had come one at a time, or so it seemed in retrospect. But since Jason Chambers' death, the entire company appeared to be falling apart, piece by piece. Somehow, Brig was expected to hold it steadfastly together. A sad smile curved his lips as he now understood that maybe his father had only made running the company seem simple. "I've got to hand it to you, old man," Brig whispered as he held his drink upward in silent salute to his father.

Maybe I'm just not cut out for this, he thought to himself as his lips pulled into a wry grimace. *Maybe I just don't have what it takes to run an oil conglomerate.*

As he sat in his father's favorite worn chair, his elbows rested on the scarred wooden desk, the same desk he remembered from his childhood. Brig took a long swallow from his warm scotch. It was his third drink in the last hour. He rubbed the back of his neck mechanically and rotated his head before tackling the final task of the day. His frown deepened as he stared at the untidy stack of papers banded loosely together in the bottom drawer of the desk. A few moments earlier Brig had discovered that this drawer, and this drawer only, had been kept locked. So this was where Jason Chambers had kept all of his personal records—the transactions that were hidden from the disapproving eyes of the company auditors and the disdainful glare of tax attorneys. Brig had suspected that the papers existed, but he had always figured that they were the old man's business, no one else's concern. He smiled sadly to himself and silently cursed his father for the reckless, carefree lifestyle that had ultimately taken his life. "You miserable son-of-a-bitch," Brig whispered fondly. "How could you do this to me?"

His gray eyes lowered to the first scrap of paper in the stack, a yellowed receipt from a furrier for a sable coat. Brig couldn't help but wonder which one of the dozen or so women his father had dated over the last few years had ended up with the expensive prize. With an oath of disgust, leveled for the most part at himself, Brig tossed the papers back into the drawer, slammed it shut, and locked it. He was too tired to think about his father or the string of women who had attracted Jason Chambers since his wife's death.

"If I had any sense I'd burn those blasted papers and forget about them," he muttered to himself; to open that portion of his father's life seemed an intrusion of the old man's privacy. Unfortunately, the inheritance tax auditors didn't see things from the same perspective. He dimmed the desk lamp, picked up his drink, and walked to the window to draw the shade. Flickering lights in the distance caught his attention and he left the shade open. He narrowed his eyes and squinted

to be sure just as the twin beams of light flashed once
again. Headlights. Someone was coming. *Who?* Brig's
thoughts revolved backward in time to earlier in the
afternoon. He was certain he had ordered his secretary
to keep his whereabouts under wraps. Hadn't Mona
understood him; he didn't want to be disturbed. He
needed this weekend alone.

Don't get crazy, he told himself as the car drove up
the long gravel road. Brig Chambers couldn't hide, not
since he took command of Chambers Oil. If someone
wanted to find him badly enough, it wouldn't be hard
to do. It didn't take a genius to guess that he would be
spending a quiet weekend in Jason's rustic cottage in
the mountains. Brig had hoped that the two-hour drive
from Denver would discourage most people interested
in contacting him. He had the foresight to take the
phone off the hook, and he hadn't expected to be interrupted. From the looks of the strong headlights winking through the trees, he'd been wrong. Perhaps it was
critical business. He checked his watch. Why else would
someone be coming to the cabin at nearly ten o'clock
at night?

The car rounded the final curve in the driveway and
Brig strained to get a glimpse of the driver. Who the
hell was it?

Becca's heart was racing as rapidly as the engine of
the rental car she had picked up at the airport. All of
the confidence she had gathered at dawn had slowly
ebbed with the series of problems she had encountered
during the day. It was almost as if she were fated not to
meet Brig again. To start off her day, the flight had been
delayed, then there was a mixup in her hotel reservation, not to mention that the rental car which was sup-

posed to be waiting for her had never been ordered, according to the agency's records. It had taken an extra four hours to get everything straightened out. To top off matters, when she had finally managed to arrive at Chambers Oil, she had been politely but firmly rebuked. The efficient but slightly cool secretary had informed Becca that Brig Chambers was gone for the remainder of the day and wasn't expected back into the office until Monday morning. If no one else could help her, then Becca was out of luck. No, the silver-haired woman had replied to her query, Mr. Chambers hadn't left a telephone number where he could be reached . . . if Becca would kindly leave her name and number, Mr. Chambers was sure to get back to her early next week. Becca had declined. It had seemed imperative at the time that she see Brig in person. Right now, she wasn't so certain.

After cresting the final hill and following the road around an acute turn, Becca stepped lightly on the brakes of the rented sedan. In front of her, silhouetted against a backdrop of rugged, heavy-scented pine trees, stood the rustic cedar cabin of Jason Chambers. Soft light from the paned windows indicated that someone was inside. Becca swallowed with difficulty as six abandoned years without Brig stretched before her. After all of the pain, would she be able to see him . . . or touch him? There was no doubt in her mind that he was in the house; she only hoped that he was alone and that he would see her. The angry years apart from him dampened her spirits and she wondered fleetingly why she had decided to come to the lonely cabin to seek him out. She had even brought her overnight bag with her. Was it an oversight or had Dean been right all along?

Before the questions that had been nagging at her could steal all of her determination, Becca switched off the ignition, opened the car door, and stepped into the night.

As Brig sipped his scotch he watched the idling car sitting in the driveway. The engine died and Brig strained to identify the driver. When the car door opened and the interior light flashed for a second, he caught a quick glimpse of a woman stepping from the car. Brig's jaw tensed. This wasn't just any woman, but a tall, graceful woman with a soft mane of golden hair, which shimmered in the moonlight. He didn't catch sight of her face, but he knew intuitively that she was incredibly beautiful. The pride with which she carried herself spoke of beauty and grace. Hazy, distant clouds of memory began to taunt him, but he savagely thrust aside his cloudy thoughts of another striking blonde, knowing that she was lost to him forever. Though she still occupied his dreams, he denied himself conscious thoughts of her. Why did she still haunt him so? And why could he remember every elegant line of her face with such breathtaking clarity? He was a damned fool when it came to Becca Peters. He always had been.

Brig cocked an interested black eyebrow as he stared voyeuristically at the well-shaped stranger hurrying to the porch. What *woman* would be looking for him in the middle of the night, at this secluded mountain home? An expectant smile lit his face only to withdraw into a suspicious frown when he realized that the gorgeous creature now rapping upon his door was probably another one of his father's mistresses, coming to claim what she considered rightfully hers. Brig drained his drink as he advanced toward the door. He hoped to hell that the blonde wasn't wearing a sable coat.

In the past week Brig had secretly dealt with one of his father's mistresses. Nanette Walters was a calculating bitch who was ready to spill her guts about her relationship with Jason Chambers to any interested gossip columnist for the price of a oneway ticket to the Bahamas. Fortunately, Brig had gotten to her first. The thought of Nanette's aristocratic beauty and easily bought affections soured Brig's stomach and he clenched his jaw in determination as he steeled himself against what would certainly be another cold, expensive demand by one of his father's latest women.

Every muscle in Brig's body had tensed in anticipation by the time he reached the door. The insistent rapping had stilled, but the woman was persistent. Brig hadn't heard her restart the car and leave. He jerked the door open and let the light from the interior of the house spill into the night. The pale lamplight rested on the long, tawny hair of the woman standing on the porch and a familiar scent hung in the night air. Brig felt himself waver. He couldn't see her face; her head was bent over her purse and she was rummaging through it as if she was looking for something. Disgust forced a smile of contempt to Brig's lips when he understood: The blonde obviously had her own key to his father's private retreat.

The stranger lifted her bewitching green eyes and Brig's breath caught in his throat. Memories of making love to her in a fragrant field of spring clover clouded his mind. Was she an illusion? As his stunned gaze met and entwined with hers, Brig couldn't help but slip backward in time. It was as if six long years of his life had suddenly disappeared into the darkness. He damned himself for the stiff drinks. *It couldn't be Becca, not after six unforgiving years.*

"Rebecca?" he whispered, not believing the trick his mind was playing on him. He must have had more to drink than he thought. A thousand questions surfaced as he stared at her and just as quickly those questions escaped, unanswered. It had to be Rebecca—the resemblance was too perfect for it to be unreal. What was she doing here, at his father's private cabin in the middle of the night?

Wasn't it just yesterday when they had made love in the rain? Couldn't he still taste the warm raindrops on her smooth skin? He closed his eyes for just a moment—to steady himself—and his dark brows knitted in the confusion that was cutting him to the bone. Why the hell couldn't he think straight?

The sound of his disbelieving voice whispering her name moved Becca to tears. Her answer caught in her swollen throat. Why hadn't she sought him out sooner? Why had she waited so long? Was pride that important?

A wistful smile, full of the memories they had shared together, touched her lips. He looked so tired . . . so worried. Her lips trembled when she realized that he, too, might be vulnerable. He had always been so strong. Without understanding the reasons behind her actions, she reached up and touched his rough cheek with her fingertips.

His eyes flew open. They were as she had remembered them: deep-set and steely gray. They touched her as no other eyes had dared. They held her imprisoned in their naked gaze, encouraged rapturous passion.

"Brig," she murmured, her voice raw. "How are you?" Her hand still caressed his cheek.

He studied her for an endless second, but ignored her concerned inquiry. His eyes probed deeply into hers, asking questions she couldn't hope to answer. "What are you doing here, Rebecca?"

"I came to see you."

It was so simple and seemed so honest. For an instant Brig believed her. He needed to trust her. Perhaps it was the look of innocence in her found, verdant eyes, or maybe it was the effect of more than one too many drinks. But that didn't entirely explain his feelings. More than likely it was because, in the past few weeks, he had felt so incredibly alone. Whatever the reason, Brig couldn't resist the look of naive seduction in her eyes. "God, Rebecca, why did you wait so long to come back?"

Chapter 3

He didn't think about the past and gave little consideration to the future. Instead, Brig took Becca into his arms and crushed her savagely against him. He couldn't let her vanish as quickly as she had come. His lips captured hers almost brutally, as if he could reclaim in a single kiss what had been lost to him for so long.

Becca's knees weakened in his embrace and she wound her arms possessively around his neck to cling to him in silent desperation. She returned the fever of his kiss with the same passion she felt rising in him. Tears of joy ran unashamedly down her cheeks and lingered on her lips. He tasted the depth of her longing in the salt of her tears.

Becca didn't resist when he lifted her from the porch and carried her inside the cabin. Instead she held him more tightly than before and wondered if she would feel the ecstasy of dying in his arms.

The room into which Brig took Becca was shadowed in darkness. There was the slight hint of an expensive blend of pipe tobacco in the air that reminded Becca of Brig's father and her reason for seeking him out. She knew she should tell Brig about Gypsy Wind now, before things got out of hand. But she couldn't. It felt too right being held by the man she loved. She couldn't tear herself from his embrace.

A thin stream of moonglow pierced through the skylights and gave the room some visibility. As Becca's eyes became adjusted to the darkness, she realized that she was in a bedroom: Brig's bedroom.

Brig walked unerringly to the bed. He dropped Becca on a soft down comforter and let his weight fall against her body. He crushed her to him, holding her fiercely to him. His lips brushed hers in tender kisses flavored with scotch and warm with need. His hands pressed intimately against the muscles of her back and through the light jersey fabric of her dress, Becca could feel the heat of his fingertips. They sparked fires in her she had thought dead and rekindled a passion she had buried long ago.

He tasted just as she remembered and the roughness of his unshaven face reminded her of lazy mornings spent waking up in his arms, arousing desires smoldering from the night. His kisses were the sweetest pleasure she had ever known.

"Rebecca," Brig moaned, tortured by the demons playing in his mind. "Rebecca . . . God, how many nights has it been?" His warm breath fanned her face.

"Since what?" she prodded, her breath torn from her throat.

"Since we made love?"

She swallowed the lump in her throat. "Too many," she admitted. His fingers entwined in the strands of her honey-gold hair. She couldn't read his expression in the darkness, but she could feel his unchallenged sincerity. Slowly, she touched his lips and felt the hard angle of his masculine jaw. His hand reached up and covered hers and he kissed it.

"Why did you wait to come back?" he asked.

"I don't know . . . I was afraid, I suppose."

"Of me?"

"No!" She tried to think, tried to explain what she felt, but she couldn't.

"You had the right to be." He pulled his head away from her hand, putting a little distance between them. He let go of her hand and rolled away from her. Why was she here? Why now?

"Don't!" she cried, refusing to release him. Her arms wrapped around his back and she whispered against the back of his neck. "It was my pride. . . . Let's not talk about it. Not here. Not now."

He tried to disentangle her arms. "Rebecca. Don't you think we should talk things through?" He tried to keep his wits about him, attempted to think logically, but he couldn't. The feel of her breasts crushed against his back and the warmth of her arms around his chest made his blood begin to race.

"Please, Brig. Can't we just forget . . . just for a little while?" Her heart was pounding so loudly she knew he could hear it. Her breath was barely a whisper, a small plea in the middle of a clear mountain night.

"Dear God, woman. Don't you know how you torture me?" he asked raggedly. Becca let the air out of her lungs. He was about to deny her, again . . . she could feel it. "I wish I could forget you," he said as if she weren't listening. The bed sagged as he shifted again. He loomed over her in the darkness as he planted one hand on either side of her body. "Do you know what you're asking?"

"Yes," she said.

Cold suspicion had begun to form in his mind, but as he gazed down upon her his doubts fled. The moonlight caressed her face in its protective radiance and her eyes took on a heavenly silver-green purity that begged him to believe her. As she lay upon the bed staring trustingly at him, he knew her to be the most beautiful and beguiling woman he had ever had the misfortune to meet.

Becca couldn't see the pain in Brig's gray eyes, couldn't hope to read his expression, but she knew that he was gazing down upon her, trying to find the strength to pull away again. That knowledge was a dull silver blade twisting slowly in her heart. He wanted to love her, but was denying himself.

"Why did we let it go sour?" he asked, his fists clenching in the restraint he was holding over his body. Dear God, she was beautiful. His question was rhetorical; he didn't expect an answer.

"We made mistakes . . ."

"Like tonight?" he asked cruelly.

"Does this feel like a mistake to you, Brig?" If only she could look into his eyes. If only he would let her.

"Nothing has ever felt wrong with you," he conceded as he lowered his head and his lips met hers in a kiss that spanned the abyss of the six lonely years separating them. The warmth of his lips filled her and she let them part to encourage more intimacy. Everything felt so right with him; it always had. As his mouth claimed hers it was as if all the doubts and fears she had furtively harbored had disappeared. *He wanted her.* Her heart clamored joyously and her blood began to run in heated rivulets through her veins. The love she had chained deep in the shadowy hollow of her heart became unbound in the knowledge that he wanted her. She wrapped her arms around his neck and enjoyed the comfort of his caress.

His tongue slid familiarly through her teeth, touching hers and mating with it in a passionate dance once forgotten. He explored her mouth, groaning softly in pleasure at her heated response. "I've missed you," he admitted roughly, drawing his head away from hers for a moment. He brushed back the silken strands of her hair and kissed her forehead lightly before letting his lips trail down her cheeks to recapture her mouth. "Let me love you."

The jersey dress buttoned on the shoulders. Brig's fingers slid the pearl-like fasteners through the holes and the soft fabric parted to expose her neck and shoulders. He kissed the white column of her throat, nuzzling gently against her neck. Without thinking she tilted her head, letting her sun-streaked hair fall away from her throat and offering it to him willingly. His moist tongue pressed against her skin and he tasted the bittersweet tang of her perfume—the same scent she had worn in the past. It was a fragrance he would never forget. Once he had been with a woman who was wearing Rebecca's fragrance; he had left that woman before the evening had begun. The perfume had evoked too many unwanted memories and destroyed any possible attraction he may have felt for the poor woman.

But tonight was different. Tonight he would drown in the gentle fragrance of wildflowers that filled his nostrils. Tonight in the dusky bedroom, the scent that clung to Rebecca's hair fired his blood and summoned a passion in him he had thought was lost long ago. No other woman had reached him the way Rebecca had, and he had vowed that none would. No other woman had dared enrage him so dangerously. Her soft moan of pleasure encouraged him. He felt her body trembling beneath his persuasive hands.

With a gentle tug the dress slid lower on her body. Lace from a cream-colored slip partially obscured the swell of her breasts and highlighted the hollow between them. He moved over her and his mouth moistened that gentle rift.

"Brig," she whispered, closing her eyes and letting him touch her soul. His hands slid over the silky fabric of her slip, arousing in her aching breasts a need that seemed to consume her in its fire. The satin fabric teased her nipples into hard, dark points that strained against the lace. His warm lips touched the gossamer cloth and Becca moaned her gratitude as the moist heat of his mouth covered her nipple.

Dizzy sensations of a lost past whirled in her mind. Images of a moonlit night and a cascading waterfall filled her thoughts. "I'll always love you," she had heard him say, but that was long ago, in a time before treachery and deceit had ripped the two of them so ruthlessly apart.

His tongue moistened the lace and his lips teased her breast through the gentle barrier of silk and satin. Slowly, he turned their bodies, pulling her over him so that her breasts would fall against him and he could take more of her into his mouth. He groaned in satisfaction when the strap of her slip slid down her shoulder and her breast became unbound. She wore no bra to encumber her, and as the rosy-tipped breast spilled from the slip, Brig captured it in his lips and let his teeth tease the engorged nipple.

"Please love me," she gasped, praying that he understood her needs were not only physical. She wanted to relive the happiness they had shared. She needed to claim again the time when he was hers.

His hands were warm as they pressed between the slip and her ribcage. So slowly that it seemed pure agony, he pushed the fabric past her hips and onto the floor. He disposed of each piece of her clothing as if it were a useless piece of cloth, used only to impede him in his quest to claim her. When at last she was nude, lying trembling in his arms, he took her hands and guided her to the buttons of his shirt.

With whispering softness he brushed kisses over her eyelids as she opened his shirt and slid her hands under the oxford fabric. Her fingers touched him lightly at first, gently outlining each of the muscles of his chest. His groan of satisfaction as she traced each male nipple made her more bold and she slid the shirt over his shoulders, letting her fingers glide down his arms and trace each hard, lean muscle. When his shirt dropped to the floor he gripped her savagely, pushing her naked breasts against the furry mat of his chest. His lips rained liquid kisses of pulsing fire over the top of her breasts before returning to her mouth. Once more his tongue pushed insistently through her teeth to capture and stroke its feminine counterpart. Becca wanted to blend with him and break the boundary that separated his body from hers. She wanted to become one with him, to feel his heart beat in her blood. An ache, deep and primal, began to burn within her, igniting her blood until she felt it boil in her veins.

Brig had never stopped kissing her and his hands hadn't halted their gentle, possessive exploration of her body, but he had managed to remove his pants. She didn't know the exact moment when he had discarded his clothes, but rather became slowly conscious of the fact that he was naked, lying under her and matching her muscles with the rock-hard flesh of his own. His hands moved in slow circles over her back and his lips left none of her untouched as he caressed her.

She felt herself tremble at the familiarity of his touch, the intimacy of his skin on hers. A flush of arousal tinged her skin and she felt the warm glaze of his sweat mingling with her own.

His hand passed over her thigh and her body arched against him, pleading for more of his touch. He wrapped his arms around her and rotated both of their bodies on the comforter, so that once again he was leaning over her, looking at her eyes, misty in moonglow.

Words of love threatened to erupt from her dry throat, but before she could utter them, his knee wedged between her thighs and took her breath away in a rush of desire.

"Becca," he moaned into the tawny length of her hair, "are you sure this is what you want . . . really sure?" All of his muscles had become rigid with the restraint he placed upon himself. Beads of sweat, tiny droplets of self-denial, formed on his upper lip as he awaited her response.

In answer, she threaded his dark hair between her fingers and pulled his head down on hers. She kissed him with the fervid desire so long repressed. Six years she had waited for him. Six years she had yearned for his caress.

He groaned in relief as he gently came to her and found that portion of her no other man had touched. She seemed to melt into him, joining him in a pulsating rhythm that they alone had explored in the past and had now rekindled in the darkness of his bedroom.

The sweet, gentle agony began to build in her as she captured every movement of his body. The fire within her burned more savagely with each persuasive stroke of love, until she felt herself erupt. When he felt her release, he exploded with a passion that shook both of them and left him drained of the frustration that had been with him for the past few weeks. He held her tightly, softly pressing his lips to her hair.

"Stay with me tonight," he coaxed.

She sighed in contentment, warm in the cradle of his arms and the luxury of afterglow. It was moments later, when the beating of her heart had slowed, when the reality of what she had done brought her brutally back to the present. Brig's breathing was regular, but he wasn't asleep. When she attempted to free herself of his embrace, he tightened his grip on her, imprisoning her against him.

"Brig . . . I think we should talk," she whispered, hoping to find the courage to bring up her reasons for seeking him out. She felt him stiffen.

"Later."

"But there are things that I—"

"Not now, Rebecca! Let's wait, at least until the morning." Her resolve began to waver. She closed her eyes and tried to content herself by resting her head against his chest and listening to the steady beat of his heart.

The image of a dark horse, racing dangerously along the ocean's shore, hoofbeats thundering against the pale sand, formed in her tired mind. Lather creamed from the horse's shoulders and foam from the sea clung to the speeding legs. Sentimental Lady ran with the wind. The image of the horse compelled Becca—she had to tell Brig all of her secrets. He had to know about Gypsy Wind.

"Brig, we *have* to talk."

"I said not now!"

"But it's important. Remember Sentimental Lady?"

"How could I forget?" His voice was coated in contempt. He made a derisive sound in the back of his throat. "Let's just leave this conversation until later."

"I can't."

"We've waited for six years, Becca. One more night isn't going to make much difference."

"But you don't understand—"

"And I don't want to!" His voice was stern, his eyes flashed anger. She felt herself tense at his cutting reprimand.

"I just want to talk to you. Don't treat me like a child. It didn't work before, and it won't work now," she whispered.

His voice softened. "Look, Becca, the past couple of weeks have been a little rough. I'm only asking that you put whatever it is you want to talk about on hold—until the morning." He knew what it was she wanted to discuss, but he was too tired to go through the argument of six years past. He didn't want to think about her deception, nor the ensuing scandal, didn't want to be reminded of how deep her betrayal had been. All he wanted was to hold her and remember her as she had been before all of the damned controversy. His arms bound her tightly as he tried to forget the lies and anguish. "If you really want to talk about anything right now, of course I'll listen . . . " Brig pressed his lips to her eyelids and he felt her begin to relax. If only he could concentrate on anything other than that last hellish race.

For the first time that night, Becca realized how much Brig had aged. The years hadn't been kind to him, especially now, right after the death of his father. Her confidence began to waver.

"I want to talk to you about your father."

Brig's arms tightened around her and in the moonlight Becca could see his eyes opening to study her. "What about my father?" he asked.

Becca sighed deeply to herself, but it wasn't a moan of contentment. It was a sigh of acceptance: Brig would never love her, never trust her. She could feel it in the firm manacle of his embrace, read it in the skepticism of his gaze. The tenderness she had once found in him was buried deeply under a mound of suspicion and bitterness. "I owe your father some money."

No response. Her heartbeat was the only noise in the room. The seconds stretched into minutes. Finally he spoke. "Is that why you came here tonight, because of some debt to my father?"

"It was the excuse I used."

His gray eyes held her prisoner. "Was there any other reason?"

"Yes," she whispered.

"What was it?"

"I wanted to see you, touch you . . . feel for myself that you were alive. When I first heard about the plane crash I thought you might be dead." It was impossible to keep her voice even as she relived the nightmare of emotions that had ripped her apart. Even with his powerful arms about her, she could feel her shoulders beginning to shake.

"So you waited nearly two weeks to find me."

"I didn't want to intrude. I knew things would be hectic—the newspapers couldn't leave you alone. I didn't want to take any chance of dredging everything up again, not until I'd talked to you alone."

"About the money?" His voice was cynical in the darkness.

"For one thing."

"What else?"

"I needed to know that you were all right . . ."

"But there's more to it, isn't there?"

She nodded silently, her forehead rubbing the hairs of his chest. All of his muscles stiffened. Her voice was steady when she finally spoke. "I had to borrow the money to breed another horse."

"So you came to the old man? What about the banks?"

"I didn't have enough collateral—the stud fee was a fortune."

"You could have come to me," he offered.

"I don't think so. You made that pretty clear six years ago."

"People change . . ."

"Do they?" She laughed mirthlessly. "It took all of my courage to come to you now. . . . It would have been impossible three years ago. I didn't even want to approach your father, but it was the only solution. Even Dean agreed, although now he's changed his mind."

"Your brother? He was in on this?" The softness in Brig's voice had disappeared and was replaced by disgust. "I would have thought that by this time you would have gotten enough sense to fire that useless bum."

"Dean was there when you weren't," she reminded him, a touch of anger flavoring her words.

"I wasn't there because you shut me out."

"You weren't there because you chose not to be!" she retorted, shifting on the bed and trying to wiggle free of his embrace.

"After all these years, nothing's changed, has it? You're still willing to believe all the lies in the gossip tabloids, aren't you?" He gave her an angry shake and his eyes blazed furiously.

"Dean was there."

"Dean lied."

"Dean lied and the newspapers lied?" she repeated sarcastically. "What kind of a fool do you take me for?"

"A woman who's foolish enough not to be able to sort fact from fiction or truth from lies."

"I didn't come here to argue with you."

"Then why did you come?" His thumbs slid slowly up her ribcage, outlining each delicate bone as it wrapped around her torso. "Did you come here to seduce me?"

"No!"

"No?" His fingers inched upward until they touched the underside of her breast, teasing the sensitive skin.

"I came here to explain about the money—and about Gypsy Wind."

"The horse?"

"Yes—please, don't touch me. I can't think when you touch me."

"Don't think," he persuaded, his lips and tongue stroking the flesh behind her ear. Her breath became ragged as much from desire as from the frustration she was beginning to feel.

"But I want you to know about the money . . . I want you to understand about Gypsy Wind . . . I want . . ."

"You want me."

How could she deny what her body so plainly displayed? Her nipples had hardened, anticipating his soft caress, her skin quivered beneath his touch and the fire in her veins was spreading silently to every part of her body. "Oh, Brig, of course I want you," she said. "I've wanted you for so long . . ."

Desire lowered his voice. "I don't care about the money and I don't give a damn about your horse—"

"But you will. In the morning, when you're sober—"

"I am sober and the only thing I care about is that you're with me. I don't care how you got here, and I'm not all that concerned with why you came. It only matters that you're here, with me, beside me . . . alone. Just let me love you tonight and tomorrow we'll discuss whatever you want to."

"I just wanted you to know why I had to see you."

"It doesn't matter. What matters is that you did." His lips touched her familiarly, softly tracing the line of her jaw, the curve of her neck. His hands gently shaped her breasts, feeling anew the silky flesh beneath his fingertips. He wasn't hurried when his mouth descended to her nipple. It was as if the slow deliberation of the act increased its intensity and meaning. Becca turned her head and groaned into the pillow as his lips molded over her breast.

"Just love me, Brig!" she cried desperately as his hands slid leisurely down her backside to rest on her buttocks.

"I will, Rebecca," he vowed, moving his body over hers and gently parting her legs. "I will."

Chapter 4

Brig had long since fallen asleep, but Becca was restless. She had tried to unwind in the comfort of Brig's embrace, but found it impossible. Continuing doubts plagued her. Though she had tried to tell him about Gypsy Wind, she was sure that she hadn't really gotten through to him. In the morning, when the scotch he had consumed wouldn't cloud his mind, he would see things in a different light. Nothing would change. If anything, the doubts he felt for her would only be reinforced. He wouldn't forget the agony of the past, nor would he be able to rise above his long-festering suspicions of her. The night had only softened the blow slightly. Under the light of a new day his old doubts would resurface.

Becca shuddered as she anticipated his response to the fact that she owed him more than fifty thousand dollars for a horse that would remind him of the tragedy of Sentimental Lady. The fact that Becca had planned Gypsy Wind's conception and borrowed money from Brig's father to have her conceived would feed Brig's gnawing doubts. Becca closed her eyes and tried to drift off to sleep, attempted to be lulled by the sound of Brig's rhythmic breathing. But sleep was elusive; her fear kept it at bay.

Her love for Brig was as deep as it had ever been, his just as shallow. If Becca had hoped to find a way back into his heart, she had destroyed it herself. Gypsy Wind would become the living proof of Becca's deceit, a reminder of the grim past. Tears of frustration burned hotly behind Becca's eyes and slid silently over her cheeks.

Sleep refused to come. Becca was still awake when the first ghostly rays of dawn crept into the room and colored it in uneven gray shadows. Slowly she extracted herself from Brig's arms, careful so as not to disturb him. She reached for a blue terry robe hanging on a nearby chair and pulled it over her shivering body. Without the warmth of Brig's arms around her, the room seemed frigid and sterile. She rolled up the sleeves of the robe, cinched the tie around her waist, and walked across the thick, ivory pile of the carpet to stand at the bay window. After pulling the heavy folds of cloth around her neck, she sat on the window ledge and stared vacantly out the window to watch the sunrise.

The sun crested the horizon and flooded the mountainside with golden rays that caught in the dewdrops and reflected in the snow of the higher elevations. Becca restlessly ran her fingers over the moisture that had collected on the panes of the windows. How many nights had she dreamed of falling back into Brig's arms? How many unanswered prayers had she uttered that she would find a way back into his heart? And now that she was here, what could she do to stay in his warm embrace? Brig's words of the night before came back to taunt her: *"Why did we let it go so sour?"* If only she knew. How had something so beautiful turned ugly? Becca smiled grimly to herself as she reconstructed the events that had drawn Brig to her, only to cruelly push him away.

The party had been Dean's idea, a way to gain more national press coverage for his sister and the filly. Until that night, not much attention had been given the tall girl from California with the small stables and what was rumored to be the fastest Thoroughbred filly ever bred on California soil. The wiser, more sophisticated breeders in the East had considered Becca Peters and Starlight Breeding Farm much the way they did with any new West Coast contender: a lot of California hype. Until the untried filly had proved herself, few gave her much notice, with the one glaring exception of Brig Chambers.

When Becca had received word that Brig Chambers, himself a horse breeder of considerable reputation, wanted to see Sentimental Lady, she had agreed and Dean had suggested the party. Dean's arguments had included the fact that news coverage would be good business for the Lady as well as Starlight Breeding Farm. He had also mentioned that Brig Chambers, part of the elite racing social set, deserved more than a smile and a handshake for flying across the continent to see Becca's horse. Becca had reluctantly agreed.

The celebration had taken place on a private yacht harbored in San Francisco Bay near Tiburón. The owner of the yacht, a rich widow of an insurance broker and friend to the California racing set, had been more than delighted to host the gala event on her late husband's gleaming white vessel. Brig Chambers wasn't often on this side of the continent, and rarely accepted invitations to posh gatherings, but this night was different.

Becca caught her first glimpse of him when he was ushered through the door by Mrs. Van Clyde. The short woman with the perfectly styled white hair and sparkling blue eyes looked radiant as she escorted Brig through the crowded, smoke-filled salon. He was taller than Becca had imagined . . . with a leanness that Becca hadn't expected from the spoiled son of an oil baron. In his sophisticated black tuxedo, Brig Chambers looked more than a pampered only son of wealth; he seemed *hungry* and *dangerous,* exactly the antithesis of the image he was attempting to portray in his conservative black suit. Becca had heard him referred to as "stuffy"; she didn't believe it for a moment.

Nina Van Clyde, in a swirl of rose-colored chiffon, introduced him to each guest in turn, and though he attempted to give each one his rapt attention, Becca noticed a restlessness in his stance. It wasn't particularly obvious, just a small movement such as the tensing of his jaw or his thumb rubbing the edge of his first finger, but it clearly stated that he wasn't comfortable. His smile was well-practiced and charming, a brilliant, off-center flash of white against bronze skin, but his eyes never seemed to warm to the intensity of his grin.

Becca studied his movements over the rim of her champagne glass. He reminded her of a caged panther, waiting for an opportunity to escape, watching for just the right prey. He definitely intrigued her, and when his dark head lifted and he met her unguarded stare, the corners of his mouth turned downward in amusement.

After a brief apology to Mrs. Van Clyde, he advanced on Becca, ignoring any of the other guests.

"You're Rebecca Peters," he said coldly.

"And you're Mr. Chambers."

"Brig."

Becca inclined her head slightly, accepting the use

of first names. Perhaps he didn't like to become confused with his famous father.

"I guess I should thank you for all this," he stated, cocking his head in the direction of the other guests and the well-filled bar.

"It was my brother's idea."

He seemed to relax a bit, and his gray eyes softened. "You may as well know, I'm not crazy about this sort of thing."

Becca's full lips curved into a smile. "I could tell."

He answered her smile with one of his own. "Shows, does it?"

"Only to the practiced eye."

"Were you watching me that closely?" His eyes traveled over her face, lingered in the depths of her green gaze, before trailing down her body and taking in all of her, the way the sea-blue silk dress draped over one of her shoulders to hug her breasts before falling in soft folds of shimmering fabric to her ankles.

Becca felt the heat of her embarrassment burn her skin. "Of course I was watching you," she admitted. "You're the center of attention."

As if to give credence to her words, several men Becca recognized as San Franciscan breeders came up to Brig and forcefully stole his attention.

Becca wandered through the crowd, politely conversing with several other California breeders. She sipped lightly at her champagne, never once losing her feel for Brig's presence in the room. Presently he was talking with a reporter from a San Francisco newspaper. Though Becca didn't openly stare at him, she knew where he was in the throng of elegantly dressed people dripping in jewels.

The music from a small dance band was nearly

drowned in the clink of glasses and chatter of guests. A hazy cloud of cigarette smoke hung in the salon where knots of people congregated while sipping their drinks from the well-stocked bar. Becca was alone for the first time and she took the chance to escape from the stifling room.

Once on the deck, she took in a deep breath of sea air and tried to ignore the muted sounds of the party filtering from the salon. A breeze caressed her face and lifted the wisps of hair that had sprung from their entrapment in a golden braid pinned to the back of her neck. Water lapped against the sides of the slowly moving vessel, and Becca could see the glimmering lights of San Francisco winking brightly in the moonless night.

She leaned her bare forearms against the railing and smiled to herself, glad to be free of the claustrophobic crowd in the main salon. She felt Brig's presence before he spoke.

"I should apologize for the interruption of our conversation," he announced, leaning next to her on the railing. He didn't look at her, but rather concentrated on the distant city lights and the sounds of the night.

"It wasn't your fault," she replied with a sincere smile. "I'm willing to bet it will happen again."

"I don't think so." He sounded sure of himself and his opinions.

"You underestimate the persistence of we Californians, especially the press."

"I'm used to dealing with the press."

"Are you?"

Brig smiled and clasped his hands together. "I've already had the . . . pleasure of meeting a few reporters tonight. Were they your idea?"

Becca shook her head and her smile faded.

"Don't tell me," Brig continued. "Your brother had something to do with that, too."

Becca was intrigued. "How did you know?"

"Lucky guess," was the clipped reply.

"Dean thought the publicity would be good for the stables and Sentimental Lady. I didn't see that it would hurt."

Brig's hand reached out and touched Becca's wrist. He forced her to turn away from the view to look into his eyes. "There's a subject I've been wanting to discuss all night. I'd like to see your horse. She's the reason I'm here."

Becca tried to manage a smile. "I know," she replied, wondering if he was going to release her wrist. He did.

"Then you'll show her to me?"

"Of course. We can drive there tomorrow."

"Why not tonight?" he demanded.

"It's a three-hour drive," she responded before she began to think clearly. Was he serious? "Besides, it's late . . . and then there's the party. Mrs. Van Clyde would be offended if we left. That is what you're suggesting, isn't it?" Becca wasn't really sure she had understood him correctly.

"That's exactly what I'm suggesting."

"I don't know . . ." The night wasn't going as she and Dean had planned.

"Don't worry about Mrs. Van Clyde. I can handle her."

"But my brother . . ." Becca was grasping at straws, but things were moving too fast. There was an arrogant self-assurance to Brig Chambers that unnerved her. And then there was Dean—he had wanted to talk to Brig in private about a job with Chambers Oil.

Brig's smile became cynical. "I'm sure your brother can take care of himself." His hand touched her bare elbow, guiding her toward the door to the salon and the noisy crowd within. "Make your apologies, get your coat and whatever else you brought here, and meet me on the starboard deck."

"What about transportation? We've got to be more than a mile out."

His gray eyes stared at her as they reentered the room and the din of the party made it impossible to converse. Brig leaned over to whisper into her ear. "I've already arranged it. Trust me."

For the first time in Becca's twenty-six years, she wanted to trust a stranger, completely. She found Dean leaning over a well-endowed brunette, and pulled him aside to tell him of the change in their plan. Dean wasn't pleased and had trouble hiding his anger, but he didn't argue with Becca. He couldn't. He was smart enough to realize that Brig Chambers was used to doing things his way. Any argument would fall on deaf ears and only serve to anger the son of one of the wealthiest men in America. Dean could afford to be patient.

A motor launch was waiting and took Brig and Becca over the cold water to the dock, where Brig's car was parked. The drive through the dark night should have taken nearly four hours, but was accomplished in less than three. Becca should have been nervous and restrained with the enigmatic driver of the car, but wasn't. Their conversation flowed naturally and the only fragments of tension in the air were caused by the conflicting emotions within Becca. The man driving so effortlessly through the winding, country roads was a stranger to her, but she felt as if she had known him all of her life. She had never felt so daring, nor so trusting.

His laughter was rich and genuine, yet there was a dangerous glint in his gray eyes that made Becca tremble in anticipation. How many of her thoughts could he read in her smile? She couldn't dismiss the awareness she felt for his masculinity. It was a feeling that entrapped her and sent shudders of expectation skittering down her spine.

Throughout the long drive, she had managed to keep her poise intact and tried to ignore the voice of femininity that begged her to notice Brig Chambers as a man. But as the sleek car began to twist down the rutted lane toward the farm, she felt all of her composure beginning to slip away. The headlights flashed against the white buildings near the paddock and Becca's pulse jumped. The disrepair of the little farm seemed glaring. Perhaps it was better that Brig had come at night. Perhaps he wouldn't notice what was so painfully obvious to her: rusty gutters, wooden fences mended with baling wire, and chipped paint, which was peeling off the boards of the barns. She swallowed back her embarrassment. It was all worth it. Money that should have gone to renovation and repair was well-spent on Sentimental Lady and her training. Becca knew deep within her heart that all of the money used on the horse would come back a hundredfold once the filly began to race.

Becca attempted to disregard her hammering heart. She was home; that thought should calm her, but it didn't. The fact that she was virtually alone with a stranger, a pampered rich boy of the social elite, unnerved her. He would walk through the barns and into her life, scrutinizing it under the same standards of the Kentucky breeders. Starlight Breeding Farm was a far cry from the glamorous blue-grass establishments of the East.

The tires ground to a halt on the gravel, and Brig cut

the engine. He reached for the handle of the door, but Becca reached out to restrain him. "Wait."

Brig's hand paused over the handle. "Why?" He turned to face her. She could feel his eyes upon her face in the dark interior.

"This isn't . . . I mean, we don't handle things the same way you do."

"Pardon?"

"I mean we don't have the facilities or the staff to . . ."

His fingers touched her shoulder. "I just came here to look at your filly, Rebecca. I'm not here to judge you."

"I know Oh, damn! *Why* are you here?" The question that had been teasing her for the past week leapt to her lips.

"I told you, I came here—"

"I know, 'to see the horse.' That's what has been bothering me," she admitted. Was it her imagination, or did his fingers tense over her shoulder?

"Why?"

"This doesn't make much sense, at least not to me."

He removed his hand and Becca felt suddenly cold. "What doesn't make sense?"

"The fact that you came here. No one, not even Brig Chambers, flies more than two thousand miles to 'look at a horse,'" she accused. Her words were out before she had a chance to think about them.

Brig leaned back against the leather cushions of the Mercedes and touched her cheek lightly. He hesitated and frowned. "Someone might if he thought the horse was a threat to one of his own."

"Is that why you're here?"

His hand reached out in the darkness and his fingertips caressed her cheek. Becca took in a deep breath and he dropped his hand, as if suddenly realizing the intimacy of the gesture.

"It's one reason," he conceded. His voice seemed deeper. "I have a pretty decent stable of two-year-olds. I'm sure you already know that."

"Who doesn't? Every racing magazine in the country has run at least one article on Winsome." What kind of game was Brig Chambers playing with her, Becca wondered. He wasn't being completely honest, Becca could feel it. She hadn't earned her reputation at twenty-six without some degree of insight into the human psyche, and she knew intuitively that there was more to Brig Chambers than met the eye. He hadn't flown across the United States to "scope out the competition." The owner of a Thoroughbred the likes of Winsome didn't waste valuable time.

"Are we going to look at your Lady?" Brig asked.

"If you level with me."

She could see the gleam of his white teeth in the darkness as he smiled. "You're not easily fooled, are you?"

"I hope not," she shot back. "Is that what you're trying to accomplish?"

"No. But there is another reason why I'm here," he allowed. "If I like the looks of Sentimental Lady, I'm prepared to offer a good price for her."

The bottom dropped out of Becca's heart, and angry heat rushed through her veins. "She's not for sale." As quick as a cat, Becca opened the car door, stepped outside, and slammed the door. She picked up her skirt and began to march to the house.

Brig had anticipated her move and was beside her in three swift strides. "Is there a reason why you're so angry?" he asked as he grabbed her arm and turned her to face him. In the dim light from a shadowy moon, he saw the glint of determination in her wide eyes.

"I loathe deception." She tried to pull her arm away from the manacle of his grip, but failed. "Let go of me!"

"I didn't deceive you." His fingers dug into the soft flesh of her arm.

"Bull! Dean set this up, didn't he? He's wanted to sell Sentimental Lady from the moment she was born."

"No!"

"Liar!"

Brig's eyes narrowed as he looked down upon her fury. Even enraged, she was gorgeous. "Your brother mentioned that you might be interested in selling—nothing more."

"Well, he was wrong! She's not for sale!"

"That's too bad," he said softly.

"I don't think so." Her anger began to ebb. There was something about him that soothed her rage. She knew he was going to kiss her and she knew she should stop him, but she couldn't. When his head bent and the fingers of his free hand wrapped around her neck to cradle her head, she began to melt inside. And when his lips brushed hers in a tender kiss that promised a night of unbound passion, she had to force herself to pull away from him.

"Was this part of Dean's plan, too?"

His jaw tensed and the corners of his mouth turned down. "Your brother had nothing to do with this."

Her silent green eyes accused him of the lie. He dropped her arm with a sound of disgust. "You don't know the truth when it stares you in the face, do you? I came out here to see your horse, and perhaps offer to purchase her. Period. Yes, it was your brother's suggestion, but I did know a little about Sentimental Lady, and if I hadn't already been interested, I wouldn't have come, and that's the end of it."

He took a step away from her before continuing. "I put up with that ridiculous party and talked to a crowd of people I hope to God I'll never have to face again. And then I arranged for transportation out here, wherever the hell we are. Now you turn paranoid on me. You asked for the truth, Rebecca, and I've given it to you. If anyone's scheming to take your horse away from you, it isn't me!"

"Didn't you just say you planned to buy her?"

"Only if you're willing to sell! I might consider making an offer on her, *if* I like what I see." He stopped his tirade to take in a deep breath. "Look, Rebecca, I don't know what problems you've been having with your brother, and frankly I don't want to get involved in family disputes. If it's too much trouble for me to look at your filly, then forget it. I think I can find my way back to civilization."

He turned on his heel and began to return to the car. "Wait," Becca called. Brig stopped. "If you want to see Sentimental Lady, I'll take you to her." He followed her to the largest of the buildings surrounding the paddocks.

The door creaked when she opened it and there was a restless stirring when Becca flicked on the lights. A few disgruntled snorts greeted her as she passed by the stalls of the awakened horses. Becca murmured soothing words to the animals and stopped at Sentimental Lady's stall. "Come here, girl," she called to the dark filly and made soft clucking sounds in the back of her throat.

Sentimental Lady's nostrils flared and she backed up distrustfully as she eyed Brig. She stamped her foot impatiently and flattened her dark ears against her head. "She doesn't like strangers," Becca explained to

Brig before softly coaxing the highspirited horse to come forward.

Brig's gray eyes never left the horse. He studied the filly from the tip of her velvet-soft nose to her tail. Lady tossed her near-black head and snorted her contempt for the man appraising her.

"Is she as fast as she looks?" Brig asked.

"She's fast." Becca found it impossible to put into words how effortlessly Sentimental Lady ran, how rhythmically her black legs raced, or how fluidly her muscles worked. The horse was a study in grace when she lengthened into her stride.

"Is she strong?"

Becca snapped off the lights and closed the door. "She's strong."

"And big," Brig murmured. He rubbed his thumb pensively over his jawline. "She's one of the tallest fillies I've ever seen. What's her girth?"

"Seventy-five inches."

Brig shook his head and scowled. "Have you had any trouble with her legs?"

Becca was a little defensive. "We've had to watch her ankles."

"She's too big," was Brig's flat, emotionless statement. "Her legs won't be able to carry her the distance."

"Because she's a filly?" Becca shot back.

"Because she's a *big* filly. Her girth is over an inch larger than Winsome's and his legs are stronger."

"You haven't seen her run," Becca whispered as they walked toward the house.

"I'd like to."

"Why? I told you she wasn't for sale."

Becca placed her hand on the doorknob, but Brig took hold of her arm, catching the warm flesh and forcing her to turn and look at him. "I came all this way; I'd like to see her run." His eyes touched hers and in the darkness she could read more than interest for a horse in his gaze. Passion burned deep within him, Becca saw it as clearly as if he had whispered, "I want you." Becca managed to unlock the door and it swung open, inviting them both into the comfort inside.

Her pulse was racing and her lips desert dry. She tried to think calmly, but found it impossible. Her smile trembled with the confusion that was overtaking her. "Sentimental Lady has a workout scheduled for tomorrow morning . . ." Was he listening? He was looking at her lips, but Becca doubted if he had heard a word she said. "You could come and see her then." She began to retreat into the house, but felt the muscles in her back press up against the doorjamb. "She . . . runs at six."

His hands captured her bare shoulders. His face was only inches from hers and his clean scent filled her nostrils. "It's already after two."

"I know . . ."

His lips pressed hotly against hers and the delicious pressure of his fingers on her shoulders increased. His warm breath fanned her face as he pulled his head away from hers to look into her eyes. "I can't go back to the city tonight. It will be nearly dawn when I get there," he pointed out.

Becca's senses were swimming and she found it impossible to think clearly. "But . . ." *What was he asking?*

His fingers touched the hollow of her throat and her pulse jumped. He gazed down upon her through heavy-lidded eyes. "Let me stay with you," he suggested throatily, and softly nuzzled the inviting column of her neck. She had to fight the urge to collapse into him.

She pressed her palms against his chest. Her eyes searched his face. "I find you very attractive," she admitted.

"Why do I expect the word *but* to preface the rest of your response?" He smiled, and in the pale light from an uneven smattering of stars, Becca returned his grin.

"Because I don't know you . . ."

His fingers toyed with the neckline of her dress, rimming the silken fabric. "Tell me you don't want me," he commanded, softly, before pressing a kiss to her bare skin above the edge of the dress.

"I can't," she conceded breathlessly. Why did she feel that the edge of her soul was exposed to his knowing gaze?

"Why not?"

"Because I do want you," she replied honestly.

The corners of his mouth quirked.

"But that's not enough."

"There's nothing wrong with physical need."

The stillness of the night seemed to close in on Becca. Brig's touch was warm and inviting. It seemed as if they were alone in the universe: one man and one woman. His lips once again brushed hers, caressing her with a passion she had never known, promising a night of rapture and warmth, if only she would take it. She had been lonely so long. "Physical need is important," she agreed quietly. "But there has to be more."

"What is it you want, Rebecca? Are you waiting to fall in *love?*" he asked contemptuously.

"I'm not *waiting* for anything. It . . . it just has to be right for me."

He took his hands off of her and planted them firmly on either side of her head, bracing himself on the doorjamb. His gray, brooding eyes forced her to hold his unwavering gaze. "I'm not asking for anything you're not willing to give. I would never push you into any-thing you don't want. Believe it or not, I know that this isn't easy for you."

"Do you?" She wanted to believe him, needed to hear that he understood her.

"Of course I do. It's written all over your face."

"It's not that I'm a prude."

He smiled. "I know. And I'm not looking for a one-night stand. If that's what I wanted, I could have stayed in San Francisco, or New York, for that matter. The truth of the matter is that you intrigue me, Rebecca Pe-ters. Just who are you?" His finger came up to trace her lips. Shivers of anticipation traveled hurriedly down her spine. "I've read about you and your farm out here. A beautiful young woman with an impoverished breed-ing farm somehow has the brains to breed Night Dancer, one of the greatest racing studs of all time, to a little-known mare called Gypsy Lady and ends up with per-haps the fastest Thoroughbred filly ever bred. I want to know about you, Ms. Peters, all about you."

"And that includes sleeping with me?" she asked. "Are you stupid enough to think that you could possi-bly understand me by sleeping with me?" She knew she should feel outraged, but she didn't.

"I had no intention of sleeping with you when I came out here. I was only interested in you because of business."

"But?" she coaxed, lifting her elegant eyebrows.

"But you happen to be the most intriguing woman I've ever met." His hand slipped under her head, and he deftly removed the clasp that held her hair restrained. With one quick movement of his fingers, her golden hair spilled down past her shoulders, still wound loosely in a thick braid. "Trust me," he pleaded as his lips met hers in a kiss that was bold rather than tender. His mouth found the moistness of hers and he held her against him hungrily. "Let me love you, Rebecca," he whispered.

"Oh, Brig . . . I . . ." His lips stilled her response and the heat of passion began to race through her veins. She gasped when his hands found the clasp of her dress and the blue silk fabric parted, leaving her upper shoulder bare. His lips were warm and moist where the fabric had once been, and Becca felt her bones beginning to melt. She couldn't think, couldn't stand. Before she swayed against him, Brig reached down and captured her sagging knees with the crook of his arm. He lifted her off of her feet and touched his lips to her forehead as he carried her inside the old farmhouse.

Becca's heart was racing, but she didn't protest as he carefully mounted the stairs. When he hesitated on the landing, she encouraged him by indicating the direction of her room. He didn't turn on the light and Becca's eyes grew accustomed to the shadowy light cast by a cloud-covered moon. Carefully, Brig set her on her feet and let the elegant blue dress slip into a puddle of silk on the floor. His hands moved downward over her body, as if he were memorizing each soft contour of her muscles, every rib in her ribcage. His groan was primal when he cupped her breast and felt the weight of it in his hungry palm. Her answering sigh of expectation fired his blood and his lips, hungry with unsatisfied desire, pressed forcefully against hers. She felt the tip of his tongue press through her teeth to touch the inner reaches of her mouth.

His lips devoured her, spreading a trail of demanding kisses across her cheeks, inside her ear, and down the column of her throat. His tongue touched the delicate bones surrounding the hollow of her throat and drew lazy, wet circles of delicious torment that forced her to cling desperately to him, hoping the sweet agony would never stop.

"Love me," she whispered, her hoarse voice breaking the stillness of the night. She entwined her arms possessively around his neck and let the tips of her fingers delve below his collar. Her eager hands encountered shoulder muscles tense with desire. "Touch me, sweet lady," he pleaded. Deliberately he forced her onto the bed with the weight of his body. The mattress sagged as their combined weight molded together. Impatiently he discarded his clothes, damning the frail barrier holding them apart.

His body was damp with perspiration. The beads of sweat collected on his forehead and ran down his spine. A gentle breeze lifted the curtains and whispered through the pine trees to scent the room, but it did nothing to cool the passion storming between them.

Heated torment inflamed Becca's veins and pounded in her eardrums. The dim light from a pale moon let her see the man she was about to love, let her read the fire in his eyes, let her witness the rising tide of his emotions.

His hands slid possessively over her body, molding his skin to hers. The sweat that clung to his body blended with hers as he moved his torso over hers, claiming her body. Becca moaned when he took her breast into his mouth and teased the nipple with his tongue and teeth. Her fingers dug into the muscles of his back as she gave in to the sweet ecstasy of his caress.

His eyes were glazed in barely restrained passion when he took her face between his hands and stared into her soul. "I want you," he whispered. "Please let me know that you want me."

"Oh, Brig, please . . ." She didn't have to finish; her eyes pleaded with him to take her.

"May this night never end," he whispered savagely before once again molding his swollen lips to hers.

He braced himself so that he could watch her face as he found her. She gasped with satisfaction at the moment they became one, feeling a delirious triumph at the union of their flesh. The ache within her began to ebb and the words of love forming on her lips died as he slowly urged her to sensuous new heights of passion. They moved as one, together in rapturous harmony, blending flesh to flesh, skin to skin, muscle to muscle until the tempo began to quicken and the pressure within Becca's body began to thunder and echo in her heartbeat.

She felt the fires within her begin to flare and Brig's answering shudder of surrender.

"I love you," she whispered, while tears of relief filled her eyes. "I know it's irrational, but I think I love you."

"I know," he murmured, kissing the wet strands of her sun-streaked hair and holding her trembling body as if life itself depended on it.

Chapter 5

When Brig opened his eyes, he noticed that his body was covered in sweat, evidence of his recent nightmare—the vivid and brutal dream that had interrupted his sleep repeatedly during the last six years. The nightmares had become less frequent, but being with Rebecca again had triggered the ugly, painful dream. He lifted his arm to touch her, to find comfort in the softness of her body and to convince himself that his memory of making love to her hadn't been part of the dream, hadn't been conjured by his imagination. His hand touched the crumpled sheets, cold from the morning air. The bed was empty.

Brig's eyes flew open with the realization that she was gone. He lifted his head from the pillow too quickly, and a ton of bricks pressed on his skull in the form of a hangover. Then he saw her—as beautiful as he remembered. It wasn't part of his dream. Rebecca was really here, in his father's cabin in the foothills of the Rockies. She was huddled in his favorite blue robe, her fingers drawing restless circles on the window ledge where she sat as she stared out the window. She appeared absorbed in thought. Pensive lines of worry marred the smooth skin of her forehead. Her honey-blond hair was unruly and tangled as it framed her delicate face. Her green eyes stared, but saw nothing. What was she thinking?

He started to call her name, but withheld the impulse as he recalled the first time he had seen her. Dressed elegantly in shimmering blue silk, her hair coiled regally upon her head, Rebecca had combined beauty with grace. She had been refined and yet seductive.

Brig hadn't fallen in love with her then. It had come much later when the feelings of respect and trust had grown into love. They had worked together side by side, day after day, in the sweat and grime of training a headstrong bay filly to become the racing wonder she was. With Rebecca's fiery Thoroughbred and Brig's money, they had formed a partnership intent on taking the racing world by storm. They planned to shake up the elite world of horse racing with Sentimental Lady, a filly who could outdistance the colts.

At the thought of the elegant horse, Brig's stomach turned over and the taste of guilt rose in the back of his throat. For the first time in his life, Brig had allowed himself to be shortsighted. Perhaps his clear thinking had been clouded with love, but nevertheless it was a poor excuse for letting his emotions override his logic. He had known from the moment he laid eyes upon Sentimental Lady that her legs weren't strong enough to carry the weight. If only he'd used his head instead of trusting a woman with beguiling green eyes!

His nightmares were a surrealistic replay of the events that had shattered his life. It was always the same. He was with Rebecca in a crowd of thousands of cheering people. The track was dry and fast—Sentimental Lady's favorite. The warm California sun glistened on the flanks of a blood-bay horse as she nervously pranced toward the starting gate. The other horse in the match race, Winsome, had already won top honors as a three-year-old. His list of victories included two of the three jewels of the triple crown and now he faced an opponent he had never previously encountered. Although Sentimental Lady had stormed into the racing world as a two-year-old, and at three had won all of her starts, including the Kentucky Oaks, the Black-eyed Susan, and the Coaching Club American Oaks, she hadn't raced against the colts. She had shattered several world records, and was clocked faster than Winsome. The press and the fans demanded a match race of the two most famous three-year-olds of the season: Sentimental Lady challenging Winsome.

There was another side to the story, an interesting twist that headlined the gossip columns. The filly, renowned favorite of the feminist fans, was bred and owned by Rebecca Peters, a young woman making her way in a man's world. The colt belonged to the stables of Brig Chambers, heir to an oil fortune and rumored to be romantically involved with Ms. Peters. It was a story the press loved, a story that extended the bounds of the racing world and included the romantic glitter of the very rich. Pictures and articles about the famous couple and their rival horses were flashed in both racing tabloids and gossip columns alike. Reporters couldn't get enough information on the horses or their owners. Speculation ran high on the future mating of Sentimental Lady to Winsome.

As the world saw it, Brig Chambers had it all: a beautiful, intriguing woman and two of the fastest horses ever run. Nothing could go wrong, or so he was told. So why then did he argue against the race, and when he finally relented, why did doubt keep filling his mind as he watched a lathered Lady being led into the starting gate? Why was there an uneasy sense of dread? Where was the exhilaration; the excitement? The false sense of security he had felt earlier in the week began to crumble. The race was a mistake—a terrible mistake.

Winsome, veteran of many victories and known for his calm temperament, was led into the starting gate. The crowd roared its approval and Sentimental Lady spooked at the sound. She skittered across the track and shied as her jockey attempted to urge her toward the gate. Nervous sweat lathered her withers and she tossed her head in apprehension.

"She's too nervous," Brig muttered, but his words of concern were lost in the approving roar of the crowd as Sentimental Lady sidestepped into the starting gate. The gate closed and the Lady reared, striking her head. It was too late; the door opened with the ringing of bells and shouts from the crowd. An empty track stretched out before her and Sentimental Lady bolted. Brig yelled at the officials, but his voice was drowned in the jumble of noise from the fans.

"No!" Brig shouted at the jockey, watching the race between colt and filly in silent horror.

Winsome was ahead, but Sentimental Lady seemed to get her footing. She was astride the black colt before the first turn. The speed of the race was incredible and Sentimental Lady finished the first quarter faster than she had ever run. Winsome liked to lead and was known for crushing his opponents early in the race, but Sentimental Lady hung on, holding her own against the powerful black horse.

The blood drained from Brig's face as he watched the horses, racing stride for stride, heartbeat for heartbeat. "This is a mistake," he screamed at Rebecca. "She's not going to make it . . ."

"She will!" Rebecca disagreed, her eyes shining in pride at the way the Lady was running. The crowd seemed to agree, roaring, urging the horses onward in their blinding pace.

"We've got to stop the race!" Brig shouted, shaking Becca.

"It's too late—"

"We've got to! Lady hit her head in the gate. Her stride's off!"

"You're crazy," Becca screamed back at him, but a flash of doubt clouded her green eyes. "Look at her— she's running with the wind!"

Sentimental Lady was a neck ahead of the colt, but he was pushing her, driving her to greater speeds, forcing her to run faster than she ever had. The horses were halfway down the backstretch, their legs pounding the track furiously, their dark tails trailing behind. Nostrils distended, they ran, neck and neck, stride for stride, eyeball to eyeball. The white fence inside the track hampered Brig's view, but still he saw the misstep as clearly as if he had been astride her rather than on the sidelines.

The blow to the leg came with a sickening snap that Brig imagined rather than heard. It was the brittle crack of bone as nearly twelve hundred pounds of horse came crushing down on fragile legs.

For a moment Brig stood transfixed, watching in sickened dread. "She broke down," he yelled at Rebecca, who had witnessed the fateful step.

Winsome pressed on, and Lady, her spirit and courage refusing to be extinguished, continued to race on her three good legs. The jockey fought desperately to pull her up, knowing that her competitive fires would carry her on and further injure her. Each stride pushed her tremendous weight on the shattered bone, further pulverizing the bone into tiny fragments ground into tissue, dirt, and blood.

Brig didn't see Winsome finish the race. He ran across the track to the site of the injury, where the jockey was trying to calm the frightened animal. The veterinarian arrived and tried to soothe the horse, while attempting to examine the break. The Lady reared and Rebecca, with frightened tears running down her face, softly called to the horse, hoping to somehow forestall the inevitable.

"Good girl. That's my Lady," she said tremulously. "Let the doctor look at you, girl."

The frightened horse reared. Blood was smeared on her regal white star, and her right foreleg was a twisted mass of flesh and bone. The whites of her dark eyes showed the fear and pain.

Rebecca reached for the horse's reins but Sentimental Lady reared again. The injured leg glanced Becca's shoulder, leaving her ivory linen suit stained with blood and her shoulder bruised.

"Get away from her," Brig shouted, pushing Becca away from the terrified horse.

"I can't . . . oh, Lady . . . Lady," Becca called as she backed away. "Calm down, girl, for your own sake . . ."

The veterinarian looked grimly at Brig. He nodded toward Becca. "Get her out of here." He spoke rapidly as he placed a clear, inflatable cast over the horse's damaged leg. It quickly turned scarlet with blood.

"It's all my fault," Becca screamed as Brig put his arms around her shaking shoulders and led her away from her horse.

"Don't blame yourself."

"It's all my fault!" she cried over and over again,

hysterical. "She should never have run. I knew it—I knew it. Damn it, Brig, it's all my fault!"

Brig hadn't understood her overwhelming sense of guilt. He dismissed it as an overreaction to a tragic event, until twelve hours later Sentimental Lady was dead and the results of the autopsy proved Becca right. Only then did he understand that she was, indeed, responsible for the courageous horse's death.

Brig rubbed his hands over his eyes and tried to dispel the brutal apparition that destroyed his sleep. How many nights had he lain awake and wondered how he could have prevented the gruesome tragedy; how many days had he tried to find a way to absolve Rebecca of the guilt? How much of the guilt was his? He should never have agreed to the match race; it was a devil's folly. Even if the tragedy hadn't occurred, there was the chance that the beaten horse would never have been the same.

As it was, a beautiful animal had been ruined unnecessarily, a waste due to the poor judgment of humans. If that wasn't enough to torture him, the truth he had learned after Sentimental Lady's death should have kept him away from Rebecca Peters forever. And yet, last night, without thinking of any of the horrors of the past, Brig had made love to her as if the deception had never existed.

Brig wanted to hate her. He wanted to curse her in the darkness and throw her out of his life forever, but he couldn't. As he watched her staring vacantly out the window, the sadness in her eyes touched his soul. How had she ever been caught in such an evil trap? Why had she drugged her own horse in an expensive attempt to quicken Sentimental Lady's speed? His stomach soured at the thought. Why did she seem so innocent and honest, when he knew her to be a liar? She was a dichotomy of a woman, beguiling and treacherous.

"Rebecca?"

Brig's voice called to her from somewhere in the distance.

"Rebecca, are you all right?"

Becca cleared her mind and found herself staring out the bay window of Jason Chambers' mountain cabin. Brig's concerned voice had brought her crashing back to the present. How long had she been daydreaming about a past that was so distant? She cast a quick glance at Brig. He was still in bed, propped up on one elbow and staring intently at her. He seemed anxious and didn't appear to notice that the navy blue comforter had slid to the floor. How long he had been watching her, Becca couldn't guess.

She shivered and wrapped her arms around herself, to build her courage rather than create warmth. "I guess I was just thinking," she replied evasively. She turned her head away from him and hid behind the thick curtain of her hair, where she brushed aside a lingering tear that had formed in the corner of her eye. She had loved him so desperately and the bittersweet memories of their past caught her unprepared to meet his inquisitive gaze.

His dark hair was rumpled and a look of genuine concern rested in his unguarded stare. "What were you thinking about?" he asked. He didn't attempt to hide the worry he felt for her.

Her lips trembled as she attempted a smile. "Us."

"What about *us?*"

Her voice was frail, but she forced her eyes to remain dry as she found his gaze and held it. "I . . . I was thinking about how much love we had, once," she admitted.

"Does that make you sad?"

She had to swallow to keep her tears at bay. He couldn't understand, he never had. She averted her gaze and stared sightlessly out the window. "It's just that I loved you so much," she admitted raggedly.

His brows knit in concentration as he drew his knees beneath his chin and studied her. Why was she here, opening all the old wounds? What did she want? "I loved you too," he said.

"Not the same way." It was a simple statement of fact.

"You're wrong."

"You still don't understand, do you?" she charged, as she whirled to imprison him with her damning green stare. "I wanted to spend the rest of my life with you. I wanted to share all of the expectations, the joys, even the disappointments with you." Her voice caught in the depth of her final admission. "I wanted to bear your children, Brig. I wanted to love them, to teach them, to comfort them when they cried. . . . Dear God, Brig, don't you see? I wanted to be with you forever!"

"And I let you down?"

"I . . . I didn't say that . . ."

His gray eyes challenged her from across the room. The silence was heavy with unspoken accusations from a distant past. With an utter of vexation, Brig fell back against the bed and stared, unseeing, at the exposed beams in the ceiling. "I wanted those things, too," he conceded.

"Just not enough to trust me."

"Oh, Rebecca . . . don't twist the truth." He felt raw

from the torture of her words. "I asked you to marry me, or have you conveniently forgotten that, too?"

"I remember," she whispered.

"Then you can recall that *you* were the one who couldn't make a commitment. *You* were the one who had to prove yourself to the world." The rage that had engulfed him six years before began to consume him once again, and he had to fight to keep his temper under control. How many times would he let her deceive him? His fingers curled angrily around the bed sheet.

"I needed time."

"I gave you time, damn it!" He sat upright in the bed and his fist crashed into the headboard. "You asked for time, and I gave it to you!" His ghostly gray eyes impaled her, daring her to deny the truth.

"But you couldn't give me your trust, could you?"

"Do you blame me?" Pieces of their last argument pierced Brig's mind. His accusations, her violent denials. If only she could have told him the truth! He didn't wait for her to respond to his rhetorical question. Instead he grabbed his clothes and stood beside the bed. He was still naked and Becca could see the tension in all of his rigid muscles. His voice was uneven, but he managed to pull together a little of his composure. "Look, Rebecca, this argument is getting us nowhere. I'm going to take a shower and get cleaned up. I drank a little too much last night and I'm paying for it this morning. When I clear my head, we'll talk."

He turned toward the bathroom, but paused at the door and faced her once again. His voice was softer and his smile wistful. "I'm glad you're here," he admitted, wondering why he felt compelled to explain his feelings to her.

She didn't move from her seat on the window ledge until she heard the sound of running water. Once she knew he was in the shower and she had a few minutes to herself, her tense muscles relaxed and the tears burning at the back of her eyes began to flow in uneven streams down her cheeks. She pinched the edge of her thumb between her teeth and tried not to think about the love they had found, only to lose.

Was it her fault, as Brig insisted, or was it fate that held them so desperately apart? If only she hadn't been so blind when it had come to Sentimental Lady, if only she had listened to Brig's wisdom. Perhaps they would still be together, would have married, and would share a child. Perhaps Sentimental Lady would still be alive. But Becca had been young and hellbent on making a name for herself as a horse breeder. Sentimental Lady had been her ticket to success. How was Becca to know that Brig's prophecies would be proven correct, that Sentimental Lady's legs were too weak for her strong body? Not even her trainer had guessed that the Lady would break down. And how was Becca to know that someone would inject her horse with an illegal steroid, a dangerous drug that alone might have permanently injured her horse? In the end, Becca had not only lost the fastest horse she had ever owned, but also the trust of the one man she loved. Was it her punishment for being overly ambitious, for fighting her way to the top in a man's domain?

Becca stiffened her spine and tried to ignore the unyielding pain in her heart. Perhaps she was overreacting. Last night Brig hadn't been overly upset when she had tried to explain about the horse; maybe she was blowing the problem out of proportion. But then again, last night Brig had been drinking and was shocked to see her. Everything that had happened between them

was somewhat unreal, an unplanned reunion of two
lovers suffering from the guilt of the past. This morning things were different. Gone were the excuses of the
night, the passion of six lonely years, the feeling of
isolation in the mountains. Today, the world would intrude and the mistakes of the past would become blind-
ingly apparent.

She had decided to accept Brig's decision concerning Gypsy Wind and the money. She realized that,
legally, she had virtually no say in the matter. If Brig
demanded repayment, she would have to sell the Gypsy.
Nothing she owned even approached fifty thousand
dollars. However, she would try her damnedest to make
Brig understand what the horse meant to her, what
Gypsy Wind represented. Before her resolve could
waver, she went to her car and grabbed the overnight
bag she had stashed in the back seat. She cleaned herself in the guest bath and changed into her favorite forest green slacks and soft ivory blouse. The outfit was a
little dressy for the rugged mountains, but this morning
Becca wanted to look disturbingly feminine. She wound
her hair into a gentle twist and pinned it loosely to the
back of her neck before touching a little color to her
pale lips and cheeks.

Without consciously listening, she knew the exact
moment when the shower spray was turned off. Apprehension rose in her throat. She had to keep busy and
hold her thoughts in some sort of order, because like
it or not, she knew that she and Brig were about to
become embroiled in one of the most important arguments in her life. She planned her defense while putting together a quick breakfast from the sparse contents
of the refrigerator. By the time she heard the bedroom
door opening, the hasty meal was heated and the
aroma of freshly perked coffee mingled with the scent

of honey-cured ham to fill the rustic kitchen and dining alcove.

She thought she heard Brig coming, but his footsteps paused, as if he had entered another room in the house. She waited and then heard him continue toward the kitchen. She was just sliding the eggs onto a plate when he strode past the dining alcove and through the door. She was concentrating on her task and didn't look up.

"What's this?" he asked, just as she set the plates on the table.

"What does it look like? It's breakfast." She turned to face him and found that he wasn't looking at the table. Instead he was staring intently at her, as if he were trying to put together the pieces of a mysterious puzzle. He looked more like the man she remembered from her past. Clad only in jeans and an old plaid work shirt, he seemed younger. His head was still wet from the shower and his jaw cleanly shaven. The slight hint of a musky aftershave brought back provocative memories of living with him in a rambling beach house overlooking the moody Pacific Ocean.

"I'm not talking about the food," he replied cautiously. His eyes turned steely gray. "Your clothes, did you bring them with you?"

Her eyes met his and refused to waver. "Yes."

"Wait a minute. Are you saying that you *intended* to spend the night with me? Don't you have a hotel or something?" When she didn't immediately respond, he grabbed her arm and his fingers tightened painfully. Suspicion clouded his gaze. "Just what's going on here?" he demanded.

"What do you think?"

"I *think* that you planned last night."

"I only planned to find you . . . not seduce you, if

that's what you're implying. I didn't even know if you would see me. I had no idea that we would end up making love."

His grip tightened on her arm. "Then why the change of clothes?"

She couldn't help but blush. "I really didn't know where I'd be spending the night. I only guessed that you would be here, and I knew that it was too late to head back to a hotel in Denver."

"And what if you hadn't found me? Did you plan to sleep in the car?" He couldn't hide the sarcasm in his voice.

"I don't know."

"I'm just trying to understand you." He sighed, releasing her arm.

"I tried to explain everything last night, but you wouldn't listen."

"I'm listening now." He crossed his arms over his chest and leaned against the counter.

Becca took a deep breath before she began. "I told you that I owed your father some money . . . fifty thousand dollars to be exact." She watched his reaction, but he didn't move a muscle, stoically waiting for her to continue. "I needed the money to breed a horse."

"And I assume that your mare conceived and now you have yourself a Thoroughbred."

Becca nodded.

"Colt or filly?"

She met his gaze boldly. "Filly. Her name is Gypsy Wind."

Brig's jawline hardened. "You told me that much last night. But you neglected to tell me that she's a full-blooded sister to Sentimental Lady."

Becca hid her surprise. "I tried to tell you everything last night. You weren't interested."

In frustration, Brig raked his fingers through his hair. He shifted his eyes away from Becca for just a minute. "I can't believe that you would be so stupid as to make the same mistake twice, *the same damned mistake!*"

"Gypsy Wind is no mistake."

"Then why are you hiding her?"

"I'm not."

"Come on, Rebecca. Don't deny it. If you'd let out the word that *you* were breeding another horse, a full sister to Sentimental Lady, the press would have been on you like fleas on a dog. That's why you hid her, came to a private source for money."

"I came to your father as a last resort."

"Sure you did," was Brig's contemptuous response. "I bet the old man really ate it up, didn't he? He never could pass up the opportunity to pull one over on the press." The smile that tugged at the corners of Brig's mouth didn't touch his eyes. There was a sullen quality, a bitterness, that made his features seem more angular.

Becca's chin lifted and a defiant glimmer rested in her round eyes. "How did you know that Gypsy Wind is Sentimental Lady's sister?"

"Because I knew there was more to the story than what you admitted last night." His raised palm stilled her protests. "And I admit that I didn't want to discuss anything with you last night, including your horse or the money you owed my father." Brig noticed that the defensive gleam in her eyes wavered. "But you did pique my interest, and after my shower I went into the old man's den. That's where I found this." He extracted a neatly folded document from his back pocket.

"The note," she guessed aloud, staring at the yellowed paper.

"That's right." He tossed the note onto the table and it slid across the polished oak surface to rest next to Becca's mug. The figure of fifty thousand dollars was boldly scrawled on the face of the document; Becca's signature attested its authenticity.

As Becca reached for the paper, Brig's words arrested her. "Check out the back." Becca turned the note over and saw Jason Chambers' notation. *Proceeds to be used for breeding of Night Dancer to Gypsy Lady.*

"When did you plan to tell me about her, Becca?"

"I did—"

"Because my father died! What if he hadn't?" Brig's voice was deadly. "How long would you have waited? Until she began racing?"

"I don't know," she whispered honestly.

Brig reached for a chair, turned it around, and dropped into it. He straddled the seat and rested his arms against the back while his eyes impaled her. "Why don't you tell me all about it," he suggested, ignoring the now-cold breakfast. "We've got all weekend, and I can't wait to hear why you took it upon yourself to flirt with tragedy all over again."

Chapter 6

While Becca tried to collect her thoughts, the meal was started and finished in suffocating silence. All of her well-rehearsed speeches, all of her defenses for breeding Gypsy Wind fled under Brig's stony gaze. The tension in the air was difficult to ignore, although Brig tried to appear patient, as if he understood her need for silence.

When they finished breakfast, Brig opened one of the French doors in the small alcove and quietly invited Becca to join him on the broad back porch that ran the length of the cabin. Becca carried her cup of coffee, cradling the warm ceramic in her palms as she stepped outside into the brisk mountain air. She couldn't help but shiver. It was still early in the morning and a chill hung in the late autumn air. Becca took a long sip from her coffee, hoping it would warm her and give her the strength to face Brig with the truth concerning Gypsy Wind. There was little doubt in her mind that Brig would be angry with her and she half-expected him to push her out of his life again and this time keep the horse.

Brig followed Becca onto the porch. He leaned his elbows on the hand-hewn railing and his gray eyes scanned the secluded valley floor. A clear stream curled like a silver snake along a ridge near the edge of the woods. Already the aspens were beginning to lose their golden leaves to the soft wind. Brig's gaze followed the course of the creek and a wistful smile pulled at the corners of his mouth. It was in that stream where he had caught his first native brook trout. He hadn't done it alone. His old man had taught him how to cast and watch for the fish to strike. God, he missed that cuss of a father.

Abruptly Brig brought his wandering thoughts back to the present. He turned to face Rebecca and caught her watching the play of emotions on his face. He had hoped that in the morning light, without the blur of too many drinks, Rebecca Peters would lose her appeal to him, but he had been wrong. Dead wrong. Even the condemning proof of her treachery, the note to his father, couldn't mar her beauty. He supposed that if anything, it had added to her intrigue. Becca had always been a woman of mystique. The six years he had been away from her had given a maturity to her expressive green eyes, which made her captivating. He knew that he shouldn't be susceptible to her, that he should outwardly denounce her, but he couldn't. Instead he tried a more subtle approach. "I guess I should apologize for last night."

"Why?" she asked, observing him over the rim of her cup. Dread began to inch up her spine as she wondered which way the conversation was heading.

"It's been a long week. A lot of problems. I didn't expect to see you last night and I had no intention of getting so carried away."

Why was he apologizing for something so right as making love? "It's all right ... . really."

"I didn't think you would come here."

She shook her head and the sun glinted in the golden strands of her hair. "I know. Look, everything's okay."

"Is it?" A muscle began to jump in his jaw. "Is spending the night with a man so easy for you that you can shrug it off?"

Her gaze hardened. "You know better than that."

"Did you plan last night?"

A hint of doubt flickered in her eyes. "I don't really know," she said honestly. "I ... I don't think so."

"I'm not usually so easily seduced." His voice was cold.

"Neither am I."

For the first time since she had come to him, Brig allowed himself the fleeting luxury of a smile. It was just as she had remembered, slightly off-center and devilishly disarming. "I know," he admitted begrudgingly. He hoisted himself onto the railing and stared at her. His eyes pierced her soul. "Why don't you tell me about your horse."

"She's the most beautiful animal I've ever bred."

"Looks don't count. Remember Kincsem, an ungainly filly who won all fifty-four of the races she entered."

"Gypsy Wind is fast."

"Sentimental Lady was fast."

"But she's stronger than Lady—"

"She'll have to be." Brig's eyes implored her. "Good Lord, Becca. What I can't understand is why you want to put yourself through all of this again. And the horse. Jesus, Becca ... what about your horse? The minute she begins to race the press will be all over her. And you can bet that they won't forget about Sentimental Lady, not for a second! Damn it, the entire nation was affected by Lady's last race." His voice had increased in volume and he could feel the splinters of wood imbedding into his palms as he curled his fingers around the rough wood of the railing. His eyes were angry as he remembered Sentimental Lady. "I just don't understand you, Rebecca Peters . . . I don't know what you're trying to prove." His voice was softer as he added, "Maybe I never did."

Despite Brig's violent display of emotion, Becca remained calm. It was imperative that he understand. "Rebreeding Gypsy Lady to Night Dancer was a logical move," she stated softly. "Hadn't you ever considered it?"

"Never!"

"Your father understood."

Brig's gray eyes flashed dangerously. "My father understood only two things in the past few years: How to make a helluva lot of money and how to spend it on a pretty face."

"You know that's not true."

Brig laughed humorlessly. "Maybe not, but I can't understand for the life of me why he agreed to loan you so much money—just to see it thrown away on some fiasco."

Becca could feel her anger starting to seethe. "Gypsy Wind is no fiasco, Brig. She's probably the best racing filly ever bred."

"You said the same thing about Sentimental Lady."

"And I believed it."

"You were wrong!"

"I wasn't! She was the best!"

"She broke down, Becca! Don't you remember? She couldn't take the pressure—she wasn't strong enough. Her leg snapped! Are you willing to put another horse through that agony?" Brig's eyes had turned a stormy gray.

"It won't happen," she whispered with more conviction than she felt. Something disturbing in Brig's gaze made her confidence waver.

"You said that before."

Becca's stomach was churning with bitter memories of the Lady and the grueling, treacherous race. "In that instance, I was mistaken," she admitted reluctantly.

"And what makes you so sure that this time will be any different?"

"Gypsy Wind is not Sentimental Lady." Becca's voice was thin but determined. Brig recognized the pride and resolve in the tilt of Becca's face.

"You just admitted your mistake with Sentimental Lady."

"We aren't talking about Lady. If we were, I'd probably agree with you. But Gypsy Wind is an entirely different horse."

"A full-blooded sister."

"But she's stronger, Brig, and fast—"

"What about her temperament?" Brig demanded.

For the first time that morning, Becca hedged. "She's a winner. Ian O'Riley is training her. You know that he wouldn't bother with a horse if she didn't have the spirit."

"That was Lady's problem: her spirit. Ian O'Riley should know better than anyone. After all, as her trainer, he paid the price."

"For the last time, we are not talking about Sentimental Lady!"

Brig was pensive as he sat on the railing, his hands supporting his posture. Becca's large green eyes were shining as she talked about the filly. She was proud of Gypsy Wind, sure of her. Brig found himself wanting to believe Rebecca, to trust her as he once had. If only he could. Instead he voiced the question uppermost in his mind. "So why did you come here to tell me about her—why now?"

"I wanted you to know. I didn't want you to hear it from someone else."

"But the old man knew. What if my father hadn't died?"

"I would have come to you."

"When? If that horse is as good as you say she is, why didn't you start her as a two-year-old?"

She avoided his gaze for a moment. "I didn't think she was ready. I don't know when I would have come to you." When she looked up and her eyes met his, they were once again steady. "It would have been soon. I wouldn't have allowed her to race until I had told you about her. I just wasn't sure how to approach you. When I found out that Jason had been killed, I knew I had to see you, as much for myself as for the horse. I wanted to know and see with my own eyes that you were all right."

"You knew that much from the papers."

"I wanted to touch you, Brig, to prove to myself that you were unhurt. I *had* to see for myself. Can't you understand that?" Her honesty rang in the clear air and Brig had to fight the urge to take her into his arms and crush her against his chest.

"Now that you're here, what do you expect of me?"

Becca drew in a deep breath, forcing herself to be calm and think clearly. "I want you to let me race the horse. I'm going to be honest with you, Brig, because I really don't know how else to handle this. I don't own a lot in this world, and most of what I do have is mortgaged to the hilt. But I do own Gypsy Wind, and I'd stake my life on the fact that she's the finest two-year-old alive. When she begins to race, I'll be able to repay you, but not before."

"Are you asking me to forget about the note?" His dark eyes watched her, waited for any emotion to appear on her face.

"No. I'm only asking that you hold onto it a little longer. You can't possibly need the money."

"Do you really think I would try to take your horse away from you?"

She swallowed with difficulty. "I hope not."

His eyes clouded. "You never have understood me, have you?"

"I thought I did once." Becca's throat began to tighten as she looked at him. Why did she still love him with every breath of life within her?

"But you were wrong?" he prodded.

"I never thought you would . . . crucify me the way you did."

"Crucify you? What are you talking about?"

She couldn't hide the incredulous tone in her voice. "You tried to destroy me six years ago."

"I had nothing to do with that—"

"Don't deny it, Brig. Almost single-handedly, you ruined my reputation as a horse breeder."

"No one can tarnish another's reputation. What happened to you was a result of *your* own actions," he spat out angrily.

Becca felt the insult twist in her heart like a dull blade. All these years she had hoped that Brig's condemning silence wasn't what the newspapers had made it. Her hands were shaking and she had to set down the cup of coffee for fear of spilling it. "You really thought I drugged Sentimental Lady?" she asked, her voice barely audible in the still mountain air. Her green eyes accused him of the outright lie.

"I think you know who did."

Becca couldn't resist the bait. "I have my own suspicions," she agreed.

"Of course you do. Because it had to be someone who had access to the horse before the race, someone you employed. Unless of course you injected her yourself."

"You don't believe that!" she cried, desperately holding onto a shred of hope that he could still trust her.

"I didn't want to."

"Then how can you even suggest that I would purposely harm my horse?" Bewilderment and the agony of being unjustly accused twisted her features. Brig lifted his body from the railing and stepped toward Becca. He was so close that she could feel the warmth of his breath against her hair.

"Because I think you know who did, Rebecca, and with your silence, you've become an accomplice to a crime too grotesque and inhumane to understand." Her eyes flashed green fire, but he persisted. "Whether you actually injected Sentimental Lady or not, you were responsible for her well-being and should have protected her against the agony she had to suffer."

Becca reacted so quickly, she didn't have time to think about the result of her actions. Her hand shot up and she flexed her wrist just as her palm found Brig's cheek. "You bastard!" she hissed, unable to restrain her anger.

Brig grabbed her wrist and pulled her roughly to him. "I'm only reminding you of what happened."

"You're twisting the truth to suit yourself."

"Why would I do that, Rebecca? It doesn't make any sense."

"Because you knew that she'd been drugged. Weren't you the one who wanted the race stopped just after the horses were out of the gate?"

"Because Lady hit her head."

"Because you had second thoughts!" she accused, the words biting the cold air.

He jerked her savagely, as if he would have liked to shake her until she began seeing things his way. "Second thoughts?" he repeated, trying to understand her damning stare. His dark eyes narrowed. "What do you mean?"

"I mean that you don't have to lie anymore, Brig. Not with me. There's no one here but you and me, so you may as well confess. Your secret will remain safe. Hasn't it for the last six years?"

The fingers digging roughly into the soft flesh of her upper arms slowly relaxed. A quiet flame of fury burned in Brig's eyes, but the ferocity of his anger ebbed and he slowly released her. His whisper was rough and demanding. "What secret?" he asked. To his credit, he was a consummate actor. The confusion flushing his face seemed genuine.

Rebecca could feel tears pooling in her eyes, but she blinked them back, reminding herself not to trust this man who had passed his guilt on to her.

"What secret?" he asked again. A portion of his

anger had returned as he guessed the twisted path of her defense.

She pleaded with him to be honest with her; her eyes begged for the decency of the truth. "You know that I didn't do anything to Sentimental Lady, Brig, and you also know that no one employed by me would have dared to harm that horse. The reason you know it is that you were the one who paid someone to inject her."

"What?" he thundered.

"There's no reason to deny it."

"You're out of your mind!"

"Not anymore. I was once, when I thought I could trust you."

His anger faded into uncertainty. "You've actually got yourself believing this, haven't you?"

"It's the only thing that makes any sense—"

"You mean it's the only way you can absolve yourself of the guilt."

Becca's slim shoulders sagged, as if an insurmountable weight had been placed upon her. The reasoning she had hoped would prove false came easily to her lips. "You were the one who had invested all the money in Sentimental Lady's training, and you were the one who received the lion's share of the insurance against her," Becca pointed out. When Brig tried to interrupt, she ignored him, allowing the truth to spill from her in an unbroken wave. "If Sentimental Lady hadn't broken down, but gone on to win that race, you knew that she would be disqualified because of the drugs. They would have shown up in the post-race urine sample. Winsome would have come out the victor. Either way you won. Once again, the stables of Brig Chambers would have come out on top!"

"You scheming little bitch!" he muttered through tightly clenched teeth. "You've got it all figured out, haven't you? It may have taken you six years to come up with an alternative story, but I've got to give you credit, it's a good one."

"Because it's true."

It was difficult to keep his anger in check, especially under the deluge of lies Becca had rained on him, but Brig Chambers was usually a patient man and he forced himself to remain as calm as possible under the circumstances. He told himself to relax and with the exception of a tiny muscle working in the corner of his jaw, he seemed outwardly undisturbed. He watched Rebecca intently. Damn her for her serene beauty, damn her for her quick mind, and damn her for her pride, a pride that couldn't suffer the pain of the naked truth. He hoped that he appeared indifferent when he spoke again.

"You've convinced yourself that this story you've fabricated really happened.

"It did."

"No way. If I wanted Winsome to come out a victor, I wouldn't have spent so much money on the Lady."

"And if you hadn't spent so much time with her, with me, there wouldn't have been all of the hype. The press and the public might not have demanded a match race."

"What good was the race to me? I had the best three-year-old colt of the year. If it was money I was after, I could have sold Winsome to a syndicate and put him out for stud, instead of gambling on another race."

"But he wouldn't have been nearly as valuable."

"What if he had lost?"

"You made sure that he didn't." Her voice was cold and nearly convincing.

"I didn't touch Sentimental Lady—"

"But you know who did," she cut in quickly, sensing his defeat. "You paid them off." Her eyes, lifted to his, were glistening with tears.

For a moment his fists doubled and he slammed one violently against a cedar post supporting the roof of the porch. Startled birds flew out of a nearby bush. He stopped, and restrained his fury before walking back to her. When his hands lifted to touch her chin, they were unsteady, and when his thumbs gently brushed one of her hot tears from her eye, she thought she would crumble against him. She wanted to tell him nothing mattered, that the pain of the past should be forgotten; but pride forbade her.

"Don't twist the truth and let it come between us," he pleaded, his voice as ragged as Becca's own fragile breath. He gently took her into his arms and folded her tightly against his chest. "It's kept us apart too long."

Pressed against him, Becca could hear the steady beat of his heart. She could feel the comfort and strength of his arms around her, shielding her from the pain of the past. She understood his need to be one with her, but she couldn't forget what had held them so desperately apart. Perhaps it was because she had been so young and vulnerable. Maybe she hadn't had the maturity or courage to handle the situation surrounding Sentimental Lady's death.

When Brig's uncompromising silence had condemned her for allowing someone to drug her horse, she should have been more vocal in her denial. When the press had hounded her for the truth, she should have held a press conference to end the brutal conjecture about the accident. If she had, perhaps the newspapers wouldn't have had such a field day with the coverage of the tragic incident. As it was, it had taken months for the story to die down. Even after the investigation, when Ian O'Riley had proved by a preponderance of evidence that he made every reasonable effort to protect the horses in his care from any foul deed, the reporters wouldn't give up.

If Becca had been stronger, she might have been able to deny, more vehemently, any knowledge of the crime. As it was, with the death of the great horse and the pain of Brig's accusations, Becca had taken refuge from the public eye. Her brother Dean had helped her piece together her life and slowly she had regained her courage and determination. The gossip had finally quieted. She and Dean had survived, but Brig's brutal insinuations hung over her head like a dark, foreboding cloud.

The worst part of it was that Brig knew she was innocent. He had to. As Becca's tired mind had sifted through the evidence of those last painful days before the race, it became glaringly apparent that Brig Chambers was the one who would most benefit by drugging Sentimental Lady. Only one reasonable solution could be deduced: Brig Chambers paid someone to inject the horse.

In the first few weeks after the race, Becca thought she would die from the torture of Brig's deception and accusations. She hadn't been interested in anything in her life when she realized that Brig, or someone who worked for him, had purposely set her up. Because she had been so devastated by Brig's ruthlessness, and because she didn't know how to defend herself, Becca had unwittingly taken the blame for the deed by her silence. There hadn't been enough evidence to indict anyone in the crime, but the scandal and mystery of

Sentimental Lady's accident remained to cripple Rebecca's career. If it hadn't been for her brother Dean and his care for her, Becca doubted that she would have ever gathered the courage to return to horse racing and the life she loved.

As she stood in the shelter of Brig's arms, she knew that she should hate him, but she was unable. Her bitterness toward him had softened over the years, and then, when for a few lonely, wretched hours she had thought him dead, she finally faced the painful truth that she still loved him. As she gazed upward at him, wondering at the confusion in his brow, she agonized over the fact that he had treated her so callously. How could he have abused her? After all, she had held her tongue and when the press had accused her unjustly, she hadn't defended herself by smearing his name. Despite the silent rage and humiliation, she hadn't lowered herself to his level nor dragged his famous name through the mud. Meticulously, she had avoided fanning the fires of gossip as well as steadfastly refusing to give the columnists the slightest inklings of her side of the argument. It was no one's business. Her affair with Brig had been beautiful and intimate. She wasn't about to tarnish that beauty by making their personal lives public. Her dignity wouldn't allow it. Instead she had gone home and licked her wounds with the help of her brother. Dean was right; by all reasonable standards she should loathe Brig Chambers for what he did to her.

Why then did the feel of his arms around her give her strength? Why did the steady beat of his heart reassure her? Why did she secretly long to live in the warmth of his smile?

They stood holding each other in the autumn sunlight, as if by the physical closeness of their bodies they could bridge the black abyss of mistrust that silently held their souls apart. They didn't speak for a few breathless moments, content with only the sound of their hearts beating so closely together and the soft whisper of the cool breeze rushing through the pines.

"I've never stopped loving you," Brig whispered in a moment of condemning weakness. The muscles in his arms tightened around Becca with his confession. He hated himself intensely at that moment. For six years he had ignored his feelings for Rebecca, hidden them from the world and from himself. In one night of revived passion, she had managed to expose his innermost secrets.

Becca's knees sagged. So long she had waited to hear those words of love from this proud man. She had yearned for this moment, and when it was finally hers, she grasped it fleetingly, only to release it. The words sounded too hollow, a convenient excuse for a night of passion. "I don't think we should talk about love," she managed to say, though her throat was unreasonably dry.

His hands moved upward to her chin and tilted her face to his. Dark eyes, gray as the early morning fog, gazed into hers. "Why not?"

"Because you and I have different meanings for the word. We always have."

His dark eyebrows drew pensively together. "I suppose you might be right," he reluctantly agreed. "But I can't believe that you're denying what you feel for me."

"I've always known that I'm attracted to you and I thought that I loved you once . . . sometimes I think I still do."

"But you're not sure?"

She wanted to fall back into his arms and reassure him, to pledge the love she felt welling in her heart, but reason held her words at bay. "I'm just . . . trying not to get caught in the same trap I fell into before."

A fleeting expression of pain crossed his face, but was quickly hidden beneath the hardening of his rugged features. "Is that what I did to you—'trapped you'?" The thin thread of patience in his voice threatened to snap.

"I trapped myself."

"And you're not about to let it happen again."

Her attempt at a frail smile faded. "I try not to repeat my mistakes."

"With the one glaring exception of Gypsy Wind."

Becca pursed her full lips. "If there's one thing I'm sure of in this world, it's that Gypsy Wind is no mistake."

"What about your feelings, Rebecca? Can't you trust them?"

"About horses, yes."

"But not men?" He cocked an angry black brow.

"They're more difficult," she admitted.

He stepped back from her, leaned insolently against the railing, and crossed his arms over his chest. *"They?* I'm not talking about the other men in your life, Rebecca. I'm just trying to sort out how you feel about me . . . about what happened last night."

She drew in an unsteady breath. "That's not easy."

His eyes narrowed and the gray pupils glittered like newly forged steel. Every muscle in his body tensed. "So what you're attempting to say is that you have become the kind of woman who keeps all of her emotions under tight rein. Everything you do is well thought out in advance."

"I mean that I try not to see the world through rose-colored glasses anymore—"

He cut her off. "So you've become a bitter, calculating woman who works men into her life when it's convenient, or when she needs a favor."

It took every ounce of strength in Becca's heart to rise above the insult. "I hope not."

Again he mocked her as he continued, "The kind of woman who can hop into bed with a man as part of a business deal."

Her face flushed with anger. "Stop it, Brig. I'm not like that. You know it as well as I do."

"I don't think I know you at all. Not anymore. I was hoping that what we did last night meant something more to you than a quick one-night stand."

"It does."

"What?" he demanded. His voice was low, his eyes dangerous, his jaw determined.

"It would be easy for me to excuse what we did last night as an act of love."

"Excuse? For God's sake, woman, I'm too old for excuses!"

"Brig, what I feel for you is very strong and sometimes I delude myself into believing that I still love you," she began hesitantly. "What happened last night happened because of a set of circumstances and the fact that we care for each other—"

"Care for?" he echoed. "What the hell is that supposed to mean? 'Care for' is something you do for an elderly aunt!"

"Don't insult me, Brig. I said that I care for you; it means exactly what it implies."

Brig ran his fingers impatiently through his dark hair. Hot spurts of jealousy clouded his thinking. "Tell me this, Becca, just how many men have you *cared for* in the last six years?"

Becca's eyes flashed dangerously. "Is that what you want to know? Why don't you come straight to the point and ask me how many men I've slept with?"

"One and the same," he threw back.

"Not necessarily."

"Okay, then, how many men have you slept with?" He watched the disbelief and anger contort her even features. Wide eyes accused him of being the bastard he was. The thought of another man kissing those lips or touching her golden hair made his stomach knot.

"That's none of your business, Brig. You gave up all of those possessive rights when you threw me out of your life."

"You walked away."

Her lower lip began to tremble, but she held back her hot angry tears. "I had to, Brig. Because you thought so little of me that you honestly contended that *I* destroyed Sentimental Lady. Even with everything we had shared together, you never trusted me. In my opinion, without trust, there is no love." Her voice cracked, but she continued. "Just who the hell do you think you are? You have no right to ask me about my love life."

"I'm just *someone who cares for you,*" he mocked disgustedly.

Becca felt her entire body shake. "You really can be a bastard when you want to be."

"Only when I'm pushed to the limit."

"It's reassuring to know that I bring out the best in you," she tossed out heatedly. She could feel her anger coloring her cheeks. "I think this discussion is over. We don't have much to say to each other, do we?" She pivoted on her heel and started toward the door. As quick as a springing cat, Brig was beside her. His grasp on her arm forced her to spin around and face the rage contorting his chiseled features. His lips were thin, his eyes ruthlessly dark.

"You'd like to run out on me again, wouldn't you? After all, it is what you do best."

"Let's just say that I don't like to waste my time arguing with you. There's no point to it."

"Counterproductive, is it? Not like sleeping with me?"

She slid her eyes disdainfully upward. "Let it go, Brig. We have nothing more to discuss."

Angrily, he jerked on her arm and she lost her balance. She fell against him and her hair came forward in a cloud of honey-colored silk. "I've never met a woman who could infuriate me so," Brig uttered through his clenched teeth. For the most part his anger was leveled at himself for his weakness.

Becca tossed her hair out of her resentful green eyes. "And you've met your share of them, haven't you? What about Melanie DuBois? Didn't she ever 'push you to the limit'?" The minute the jealous implication passed her lips, Becca knew she'd made a grave error in judgment. The rage in Brig's eyes took a new dimension, one of piteous disgust.

"You really know how to hit below the belt." Brig released her as if holding Becca was suddenly repulsive. She rubbed her upper arms in an effort to erase the pain he had caused.

"I'm sorry," she whispered. He had walked away from her, putting precious space between their bodies. "I had no right to say anything about her." Becca detested anything as petty as jealousy, and she realized that her remark about the dead woman was not only childishly petulant, but also deplorable and undignified. She had to make him understand. "Brig—"

He waved off her apology with the back of his hand. "Don't worry about it." His jaw hardened and his lips thinned as he pressed his hands into the back pockets of his jeans.

"I just didn't mean to say anything that mean." Her animosity faded. "I . . . I don't want to argue with you and I don't want our discussions to deteriorate into a verbal battlefield; where we just try and wound each other for the sake of some shallow victory." She took a step toward him, wanting to touch him, but holding her hands at her sides.

His voice was coldy distant. "You didn't wound me, if that's what you're afraid of."

"What I'm afraid of is that I look like a hypocrite."

He arched his eyebrows, silently encouraging her to continue.

"I didn't want to discuss my . . . past relationships with men, and then in the next moment I brought up one of the women in your life."

He shrugged. "Forget about it."

"But I know that you and Melanie were close—"

"I was never close to that woman," he cut in sharply.

Becca was taken aback. "But I thought—"

Again he interrupted, this time more harshly. "You thought what the rest of the world thought, what Melanie DuBois wanted the world to think. If you would have had the guts to come to me before my father was killed, before your back was up against the wall, you would have realized that everything in those cheap gossip tabloids was a hoax. A carefully arranged hoax."

"You never publicly denied it."

"Isn't that a little like the pot calling the kettle black? Besides, why would I? Any statement or contradiction I might have made would only have worsened an already bad situation. I decided it just wasn't worth the effort." Brig read the look of doubt on Becca's elegant face. "I can't deny that initially I was attracted to Melanie. Hell, she was a beautiful woman. But it didn't take me long to figure out what she was really after."

Brig paused, but Becca didn't interrupt, afraid to learn more than she wanted to know about the glamorous woman romantically linked to Brig, and yet fascinated with Brig's denials. A severe smile made him appear older than his thirty-five years.

"Anything you read about Melanie DuBois was precisely engineered by Ms. DuBois and that snake she called an agent." Brig leaned more closely to Becca. He withdrew his hands from his pockets and captured her shoulders with the warmth of his fingertips. She felt the muscles in her back begin to relax. "Don't tell me you believe everything you read in the papers." His gaze was coldly cynical.

Becca cocked her head and eyed him speculatively. Her hair fell over his arm. She knew he was referring to her vehement denouncement of the press coverage of Sentimental Lady's last race. "Of course not," she whispered.

"Then trust me. I have never had anything other than a passing interest in Melanie DuBois."

Her wistful smile trembled. "I'm sorry I made that stupid remark and brought her up. It was . . . unkind."

Brig recognized the flicker of doubt that darkened Becca's green eyes. "You still don't believe me, do you?"

"I'm just trying to understand, Brig. If Melanie had no connection with you, why was she in the plane with your father?"

For a moment he returned her confused stare: She seemed so vulnerable, so genuinely perplexed. He brushed aside an errant strand of her blond hair, pausing only slightly to rub it gently between his fingers. "Do you want me to tell you all about Melanie?" he asked softly.

She hesitated only briefly. "No." It wouldn't be fair. Hadn't she just told him that her love life was none of his business? She had no right to his.

"What if I told you it was important to me that you know?" His eyes moved from the lock of hair he had been studying and gazed intently into hers. He pushed the golden strands back into place.

"I'd listen," she sighed.

His intense gray eyes didn't leave hers. "I met Melanie at a cocktail party in Manhattan. It was one of those sophisticated affairs that everyone dreads but still attends."

"Not exactly your cup of tea."

"That's right. But I was forced to go. Business. Melanie was there. After I'd made the proper appearance and taken care of the Chambers Oil business, I got ready to leave. Melanie came up to me and asked me to take her home. I complied."

Becca's throat became dry, but something in his gaze reassured her. A sick feeling took hold of her as she realized she didn't want to hear about the other women in Brig's life. "I understand," she murmured, hoping to close the subject.

"No, you don't."

"I don't want to hear what happened, Brig. It's your business and I don't want to know about any of your affairs."

"Yes, you do," he persisted. "The business deal had gone sour, and I was dead tired from a flight earlier from the Middle East. That night I had no interest in Melanie."

"But there were other nights."

"Not with her."

Becca shook her head. "Brig, just let it alone. The woman is dead and I don't want to hear about it. Not this morning."

"It's important, Rebecca, because I never did sleep with Melanie."

"I find that hard to believe."

"That's understandable. She was a gorgeous woman . . . desirable, I suppose, but I just wasn't interested."

"Why not?"

"There wasn't any chemistry between us. Do you understand that?" His fingers touched her neck, stroking the soft skin familiarly. It was a warm caress shared only by lovers.

"Yes," she admitted. How many times had she dated wonderful, kind, intelligent men and found that she felt no passion for them. It was as if she was cursed to love only Brig. Only Brig had been able to catch her soul. He looked into her eyes as if he could see into the darkest corners of her mind.

"At first I made the mistake of thinking that Melanie was all right. She was a little vain, but I chalked that up to her being a model. We dated casually, but it wasn't anything serious. The papers got wind of it and blew it out of proportion, but I really didn't care. Not until I understood what it was that Melanie really wanted."

"Which was?"

"My father." Brig let the full impact of his statement settle upon her before continuing. "As a model, Melanie was hot, starting to climb toward the pinnacle of her profession. But she wasn't getting any younger, and modeling is a young woman's game. Melanie was smart enough to realize that her career would only last a few short years at best. She liked the good life. Even with the money she earned, she was always in debt. It takes a lot of cash to keep a townhouse in New York, a condo in L.A., and a cabin in Aspen. That woman could spend money faster than the treasury department could print it."

"And so she became romantically involved with your father," Becca guessed with a sickening feeling of disgust.

"More than that. She was pressuring Dad into marrying her."

"But the press . . . why didn't they know? This sounds like something the gossip columnists would get wind of."

"Melanie had to be patient. Dad insisted on it." Brig looked away and squinted against the rising sun. "Patience wasn't Melanie's long suit, but she played her cards right. When she knew I wasn't interested in her, she moved in on Dad. He was probably her target all along. Anyway, Melanie had to wait in line."

Becca understood. "Because he was involved with Nanette Walters."

Brig frowned and shook his head. "I can't for the life of me understand Jason's choice in women, not since Mom died. But there it was. And even though

Nanette was just one in a long succession of women, my father cared for her." Brig's hands slid down Becca's spine and he pulled her close to him. "Jason made sure that all the women in his life were . . . comfortable. He gave Nanette her walking papers along with a sizable gift of jewelry."

"Why are you telling me all of this?" she asked, aware of the soft touch of his hands against the small of her back.

"I wish I knew," he admitted, kissing the top of her head.

Chapter 7

Nothing was resolved, and, for the moment, it didn't seem to matter. Becca accepted Brig's silent invitation to stay with him for the remainder of the weekend. Upon his suggestion, she donned her jeans and sneakers and they hiked together through the leaf-strewn trails of the lower slopes, holding hands and flushing out a frightened doe and twin fawns who quickly bounded out of sight and into the protection of the dense woods. Brig held her hand warmly in his and with the other, pointed out secret treasures from his boyhood. The abandoned tree house he had unskillfully crafted at twelve was missing more than a few of its floorboards. It looked weathered and discarded in the ancient maple tree. The bend in the path where he had discovered a broken arrowhead was now overgrown. The deep pool in the mountain stream was as crystal clear as it had ever been, though it had been twenty years since he had last caught a native trout in it or swum naked along its bank.

Becca felt that Brig was showing her a secret side to his nature. A dimension she had never before been al-

lowed to see. It warmed her heart to think that he
would share his fondest memories with her. She
walked with him until her muscles ached, and they
laughed into each other's eyes as if they were the only
man and woman in the universe. They were alone,
male and female, basking in shared affection, afraid to
call their feelings love.

When twilight began to darken the hillside, they
raced back to the cabin. Becca lost by a miserable margin, and Brig's gray eyes danced with his victory. She
pretended wounded anger, but he saw through her ruse
and as she attempted to brush past him into the cabin,
his hand shot out and captured her waist. Her head
tilted backward and her golden hair fell away from her
face, framing her twinkling green eyes in tousled,
tawny curls. Her cheeks were pink from the cool fresh
air and her lips parted into a becoming smile more sensual than any Brig had ever seen.

"You love to win, don't you?" she asked.

"I love to be with you," he responded, his eyes darkening mysteriously.

Her arms entwined around his neck. "I can't think
of another place I'd rather be."

"That, Ms. Peters, is an invitation I can't ignore," he
replied, tightening his grip on her waist and bending
his head to mold her chilled lips to his. She closed her
eyes and let the taste of him linger on her lips. She savored every moment she shared with him. Too long
she had waited for the intimate pleasure of his touch.

His fingers spanned her waist to grip her possessively. His tongue slid between the serrated edges of her
teeth to explore the warmth of her mouth. He groaned
when the tip of her tongue found his. The pressure of
his mouth against hers hardened with the passion that
fired his blood.

When he lifted his head, it was to smile wickedly into her passion-glazed eyes. "Sometimes I wonder if I'll ever get enough of you," he mused against her ear.

"I hope not," she breathed fervently.

They walked into the cabin silently, arms entwined, bodies barely touching. While Brig started the fire, Becca managed to put together hodgepodge sandwiches from the dwindling supply of food in the refrigerator. Together they drank chilled wine, nibbled on the sandwiches, and warmed their bare feet near the glowing embers of the crackling fire. The tangy scent of burning pitch filled the air. Sitting on the floor, her head nestled against Brig's shoulder, Becca felt more at home than she had in years.

She watched him as he finished the last of his wine. The firelight sharpened the lines of his face, but even in the hard light, the charm of his smile was undiminished. The last six years had added a rugged quality to his masculinity. He was as lean as he had ever been and his hair was still near black with only the slightest sprinkling of gray.

He turned his gaze to her and found her staring intently at his profile. His eyelids lowered and his smile became provocative. "You're an interesting woman, Rebecca," he whispered hoarsely. With his finger he traced the line of her jaw and let it lower to the column of her neck. His finger stopped its descent at the hollow of her throat where it began drawing sketchy, lazy circles. "I'm not sure I like what you do to me."

Her eyebrows raised, prompting him onward. She couldn't find her voice, it was lost in the soft swirl of emotions generated by his feather-soft touch.

"I'm not in control when I'm around you, not in complete command of myself."

His fingers found the top button of her blouse, released it, and toyed with the edge of her collar. Becca closed her eyes and she felt her body warming from the inside out, heard the ragged sound of her uneven breathing as he unhooked another button and then another. She had to draw in her breath quickly when his hand slipped under the soft fabric of her bra to lovingly cup a breast.

"Oh, Brig," she sighed, turning her body, twisting in his arms in order to move closer to him. She felt her nipple harden, and moaned in contentment, when his head lowered and he took her breast in his mouth. The soft movements of his tongue and lips comforted her and helped increase the thundering tempo of her heartbeat.

Slowly he undressed her and then when she was naked, he discarded his own clothes. He lowered himself beside her, letting the hard length of his body mold against the soft tissues of hers. His arms wrapped around her, his hands kneaded the soft muscles in her back. "You're mine," he whispered roughly against her neck. His lips warmed a trail of hungry kisses down her throat, over the hill of her breasts, around her navel. "You've always been mine."

The possessive sound of his voice made her blood thunder in her ears and the moist warm heat from his swollen lips ignited her skin. She ached to be a part of him. The void within her yearned to be filled with the depth of his passion. She began to yield with the persuasive touch of his hands on her buttocks.

"Stay with me," he pleaded. Heavy-lidded eyes held hers in a heated gaze that promised a lifetime of love. If only she could believe those eyes.

"Forever," she whispered, pushing aside her doubts and letting herself become swept up in the tide of rising passion. She felt the weight of his body as he shifted to part her legs and claim once again what had always been his.

Sunday afternoon came far too quickly. Isolated in the cozy mountain cabin, Becca had felt secluded from the rest of the world. She had forced herself to forget the pain of the past and the brutal anger of her argument with Brig concerning Gypsy Wind. Now it was time to face the truth and unwrap the shielding cocoon of false security she had willingly used to cover herself from the pain of past deceits.

From her vantage point in the kitchen, she could look out the window and see Brig. He was sitting on the porch steps, gazing intently across the valley floor. He rested his elbows on his knees and cradled a cup of steaming coffee in his hands. His wavy hair was rumpled, and despite the fact that he had shaved earlier, already there was evidence of his beard darkening his hard jawline. He squinted past the rising fog and his breath misted in the crisp autumn air.

He must have heard her footsteps as she approached. Though he didn't turn his head to look in her direction, he spoke. His eyes remained distant. "You've come to tell me that it's time you left," he stated flatly.

She sat down next to him, wedging her body between his and one of the strong supports for the roof. "We can't hide up here forever." She huddled her arms around her torso. Though wearing a moss-colored bulky knit sweater, the chill in the air made her shiver.

"I suppose not." Again his voice was toneless. He took a long scalding sip of his coffee.

"It would be nice to spend the rest of our lives up

here," she mused aloud while watching the flight of ducks heading southward.

"But impractical."

"And irresponsible."

His mouth quirked downward. "That's right, isn't it? We both have pressing responsibilities."

She tilted her head and studied his features. This morning he seemed suddenly cold and distant. "Is something wrong?"

"What could be wrong?"

"I don't know . . . but you look as if something's bothering you."

"Any guesses as to what it might be?"

Her smile faded. "Gypsy Wind."

"That's a good start." Brig's lips compressed into a tight, uncompromising line.

Becca's heart missed a beat. "What do you want to do with her?"

"Nothing."

"Nothing?" she repeated.

"I don't want you to race her, Becca. I don't want you to go through all of that pain again."

"A race doesn't have to end in pain and death."

"You're tempting fate."

"Don't tell me you believe in that nonsense. I've never thought of you as a man who put stock in fate or destiny, or whatever else you might call it."

"Not usually. But we're not dealing with a usual set of circumstances here." He set his cup down and grabbed her by the shoulders as if he intended to shake some sense into her. "Damn it, Becca. You don't have to prove anything to me or the rest of the world. There's no need to try and purge yourself of this thing."

"I'm not," she argued, her face tilted defiantly. "I'm only attempting to do what any respectable breeder would if he were in my shoes. I'm trying to race the finest filly ever bred."

"Forget it!"

Becca's anger flashed in her eyes like green lightning. Her fingers dug into her ribs. "Just what is it you expect me to do?"

The severity in his gaze faded. "I want you to hang it up," he implored. His fingers were gentle on her shoulders as he tried to persuade her. "Sell Gypsy Wind if you have to, or better yet, keep her, but for God's sake and hers, don't let her race!"

"That's crazy."

"It might be the sanest thing I've ever suggested."

"It's impossible. Gypsy Wind was bred to run."

"She was bred to absolve you of Sentimental Lady's death."

The insult stung, but she didn't let go of her emotions. "There's no point in arguing about this," she stated, attempting to rise. His hands restrained her.

"There's more." His voice was low.

"More to what?"

"I want you to stay with me."

"Oh, Brig," she said, thinking of a thousand reasons to stay. "Don't do this to me. You know I want to stay with you . . ." Tears began to gather behind her eyes.

"But you can't?"

She shook her head painfully, thinking of Starlight Farm, her brother, Dean, and Gypsy Wind. She had worked six long, tedious years to get where she had, with no help from Brig Chambers. In the beauty of one quiet weekend, he expected her to change all of that. "I've got to go home."

He struggled with a weighty decision. His eyes grew dark. "Stay with me. Make your home with me. Be my wife."   .

The tears that had pooled began to spill from her eyes and her chin trembled. "I wish I could, Brig," she said. "But it's just not possible. You know it as well as I."

"Because of Sentimental Lady."

"Because you lied to the press. You accused me of killing the horse—"

"I knew that you didn't intend to kill her. I never for a moment thought that you intended to hurt her."

"You know that I didn't hurt her."

"But someone who worked for you did."

"Is that what you're doing? Trying to convince me that it was one of the grooms . . . or maybe Ian O'Riley . . . or how about my brother, Dean, or the vet? You know who did it, Brig. Don't point the finger somewhere else. I might have been gullible enough to believe you once, but not any longer."

"Becca, I'm telling you the truth. Why can't you accept that?"

His eyes were steely gray, but clear, his expression exasperated. Becca longed to trust him. She wanted to believe anything he told her. "Maybe because you never came after me."

"Only because you didn't want to see me."

"That's a lie."

"I called, Rebecca. You refused to speak to me."

Becca shook her head, trying to dodge his insulting lies. "You never called. Don't start lying to me, Brig. It's too hard a habit to break."

The pressure on her arms increased. "I did call you, damn it. I talked with your brother once and that old trainer O'Riley a couple of times. I even talked with your cook, or housemaid, or whatever she is."

Doubt replaced her anger. "You talked to Martha? When?"

"I can't remember exactly."

"But she's been gone for over five years."

"I spoke to her about six months after the accident," Brig replied thoughtfully. "It was the second call I'd made."

Becca drew in her breath. "No one told me that you'd phoned."

Brig's eyes narrowed suspiciously. "And that's why you didn't phone me back?"

"I couldn't very well return what I'd never received."

"Then someone—no, make that everyone in your house is lying to you."

"Or you are," she thought aloud.

His fingers carefully cupped her chin. "Why would I? What purpose would it serve. As soon as you go back to California you could check it out."

"I don't know."

"Face it, Becca. Someone is covering up. Probably the same person who drugged Sentimental Lady."

"It just doesn't make any sense. Why would anyone working with me to make Sentimental Lady a winner want to throw the race?"

Brig got up and began pacing on the weathered floorboards of the porch. He ran his fingers thoughtfully through his hair. "I don't know," he said quietly. "Unless someone had it in for you. Did anyone have an ax to grind with you? It could be something that you might think insignificant like . . . an argument over a raise . . . or the firing of a friend."

Becca rested her forehead on her palm and forced her weary mind to go backward in time, past the ugly race. It was futile. She shook her head slowly.

Brig was desperate. He came back to her and forced her eyes to meet the power of his gaze. "You've got to think, Rebecca. Someone deliberately tried to keep us apart, probably for the single reason of keeping the truth of the race secret. As long as we suspected each other, we wouldn't think past our suspicions. We wouldn't be able to find the real culprit, even if he left a trail of clues a mile long."

"But the racing commission . . . certainly its investigation would have discovered the truth."

"Not necessarily—not if the culprit were clever. And remember, the commission was more concerned about Sentimental Lady's recovery than the drugging. By the time all of the havoc had quieted, the culprit could have covered his tracks."

She wanted to believe him but couldn't think past the six lonely years she had spent in the shadow of that last damning race without Brig's strength or support. "I don't know," she whispered. "It all seems so far-fetched."

"No more so than your half-baked accusations that I had something to do with it!"

"But why? Why would anyone want to disqualify the Lady?"

Brig closed his eyes for a moment and tried to clear his head. Nothing was making any sense. "I don't know." His eyes snapped open. "But you must. Think, Rebecca, think!"

"I have, Brig. For the past six years I've hardly thought of anything else. And the only logical answer to the question of who injured Sentimental Lady was you."

"But you don't believe that anymore, do you?"

Her smile was thin. "I don't know what to believe. But if it's any consolation, I never wanted to think that you had anything to do with it."

"But you still have doubts."

She looked bravely into his eyes. "No."

For the first time that morning, the hint of a smile lightened his features. He took her into his arms, and held her body close to his. The power of his embrace supported her. "Then you'll stay with me?"

"Not yet," she said, dreading the sound of her own voice.

The arms around her relaxed and Brig stepped away from her. "Sometimes I don't think I know what you want, lady, but I assume this has something to do with your filly. You still intend to race her, don't you, despite what happened to Sentimental Lady."

"I have to." Couldn't Brig understand? Gypsy Wind had more than mere potential for winning races—she was a champion. Becca would risk her reputation on it.

"No one's holding a gun to your head."

Becca put her hands on her hips and tried a different approach. "Why don't you come to the farm and see first hand what it is that makes Gypsy so special? Come and watch her work out. See for yourself her power, the grace of her movements, the exhilaration in her eyes when she's given her head. Don't judge her before you've seen her."

Brig tossed the idea over in his mind. His work schedule was impossible. He had no time for horses or horse racing. He'd ended that folly six years ago. But Rebecca Peters was another thing altogether. He wanted her. More than he had wanted her six years ago. More than he had ever wanted anything. He saw the look of pride on her face and he noticed the defiant way she stood as if ready to refute anything he might say. Thoughtfully, he rubbed his thumb slowly under his jaw. "What if I disagree with you?"

"You won't." Becca wondered if she looked as determined as she sounded.

Brig cocked his head but didn't argue. "If I do decide to go to California and I think that Gypsy Wind is unsound, will you promise not to race her and give up this foolish dream?"

"Not on your life." Her eyes glittered with fierce determination.

"And you're not afraid that someone might do to her what was done to Sentimental Lady."

"I've been racing horses ever since Sentimental Lady's death. The incident hasn't recurred."

Brig's voice was edged in steel. "Then I guess we're at an impasse."

"Only if you want to be." Her hand reached out and her fingers touched his arm. "Don't shut me out, Brig. Not now. I don't think I'm asking too much of you. Please come and see my horse. Reserve your judgment until then. If you think she's not as fine as I've been telling you, we'll work something out."

"Such as?"

"I'll find a way to repay your loan within the year. Is that fair?"

"I suppose so. Now, what about my proposition? Will you marry me?"

"Give it time; Brig. We both need time to learn to love and trust each other again. Six years is a long time to harbor the kinds of feelings we've had for each other. You can't wash them away in one weekend in the mountains."

"Nor can you prove to the world that you're one of the best Thoroughbred breeders in the country. I was wrong about you, Rebecca. You haven't changed at all. You're still giving me the same flimsy excuse you did the last time I asked you to marry me. I'm not a man who's known for his patience, nor am I the kind of man who gets a kick out of rejection. I've asked you twice to marry me, and I won't do it again."

Becca struggled with her pride. When she spoke her voice was strangely detached and the words of reason seemed distant. "I didn't come to you to try and coerce a marriage proposal from you, Brig, nor did I intend to have another affair with you. All I wanted was to know that you were safe and to tell you about Gypsy Wind. I've done those things and I've also told you that I intend to repay my note to your father. Business is done. My plane leaves in less than four hours from Denver. I have to go."

His face was a mask of indifference. "Just remember that you made your own choices today. You're the one who will have to live with them."

Chapter 8

The trip back to Starlight Breeding farm was uneventful, and Becca had to force herself to face the realization that she had no future with Brig Chambers. If ever she had, it was gone. She had thrown it away. Becca knew that Brig cared for her, in his own way, but she also knew that he didn't trust her and probably never would. The best thing to do was to forget about him and concentrate on paying back the debt to him as quickly as possible. She frowned to herself as she unpacked her suitcase. Forgetting about Brig and what they had shared together was more easily said than done. In the last six years she had never once forgotten the tender way in which he would look into her eyes, or his gentle caress.

"Cut it out," she mumbled to herself. The last thing she should do was brood over a future that wasn't meant to be. With forced determination, she pulled on her favorite pair of faded jeans and started toward the paddock. The first order of business was Gypsy Wind.

Becca clenched her teeth together as she thought about training Gypsy Wind to be the best Thoroughbred filly ever raced. She may have already made a monumental mistake by not racing the filly as a two-year-old, and if she were honest with herself it had something to do with Brig and the fact that, at the time, he didn't know about Gypsy Wind. At least the secret was now in the open, and Becca vowed silently to herself that she would find a way to make Gypsy Wind a winner with or without Brig's approval.

She found Ian O'Riley in the tack room. His short fingers were running along the smooth leather reins of a bridle last worn by Sentimental Lady. He turned his attention toward the door when Becca entered.

"I heard you were back," he said with a smile.

"Just got in a couple of hours ago."

Ian's smile faded. "And how did it go . . . with Brig, I mean?"

Becca tossed her blond braid over her shoulder and shrugged. "As well as can be expected, I guess." She took a seat on a scarred wooden chair near the trophy case. The award closest to her was now covered with dust, but Becca recognized it as belonging to Sentimental Lady for her record-breaking win of The New York Racing Association's Acorn Stakes. Absently, Becca rubbed the dust off the trophy.

"What does he think of Gypsy Wind?"

"Not much," Becca admitted. "Oh, Ian, he thinks I was foolish to breed her. He accused me of trying to absolve myself of her death."

"He thinks that's why you did it?"

Becca nodded mutely.

"And he's got you believing it, too."

Becca shook her head and put the trophy back in the case. "No, of course not, but he did make me question my motives. He even suggested that I didn't race her as a two-year-old because I was afraid of his reaction."

"Nonsense!" Ian's wise blue eyes sparked dangerously. "He knows better than that—or at least he should! Sentimental Lady's legs weren't strong enough, and I'm not about to make the same mistake with Gypsy Wind. That's the trouble with this country! In Europe many Thoroughbreds never set foot on a racetrack until they're three. And when they do, they run on firm but yielding turf.

"Gypsy Wind's legs won't be fully ossified until she's three, and I'm not about to ask her to sprint over a hard, fast track. It's a good way to ruin a damned fine filly!"

Becca smiled at the wiry man's vehemence. "I agree with you."

Ian's gray eyebrows raised. "I know . . . and I'm proud of you for it. It would have been easier to run her this year and make a little extra money. I know you could use it."

"Not if it hurts Gypsy Wind."

Ian's grizzled face widened into a comfortable grin. He winked at Becca fondly. "We'll show them all, you know. Come early next year, when Gypsy Wind begins to race, we'll have ourselves a champion."

"We already do," Becca pointed out.

"Have you given any thought to moving her to Sequoia Park?"

The smile left Becca's face and she blanched. "I was hoping that we could keep her somewhere else."

Ian put a gentle hand on her shoulder. "It holds bad memories for me, too, Becca. But it's the closest to the farm and has the best facilities around. I thought we would start her in a few short races locally before we headed down the state and eventually back East."

"You're right, of course. When would you want to move her?"

"Soon—say, right after the holidays."

Becca felt her uncertainty mount, but denied her fears. "You're the trainer. Whatever you say goes."

Ian paused and shifted the wooden match that was forever in his mouth, a habit he'd acquired since he'd given up cigarettes. "I appreciate that, gal. Not many owners would have stood up for a trainer the way that you did."

It was Becca's turn to be comforting. "Don't be ridiculous. We've been over this a hundred times before. You and I both know that you had nothing to do with what happened to Sentimental Lady. I never doubted it for a minute."

"She was my responsibility."

"And you did everything you could do to protect her."

His wizened blue eyes seemed suddenly old. "It wasn't enough, was it?"

"It's over, Ian. Forget it."

"Can you?"

Becca smiled sadly. "Of course not. But I do try not to brood about it." She stared pointedly at the bridle Ian held in his gnarled hands. "Is there something else that's bothering you?" It wasn't like Ian to be melancholy or to second-guess himself.

Ian shook his gray head.

"How did the workout go this morning?" Becca asked, changing the subject and hoping to lighten the mood of the conversation.

Ian managed a bemused smile. "Gypsy Wind really outdid herself. She wanted to run the entire distance."

"Just like Lady," Becca observed.

"Yeah." Ian replaced the bridle on a rusty hook near a yellowed picture of Sentimental Lady. He stared wistfully at the black and white photograph of the

proud filly. "They're a lot alike," he mumbled to himself as he turned toward the door. "Got to run now, the
missus doesn't like me late for supper."

"Ian—"

His hand paused over the door handle and he rotated
his body so that he could once again face Becca.

"After the race at Sequoia . . ."

Ian pulled his broad-billed cap over his head and
nodded to encourage Becca to continue.

Becca's voice was less bold than it had been and her
cheeks appeared pinker. "After all the hubbub had died
down about the horse, did you ever take a call from
Brig . . . a call for me that you never told me about?"

Ian's lips pursed into a frown. "He told you about
that, did he?" Ian asked, pulling himself up to his full
fifty-four inches. "I figured he would, should have expected it." Ian rubbed the silver stubble on his chin.
"Yeah, Missy, he called, more than once if I remember
correctly."

"Why didn't you tell me?"

Ian leaned against the door and had trouble meeting
Becca's searching gaze. "We thought about it," he admitted.

"We?"

"Yeah, Martha, Dean, and I. We considered it, talked
a lot about it. More than you might guess. But Dean,
well, he insisted that we shouldn't bother you about the
fact that Brig kept calling—said that after all you'd
been through, you didn't need to talk to him and start
the trouble all over again." Ian shifted his weight from
one foot to the other.

"Someone should have asked me."

Ian nodded his agreement. "That's what Martha and
I thought, but Dean disagreed. He was absolutely cer-

tain that anything Brig might say to you would only . . .
well, open old wounds."

Becca lifted her chin. "I was old enough to care for
myself."

The old man flushed with embarrassment. "I know,
Missy. I know that now, but at the time we were all a
little shaken up. Martha and I, we never felt comfortable about it."

"Is that why Martha quit so suddenly?"

Ian's faded eyes darkened. "I don't rightly know."
He considered her question. "Maybe it helped her with
her decision to move in with her daughter. Leastwise,
it didn't hurt."

"Did Dean speak with Brig?" Cold suspicion
prompted her question.

Ian thought for a moment and then shrugged his
bowed shoulders. "I can't say for certain—it's been a
long time. No, wait. He must have, 'cause right after
he told me he'd taken care of Brig, we didn't get any
more calls."

"How many calls were there?" Becca's heart was
thudding expectantly. Brig hadn't lied.

"Can't recall. Four—maybe five. Dean was afraid
you might take one yourself."

"So he told me not to answer the phone, in order
that he could 'protect' me from nosy reporters," she
finished for him.

"Is that what he told you?"

Becca nodded, her thoughts swimming. Why would
Dean lie to her? "So Dean was the one who made the
final decision."

"Yeah. Martha and I, we agreed with him."

"Why?"

"He was only looking after you . . ." His statement
was nearly an apology.

"I know," Becca sighed, trying to set the old man's mind at ease. "It's all right."

Ian gave her an affectionate smile before leaving the tack room and shutting the door behind him. Becca bit at her lower lip and stared sightlessly into the trophy case. Why would Dean hide the fact that Brig had called?

Swallowing back the betrayal that was rising in her throat, she tried to give her brother the benefit of the doubt. Surely he had only wanted to protect her, in his own misguided manner. But that had been six years ago. With the passage of time, Becca would have expected him to tell her about the calls. Why not tell her after the shock of the race had worn off? Was he afraid she would relapse into her depression? For a fraction of a second Becca wondered if there were other things that Dean had hidden from her. Was he responsible for the money missing from petty cash? And what about the roofing contractor he had suggested, the bum who had run off with her down payment for a new roof on the stables.

"Stop it," she chided herself. She was becoming paranoid. Though she didn't understand her brother at times, she couldn't forget that he had been the one who had helped her put her life back together when it had been shattered into a thousand pieces six years ago at Sequoia Park.

Still troubled about the fact that Dean had purposely lied to her, Becca left the tack room and tossed aside the fears that were beginning to take hold of her. She made her way upstairs to the office and tried to concentrate on the books. Though she had been gone for little over three days, she knew that the bookkeeping would be far behind, as it was near the end of the month. It was time to start organizing the journal entries for month-end posting. She opened the checkbook and realized that several checks were missing. What was happening? No entries had been made for the missing checks. A new fear began to take hold of her. Was someone at the farm stealing from her? But the checks were worthless without a proper signature: Rebecca's or Dean's.

"Dear God, no," she whispered as the weight of her discovery hit her with the force of a tidal wave. She sat down at the desk, her legs suddenly too weak to support her.

The sound of a pickup roaring down the drive met her ears. She recognized it as belonging to Dean. She waited. It wasn't long before his boots clamored up the stairs and he burst into the room, smelling like a brewery and slightly unsteady on his feet. His boyish grin was slightly lopsided.

Becca thought he looked nervous, but mentally told herself that she was just imagining his anxiety.

"Hi, sis. How was the flight?" he asked casually as he popped the tab on a cold can of beer, took a long swallow, and dropped onto the ripped couch.

"Tiresome, but on schedule," she replied, watching him with new eyes. He settled into the couch, propped the heels of his boots against the corner of the desk, and let his Stetson fall forward. Balancing the can precariously on his stomach between his outstretched fingers, he looked as if he might fall asleep.

His voice was slightly muffled. "And good ole Brig, how was he?"

Becca hesitated only slightly, carefully gauging her brother's reaction. His eyes were shadowed by the hat, but there appeared to be more than idle interest in his gaze. Becca supposed that was to be expected, considering the situation. "Brig was fine."

Her noncommittal response didn't satisfy Dean. "And

I suppose you told him about the horse," he said sarcastically.

"You know I did."

His boots hit the floor with a thud, and beer slopped onto his shirt before he could grab the can. He stood to his full height and looked down upon her with his ruddy face contorted in rage. "Goddamn it, Becca! I knew it! You didn't listen to one word of advice I gave you, did you? I don't know what the hell's gotten into you lately!"

"Precisely what I was thinking about you," she snapped back.

"I'm only trying to look out for your best interests," he proclaimed.

"Are you?"

"You know I am." He took another swallow from the beer but it didn't begin to cool the anger in his steely-blue eyes. He shook his head as if to dislodge a bothersome thought. "I knew it," he said, swearing under his breath. "Damn it! I knew that if I let you go to Denver you'd come back here with your mind all turned around."

"If you let me?" she echoed. "I can make my own decisions, Dean, and there's nothing wrong with my mind!"

"Except that you can't think straight whenever you're near Brig Chambers!"

"You and I agreed that Brig had to know about the horse—there was no other way around it."

"We didn't agree to anything. You went running off to Denver with any flimsy excuse to look up Brig again."

"And you decided to tie one on, after taking a few checks from the checkbook."

For a moment Dean was stopped short. Then, with a growl, he dug into his pockets and threw two crumpled checks onto the desk. "I was a little short—"

"Where's the other check?"

"I cashed it. Okay? So sue me!"

"That's not the point."

"Then what is, sis? And what happened while you were in Denver? Unless I miss my guess, you started to fall in love all over again with that miserable son-of-a-bitch, and then he threw you out on your ear."

Becca rose from the desk. She had to fight to keep her voice from shaking as badly as her hands. "That's not what happened." Her green eyes deepened with her anger.

"Close enough." Dean took a final swallow of beer and drained the can before he crushed it in his fist. "So what did he tell you to do—sell the horse?" Dean's knowing blue gaze bored into Becca's angry emerald eyes.

"We considered several alternatives."

"I'll just bet you did," Dean agreed with a disbelieving smirk.

Becca swallowed back the hot retort that hovered on the end of her tongue. Trading verbal knife wounds with her brother would get her nowhere. "I've decided to keep the horse. I told Brig that we'd pay him back within the year."

"Are you out of your mind? Fifty grand plus interest?" Dean was astounded. "That'll be impossible! Even if Gypsy Wind wins right off the bat, it takes a bundle just to cover her costs. You're going to have to stable her at a track, hire an entire crew, enter her in the events—it will cost us a small fortune."

"She's worth it, Dean."

"How in the world do you think you can pay off Chambers?"

"She'll win."

"Oh God, Becca. Why gamble? Take my advice and sell her!"

"To whom?"

"Anyone! Surely someone's interested. You should have listened to me and sold her at Keeneland when she was a yearling. It's going to be a lot tougher now that she's racing age and hasn't even bothered to start!"

"And you know why," Becca charged.

"Because you didn't have the guts to let Brig Chambers know about the horse, that's why. I don't know how you've managed to keep so quiet about her, or why you'd want to. The more you build her up to the press, compare her to Sentimental Lady, the more she's worth!"

Becca's thin patience frayed. "I didn't run her as a two-year-old to avoid injuring her. As for hype about a horse, it's highly overrated. Any owner worth his salt judges an animal by the horse itself—not some press release."

"I don't understand why you're all bent out of shape about it," Dean announced as he threw the twisted empty can into a nearby trash basket.

"And I don't understand why you insist on trying to run my life!"

Dean's flushed face tensed. "Because you need me—or have you forgotten?" He paused for a moment and his face relaxed. "At least, you used to need me. Has that changed?"

"I don't know," she said. "I . . . I just don't like fighting with you. It seems that lately we're at opposite ends of any argument." Despite the tension in the room, she managed a smile. "But you're right about one thing," she conceded. "I did need you and you were there for me. I appreciate that, Dean, and I owe you for it."

"But," he coaxed, reading the puzzled expression on her face and knowing intuitively that she wasn't finished.

"But I don't understand why you didn't tell me about Brig and why you hid the fact that he called me several times."

Dean seemed to pale beneath his California tan. "So he told you about that, did he?"

"And Ian explained what happened."

A startled look darkened his pale eyes but swiftly disappeared. His thin lips pressed into a disgusted line. "Then you realize that I was just trying to protect you."

"From what?"

"From Chambers! Becca, look. You've never been able to face the fact that he used you." Becca started to interrupt, but Dean held her words at bay by raising his outstretched fingers. "It's true, damn it. That man can hurt you like nobody else. I don't know what it is about him that turns a rational woman like you into a simpering fool, but he certainly has the touch. He used you in the past; and if you give him another chance, he'll do it again. I don't think he can stop himself, it's inbred in his nature."

"You're being unfair."

"And you're hiding your head in the sand."

Becca ran her fingers through her hair, unfastening the thong that held it tied and letting it fall into loose curls to surround her face. She thought back to the warm moments of love with Brig and the happiness they had shared in the snow-capped Rockies; the passion, the tenderness, the yearning, the pain. Was it only for one short weekend in her life? Was she destined to forever love a man who couldn't return that love? Could Dean be right? Had Brig used her? "No," she whispered shakily, trying to convince herself as much as her brother. "I can't believe that Brig ever used me, or that he ever intentionally hurt me."

"Come off it, Becca!"

"That's the way I see it."

Dean's eyes were earnest, his jaw determined. "And you live with your head in the clouds when it comes to horses and men. You dream of horses that run wild and free and you try to turn men into heroes who bare their souls for the love of a woman—at least, you do in the case of Brig Chambers."

"Now you're trying to stereotype me," she accused.

"Think about it, sis." Dean gave her a knowing smile before striding toward the door.

Becca couldn't let him go until he answered one last nagging question that had been with her ever since she had spoken with Ian in the tack room. "Dean, why did Martha leave the ranch when she did?"

Dean's hand paused over the doorknob. He whirled around to face his sister, his eyes narrowed. "What do you mean?"

"I mean that she left rather suddenly, don't you think? And it's odd that I haven't heard from her since. Not even a card at Christmas. It's always bothered me."

Dean's face froze into a well-practiced smile. "Didn't she say that she left because her daughter needed her?"

"That's what you told me."

"But you don't think that's the reason?" Dean asked, coolly avoiding her penetrating gaze. How close to the truth was she? He was unnerved, but he tried his best not to let it show. Becca was becoming suspicious—all because of Brig Chambers!

"I just wondered if it had anything to do with Brig's phone calls," Becca replied. The tension in the room made it seem stuffy.

"I doubt it, Becca. Martha's kid was sick."

"The eighteen-year-old girl?"

"Right. Uh, Martha went to live with her and that's the end of the story. Maybe she's just too busy to write."

"I don't even know where they moved, do you?"

"No." Dean's voice was brittle. "Look, I've got to run—see you later." Dean pushed open the door and hurried down the stairs. He seemed to be relieved to get out of the office and away from Becca.

An uneasy feeling of suspicion weighed heavily on Becca's mind. She worked long into the evening, but couldn't shake the annoying doubts that plagued her. Why did she have the feeling that Dean wasn't telling her everything? What could he possibly be hiding? Was it, as he so emphatically asserted, that he was interested only in protecting her? Or was there more . . .

Brig sat at his desk and eyed the latest stack of correspondence from the estate attorneys with disgust. It seemed that every day they came up with more questions for him and his staff. The accident that had taken his father's life had happened more than a month ago, and yet Brig had the disquieting feeling that the Last Will and Testament of Jason Chambers was as far from being settled as it had ever been. He tossed the papers aside and rose from the desk.

Behind him, through the large plate-glass window the city of Denver spread until it reached the rugged backdrop of the bold Colorado Rockies. Brig hazarded a glance out the window and into the dusk, but neither the bustling city nor the cathedral peaks held any interest for him. No matter how he tried, he couldn't seem to take his mind off Rebecca Peters and that last weekend they had spent together.

The smoked-glass door to the office opened and Mona, Brig's secretary, entered. "I'm going down to the cafeteria—can I get you anything?" Brig shook his head and managed a tired smile. "How about a cup of coffee?"

"I don't think so."

Mona raised her perfect eyebrows. "It could be a long night. Emery called. He seems to think that the wildcat strike in Wyoming won't be settled for at least a week."

"Arbitration isn't working?"

"Apparently not."

"Great," Brig muttered. "Just what we need."

Mona closed the door softly behind her and leaned against it. She ran nervous fingers over her neatly styled silver hair. She was only thirty-five; the color of her hair was by choice. "Is something bothering you?" she asked, genuinely concerned.

"What do you think?"

"I think you're overworked."

Brig laughed despite himself. Mona had a way of cutting to the core of a problem. "I can't disagree with that."

"Then why don't you take some time off?" she suggested. "Or at least take a working vacation and spend some time in your father's cabin." She watched him carefully; he seemed to tense.

"I can't do that. It's impossible."

"I could route all the important calls to you."

"Out of the question," he snapped.

Mona pursed her lips, stung by his hot retort. It wasn't

like him. But then, he wasn't himself lately. Not since that weekend he spent alone. Maybe the strain of his father's death affected him more deeply than he admitted. "It was just a suggestion."

"I know it was, Mona," he admitted, and his shoulders slumped. "I didn't mean to shout at you."

"Still, I do think you should consider taking some time off."

"When?"

"As soon as possible—before you really chop somebody's head off."

"Do you think you can handle this office without me?"

She winked slyly at him. "What do you think?"

"I *know* you can."

"I'll remember that the next time I ask for a raise. Now, have you reconsidered my offer—how about some coffee?"

Brig's face broke into an affable grin. "If you insist."

"Well, while I'm still batting a thousand, I really do think you should take a couple of days off. Believe me, this place won't fall apart without you."

"I suppose not," Brig conceded as the pert secretary slipped out of his office and headed for the cafeteria.

Mona had a point. Brig knew he was tense and that his temper was shorter than usual. Maybe it was because he found it nearly impossible to concentrate on his position. The glass-topped desk was littered with work that didn't interest him. Even the wildcat strike in Wyoming seemed grossly unimportant. Chambers Oil was one of the largest oil companies in the United States, with drilling rights throughout the continental U.S. and Alaska. That didn't begin to include the offshore drilling. Who the hell cared about oil in Wyoming? As far as he was concerned, Chambers Oil could write off the entire venture as a tax loss.

Brig rotated his shoulders and tried to smooth away the tension in his neck and back. Who was he kidding? It wasn't his father's estate that kept him awake at nights. Nor was it the strike in Wyoming, or any of the other nagging problems that came with the responsibility of running Chambers Oil. The problem was Rebecca Peters. It always had been, and he didn't doubt for a moment that it always would be.

Though he went through the day-to-day routine of managing his father's company, he couldn't forget the pained look in Rebecca's misty green eyes when he had accused her once again of knowing who drugged Sentimental Lady. Her violent reaction to his charge and her vicious attack against him, claiming that it was he rather than she who had been involved in the crime, was ludicrous. But it still planted a seed of doubt in his mind.

Brig tucked his hands into his back pockets and looked down the twenty-eight floors to the streets of Denver. Was it possible that Becca didn't know her horse had been drugged? Had he been wrong, blinded by evidence that was inaccurate? Even the racing board could level no blame for the crime. Ian O'Riley's reputation as a trainer might have been blemished for carelessness, but the man wasn't found guilty of the act of stimulating the horse artificially.

As he stared, unseeing, out the window he thought about Becca and her initial reaction to the race. She had been afraid and in a turmoil of anguished emotions. He could still hear her pained cries.

"It's all my fault," Becca had screamed, "all mine."

Brig had dragged her away from the terror-stricken filly, holding the woman he loved in a binding grip that kept her arms immobilized. Becca had lost a shoe on the track. He hadn't bothered to pick it up.

Could he have misread her self-proclaimed guilt? Could her cries have erupted from the hysteria taking hold of her? Or was it an honest acceptance of blame, only to be denounced when she had finally calmed down and perceived the extent of the crime? He had always known that she would never intentionally hurt her horse; cruelty wasn't a part of Rebecca's nature. But he hadn't doubted that she was covering up for the culprit. Now he wasn't so sure.

Rubbing his temples as if he could erase the painful memory, he sat down at the desk. There was a soft knock on the door and Mona entered with a steaming cup of coffee.

"Just what the doctor ordered," she chirped as she handed it to her boss.

"What did I do to deserve you?" Brig asked gratefully.

She winked slyly. "Inherited an oil fortune."

Brig took a sip from the steaming mug and smiled fondly at his father's secretary. He had inherited Mona along with the rest of the wealthy trappings of Chambers Oil. "You were right, Mona, I needed this." He held up his cup.

"Was there any doubt?" she quipped before her eyes became somber with genuine concern. She liked Brig Chambers, always had, and she could see that something was eating at him. "I'm right about the fact that you need a vacation, too," she observed.

"I'm not denying it."

"Then promise me that you'll take one."

Brig cracked a smile. "All right, you win. I promise, just as soon as I can get the estate attorneys and tax auditors off my back *and* we somehow settle the strike in Wyoming."

"Good." Mona returned Brig's grin. "I'll keep my fingers crossed," she stated as she walked out of the office.

Chapter 9

The first break came three weeks later. The season had changed from late summer into early autumn and Brig wondered if the promise of winter had cooled the angry tempers in Wyoming. Whatever the reason, the wildcat strike had been resolved, if only temporarily, and although anger still flared on both sides of the picket line, it seemed that most of the arguments and threats of violence had been settled.

As for his father's estate, it was finally in the lengthy legal process known as probate. Brig and the rest of the staff of Chambers Oil had given the tax attorneys every scrap of information they could find concerning Jason Chambers' vast financial holdings. Brig had reluctantly included the stack of personal notes and receipts he had found in his father's locked desk drawer. Brig had to suppress a wicked grin of satisfaction as he handed the private papers to the young tax attorney and the nervous man's face frowned in disbelief at the unrecorded transactions.

The only intentional omission was the note signed by Rebecca Peters. Brig had substituted it with one of his own in the amount of fifty thousand dollars. He considered the original note to Jason as his personal business. It had nothing to do with the old man's estate. This was one matter that only involved Rebecca and himself.

It had been difficult to concentrate on running the oil company the past few weeks. The mundane tasks had been impossible as his wayward thoughts continued to revolve around Rebecca Peters. He couldn't get her out of his mind, and cursed himself as a fool for his infatuation. In the last six years he had thought himself rid of her, that he had finally expunged her from his mind and soul. One weekend in the Rockies had changed all of that, and he couldn't forget a moment of the quiet solitude at the cabin near Devil's Creek. To add insult to injury, he began picking up horse-racing magazines, hoping to see her name in print and catch a glimpse of her. He was disappointed. He found no mention of a two-year-old filly named Gypsy Wind, nor of the entrancing woman who owned her.

When the call came through that the strike was settled, Brig didn't hesitate. He was certain that his man in Wyoming could handle the tense situation in the oil fields and he knew that Mona was able to run the company with or without him for a few days. He took the secretary's advice and made hurried arrangements to fly to San Francisco. After two vain attempts to reach Becca by phone, he gave up and found some satisfaction in the fact that he would arrive on her doorstep as unexpectedly as she had on his only a few short weeks ago.

Without taking the time to consider his motives, he drove home, showered, changed, and threw a few clothes into a lightweight suitcase. After a quick glance around his apartment, he tossed his tweed sports jacket over his shoulder and called a cab to take him to the airport. He didn't want to waste any time. He was afraid his common sense might take over and he would cancel his plans. He kept in motion so as not to think about the consequences of his unannounced journey.

Ominous gray clouds darkened the sky over the buildings of Starlight Breeding Farm. It hadn't changed much since the last time Brig had visited. A quick glance at the buildings told him that only the most critically needed repairs had been completed in the last six years. All in all, the grounds were in sad shape. Brig had to grit his teeth together when he noticed the chipped paint on the two-storied farmhouse and the broken hinge on the gate. With a knowledgeable eye, he surveyed the stables. It seemed as if the whitewashed barns were in better shape than the living quarters; a tribute to Rebecca's sense of priority. A windmill supporting several broken blades groaned painfully against a sudden rush of air blowing down the valley. Brittle dry leaves danced in the wind before fluttering to rest against the weathered boards of a sagging wooden fence.

It was glaringly apparent that because of Sentimental Lady's short racing career and the fact that Rebecca hadn't owned another decent Thoroughbred, she wasn't able to make enough money to run the farm properly. That much was evidenced in the overgrown shrubbery, the rusted gutters, and the sagging roofline of the house. It would take a great deal of cash to get the buildings back into shape, money Rebecca was sadly lacking. It was no wonder she had been forced to go to Jason for a loan. No banker in his right mind would loan money to a has-been horse breeder with only a run-down breeding farm as collateral. Guilt, like a razor-sharp blade, twisted in his conscience.

Brig made his way up the uneven steps of the porch and knocked soundly on the door. His face was set in a grim mask of determination. No matter what had happened between himself and Rebecca, he couldn't allow her to live like this! No one answered his knock. He pressed the doorbell and wasn't surprised when he didn't hear the sound of a chime inside the house. After one last loud knock, he turned toward the stables. Several vehicles parked near the barns indicated that someone had to be on the property.

Rather than explore the stables, he decided to walk through the familiar maze of paddocks surrounding the barns. The first paddock had once held broodmares. Today it was empty. With the exception of a few animals, the paddocks were vacant. The last time Brig had walked through these gates, the stables had been filled to capacity with exceptional Thoroughbreds. But many of the horses were only boarded at Becca's farm, and when the scandal over Sentimental Lady had cast doubt on Becca's reputation, most of the animals were removed by conscientious owners.

Becca had never recaptured her reputation as being a responsible, successful horse breeder. A muscle in the corner of Brig's jaw worked and his eyes darkened as he wondered how much of Rebecca's misfortune was his fault. Had he truly, as she had once claimed, destroyed her reputation and her business with his unfounded accusations? How much of her burden was his?

Unconsciously he walked toward the most removed pasture, a corner paddock with the single sequoia standing guard over it. That particular field, with its lush grass and slightly raised view of the rest of the farm, had been Sentimental Lady's home when she hadn't been on the racing circuit.

As Brig neared the paddock he stopped dead in his tracks, barely believing what he saw. The first drops of rain had begun to fall from the darkened sky, but it wasn't the cool water that chilled his blood or made him curse silently to himself. Color drained from his face as he watched the coffee-colored horse lift her black tail and run the length of the far fence. She stopped at the corner, impeded in her efforts to run from the stranger. She stood as far from Brig as was possible, flattened her ebony ears against her head, and snorted disdainfully.

"Sentimental Lady," Brig whispered to himself, leaning against the top rail of the fence and watching the frightened horse intently. "I'll be damned." There was no doubt in his mind that this horse was Gypsy Wind.

He ran an appreciative eye from her shoulders to her tail. She was a near-perfect Thoroughbred, almost a carbon copy of Sentimental Lady. For a fleeting moment Brig thought the two horses were identical, but slowly, as his expert gaze traveled over the horse, he noted the differences. The most obvious was the lack of white markings on Gypsy Wind. Sentimental Lady had been marked with an off-center star; this dark filly bore none. But that wasn't important, at least not to Brig. Coloring didn't make the horse.

The most impressive dissimilarity between the two animals was the slight variation in build and body structure. Both horses were barrel-chested, but Gypsy Wind seemed to be slightly shorter than her sister and her long legs appeared heavier. That didn't necessarily mean that Gypsy Wind's legs were stronger, but Brig hoped they were for the nervous filly's sake.

The shower increased and Brig wondered why Becca would allow her Thoroughbred to stand unattended in the early autumn rain. It wasn't like Becca. She had always been meticulous in her care of Thoroughbreds, a careful breeder cautious for her horses' health. That was what had puzzled Brig and it made it difficult for him to believe that Becca was responsible for harming Sentimental Lady . . . unless she was protecting someone.

Slowly moving along the fence so as not to startle the horse, Brig called to her. She eyed him nervously as he approached. With the same high spirit as her sister, Gypsy Wind tossed her intelligent head and stamped her right foreleg impatiently. *Just like Lady.* The resemblance between the two horses was eerie. Brig felt his stomach knot in apprehension. He couldn't help but remember the last time he had seen Sentimental Lady alive. It was a nightmare that still set his teeth on edge. He remembered it as clearly as if it had just happened.

Sentimental Lady had virtually been lifted into her stall by Ian O'Riley and his assistants. She tried to lie down, but was forced to stay on her feet by a team of four veterinarians. A horse resting on its side for too long might develop paralysis.

Her pain was deadened with ice while the chief veterinarian managed to sedate the frantic animal. She was led to the operating room where she nearly died, but was kept alive by artificial respiration and stimulants. Brig concentrated on the slow expansion and contraction of her chest. He and Rebecca had agreed with the veterinarians. They had no choice but to operate because of the contamination in the dirt-filled wound. Though the anxious horse needed no further trauma, there were no other options to save her.

Brig watched in silent horror as the veterinarian removed the fragments of chipped bone and tried to repair the severely torn ligaments. After flushing the wound with antibiotics and saline solutions, drains were inserted in the leg. Finally an orthopedist fit a special shoe and cast onto Sentimental Lady's damaged foreleg. At that moment, the operation appeared to be successful.

The agonizing minutes ticked by as Sentimental Lady was eased out of anesthesia. When she regained control of her body she awoke in a frenzy. She struck out and knocked down the veterinarian who was with her. As her hoof kicked against the side of the stall, she broke off her specially constructed shoe. Within minutes, while Ian tried vainly to calm her, the flailing horse had torn her cast to shreds and her hemorrhaging and swelling had increased. Blood splattered against the sides of the stall.

"It's no use," Ian had told Brig. "She was too excited from the race and the pain—they'll never be able to control her again. It's her damned temperament that's killing her!" He turned back to the horse. "Slow down, Lady! Slow down." For his efforts he was rewarded with a kick in the leg.

"Get him out of there!" the veterinarian ordered, and Dean helped Ian from the stall. "I don't think there's anything we can do for her."

The options had run out. All four veterinarians agreed that Sentimental Lady couldn't withstand another operation. Even if she were stable, it would be difficult. In her current state of frenzied pain, it was impossible. An artificial limb was out of the question, as was a supportive sling: Sentimental Lady's high-strung temperament wouldn't allow her to convalesce.

Brig walked back to the waiting room where Rebecca sat with Martha. Her green eyes were shadowed in silent agony as she waited for the prognosis on her horse. Brig took one of her hands in his as he explained the options to Rebecca. Her small shoulders slumped and tears pooled in her eyes.

"But she's so beautiful," she murmured, letting the tears run down her cheeks to fall onto the shoulders of her blood-stained linen suit. "It can't be . . ."

"This is your decision," he said quietly. Martha put a steadying arm over Becca's shoulders.

"I want to see her." Becca rose and walked hesitantly to the other room, where she could observe Lady. One look at the terrified horse and the splintered cast confirmed Brig's tragic opinion. "I can't let her suffer anymore," Becca whispered, closing her eyes against the terrible scene. She lowered her head and in a small voice that was barely audible repeated, "It's all my fault . . ."

Sentimental Lady's death had been the beginning of the end for Rebecca and Brig. He couldn't forget her claims that she had been responsible for the catastrophe, and hadn't fully understood what she meant until the postmortem examination had revealed that there were traces of Dexamethasone in Sentimental Lady's body. Dexamethasone was a steroid that hadn't been used in the surgery. Someone had intentionally drugged the horse and perhaps contributed to her death.

Because of Rebecca's remorse and the guilt she claimed, Brig assumed that she knew of the culprit. The thought that a woman with whom he had shared so much love could betray her horse so cruelly had ripped him apart. He tried to deny her part in the tragedy, but couldn't ignore her own admission of guilt.

The next day, when he read the newspaper reports of the event, the quote that wouldn't leave him was that of his father as Winsome had galloped home to a hollow victory. "We threw a fast pace at the bitch and she just broke down," Jason Chambers had claimed in the aftermath and shock of the accident. The cold-blooded statement cut Brig to the bone.

That had been six years ago, and with the passage of time, Brig had sworn never to become involved with Rebecca Peters again. And yet, here he was, in the pouring rain, attempting to capture a horse whose similarities to Sentimental Lady made him shudder. He was more of a fool than he would like to admit.

"Come here, Gypsy," he summoned, extending his hand to touch the horse's wet muzzle. "Let me take you inside."

Gypsy Wind stepped backward and shook her head menacingly.

"Come on, girl. Don't you have enough sense to come in out of the rain?" He clucked gently at the nervous filly.

"Hey! What's going on here?" an angry voice called over the rising wind. *"You leave that horse alone!"*

Gypsy Wind shied from the noise and Brig whirled around to face Rebecca's brother striding meaningfully toward him. When Brig's cold gray eyes clashed with Dean's watery blue gaze, a moment's hesitation held them apart. A shadow of fear darkened Dean's eyes but quickly disappeared and was replaced with false bravado.

"You're just about the last person I expected to see," Dean announced as he climbed over the fence and reached for Gypsy Wind's halter. She rolled her eyes and paced backward, always just a few feet out of Dean's reach.

"This trip was a spur of the moment decision," Brig responded. Dean managed to catch the horse and snapped on the lead rein, giving it a vicious tug.

"Plan on staying long?" Dean asked. He led the filly into the barn and instructed a groom to take care of her.

"I haven't decided yet."

Dean shrugged as if it made no difference to him one way or the other, but his eyes remained cold. "Was Becca expecting you?" he inquired cautiously.

"No."

"Well, you may as well come up to the house and dry off. She and Ian are in town. They should be home any time."

"They left you in charge?" Brig asked pointedly.

Dean's jaw hardened and he slid a furtive glance in Brig's direction. The man had always made him uneasy. Brig Chambers was in a different league than was Dean Peters. Whereas Dean was only comfortable in faded jeans, Chambers was a man who looked at ease in jeans or a tuxedo. Even now, though he was drenched from the sudden downpour, Brig looked as if he owned the world in his tan corduroy pants, dark blue sweater, and tweed sports coat. Easy for him, Dean thought to himself, he did own the world . . . practically. Chambers Oil was worth a fortune! Dean didn't bother to hide the sarcasm in his voice. "Every once in a while, when Ian and Becca have to do something together, they let me run the place."

"I see," Brig stated as if he didn't and added silently to himself, *and you pay them back by leaving Rebecca's prized Thoroughbred unattended in the rain.*

Dean wasn't easily fooled. He could see that Brig was unhappy; it was evidenced in the dark shade of his unfriendly eyes. Dean also realized that it was a bad break having Brig find Gypsy Wind in the rain, but it couldn't have been helped. The forecast had been for sunshine and Dean had gotten wrapped up in the 49ers game on television. He had a lot of money riding on the outcome of the game. The last thing he needed was Brig Chambers nosing around here. Dean couldn't trust Chambers as far as he could throw him and Becca always went a little crazy whenever she was with Brig. *Why the hell had Brig come to the ranch now?* Dean's throat went dry as he considered the note. Maybe Chambers had changed his mind. Maybe he wanted his loan repaid on the spot! How in the world would Becca put her hands on fifty grand?

Dean stopped at the gate near the front of the farmhouse. "You know your way around, let yourself in, make yourself comfortable." He stood on one side of the broken gate, Brig was on the other. "The 49ers are playing on channel seven."

Brig's smile was polite, but it made Dean uncomfortable. There was a barely concealed trace of contempt in Brig's eyes. "I think I'll dry off and then check on the horse."

Dean raised his reddish brows. "Suit yourself," he said while pulling his jacket more tightly around him. "But take my word for it, the Gypsy will be fine. Garth knows how to handle her." With his final remark, Dean turned toward the stables and headed back to the warm office over the tack room where the final quarter of the 49ers game and a welcome can of beer waited for him.

Brig walked into the farmhouse and smiled at the familiar sight. Some of the furniture had been replaced, other pieces rearranged, but for the most part, the interior seemed the same as it was six years ago. He didn't bother with the lights, though the storm outside shadowed the rooms ominously. Mounting the worn steps slowly, he let his fingers slide along the polished surface of the railing. There was no hesitation in his stride when he reached the second floor; he moved directly toward Rebecca's room. At the open door he paused.

A torrent of long-denied memories flooded his senses. He remembered vivid images of a distant past: the smell of violets faintly scenting the air, a blue silk dress slipping noiselessly to the floor, the moonlight reflecting silver light in Rebecca's soft green eyes, and the powerful feeling of harmony he had found when he had taken her body with his. The reflection had an overpowering effect on him. He braced his shoulder against the doorjamb and plunged his fists deep into his pockets while he stared vacantly into the room. He had been a fool to let Rebecca slip away from him, a damned fool too blinded with self-righteousness to see the truth.

After letting the bittersweet memories take their toll on him, he went into the bathroom and towel-dried his hair. He tossed on his jacket and ran back to the barns, his head bent against the wind. Garth had indeed seen to the horse. Once Brig was satisfied that Gypsy Wind was comfortable, he headed back to the house.

Headlights winding up the long drive warned him that Rebecca was returning. An ancient pickup with a trailer in tow ground to a stop against the wet gravel of the parking lot and the driver killed the rumbling engine.

Rebecca emerged from the cab of the truck, wearing a smile and a radiant gleam in her eye when she recognized Brig huddling against the wind. She couldn't hide the happiness she felt just at the sight of him.

"What are you doing in this part of the country?" she asked, linking her arm through his and leading him toward the house.

Her good mood was infectious. "Looking for you."

She winked at him and wiped a raindrop off her

nose. "You always know exactly what to say to me, don't you?"

"Are you telling me that I haven't lost my touch?"

"If you had, it would make my whole life a lot easier."

"Is that right?" He took her hand in his and stuffed it into the warmth of his jacket pocket.

She hesitated just a moment as they climbed the porch stairs. "I've thought about the last time I saw you . . ."

He lifted his dark brows. "That makes two of us."

She was suddenly sober. "I didn't intend to argue with you. The last thing I wanted to do was fight about Gypsy Wind."

"I know."

A sad smile curved her lips as they walked through the door together. "It seems that every time we're together, we end up arguing."

They stepped into the kitchen. "It hasn't always been that way," he reminded her.

She shook her blond hair. It was loose and brushed against her shoulders. "You're wrong . . . even in the beginning we had fights."

"Disagreements," he insisted.

"Okay, disagreements," she responded. Without asking his preference, she set a cup of black coffee on the table and poured one for herself. "Anyway, the point is, I made a vow to myself on the plane back from Denver."

"Sounds serious."

"It was. I told myself that I was going to get over you."

He sat back in the chair, straddling the cane backing before taking a sip of the coffee. "Well . . . did you?"

She made a disgusted sound in the back of her throat and shook her head. How could he sit there so calmly when she felt as if her insides were being shredded? "Not yet."

"But you intend to?"

"I thought I did . . . right now, I honestly don't know." She stared into the dark coffee in her cup as if she were searching for just the right words to make him understand her feelings. She lifted her eyes to meet his. "But I think it would make things simpler if you and I remained business partners—nothing more."

Brig frowned. "And you're sure that's what you want?"

"I'm not sure of anything right now," she admitted with a sigh.

"Except for Gypsy Wind."

Becca's somber expression lightened. "Have you seen her?"

"When I first got here."

"What do you think?" Becca's breath caught in her throat. How long had she waited for Brig to see the horse?

"She's a beautiful filly," he replied, keeping his tone noncommittal. Looks were one thing; racing temperament and speed were entirely different matters.

"Where did you see her?"

"In Sentimental Lady's paddock."

"This afternoon?" Rebecca seemed surprised. Brig nodded. "I didn't know she was going to be let out," she thought aloud. "Ian didn't mention it to me . . ."

"Where is O'Riley? I thought he was with you."

"I dropped him off at his place—he lives a couple of miles down the road." She answered him correctly, but her mind was back on Gypsy Wind. "Did you talk to Dean?"

"That's how I knew you were with O'Riley."

"So Dean was with Gypsy Wind?"

"He took her inside and had . . . Garth, is that his name?" Becca nodded. "Garth took care of her. I double-checked her a few minutes ago. She looks fine."

"Garth is good with the horses," Becca said, still lost in thought. What was Dean thinking, leaving the Gypsy outside in the windstorm? It was difficult to understand Dean at times.

"What about your brother?" Brig asked.

A startled expression clouded Becca's sculptured features. "Dean?" She shrugged her slim shoulders. "Dean doesn't seem to have much interest in the Thoroughbreds anymore . . ." her voice trailed off as she thought about her brother.

"Why not?"

Becca smiled wistfully. "Who knows? Other interests, I suppose."

"Such as?"

Suddenly defensive, Becca set her mug on the table and gave Brig a look that told him it was really none of his business. "I don't know," she admitted. "People change."

"Do they?" he asked, his voice somewhat husky as he stared at her. He felt the urge to trace the pouty contour of her lips with his finger.

"Of course they do," she replied coldly. "Didn't we?"

"That was different."

"Why?"

"Because of the horse . . ."

"Dean was involved with Sentimental Lady, probably just as close to her as either one of us. It was hard on him."

"I didn't say it wasn't."

She ignored his remark. Angry fire crackled in her

eyes. "It might have been more difficult for him than for either of us," she pointed out emphatically.

"I doubt that."

"Of course you do! That's because you weren't here, were you? You were gone, afraid to be associated with a woman whom you thought intentionally harmed her horse. Dean was the one who pulled me up by my bootstraps, Brig. He was the one who made me realize that there was more to life than one horse and one man. All the while you were afraid of ruining *your* reputation, my brother helped me repair mine!"

"I never gave a damn about my reputation!" he shot back angrily. "You know that," he added in a gentler tone.

"I wish I did," she whispered. "When I was younger, I was more confident . . . sure of myself . . . sure of you." A puzzled expression marred the clarity of her beguiling features. "And I was wrong. Now that I'm older, I'm more cautious, I guess. I realize that I can't change the world."

"Unless Gypsy Wind proves herself?"

"Not even then." She smiled sadly. "Don't misunderstand me—Gypsy Wind is important. But I feel that maybe what she represents isn't the most important thing in my life, and what might have been of greater value is gone."

His chair scraped against the floorboards. He stood behind her and let his palms rest on her shoulders as she sat in the chair. "What are you trying to say?"

"That I'm afraid it might be too late for us," she whispered.

His fingers pressed against the soft fabric of her sweater, gently caressing the skin near her collarbones. He felt cold and empty inside. Rebecca's words had vocalized his own fears. "So you think that destiny continues to pull us apart?"

She slowly swept her head from side to side. The fine golden strands of her hair brushed against his lower abdomen, adding fuel to the fires of the desire rising within him. The clean scent of her hair filled his nostrils, and he had difficulty concentrating on her words.

"I don't think destiny or fate has anything to do with it," she answered pensively. "I think it's you and me— constantly at war with each other. It's as if we won't allow ourselves the chance to be together. Our egos keep getting in the way—mine as well as yours."

The line of his jaw hardened. "Are you trying to say that you want me to leave?"

She sighed softly to herself and closed her eyes. "If only it were that simple. It's not." She shut her eyes more tightly so that deep lines furrowed her brow as she concentrated. "I'm glad you're here," she admitted in a hoarse whisper. "There's a very feminine part of me that needs to know you care."

"I always have . . ."

"Have you?" She reached up and covered his hand with her long fingers. "You have a funny way of showing it sometimes."

"We've both made mistakes," he admitted. The warmth from her fingers flowed into his. He lowered his head and kissed her gently on the crook of her neck. The smell of her hair still damp from a sprinkling of raindrops filled his nostrils. It was a clean, earthy scent that brought back memories of their early autumn tryst in the Rocky Mountains.

"And we're going to make more mistakes . . . . tonight?" she asked, conscious only of the moist warmth of his lips and the dewy trail they left on her skin.

"Loving you has never been easy."

"Because you can't let yourself, Brig." With all the strength she could muster, she pulled away from his caress and stood on the opposite side of the chair, as if the small piece of furniture could stop his advances and her yearnings. "Love is impossible without trust. And you cannot to this day find it in your heart to trust me—"

"That's not true," he ground out, hearing the false sound of his words as they rang hollowly over the noise of the storm.

"Don't bother to lie to me . . . or to yourself! We're past all that, Brig, and I'm too damned old to be playing games."

There was anger in Brig's dark eyes, but also just a hint of amusement, as if he were laughing at himself. His jaw was tense, but the trace of a self-mocking smile lingered on his lips. "You are incredible, you know. And so damned beautiful . . ." he reached his hand toward her cheek, but she turned her head and clutched his fingers in her small fist. Her face was set in lines of earnest determination.

"I don't want to be *incredible,* Brig! And God knows there must be a thousand beautiful women who would die for a chance to hear you say just that to them—"

"But not you?"

Her green eyes flashed in defiance at the suspicious arch of his dark male brows. "I like compliments as well as the next woman. I'd be a fool if I tried to deny it. But what I want from you"—her fingers tightened around his as if to emphasize the depth of her feelings—"what I want from you is trust! I want you to be able to look me in the eyes and see a woman who loves you, who has always loved you—"

"And who put her career before my proposal of marriage."

The words stung, but she took them in stride. "I needed time."

"That's a lame excuse."

"Maybe you're right," she said.

"Would you do anything differently if you could?" he asked through clenched teeth.

"I don't know . . ."

"Would you?" he demanded, his face tense with disbelief.

"Yes, oh yes!"

His muscles relaxed slightly but the doubt didn't leave his face. "How would you change things, Becca?"

The question stood between them like an invisible wall, a wall that had been built with the passage of six long years. Rebecca's voice was barely audible over the sounds of the storm. "I don't think that there would have been many things I would do differently," she admitted.

"What about me?"

She fought against the tears forming in her eyes and smiled. "I've never for a minute regretted that I met you or that . . . I thought I was in love with you." She cleared her throat as she tried to remain calm. "But you have to know, Brig, that if I could, I would turn back the hands of time and somehow find a way to save Sentimental Lady."

The honesty in her eyes twisted his heart. "I know that, Rebecca. I've always known that you wouldn't intentionally hurt anything."

"But—"

"I just thought that you were covering up for someone whom you cared about very much."

"I had no idea who—"

He stepped toward her and folded her into his arms. "I know that now, and I'm sorry that I didn't realize it before this." As his arms tightened around her he realized that she was trembling. His lips moved softly against her hair. "It's all right now," he murmured, hoping to reassure her.

Becca tried to concentrate on the warmth of Brig's arms. She fought against the doubts crowding in her mind, but she couldn't forget his words. "I thought you were covering up for someone whom you cared for . . ." She had been, but it was because she had thought Brig was somehow involved. If not Brig, then who? "Someone you cared for . . ."

She closed her eyes and let her weight fall against Brig, trying to ignore the voice in her mind that continued to remind her that Dean, her own brother, had been acting very suspiciously the past few weeks. Dean had access to Sentimental Lady.

But *why?* What would Dean have had to gain by having the horse disqualified? *Or had he expected her to lose?*

"Becca—is something wrong?"

The familiar sound of Brig's voice brought Becca back to the present. She could feel his heartbeat pounding solidly against her chest. His breath fanned her hair. "Nothing," she lied. She was anxious to escape from her fears and wanted nothing more than the security of Brig's strong arms to support her.

"You're sure?" He was doubtful, and pulled his head away from hers so that he could look into her eyes.

"Oh, Brig—just for once, let's not let the past come between us."

"I've been waiting for an invitation like that all afternoon," he replied with a crooked smile.

With the quickness of a cat, he scooped her off the floor and cradled her gently against him before turning toward the stairs.

"You can argue with me all night long, Ms. Peters," he stated, as he strode slowly up the staircase. "But you *are* incredible, and beautiful, and enchanting, and . . ."

"And I wouldn't dare argue with you," she admitted with a smile. "I love every minute of this."

"Then let me show you exactly how I feel about you."

"I can't wait . . ."

Chapter 10

Brig was silent as he carried Becca into the bedroom. She was hesitant to say anything for fear it might break the gentle peace that had settled quietly between them. Instead she listened to the movement of the restless wind as it passed through the brittle branches of the oak trees near the house. Above the wind she could hear the reassuring sound of Brig's steady heartbeat.

Still carrying her lithely, he crossed the room and set her on her feet near the edge of the bed. His eyes never left hers as he slowly slid the top button of her blouse through the buttonhole. The collar opened. Brig gently touched the hollow of her throat with his index finger. Becca shivered at his touch while he stroked the delicate bone structure. She felt her pulse jump.

Knowing the depth of her response, he concentrated on the next button, slowly parting the blouse to expose the skin below her throat, and when the blouse finally opened, he gently pushed it off her shoulders. Her skin quivered as his finger slowly made a path from her neck to the clasp of her bra. Without moving his eyes from her face he opened the bra and slid it off her shoulders, allowing her breasts to become unbound.

Becca didn't move. She heard her shallow breathing and felt the rapid beat of her heart as she let his hands work their magic on her skin. She expected him to caress a breast; she yearned for him to take one of the aching nipples in his hands and softly massage the bittersweet agony. He didn't. She felt his hands move between her breasts to flatten against her abdomen. The tips of his fingers slid invitingly below the waistband of her jeans. Involuntarily, she sucked in her breath in order to make it easier for him to come to her.

The button was released. The zipper lowered. Her jeans were pushed over her hips to fall at her feet. She was standing nearly naked in the stormy night, with only the fragile barrier of her panties keeping her from being nude. A breeze from the partially opened window lifted her golden hair from her face and contributed to the hardening of her nipples. But it wasn't the wind that made her warm inside, nor was it the impatience of the brewing storm that electrified her nerve endings. It was the passion in the gray eyes of the man undressing her that persuaded her blood to run in heated rivulets through her body.

"Undress me," he whispered, refusing to give in to the urgent longings of his body. He felt the thrill of desire rising in him, but he fought against it, preferring to stretch the torment of unfulfilled passion to the limit.

She obeyed his command by silently moving her hands under his sweater and pushing it over his head. He had to reaffirm his resolve as he looked at her, standing before him with her arms stretched overhead as the sweater passed over his hands. Her breasts fell forward, their dark tips brushing against his abdomen. He gritted his teeth against the overpowering urge to kick off his jeans and take her in a frantic union of flesh that would be as savage as it was delicious. Rather than give in to his male urge to conquer and dominate, he waited. Every muscle tensed with his restraint, but the pain was worth the prize. He had to swallow when her fingers touched him lightly as they worked with the belt buckle and finally dropped his pants to the floor. He felt the trickle of sweat begin to run down his spine, though the room was cold. Her eyes had clouded with the same passion controlling his body.

She groaned as he kneeled and softly kissed her abdomen. Her weight fell against him and she trembled at his touch when he slipped the lacy underwear down her thighs and over her calves. His fingers ran up the inside of her leg as he raised himself to his full height; he gathered her into his arms before pressing against her and forcing her onto the bed with the weight of his body.

"I want to make love to you," he whispered into her hair. "I want to make love to you and never stop."

"Then do, Brig, please make love to me." Her eyes reached for his in the darkness, promising vows she couldn't possibly keep.

He studied her face, lost in the complex beauty of a woman who was intelligent and kind, strong yet vulnerable, wise though young. How could he have ever doubted her? Why had he been such a fool as to cast away six years they could have shared together?

He lowered his head and his lips pressed against hers with all of the pain and torment warring within him. He took her face in his hands as if he had to be sure that she wouldn't disappear. Her lips parted willingly and his tongue found the delicious pleasures of her moist mouth. He groaned in surrender when her fingers dug into the solid muscles of his back.

"These last few weeks have been torturous," he confided when he finally lifted his head. "I tried to stay away—Lord knows, I tried, but I couldn't. You're just too damned mystifying and I can't seem to get enough of you."

"I hope you never can," she admitted, but before she could say anything else, his fingers caressed her breast, cupping it in his palm, feeling the soft, malleable weight before taking it gently in his mouth. She sighed with the pleasure he evoked as he stroked and suckled the nipple with his tongue and lips. The pressure of his mouth made her arch against him, hoping to fill the space between his lips with her breast. She was satisfied in the knowledge that the pleasure she was receiving was given back in kind.

She wound her fingers in his hair, cradling his face against her as if giving comfort. His hands slid lower as did his lips. Her blood pounded in her eardrums as his tongue leisurely rimmed her navel while his hands parted her legs and massaged her buttocks. "You're beautiful," he whispered against her silky skin. "I want you . . ."

"Then love me, Brig," she pleaded, "love me." Her needs were more than physical. Even though her body longed for all of him, it was her heart and her mind that had to have him. Her soul was crying for him to be one with her and share a lifetime together.

He moved over her, and she could feel each of his strong hard muscles against her own. Her breasts flattened with the weight of him, the coiling desire deep within her beginning to unwind in expectation. "I want you, Brig. I want you more than I ever have," she admitted roughly.

He shifted, parting her legs with his own. Her feet curled against his calves and rubbed against the hair on his legs as he became one with her. His lips claimed hers as their bodies joined and she felt the pulse of his blood when he started his unhurried movements of union. Her body responded, pushing against his in the heated tide of sexual fulfillment. Their tongues danced and joined until he pulled his head away from hers and stared into the depths of her eyes as if he were looking for her soul.

The coupling became stronger, their bodies surging together as one. She tasted the salt of his sweat on her tongue and heard the rapid beating of his heart. She groaned in contentment as the tempo increased. His eyes remained open, watching her reaction, and when he felt her quaking shudder of release and saw the glimmer of satisfaction in her velvet green eyes, he let go of the bonds he had placed upon himself and let his passion consume him in one violent burst of liquid fire. He groaned as he sagged against her, letting his weight press her into the mattress.

"Oh, God, Rebecca," he murmured. "I *do* love you." His fingers twined in her hair and his breathing slowed. "You are incredible—whether you believe it or not."

Several minutes later, after his breathing had slowed, he rolled to her side. His arms held her tightly against him and she felt secure and warm, pressed into the hard muscles of his chest.

"Why is it that we never fight in bed?" she finally asked.

"Because we have more important things to do," he teased.

"Be serious."

"I am. Why would we fight in bed? What would be the point?" He smiled and kissed the top of her head, smelling the perfume in her tousled curls.

"What's the point when we're *not* in bed?"

He lifted his shoulders. "I don't know. Boredom?" He looked down at her and she recognized a familiar devilish twinkle lurking in his eyes.

"I doubt that . . ."

"So do I, Ms. Peters . . . so do I." He kissed her lightly on the lips before tracing their pouty curve with the tip of his finger. "Speaking of boredom," he began in a low drawl, "I've got several theories on how to avoid it."

"Do you?" She arched an elegant eyebrow as if she disbelieved him.

A wicked smile allowed just the flash of even white teeth against his dark skin. "Several," he assured her while his eyes moved lazily down the length of her naked body. He looked as if he were studying it for flaws. Satisfied that there were none, he met her gaze squarely. "Would you like a demonstration?"

"That depends."

"On what?"

Provocatively she rimmed her lips with her tongue. "On whom you're going to test your theories."

His finger slid down the curve of her jaw. "You'll do—if you're interested."

"What do you think?" She laughed, her green eyes dancing mischievously.

He grabbed her wrists playfully and pinned them to her sides. His face was only inches from hers in the gathering darkness. "I think, Rebecca, that you're a tease, an *incredible,* gorgeous, and wanton *tease. And* I think I know just how to handle you." Dangerous fires of renewed passion flared in his cool gray eyes.

"Idle threats," she mocked.

"We'll see about that, Becca. Before tonight is over, I'll have you begging for more," he growled theatrically.

"Save me," she taunted.

"You don't know when to give up, do you?"

"Sometimes I wish I did," she sighed, the merriment ebbing from her gaze.

"Don't ever give up, Rebecca," he chided. "It's one of the most wonderful things about you—that spirit of yours. It's as unbeaten and proud as the horses you race."

"Are you serious?"

"About you? Yes!" He released her wrists and kissed her forehead. "I was a fool to ever let you get away from me." He lowered his head and kissed the slope of her shoulder. "It won't happen again."

She felt her skin quiver with his low words of possession. When his lips claimed hers, she was ready and hungrily accepted everything he offered her. She returned his passion with renewed fervor, giving herself body and soul.

His hands moved over her skin, gently kneading her muscles and reigniting the fires of desire deep within her. His lips roved restlessly down her neck, across her shoulder, to stop in the hollow between her breasts. He pushed the soft flesh against his cheeks before he took one nipple and then the other between his lips.

Rebecca sighed and thought she would die in the ecstasy of his embrace. When he shifted his weight and parted her willing legs with his knee, she molded her body against his in an effort to get closer to him . . . become one with him. "That's it, Becca, let go," he encouraged by whispering against the shell of her ear. "Just love me, sweet lady," he coaxed as he entered her and began his gentle rhythmic movements.

His hands began to move in slow, sensual circles over her breasts while he slowly fanned the fires of her love until they were white hot and she groaned in frustration. When he knew that she was ready, he increased his movements against her. They found each other at the same moment, each inspiring the other to the brink of ecstasy in an explosive rush of energy that held them together until at last they were satisfied and the animal growls that came from Brig's lips were moans of contentment.

It was much later that Becca awoke from a drowsy sleep and tried to slip out of the bed unnoticed by Brig.

"Where do you think you're going?" he asked groggily, holding her against him and frustrating her attempts at escape.

"I want to check on Gypsy Wind."

"I told you she was fine." Brig ran his hand over his eyes in an effort to awaken.

"I know, I know. But that was several hours ago and the storm's gotten worse. She may be frightened."

"Is that what you're worried about?" Brig asked, propping himself on one elbow. "Or are you afraid that your brother might have let her out again?"

Becca ignored the pointed remark about Dean. It only served to reinforce her fears. "I'm worried about the horse, Brig. She's high-spirited."

"To the point that a storm would spook her?"

Becca extracted herself reluctantly from Brig's

embrace. "I'm not sure . . . I just want to check." She slipped off the bed and began dressing in the dark.

Brig snapped on the bedside lamp and smiled lazily as he watched her struggle into her clothes. "I'll come with you."

"You don't have to."

"Sure I do." He straightened from the bed and began pulling on his pants. "That's what I came here for—to look at your wonder horse."

A stab of pain pierced Becca's heart, but she ignored it. What did she expect—words of love at every turn in the conversation? For someone who had vowed to keep Brig Chambers out of her heart, she was certainly thinking like a woman in love.

Gypsy Wind stood in the far corner of her stall, eyeing Brig suspiciously and ignoring Becca's cajoling efforts to get the filly to come forward. Not even the enticement of an apple would lure the highspirited horse. Instead she paced nervously between one side of the stall and the other, never getting close enough for Becca to touch her.

"She's got a mind of her own," Brig stated while he watched the anxious filly.

Becca couldn't disagree. "I've noticed," she commented dryly.

"What does O'Riley have to say about her?"

"He worries a lot," Becca admitted almost to herself, as she clucked softly to the horse. "And he tries not to let on, but I'm sure he has some reservations about her."

"Because of her similarities to Sentimental Lady?"

Becca nodded. "Her temperament."

"A legitimate complaint, I'd venture."

Trying not to sound defensive, Becca replied, "Sentimental Lady's spirit wasn't all bad, Brig. She was bound to be a good horse, but her spirit made her great."

"And killed her." The words hung in the air.

"Sentimental Lady's spirit didn't kill her, Brig . . . *someone* did! If she hadn't been injected, she might not have misstepped, or she might not have continued to run . . . or she might have been able to come out of the anesthesia—"

"But she didn't!" His face had hardened as he judged Gypsy Wind on the merits of her sister. "And you and I . . . we let our pride get in our way. We should have figured this out long ago. We should never have let it come between us for this long."

"I don't know what we could have done to save Sentimental Lady."

"Maybe we couldn't, but the least we could have done was trusted one another enough to find the culprit."

"But—"

He turned to face her and his eyes glittered like forged steel. "I'm not blaming you—I was as much at fault as anyone. I assumed that you had something to do with it because you kept telling me that it was all your fault. I shouldn't have listened to you, should have followed my instincts instead. God, Becca, I knew you couldn't have done it, but I thought that you knew who did! That was what really got to me—that you'd protect some bum who killed your horse."

"I didn't."

"I know that now." Brig's eyebrows had pulled together as he concentrated. "We have to figure this thing out, Becca, if you really plan to race Gypsy Wind. Otherwise the same thing could happen all over again."

"I don't think anyone would want to hurt the Gypsy—"

"Just like you didn't think anyone would want to hurt Sentimental Lady," he charged.

"That was different—"

"How?"

"Different horses, different circumstances . . . I don't know."

"That's just the point; until we understand the motive behind the drugging of Sentimental Lady, we'll never be certain that Gypsy Wind is safe. And we'll never be able to comprehend the motive until we find out who was behind it."

"But that might be impossible."

"Not really. Ian O'Riley should know exactly who had access to the horse and who didn't." Brig pulled pensively on his lower lip, as if he were attempting to visualize exactly what had happened to Sentimental Lady, as if by thinking deeply enough, he could reconstruct the events leading up to the tragedy.

Becca touched his arm lightly. "Brig, be reasonable—you're talking about six years ago! You can't expect Ian to remember every person who had access to the horse." Becca was incredulous and her wide green eyes reflected her feelings.

"I think you're underestimating your trainer. I'm sure he gave the California Horse Racing Board the name of every person near the horse in those last few hours before the race. The board surely has the records . . ."

"But that list probably includes the names of grooms who have left us. I have no idea how to reach them. And what about security guards at the track, other trainers . . . what could you possibly expect to find that the board overlooked?"

Brig's smile was grim, his jawline determined. "I

doubt that the board overlooked anything that was reported. What I'm looking for was probably never brought to their attention."

Becca shook her head at the folly of his idea. "What can you possibly hope to find?"

"I don't know—maybe nothing. But there's a slim chance that we can dig up some shred of evidence that might shed some light on Lady's death."

"It's been too long."

Brig had started toward the door, but stopped dead in his tracks. "Don't you *want* to find out what happened?"

"Of course, but I think it's too late. All we would do is stir up the entire mess all over again. The only thing we would accomplish would be getting the press all riled up. Sentimental Lady's picture, along with yours and mine, would be thrown in front of the public again."

"That's going to happen anyway. Once the press gets wind of the fact that you've bred a sister to Sentimental Lady, they're going to be breathing down your neck so fast it will make your head swim. My investigation isn't going to change the attitude of the media."

Becca had reached up to switch off the lights, but hesitated when she felt Brig's hand on her shoulder. She turned to face him, but couldn't hide the worry in her eyes. "What is it?" he asked gently. "What makes you afraid?"

"I'm not afraid—"

"But something isn't right, Becca." His face was softened by concern for her.

"What do you mean?"

"I mean that there are a few things that just don't add up."

She drew in a deep breath and tried to mask the ever increasing dread. "Such as?"

"Such as the fact that, for the most part, you held your silence after the tragedy."

"I told you why. I thought you were involved."

"Thought. Past tense. You don't anymore?"

She shook her head and snapped off the lights, hoping that Brig wouldn't notice that her hands were unsteady. "No."

Becca pushed the door open with her shoulder and walked outside. She hoped that Brig would change the subject, because of the unnamed fear growing stronger within her. The wind had quieted to occasional chilly gusts that seemed to rip through Becca's light jacket and pierce her heart.

"What made you change your mind?" Brig asked after he had secured the door to the barn.

"Pardon me?"

"About my guilt—what changed your mind?"

Becca shrugged and hoped to appear indifferent. "I guess I knew it all along. It was just an easy excuse to justify your . . . change in attitude . . ."

He put his arm around her shoulder and forced her to face him. The darkness was broken only by the security lights surrounding the barns. "Rebecca, I'm sorry—God, I'm sorry. I made a horribly unjust decision about you and I've regretted it ever since. It was my mistake." He crushed her against his chest and Becca felt the burn of tears behind her eyes.

"It's all over now," she whispered, clinging to him and aware of soft drops of rain on her cheeks and hair. It felt so right, standing in the darkness, unconscious of the chill in the air, holding Brig.

"It will never be 'all over,'" he said. "But maybe we can heal the wounds by finding out what happened to Lady."

She stiffened. "I think that's impossible . . ."

"Nothing is. I shouldn't have to tell you that. You found a way to breed Gypsy Wind when all the cards were stacked against you."

"That was only possible because of your father."

"I know, and that's another one of the pieces of the puzzle that doesn't seem to fit."

"What do you mean?"

"I told you that things didn't add up and I mentioned your silence."

"Yes?"

"Well, another thing that won't seem to quit nagging me is the fact that you didn't race Gypsy Wind as a two-year-old."

"Ian and I thought it best, because of her legs—I told you all that, and what in the world does it have to do with your father?"

"Dad is just one other thing that doesn't make any sense."

"What do you mean?"

"I can understand him loaning you some money— but not that much. When my father gave or loaned something to a pretty young woman, he usually expected something in return."

"He did—repayment of the loan with interest."

Brig shook his head as if trying to dislodge a wayward thought. "Not good enough, Rebecca. Jason must have wanted something else."

"I think you're grasping at straws," Becca whispered, but the feeling of dread that had been with her for the past few days increased.

"Do you remember what Jason said after the race between Winsome and Sentimental Lady?"

"I know. But he was upset, we all were."

Brig raked his fingers through his hair and noticed it was wet from the rain. He ignored the cool water running under his collar. He watched Becca's reaction when he repeated his father's damning words: "We threw a fast pace at the bitch and she just broke down."

Becca shuddered. "He didn't know what he was saying—"

"A handy excuse . . ."

Placing her palm to her forehead, Becca tried to close out the painful memories taking hold of her. "Don't, Brig . . . let's not dredge it all up again. What's the point?"

He took her by the shoulders and shook her until she met his eyes. "You're going to have to face everything if you really intend to race Gypsy Wind, Rebecca. You won't be able to hide here at Starlight Breeding Farm and expect the reporters to respect your privacy. All the old wounds are going to be reopened and examined with a microscope."

"You still think I had something to do with it," she accused, near hysteria. The rain, Brig's dark eyes, the haunting memories all began to unnerve her.

"No, dear one, no. But I have to know why you would go to my father for money after he said what he did."

"I had no choice. There was no other way. Dean suggested your father and I picked up on it . . ."

"Your brother?"

Becca hastened to explain. She had to make Brig understand. "Originally it was Dean's idea, but when I really decided to go through with it and approach Jason, Dean tried to talk me out of it. He told me I was crazy to consider the idea, that he had only been joking when he mentioned your father as a possible source of money."

"And yet he was the first to consider Jason. Interesting. I didn't think he knew Dad."

"He didn't."

"You're sure of that?" Brig's eyes narrowed as he witnessed Rebecca's face drain of its natural color.

"I . . . I can't be sure, but I think that if Dean had ever met your father, Jason's name would have come up in conversation at some point in time . . . and I don't remember that it did."

"Did they ever have the opportunity to meet?"

"Who knows?" Rebecca replied, trying to concentrate on the elusive past. "I suppose it was possible when Sentimental Lady was racing . . . there were a lot of parties. You remember."

"Then there was a chance that Dean met my father?"

"They could have . . . but so what?"

In the distant mountains a loud clap of thunder disturbed the silence. Brig chose to ignore her question. "We'd better get inside," he suggested, letting his eyes rove restlessly over her face. He kissed her cheek, catching a drop of rain with his tongue. "If you're lucky, I might consent to drying off your body . . ."

Rebecca managed a weak, but playful smile. "You're insufferable," she whispered, "and you've got to catch me first." She pulled out of his embrace and took off for the house at a dead run, as if the devil himself were pursuing her. When Brig caught up with her, they were both breathless and laughing. He captured her face in his hands and kissed her with all the passion he felt rising within him.

Becca closed her eyes and melted against him, conscious only of the warmth of his lips touching hers and the cool trickle of raindrops against her neck.

She was too obliviously happy to notice the menacing shadow standing in the window of the office, staring down at her with furious blue eyes.

Chapter 11

The week passed too quickly for Brig and it seemed over before it had really begun. During the days he worked with Rebecca, Ian O'Riley, and Gypsy Wind. He saw, for himself, the potential of the bay filly, but also the danger. Someone had drugged a horse such as this once before. Wouldn't they be likely to do it again? If only he knew who had been involved and what the motive had been. Seeds of suspicion had sprouted in his mind, but he kept silent about his theory until it could be proved one way or another.

Dean had made himself scarce for the duration of Brig's visit. There had always been some excuse as to Dean's whereabouts, but it only strengthened Brig's suspicions. Rebecca's brother was never around the farm, with the one exception of mealtime. Otherwise, Dean was on errands into town, or fixing a broken fence in some distant field, or just plain nowhere to be found. When Brig had questioned Becca about her brother, she had seemed unconcerned. Dean had always been his own boss and Rebecca rarely kept up on his whereabouts, as long as he carried his weight around the farm. The week that Brig had visited, Dean had done more than his share. He hadn't worked this hard in several years. Becca thought the entire situation odd, but chalked it up to the fact that Dean had never been comfortable around the wealth and power represented by Brig Chambers.

For Rebecca the week had flown by with the speed of an eagle in flight. She had felt ten years younger basking in the happiness of working day to day with Gypsy Wind and Brig and making love to him long into the cold autumn nights. She found herself wishing that this precious time with Brig would never end, that he would stay with her forever. Her love and respect for him had grown with each passing day, and she no longer tried to fight the inevitable.

Rebecca had come to understand her love and she realized that it would never die, nor could it be ignored. She would have to accept the fact that she loved him, had always loved him, and probably always would continue to love him. Though their paths might take different courses in life, the depth of her feelings for him would never diminish. Not with time. Not with distance. Her love surmounted all obstacles, and if it could never be returned with the intensity of her feelings, she could accept that. She would take Brig on whatever terms he offered. She was resigned to her fate of loving him, and content in the knowledge that he cared very deeply for her.

What bothered her was the time apart from him. When Sunday evening came, and she finally faced the fact that he would be leaving within a few short hours, she wanted to scream at him to stay, plead with him to content himself for a few more days with her, beg him to love her . . . just one more night.

Instead, she donned what she hoped was a cheery

expression and put together an unforgettable meal while he talked to Ian O'Riley. She could watch them from the kitchen window. A tall, dark-haired man with laughing gray eyes hunched over the fence as he listened to the stooped form of the grizzled old jockey. She really didn't understand why, but the scene, set before the weathered receiving barn, brought tears to her eyes. Hastily, she wiped them away with the back of her hand. She had promised herself that she wouldn't give way to the sadness she felt knowing that Brig would be gone within a few hours, and it was a vow she intended to keep. She didn't want to play on his emotions, or appear as just another weepy female. Her pride wouldn't allow it.

She heard Dean's pickup before it came into view. He had been away from the farm for the afternoon and Becca hadn't expected him to return until later in the evening. Since Brig had arrived at the farm, Dean had avoided him. Dean got out of the truck, nodded curtly toward the two men who had witnessed his noisy entrance, and then headed toward the house. The back door opened to close with a thud as Dean came into the kitchen. He tossed his hat onto a hook near the door and scowled.

"I thought Chambers was leaving," he grumbled.

"He is, but he decided to take a later flight."

"Great." Dean's sarcasm was too caustic to ignore.

After seasoning the salmon with lemon butter, Becca put it into the oven and wiped her hands on her apron. "Has Brig's stay here interfered with your life, Dean?" she asked with a forced smile. "I don't see how. You've made a point of steering clear of him."

"He makes me uncomfortable."

"Why?"

"He throws his weight around too much. This is *our* farm. Why doesn't he just leave and take care of his damned oil company? You'd think he'd have more than enough to handle without coming around here and sticking his nose in where it doesn't belong."

"Brig's only trying to help."

"The hell he is," Dean cursed with an impudent snarl. "I'll tell you what he's done, Becca: He's managed to turn this entire operation around until we don't know whether we're coming or going—"

"What are you talking about?" Dean wasn't making any sense whatsoever.

"Just look at yourself, Becca! You're dancing around with a satisfied gleam in your eye, wearing aprons and smiles like some stereotyped housewife in those fifties movies!" He stared at her fresh apron and her recently curled hair in disgust. "You're a Thoroughbred-horse breeder, Becca, not some silly woman who can't think twice without asking for a man's advice!"

An embarrassed flush crept up Becca's neck and her eyes sparked dangerously. "I haven't neglected my responsibilities, if that's what you're suggesting. I've been working with Gypsy Wind every day."

"When you're not mooning over Brig."

"Brig is helping me, Dean, and I'm not going to apologize for that! Neither am I going to deny that I care for Brig."

"And you've changed, sis. You let Brig Chambers get under your skin again. I never thought you'd be so stupid!"

"You're acting like a threatened child. What is it about Brig that intimidates you?"

Dean rose to the challenge and his icy blue eyes narrowed thoughtfully. "I'm not threatened, Becca, I'm just worried—about you. I don't want to see you hurt again, that's all. I was with you the last time. Remember? I know what Brig Chambers can do to you if he wants to," Dean warned with a well-practiced frown.

"The past is gone . . ."

"Until you start resurrecting it by breeding a horse like Sentimental Lady and then add insult to injury by getting involved with Brig Chambers all over again. You're not asking for trouble, Becca, you're begging for it!"

Becca's small fists clenched. "I think you're wrong."

"Time will tell . . ."

Brig entered the room noiselessly and the conversation dissolved. If he had heard the tail end of the argument, he gave no indication of it, nor did he comment on the deadly look in Becca's green eyes and the tell-tale blush on her cheeks. He strode across the room to lean against a counter near Rebecca. After casting her a lazy, I'm-on-your-side wink, he crossed his arms over his chest and smiled tightly at Dean. Brig seemed relaxed and comfortable, except for the glitter of expectation in his stormy gray eyes.

Dean took a chair and shifted his weight uneasily under the power of Brig's silent stare. Becca could feel the tension electrifying the air of the small country kitchen. Ian O'Riley sauntered into the room and seemed to notice the undercurrents of strained energy. The wooden match between his teeth moved quickly back and forth in his mouth.

"Brig asked me to stay for dinner," Ian remarked to Rebecca. "Said he wanted to talk about the horse . . . but if it's too much bother . . ."

"Nonsense. We'd love to have you," Becca replied quickly, destroying the old man's attempt at escape. Becca thought the conversation would be less strained with Ian involved.

Ian cast Becca a rueful glance before motioning toward the hallway. "I'll just give the missus a jingle. You know, check it out with the boss." His light attempt at humor did nothing to relieve the tension in the room. He shrugged his bowed shoulders and exited as quickly as he had entered, glad for his excuse to find the telephone in the hall.

"Haven't seen much of you around," Brig observed, looking pointedly at Dean.

"Been busy, I guess," Dean retorted as he half-stood and swung the chair around in order to straddle it backward. He rested his forearms on the chair back, and Becca wondered if her brother felt shielded with the tiny spokes of polished maple between himself and Brig.

Brig nodded as if he understood. "There is a lot of work around this place," he agreed complacently. Too complacently. Becca could sense the fight brewing in the air.

"I can handle it."

The affable smile on Brig's face faded. "Ian mentioned that it was your decision not to tell Rebecca that I had called her several times after Sentimental Lady's death."

Defensively, Dean managed a strained smile. "Is that what he said?"

Becca's breath caught in her throat.

"Uh-huh. And I suppose that woman . . . what was her name?" Brig squinted as if he were trying to remember something elusive.

"Martha?" Becca whispered.

"Right. Martha—she would confirm Ian's story, no doubt."

Dean seemed to pale slightly under his deep California tan. Becca's fingernails dug into her palms.

What was Brig doing? It was as if he and Dean were playing some slow-motion game that they alone could understand. With a dismissive shrug of his broad shoulders, Dean answered. "I suppose she might."

"If I could find her," Brig added with a twisted smile. "Do you have any idea where she is?"

"Of course not!" Dean snapped angrily.

Brig's dark brows cocked in disbelief. "No one knows where she is?"

Before Becca could explain, Dean answered. "I suppose she's with her daughter somewhere. We really don't know. She doesn't work here anymore."

"But weren't you involved with that girl . . . Martha's daughter, Jackie?"

It was Becca's turn to be shocked. Dean had been involved with Martha's daughter? What did that mean?

"We dated a couple of times. No big deal. What's this all about, Chambers? What does Jackie have to do with anything?"

"Nothing really." Brig took an apple from the counter and began to polish it against his jeans. Dean's nerves were stretched to the breaking point. His blue eyes darted nervously around the room. "I just wanted you to admit that you told Martha not to let Becca know that I called."

"I already told you that much!" Dean's eyes flared with angry blue fire.

"I don't think we should discuss this now," Becca interjected.

"I want to get to the bottom of it!" Brig insisted.

"What's to get to the bottom of? I was just protecting my sister, Chambers. If you can't remember what happened, I do!" Dean's lips curled in contempt and he pointed viciously at Brig. "You tried to ruin her," he accused. "You did everything in your power to see her disgraced before the entire racing establishment! Because of you Ian nearly lost his license!"

"What the devil—" Ian had returned to the kitchen and his stubbled chin frowned at the scene before him. "I thought we were through arguing about Sentimental Lady."

"We were—until Chambers came back."

Becca's anger got the better of her. "All right. That's enough! I don't want to discuss this any longer—"

"You'd better get used to it, sis. Once the word gets out that you've been seeing Chambers again, the lid is going to come off this pressure cooker and explode in your face! The press will be on you quicker than a flea on a dog!"

Brig's eyes glittered like ice. "And who's going to tell the press?"

"It's not something that's easily hidden," Dean remarked. "Especially once Gypsy Wind starts racing— that is *if you*'re still around by then."

"Oh, I'll be around," Brig confirmed. It sounded more like a threat than a promise. "And by the time Gypsy Wind starts, I hope to have all the mystery surrounding Sentimental Lady's death resolved." Brig was beginning to sound obsessed. His bright gray eyes never left the strained contours of Dean's ruddy face.

Becca ran her fingers through her hair and her green eyes clouded in confusion. She stared at Brig, hoping to understand the man she loved so desperately. "I don't know how you expect to find out what the horse racing board couldn't."

The muscle in the corner of Brig's jaw worked, though he attempted a grim smile. "Maybe the board didn't have the same gut feeling that I have."

"What feeling?" Becca asked.

Dean stiffened and rose from the fragile protection

of the chair. "You've got a gut feeling—after all these years?" He laughed hollowly and the false sound echoed in the rafters. "It's been six years, man—forget it. It's not worth all the trouble and it would cost a fortune to dig up all that evidence again . . ." He reached for his hat, but Brig's next words made him hesitate.

"That's right, it's been six years . . . nearly seven. I'm not up on the statute of limitations. Are you?"

"What do you mean?" Becca asked, but Brig ignored the question.

"As for the cost of sifting through the evidence, I don't think money will be the problem. Any amount it might cost would be well worth the price to see justice served and Sentimental Lady revenged."

Dean whirled on his boot heel and leveled his angry gaze at Brig. "Money's never the problem with guys like you, is it?" he inquired as he pushed his Stetson onto his head. His words reeked of unconcealed sarcasm as he opened the door and tossed his final words to Becca. "I'm going into town . . . don't hold dinner!" The screen door banged loudly behind him and within a few minutes the roar of the pickup's engine filled the kitchen.

"What was that all about?" Becca asked. The strain of emotions twisted her finely sculpted face. "Why did you intentionally pick a fight with Dean?"

"I wasn't trying to argue with him," Brig responded. "I just wanted to get some answers from him, that's all."

"That isn't all," Becca refuted, her green eyes snapping. "You nearly accused him of being responsible for Sentimental Lady's death—not in so many words, maybe, but the insinuation was there."

"Now, Missy," Ian interjected kindly, "don't be jumping to conclusions."

"I'm not!" Becca retorted. "Sometimes I don't think I understand you—any of you." She tried to force her attention back to the dinner she was preparing, but found it an impossible task. Too many unanswered questions hung in the air like unwelcome ghosts from the past. It made her shudder inwardly. "What were all those questions about Martha and her daughter? Good Lord, Brig, half of the argument didn't make any sense whatsoever!" She placed a pan of rice on the stove and added under her breath, "At least not to me."

She pulled off her apron and tossed it onto the counter as she turned to face Ian. The unmasked guilt on his crowlike features added to her suspicion of collusion. It was obvious that both he and Brig knew something she didn't. "Okay, what's going on?" she demanded. "This has something to do with Dean, unless I miss my guess." She folded her arms over her chest and waited for an explanation. Fear slowly gripped her heart as the men remained silent, but she ignored the apprehension, realizing that the truth, no matter how painful it might be, was far better than the doubts that had assailed her for the past few weeks. "What is it?" she asked in a low voice that betrayed none of her anxiety.

Ian couldn't meet Becca's exacting gaze. "I shouldn't have said anything," he mumbled to himself.

"About what?" Becca asked.

"About Jackie McDonnell," Brig supplied. Ian pursed his thin lips together impatiently.

"What does Martha's daughter have to do with anything? I don't see that the fact that she dated Dean a couple of times means anything."

"It was more than a few casual dates," Brig explained.

Ian interrupted, his wise eyes anxious. "Look, Chambers, I don't think that we should say anything. We'd be out of line. It's really none of our business—"

"What are you talking about, Ian?" Becca demanded.

"He's trying to protect you, Rebecca." Brig came closer to her and she could see the worry in his dark eyes. Was it for her? He placed a steadying hand on her shoulder, but she pulled away from him in defiant anger.

"Protecting me?" she repeated incredulously. "From what? The truth?" Ian avoided her indignant gaze. "Well, I'm sick and tired of people trying to *protect* me. Just because I'm a woman doesn't mean I fall apart under the least little bit of pressure. Dean caused a major misunderstanding by lying to me and refusing to let Brig's calls get through to me, all for the sake of *protecting* me. I would think that you of all people, Ian, could trust me with the truth!"

"It's not a matter of trust, Missy."

Becca's eyes grew softer as she gazed down at the worried ex-jockey. He wore his heart on his sleeve and his face clearly reflected his concern for her. "Ian, can't you explain to me what it is that's bothering you? It's not fair for you to carry the burden all by yourself."

His silver eyebrows pinched together. "As I said, it's none of my affair."

Brig took charge of the conversation and Ian dropped his small frame gratefully into the nearest chair. The grizzled old man removed his cap and rotated it nervously in his fingers as Brig spoke.

"You thought that Martha left the farm to take care of her daughter, who was ill—right?"

Becca nodded pensively. The stern tone of Brig's voice reinforced her fears. Nervously she rubbed her thumb over her forefinger. "I wasn't here when she left," Becca whispered, her gaze locking with Brig's. "I was visiting a friend in San Francisco at the time and when I got home she had gone . . . without even a note of explanation."

"Didn't you think that was odd?"

"For a little while, and then Dean explained that Martha's daughter, Jackie, was seriously ill and Martha had taken Jackie to a specialist in L.A. They had relatives that lived in Diamond Bar, I think. Anyway, the only thing I considered strange was the fact that Martha never bothered to call or come back even for a short visit. What exactly are you saying here, anyway? That Dean lied? Wasn't his story the truth?" Her green eyes fixed on Ian.

"Partially," Brig allowed.

"Meaning what?"

"Meaning that Martha did leave to help her daughter."

"But?" she coaxed.

"But Jackie wasn't sick, not really." He paused for a moment and Becca's heart began to race.

"I don't understand . . ." Her voice was uncertain.

"The girl was pregnant."

Becca swallowed with difficulty and had to lean against the counter for support. Her voice was little more than a whisper. "And Dean was the father," she guessed. A sickening feeling of disgust rose in her stomach as Brig's dark eyes confirmed her unpleasant conjecture.

"That's right, Missy," Ian agreed in a hoarse voice. He stared at the table and coughed nervously.

"Someone should have told me . . ."

"Dean should have told you," Brig corrected.

"So what happened—to Jackie, and Martha and the

baby?" Dean's baby. Why hadn't he confided in her? Had he ever seen his own child? What had he been thinking all these years?

Ian acted as if he didn't like talking about it, but he decided to finally let the truth come out. "Martha and Jackie moved to L.A."

"So that part wasn't a lie." It was little consolation.

"No."

"But that doesn't explain why Martha never wrote me." Becca's face was filled with genuine concern and it twisted Ian's old heart painfully.

"You have to understand, Missy, that Martha blames Dean for the pain he caused her daughter."

"Because Dean didn't marry her?"

Ian nodded. "In Martha's eyes, Dean disgraced Jackie, though heaven knows what kind of a marriage it would have been." He wiped the top of his balding head with his hand. "Jackie gave the baby up for adoption, and swore she'd never have another child. That's a pretty rough statement. Martha thought she might never have another grandchild—one she could claim as her own. She offered to adopt the baby herself, but Jackie wouldn't allow it. The girl claimed she hated the baby and wanted nothing to remind her of Dean."

"And so Martha feels the same about me."

Ian gritted his teeth. His faded blue eyes were cheerless as they held Becca's gaze. "There are too many unhappy memories here for Martha. I don't think she'll ever come back."

"Then you still hear from her?"

"Only once in a while. The missus, she sends Martha a Christmas card every year—that sort of thing."

"Does Jackie know who adopted the child?"

Ian shook his head. "Wouldn't even let the doctors tell

her if it was a boy or a girl—refused to look at it when it was born. It was nearly the death of Martha. The child is better off with its adoptive parents," Ian allowed.

Becca's heart was heavy. "Didn't Dean want to know about the baby?"

Ian shook his head. "He wouldn't even talk to Jackie when she told him she was carrying his child."

"Nice guy—that brother of yours," Brig observed dryly.

When she ran her fingers over her forehead, Becca noticed that she had broken out in a sweat. She felt cold and empty inside. Why hadn't Dean confided in her? "How is Jackie now?"

Ian brightened. "She's fine, from what I understand. Married herself a young lawyer, she did."

A wistful smile curved Becca's lips. "Maybe Martha will get that grandchild yet."

"I hope so," Ian agreed.

"I'd like to call Martha or write to her. Do you have her number?"

Ian's weak smile faded. "I don't know if that would be wise," he commented, rubbing his hand over the back of his neck. "No use in stirring up hard feelings."

"Give it time," Brig suggested.

"It's been over five years!"

"Then a few more weeks won't matter, will they?" Brig asked rhetorically.

"I'll think about it—after I talk to Dean."

Ian pinched his bottom lip with his teeth. "I don't know if I'd go bringin' it up to your brother, miss. He might not like the idea that we were talkin' behind his back."

"And I don't like the idea that he didn't level with me."

"It was hard for him . . ." Ian insisted.

"Dean has a lot of explaining to do."

"Just don't do anything rash," Ian said.

An uneasy silence settled upon the room as Becca finished preparing the meal. Dean didn't return, though Becca had set him a place at the table. The conversation was stilted at first as Ian explained about his plans for racing Gypsy Wind, including the proposed move to Sequoia Park. Slowly the tension in the conversation ebbed as dinner was served and then eaten. The three of them talked about the coming racing season and the stiff competition Gypsy Wind would have to face. Brig and Ian agreed that Gypsy Wind should be started as soon as the season opened, in order to establish a name for herself since she hadn't raced as a two-year-old. They felt that the sooner she became familiar with race regimen, the better.

By the time Ian left, some of Becca's misgivings had subsided. She promised to call Grace, Ian's wife, for Martha's address and telephone number. Although Ian soundly disapproved, he patted Becca firmly on the shoulder and told her to do what she thought best.

Brig's suitcase stood by the stairs, reminding Becca that he was leaving her. She found it imposibble to think of a future without him, or of the empty days when he wouldn't be by her side.

"I have to go," he admitted, checking his watch and setting aside his coffee cup.

"I know."

"I wish I could convince you to come with me."

Her green eyes were filled with sadness. "I have to stay here with Gypsy Wind."

They were sitting next to each other on the couch. His arm was draped lazily over her shoulders, his fingertips moving silently against her shoulder. "We could board Gypsy Wind at the Chambers Stables."

Becca smiled and set her cup next to Brig's. "I can't

move to Kentucky. I don't fit in with the Eastern racing set . . . at least not anymore . . ." Her voice faded as she remembered a time when she felt at home anywhere—when the world was at her feet, before Sentimental Lady's tragic death.

"I would be with you," he stated softly as he moved her head to lay upon his shoulder. It felt so right.

She longed to say yes, to tell him that she would follow him to the ends of the earth if necessary, but she couldn't. There was too much yet to be done, here at The Starlight Farm. "Nothing sounds better," she admitted honestly. "But I think it would be best not to move Gypsy Wind until after the New Year when Ian plans to stable her at Sequoia."

"I'd feel better if you were closer to me."

"Then why not move the corporate offices of Chambers Oil out here," she teased.

"Just like that?"

"Why not?"

"Be serious."

"I am."

"And I'm nearly foolish enough to take you up on your offer."

"I'd love it if you would stay with me," Becca confided, hoping beyond hope that they could find a way to be together. He kissed her gently on the forehead.

"I'll work on it, if you promise to be careful."

"I'm always careful . . ."

The hand over her shoulder tightened. His voice was low and threatening. "I don't trust your brother."

"You never have."

"But I wasn't convinced that he was dangerous before."

Becca laughed at the severity of Brig's features. He

really believed what he was saying. "Dean might be a lot of things," she allowed. "And I admit that I've called him more than a few myself, but he's not dangerous. Irresponsible, wily, and maybe slightly underhanded, yes, but dangerous, never!"

"You're taking this too lightly."

"And you're acting paranoid. Just because my brother shirked his responsibility toward Jackie doesn't necessarily mean that he's dangerous."

"Just be careful, okay . . . and don't go getting him upset. Don't even mention that you know about Jackie."

"That's going to be impossible . . ."

"Please, Rebecca. Don't say anything until I come back."

She saw the look of concern in his eyes. "You're really worried, aren't you?"

"I just want to know what we're up against, that's all. And I don't like leaving you here alone with him."

"Brig, Dean's my brother! He would never hurt me—"

"You don't know that, Becca!" For the first time, Brig's fear infected her.

"This is more than your concern because of Jackie's baby, isn't it? You really think Dean was involved in Sentimental Lady's death."

Brig's eyes narrowed and he held her more tightly to him. "I just want to know what we're up against, and I need a couple of days to sort out a few things. Why don't you come with me, for just a few days, until I can get to the source of all this?"

"I can't leave the farm right now."

"Ian can handle it. I've already spoken with him."

"Brig, this is my home, my responsibility, my *life*. I just can't pack up and leave because you're paranoid."

Roughly, he gave her shoulders a shake. "I'm not paranoid, Becca."

"Then trust me to be able to handle myself—with my brother or anyone else."

His smile was weak. "You always were a stubborn creature," he conceded. "Do you have a gun?"

Becca paled. "*No!* And I don't need one," she asserted, her lower lip trembling.

"How can you be sure?"

"Stop it, Brig, you're scaring the hell out of me."

"Good, you should be frightened."

Her voice was as tight as her grip on the arm of the couch. "I hope this is a severe case of melodrama on your part," she whispered.

"So do I."

"Dean is my brother—"

He waved off her arguments with his open palm. "I just want you to be careful, Rebecca. You're important to me." He twined his fingers in her tawny hair and pulled her head closer to his in order to press a kiss against her lips, silently promising a shared future. "Take care of yourself, lady."

Her voice caught and she had trouble forming her response. "I will," she promised.

"There's one other thing," he said as he reluctantly rose and stepped away from her. Reaching into the pocket of his corduroy slacks, he extracted a yellowed piece of paper. Becca recognized it as the note she had signed to Jason Chambers. Brig handed the small document to her. "I've taken care of this."

She took the paper, but continued to stare into his eyes, as if she was attempting to memorize their steely gray depths. "What do you mean?"

"The note doesn't exist anymore."

"I'm sorry, Brig, but I don't quite follow you."

"It's simple. As far as anyone knows, this note was never signed. You don't owe me or Chambers Oil a bloody cent."

Becca smiled sadly. "I appreciate the offer, Brig, but I can't accept it. You don't have to buy my way out for me."

"And I couldn't live with myself if I took your money. Don't you see what I'm trying to say to you—that I love you and that what I have is yours. I don't want your money, Rebecca. I want you."

"Then stay with me," she pleaded, searching his face to try and understand him. If only she could believe that he loved her with the same intensity she felt for him.

He took her hands in his. "I'll be back," he promised. "As soon as I can . . ."

Their last embrace was a surrender to the doubts that kept surfacing in her mind. She held him as if she were afraid he would step into the dark night and never return.

Chapter 12

It was the second day affer Brig had departed that Becca's worries began to affect her work. The first night she had been anxious, but slowly her worry had developed into fear. Not only had she not heard from Brig in the last forty eight hours, but also Dean hadn't returned, and she couldn't track him down. She had known that Dean was angry when he left the farm, but she had expected him to show up before now. This wasn't the first time he had taken off in an angry huff, but it was surprising that he hadn't come home with his tail tucked between his legs and a sheepish grin on his face after he had cooled off. This time it was different.

Ian O'Riley had shrugged off her concern with a dismissive shake of his balding head. Ian figured that Dean probably just needed to go somewhere and let off steam. He would return again, the old man assured Becca, like a bad penny. Becca wasn't so sure. In her anxiety, she had called Dean's favorite haunts in the nearby town. No one had seen him since the night he had driven into town like a madman.

She was working on the books when she heard the familiar sound of Dean's pickup rattling down the drive. A smile of relief curved her lips as the truck came to a halt near the stables. Dean was known for his theatrical entrances. She closed the general ledger and was about to head outside when she heard the clatter of his boots pounding on the stairs. He flew into the office at a dead run. Breathless from his sprint across the parking lot, wearing the same faded jeans and work shirt he had donned on Sunday, he looked tired and drawn. There was the faint smell of alcohol mingled with sour sweat on his clothes. A tender bruise blackened one of his cheeks.

Becca tried to make light of the situation, though her suspicion could not be denied. "You look like something the cat dragged in and then kicked back out again," she teased, though her green eyes reflected her concern for her brother. "But I'm glad you're back. I was really beginning to worry about you."

"I'll bet," Dean ground out caustically. It was then she noticed the look of contempt that darkened his icy blue eyes.

"Is something wrong? What happened to you? Where have you been? I called all over town, but no one knew where you were. I even thought about calling the police . . ." she tried to touch him on the shoulder, but he shrank away like a wounded animal.

"The police?" he echoed. "That would have been great. Jesus, Becca, you don't have to pretend any longer. I know how you feel about me."

The sarcasm in his voice made her smile disappear completely. What had gotten into him? He acted as if she intended to hurt him. "Dean, are you in some kind of trouble?"

"I'm not sure," he admitted, dropping his insolent attitude for a second. It was replaced immediately, as if he suddenly remembered that she was the enemy. "It doesn't matter," he said. "And if I am in trouble, I know who to blame."

"I'm not sure I understand what you're getting at . . ."

"Don't give me that line, Becca. You know as well as I do that Chambers isn't going to let up on me for a minute, is he?" He wiped the sweat from his forehead with the back of his grimy hand as if he were trying to erase a haunting memory.

"What has Brig got to do with any of this?" she asked, her voice tight, her mouth dry. Apprehension slowly began to grip her heart. Dean was in trouble— big trouble—and Brig was involved. The bloody memory of Sentimental Lady's last frantic hours kept surfacing in her mind. Dean couldn't meet her eyes.

"Ah, hell, Sis. I don't have time to sit around here and swap stories with you now. I just came back for a few of my things and a couple of bucks . . ."

"What are you talking about?" she demanded in a hoarse whisper filled with dread.

Dean looked at her as if he were seeing her for the first time since entering the room. He ran his hand against the corner of his mouth as he studied her. He was skeptical. "You mean you don't know?"

She shook her head, her green eyes beseeching him as she attempted to understand the brother who had once been so dear to her. He was a stranger . . . a frightened stranger carrying a heavy burden of guilt. She could read it in his eyes. *Good Lord, Dean must have known all along what had happened to Sentimental Lady!* The brother she had known had changed more than she had been willing to admit. Her heart froze.

"Then, I'll tell you. Chambers is responsible for this," Dean stated as he pointed angrily at his discolored cheek.

"Brig?" Becca mouthed the word. She was incredulous. It was then that she noticed the dried blood smeared on Dean's plaid shirt and the slight swelling of his lower lip.

"That's right! Your friend, Brig Chambers, champion of all that is good and right with the world," he snarled. "Defender of the little people and the big bucks. That's how you see him, isn't it? As some modern-day Prince Charming?"

"I . . . I see Brig as a man, a good man . . ."

"Ha!"

". . . and I find it difficult to believe that Brig got into a fistfight with you."

"Of course you do. Because it's not his style, right? How many times have I told you that you get crazy when you're around him? Well, you're right; Chambers didn't beat me up. He wouldn't dirty his hands. One of his goons got hold of me the other night and decided to teach me a lesson."

"Why didn't you come home?" she cried.

"Because this guy, he wouldn't let me . . ."

"Oh, Dean—"

''It's true!" Dean's fist pounded onto the top of the desk. Becca nearly jumped out of her skin.

She wavered for a moment, trying desperately to understand her brother, the brother she had once trusted with her life. The question faltered on her dry lips. "How . . . how do you know that this man . . . the one that hurt you . . . how do you know that he was connected with Brig?"

"Who else?"

"Someone who bears a grudge against you . . ." she was thinking as fast as she could, hoping to find someone, anyone, other than Brig who might be responsible. " . . . like Jackie McDonnell. Maybe she was behind it."

Dean's eyes flared dangerously. "I *know* it was Chambers, Becca." He glanced around the room nervously. "Look, I don't have much time. I need a check for a couple of grand." The checkbook was lying open on the desk. Dean picked it up.

"You need two thousand dollars?" Becca repeated. Too much was happening. She needed time to think and understand what was happening. "Why?"

"Because I'm leaving, damn it!"

"Leaving? Why?" Becca felt her entire body beginning to shake.

"I just can't sit around here any longer and watch you make a fool of yourself over Brig Chambers—"

"That's not what's bothering you."

"The hell it isn't."

Becca watched her brother through new eyes, but she gave him one last chance, praying silently that her suspicions weren't founded. "This has something to do with Jackie McDonnell and her baby, doesn't it?"

Dean laughed mirthlessly before his eyes narrowed. "Leave her out of this. And as for that kid of hers . . . how do I know that it was mine? Jackie had been making it with half the guys in the county. I wasn't about to raise some other man's bastard."

"Dean!"

He shook an angry finger under her nose. "I told you not to tell Brig about Gypsy Wind, but you had to, didn't you? And he had to come back here and start digging everything up all over again. This is all your fault, Becca—"

"Oh, God, no," Becca whispered. Tears pooled in her round green eyes. "Sentimental Lady—"

"Shhh!" The sound of a car racing down the drive caught Dean's attention and he put a finger to his swollen lips to silence his sister. His eyes glittered dangerously when he glanced out the window and a bitter smile thinned his lips. "Damn!" A silver Mercedes was speeding on the gravel driveway. Dean recognized it as belonging to Brig Chambers. "I've got to get out of here, Becca, and now. Give me the money—"

"You can't run," she murmured, her trembling voice betraying her battered emotions.

Dean's eyes were filled with undisguised contempt. "That's where you're wrong."

"But I don't understand . . ."

"I just bet you don't. And you probably never will." He ripped a check out of the book and stuffed it into his pocket before grabbing the loose cash from the top desk drawer. "Just do me one last favor, will you, Becca?"

"What's that?"

"Give me a few minutes to get out of here," he requested. A small shadow of fear clouded his gaze for a split second. Becca felt her stomach begin to knot.

"What . . . what do you want me to do?"

He was undecided. "Hell, I don't know. Anything. Stall Brig. Do whatever you have to, tell him you think you saw me out in the far pasture . . . tell him anything to get him off my back and give me a running start."

Becca's hands were shaking as she stepped toward Dean and placed her palms against his shoulders. He stiffened while tears streamed down her cheeks. "I think I know what you're running from, Dean, and it's a mistake. You can't begin to hide—"

"You're a miserable excuse for a sister!" Dean screamed at her as he shook himself free of her grasp and knocked her to the floor. "I knew I couldn't count on you!" He ran to the window and opened it. Quickly he calculated the fall. It was only two stories, less than twenty feet. Surely he could make it. He poised on the window ledge and cast one last insolent glance of hatred at his sister. For the first time Becca noticed the shiny butt of a pistol peeking out of his pocket. He wrapped one hand around the gun while with the other he took hold of the ledge.

"Don't!" Becca shrieked hysterically from her position on the floorboards. Her hair was tangled, her face contorted in fear, and she sobbed uncontrollably when she witnessed Dean lower himself out of the window and finally release his grip on the ledge. *"No!"* She heard him drop, the hollow sound of a body hitting unyielding earth.

Brig burst into the room. His eyes darted from the open window to Becca's ashen face and the terror reflected in her deep green eyes. The concern on his face deepened. "Are you all right?" he asked as he raced to her side and took her into the strong security of his arms. "God, Becca, are you all right?"

"I'm okay . . ."

"You're not hurt?" His dark eyes raked her body as if he were searching for evidence to the contrary.

"Really . . . I'm . . . I'm fine," she managed to say as she wiped her tears with the back of one hand. The other was braced behind his neck, holding him near. She needed to feel the strength of his body against hers, the comfort of his arms holding her fiercely. She had to know there was something strong in the world that she could grasp.

He held her just as desperately. For the last two hours he had feared her dead, lost to him forever, and he vowed silently that he would never again let her go, should he find her alive. He pressed his lips to the top of her head. "Dear God, Rebecca," he groaned, "I was afraid that I'd lost you." His voice was husky, his vision clouded by salty tears of relief.

The next few moments were quiet, the silence broken only by her quiet sobs and the rapid beating of his heart. From somewhere nearby, he thought he heard a painful moan, but he ignored it, concentrating only on the warmth of the woman in his arms.

Slowly her thoughts became coherent. "Where have you been?" she asked in the faintest of whispers.

"In L.A."

"Then you didn't return to Denver?"

His smile was grim. "No. It's a long story. Your brother—where is he?"

Becca nodded feebly toward the window, afraid that Dean might be injured or worse. Reluctantly Brig released her, but before he reached the ledge the thought of Dean's hidden pistol entered Becca's weary mind. "Watch out," she called after Brig. "He's got a gun." Her heart twisted at the thought.

The sound of a pickup coughing and sparking to life caught her attention. Brig stood watching silently as the truck roared down the winding lane. "Stupid fool," he muttered through clenched teeth.

"Why did you let him go?" Once again confusion took hold of her.

"He won't get far, and I didn't come here chasing

him," Brig explained. "It was you I came to see. I was worried about you." He came back to her and pulled her to her feet, wrapping his arms tightly around her waist. His eyes were filled with genuine concern. "When I heard that Dean had gotten away from Charlie—"

"Then Dean was right. It was you. You were behind it!"

Brig nodded curtly. "But, as usual, your brother used less than sound judgment. He wouldn't accept Charlie's hospitality and tried to knock him out by hitting him over the back of the head. Charlie reciprocated."

"But why did you try and hold him? I think that's called kidnapping in this state."

"No one kidnapped anyone. We just invited Dean to play poker—for forty-eight hours. I guess he didn't like the game."

"But, Brig, why?"

"Because I needed time and I had to be sure that he wouldn't hurt you while I was in L.A."

Becca shook her head, rubbing the soft golden wisps of her hair against Brig's chest. "You didn't need to worry. Dean would never hurt me."

"When it comes to you, I don't take any chances. Come on, let's go into the house and I'll pour you a drink. You look like you could use one."

"What I need is answers. I want to know what it was you were after in Los Angeles."

Becca's knees were weak and she had to lean on Brig as they walked through the gathering twilight toward the old farmhouse. Brig's arm was a steadying reinforcement on Becca's slumped shoulders. She tried to think rationally, but the headache that had begun to develop between her temples and the memory of the fear in Dean's eyes clouded her mind.

Once inside the farmhouse, Brig poured two shots of brandy. Becca accepted the drink gratefully and had to hold the small snifter in both of her hands in order not to spill any of the amber liquor. She looked small and frail as she sat on the couch cradling the glass between her fingers. Brig wondered how much of her vulnerability was the direct result of his carelessness. He silently cursed himself before draining his drink in one lengthy swallow.

Her soft green eyes searched his. "I don't understand, Brig, why aren't you chasing Dean?"

"Because I'd rather stay with you—you need me right now."

She smiled weakly despite her fears. "But I thought you wanted to capture him—oh God, will you listen to me. I'm talking about my *brother!*" She dropped her head into her palm and felt the tears beginning to rise once again in her throat.

"Shhh, it's all right." He sat beside her on the couch after refilling her drink.

"How can you even think that everything's okay?"

"Because for the last six years we've all been living a lie—I'm just angry with myself for not sensing it any earlier. I let my pride get in the way of my clear thinking."

"I think we all could say that. But what about Dean?"

"He's probably already in custody."

"What?"

"I called the police and explained everything to them. They were going to pick up Dean and question him. I told them that I suspected that he would try to make a run for it after he came here."

"But how did you know that he'd be back?"

Brig's lips curved into a thoughtful frown. "Because the poker game—the one he skipped out on. It was rigged. For a while he won and big, then he started losing. By the time he took off, he didn't have a dime on him—or a credit card. He was bound to come here for some cash when he smelled that I was on to him." Brig shook his head in self-mockery. "That was a bad move on my part. He could have hurt you . . ."

"He would never hurt me."

"You don't know your brother anymore."

Becca's eyes were clear when she looked into Brig's stormy gray gaze. "Nothing that has happened has convinced me that Dean would intentionally harm me, at least not physically." She swirled the liquor in her glass and studied the small whirlpool. Her voice was hoarse when she spoke again. "All of this has something to do with Sentimental Lady, doesn't it?"

Brig set his empty glass on a side table. "Yes."

"And that was why you didn't go back to Denver?"

"I couldn't . . . not when I felt I was so close to the truth."

"But why couldn't you tell me? Why didn't you let me know what you were planning?"

Brig raked his fingers through his dark hair and his eyes closed for a moment, as if he was searching for just the right words to make her understand his motives. "Because I wanted to be sure that I was on the right track. For God's sake, Rebecca, Dean's your brother! I couldn't accuse him without the evidence backing me up."

"And now you've got it?" she asked quietly as she absently rubbed her temple. Brig's arm across her shoulder tensed and he nodded. "Oh, God," she murmured desperately. She fought against the tears threatening to spill.

"You knew, didn't you?" he asked gently.

She shook her long blond curls. "No. Not really. I . . . I had vague suspicions . . . nothing founded and I guess I really wanted to look the other way. I didn't want to believe that Dean was a part of it . . . I guess I hid my head in the sand." She turned away from him and her next words were barely a whisper. "It explains so much," she confided, taking a sip from the brandy. "Tell me what you found."

There was a dead quality in her voice that made him hesitate. "I should have known that Dean was involved when I found out that he had intentionally not told you about the phone calls. That didn't make much sense to me. It was as if he wanted to keep us apart. From what I could remember about him, he was always interested in Chambers Oil. He didn't object to your seeing me six years ago and I suspected he was secretly hoping that you and I would get married and he'd be that much closer to my father's wealth."

Becca felt that she should defend her brother, but Brig's assessment of the situation was so close to her own feelings, she couldn't deny his supposition. She silently nodded her agreement, trying to hold at bay the sickening feeling of betrayal taking hold of her. It was true. Before the tragedy, Dean had been more than pleased with her relationship with Brig.

"But something happened," Brig continued. "It had to have been the accident. At first, I thought like everyone else, that the reason for Dean's attitude toward me and the fact that he didn't let the phone calls through was because he blamed me for not supporting you during the investigation."

"What changed your mind?" she asked, though something inside her told her that she really didn't want to know.

"It was something you said."

"What?"

"You mentioned that Dean suggested you go to my father for the money to breed Gypsy Wind. That seemed a little out of character to me. If Dean wanted us apart, why would he risk getting the old man involved?"

"We had no choice," Becca reiterated. "There was nowhere else to turn and I really don't think Dean wanted me to contact Jason. When I decided to go, Dean objected."

"I think he was just blowing smoke . . ."

Becca leaned heavily against the cushions and closed her eyes. She remembered meeting with Jason Chambers in his cabin in the Rockies. He had insisted that she meet him there, away from the eyes in the office. The transaction was to be a private matter. No one would know about it except for himself and Becca. He had seemed pleased that she had come, or was it relief that had sparked in his cool brown eyes as he puffed on his pipe and let the smoke circle his head? His smile as they had shaken hands seemed vaguely triumphant and he had tucked the note away in the bottom drawer of his scarred oak desk. His response had been immediate and Becca had left the cabin feeling that if she had asked for a million dollars he would have given it to her without batting an eye. Yes, it had been strange, but she had been so elated that the oddity of the situation hadn't really taken hold of her. Until now, when Brig brought it all back to her.

"There was something else that bothered me," Brig continued. "Jason agreed to that loan . . . without any restrictions, right?" Becca opened her eyes and nodded her agreement. "He wasn't exactly the most philanthropic man around," Brig observed, tracing the line of her jaw with his fingertip, "especially when you consider his attitude after the match race. His remarks were so unfeeling and cruel. It just didn't make any sense that he would loan you the money to breed another horse like Sentimental Lady. The answer had to be in that final race, but I just didn't know what it was."

"So why did you decide to go to Los Angeles? I'm sorry, Brig, you've lost me."

"Because Ian O'Riley slipped up. When I asked him about Martha, he mentioned Jackie McDonnell and the child."

"So you went to L.A. to find Jackie," Becca surmised. "Did you locate her?"

Brig's expression remained grim. "Yeah. I found her and her mother . . ."

"Martha."

"Let me tell you, there's no love lost between Jackie and your brother."

"I know," Becca replied as she reflected on Dean's cruel statement about the girl. How had she been so blind to her own brother's deceit?

"Jackie was more than willing to tell me everything she knew about the situation, which was only that Dean had been doing a few things for my father. She couldn't, or wouldn't, admit that he had injected Sentimental Lady. Maybe she really doesn't know, or maybe she was protecting herself. If she knew about the crime, there's a chance that she could be considered an accomplice."

"So you're sure that Dean was involved," Becca whispered dryly. She held her tears at bay though they burned hotly behind her eyelids.

His fingers rubbed her shoulder. "The way I've got

it figured is that Jason paid Dean to inject Sentimental Lady within the last hour before the race, after the racing soundness examination. Dean got a bundle of money from my father and Jason Chambers' horse, Winsome, kept his flawless record intact."

"Becoming all the more valuable at stud . . ."

"Exactly."

Becca tried one final, futile denial. "But Dean, he never had any money . . ."

Brig pressed a silencing finger to her lips. "Because he spent it—"

"On what?"

"According to Jackie, your brother gambles, and I can speak from personal experience to tell you he's a lousy gambler—at least at poker."

"Then how do you know that Dean got the payoff?"

"Somehow he managed to give Jackie five thousand dollars to help with the medical costs of having the baby and to give her enough money to establish herself somewhere else, to get her off his back."

"No wonder Martha never bothered to write."

Brig's voice was soothing. "She never blamed you, but couldn't stand the sight of your brother."

Becca slumped lower on the worn couch, as if the weight of Brig's explanation was too much for her slim shoulders to bear.

"So Jackie is willing to testify against my brother and tell the police that Jason and Dean were in this together."

"I'm not sure she's that strong."

Becca's green eyes urged him to continue. "Then what?"

"I think that Dean will make a full confession when he understands that the circumstantial evidence points at him and paints a rather grim picture. He'd be smarter to play his cards right and try and keep this as quiet as possible—for everyone's sake."

"They'll be back, won't they?" Becca asked. "The reporters will be back."

"As soon as they get wind of the story."

Becca sank her teeth into her knuckles as she thought about her brother and the frightened man he had become. "Dear God," she whispered, feeling suddenly chilled to the bone. "That's why he took care of me, because of his guilt."

"And so that you wouldn't find him out."

The pain in her heart was reflected in the tortured emotions on her face. "Sentimental Lady was so beautiful . . . and so innocent. I can't believe that he would intentionally—"

"Dean never intended to kill the horse, Rebecca. He only wanted to disqualify her. It was the misstep and her temperament that finally killed her."

"But if he hadn't injected her—"

"We'll never know, will we?"

A shuddering sigh passed Rebecca's lips. "It doesn't matter; Sentimental Lady is dead."

"And you took the blame for that. You and Ian O'Riley."

"It's over now."

"And you can start fresh with Gypsy Wind."

"I don't even want to think about racing right now," Becca confided. "I'm so tired, and confused. I don't think I'll ever want to race again."

"You will."

"I'm not sure, Brig." She looked at him with eyes filled with agony and remorse. "If it wasn't for my stubborn pride and the fact that I had to prove myself to the world as a horse breeder, none of this tragedy would have taken place . . . and my brother wouldn't be on the run—"

"Don't blame yourself, Becca."

She wrapped her arms about her abdomen and rocked on the couch. "Hold me, Brig," she pleaded. "Hold me until it's over . . ."

Chapter 13

The police had taken Dean into custody that same afternoon, and when pressed with the evidence stacked against him, Dean had confessed that he had been responsible for drugging Sentimental Lady in her stall six years before.

Injecting Sentimental Lady with Dexamethasone had been Jason Chambers' idea. He had dealt with Dean in the past and knew that Becca's brother was always in debt, so he offered to pay him twenty-five thousand dollars to drug the horse. It was beneficial to both parties. Dean would be able to pay off several mounting gambling debts and an impatient loan shark. The last five thousand he would give to Jackie for the baby. The deal was sealed and Jason Chambers didn't have to worry about his horse.

According to Dean, Jason had considered Sentimental Lady strong competition and he was unsure of Winsome's ability when it came to racing against the fleet filly. To withdraw Winsome from the race was out of the question because it would be obvious that the colt was demurring to the filly. Jason couldn't take a chance on losing the race. He had to keep Winsome's racing record intact because he planned to put him out to stud and wanted to demand the highest possible fee for Winsome's services. He knew that no matter what the outcome of the race, Sentimental Lady would be disqualified when traces of the steroid were found in her test sample taken immediately after the race.

Twice Rebecca had tried to see her brother, but he had refused, preferring not to face her or the fact that he had let her shoulder the blame for his crime. It was difficult for her, but she realized that if and when Dean wanted to see her, he would contact her. She left the police station feeling drained and exhausted and was met by a bevy of reporters who had gotten wind of the story. She was grateful for Brig's strong arms and calm sense of responsibility. After a firm "no comment" to the eager press, he had whisked her away from the throng and into his car. Within minutes they had left the inquisitive reporters on the steps of the station house.

"They're not going to leave you alone," Brig pointed out, gently smoothing her hair away from her face.

"I know," she murmured, her misty eyes darkened with pain. "But I just can't face them . . . not yet." She turned her head and tried to focus on the passing landscape, but she couldn't think of anything other than her brother's lies. For six years he had hidden the truth. It was ironic, she thought quietly to herself, that six years ago, when she thought Brig had betrayed her, Dean had helped her through that rough period. As it turned out, Dean had been the culprit, and now Brig was helping pull her life back together.

She felt safe once back at Starlight Breeding Farm, but her dreams were tormented with haunting images of her brother behind bars and a terrorized Sentimental Lady rearing against the pain in her bloodied foreleg.

When Becca woke in the middle of the night, still trembling from the frightening images, Brig was beside her. His strong arms surrounded her and helped comfort her. "It's all right," he whispered against the tangled strands of her hair. "Everything's all right now. You're with me, darling Becca." And she believed him. In the desperate hours of the night, with the shadowed fragments of the dream still fresh, she believed him.

It was dawn that brought reality thundering back to her and forced her to rebuild her life. Two days after Dean's arrest, there was a sharp rap on the front door. As Becca raced down the stairs to answer it, she could hear a car idling in the drive. Since it was only seven in the morning, Becca knew it had to be someone with news of her brother. Her heart hammered fearfully as she conjured reasons for the unexpected visit. Had Dean decided to see her after all, or had he attempted to escape? Or was it worse? In his confused state of depression, could he have tried to harm himself?

She yanked open the door, expecting to face a grim police officer. Instead she stood face to face with a slim, attractive woman of about thirty-five, whose well-manicured appearance and practiced smile were neatly in place as her brown gaze swept over Becca's slightly disheveled appearance.

"Ms. Peters?" the woman inquired with a flash of near-perfect teeth and inviting smile.

Becca was instantly wary. She ran her fingers through her long golden hair, attempting to restore it to some kind of order. "Yes?"

"My name is Marian Gordon. I'm with the *Stateside Review.*" She paused for a moment, waiting for the desired effect, and then extended her hand. Becca forced a wan smile onto her face, hoping not to appear overly alarmed. The *Stateside Review* was little more than a cheap scandal sheet that boasted a healthy nationwide circulation. The stories it covered were usually the most bizarre imaginable and Becca realized that there was probably no way to put off the inevitable. One way or the other, Marian Gordon would get her story. Becca took the slim woman's hand grudgingly, and then released it.

"What can I do for you, Ms. Gordon?" she asked coolly. Her elegant dark brows arched instinctively upward.

"Your brother is Dean Peters?" Becca drew in a long, steadying breath before nodding. "I thought so." Marian Gordon seemed pleased. Her poised smile became smug. "Mr. Peters has agreed to give me an exclusive interview concerning his arrest and alleged part in the scandal concerning Sentimental Lady's death."

"He did what?" Becca replied, stunned. Then, collecting herself, she retaliated. "Is this with or without his attorney's knowledge?"

Marian shrugged, obviously not interested in minor details. "I was hoping that I would get your cooperation, Ms. Peters. It would give the story more depth and perspective if I could hear your side of it. Don't you agree?"

"I wasn't aware there were sides."

"Obviously you haven't spoken to your brother lately."

"Obviously." Becca bit back the hot retort that hovered anxiously on the tip of her tongue. "I don't think I can comment on anything at the moment," Becca hedged with a lofty arch of her brows. It took all of her control to be polite to the sharply dressed woman.

Marian Gordon smelled a story—a big story. This could be the story that would give her career the shot in the arm it so desperately needed. Rather than be taken aback by Rebecca Peters' cool reception, she pursued that elusive big story. "Your brother claims that you've . . . been keeping company with Brig Chambers again. True or false?"

"It's true that I see Mr. Chambers," Becca admitted after an initial moment of hesitation. "What does that have to do with my brother or his case?"

"Are you living with him?"

"Pardon me?"

Marian smiled sweetly. "I asked you if you were living with him." This was turning out better than the wily reporter had expected and she switched on her pocket tape recorder. She was right. The story was hot.

"Mr. Chambers has visited the farm," Becca replied evasively.

"Is he here now?"

Becca paused slightly. It was useless to lie. The Mercedes was visible in the driveway. No other vehicle on the farm compared to its luxury. It wouldn't take this reporter long to figure out that it belonged to Brig. "Yes. As a matter of fact, he is."

The woman's eyes lighted with unexpected pleasure. "Good. Then maybe I'll get a chance to have a word with him. This story involves him, too. You know, what with his father being involved and all." Marian couldn't believe her good fortune.

"I don't think so."

"But surely he has some thoughts about your brother and his father and why they drugged that poor horse."

Becca nodded her head and smiled. "I'm sure he does," she agreed. "And I'm sure that I can convince him to give you a call when he decides to make an official comment."

Marian was cagey. She tried another, more subtle tack. "Is there any truth to the rumor that you borrowed money from Jason Chambers in order to breed nearly a carbon-copy of Sentimental Lady. What was that horse's name—Gypsy Wind?"

Becca's suppressed temper began to flare. "I'm not sure I understand what you're insinuating."

The reporter looked appalled. *"Insinuating?"* she echoed. "Why, nothing, dear. According to your brother, you borrowed a rather large sum of money to produce a horse which would be a full sister to Sentimental Lady. Jason Chambers loaned you that money . . . privately of course. True?"

Forcing her fingers to unclench, Becca replied. "I bred Night Dancer to Gypsy Lady a second time. I had no idea that the offspring would be a filly, but it was. Gypsy Lady gave birth to Gypsy Wind. Now, if you'll excuse me, that's all I have to say on the subject . . . make that any subject."

"Well, one last thing. Can I see her?"

"What?" Becca had begun to turn, but spun back to face the tenacious reporter.

"I'd like a picture of Gypsy Wind for the paper. Surely you wouldn't mind a little free publicity for your horse. After all, she never raced as a two-year-old. The public will want to see if she's all she's cracked up to be."

Becca's thin patience shattered. "What she is, Ms. Gordon, is a fine racing Thoroughbred. She'll prove herself on the racetrack. And I don't want any photographs of her to be taken, not yet. She's very high-strung and there's no reason to upset her."

"You said she'll prove herself on the racetrack. What will she prove? That Rebecca Peters is still a qualified horse breeder?"

"That Gypsy Wind is a great filly."

"Prove it. Let me get a picture of her."

"No."

"The horse, *if* she is a champion, will have to get used to it sooner or later—"

"When the time comes. Not now." Becca's voice was stronger and filled with more determination than she had thought possible. The reporter had made her angry and she felt an impassioned need to protect Gypsy Wind.

Marian realized that she had blown whatever chance she had for a more in-depth interview, and she cast a hungry glance at Brig Chambers' car in the drive. Beyond the car were the barns. If only she could get one peek inside. Rebecca Peters was still lingering at the door and her expression was more than slightly perturbed, but Marian couldn't resist the chance for a final question. Why not? She had gotten far more than she had expected from the fiery blond woman.

"Well—no pictures. But tell me this, do you think your horse can duplicate Sentimental Lady's racing career?"

"That remains to be seen."

"Something bothers me, Ms. Peters."

"Just one thing?"

Marian let the pointed remark run off her back. "Why did you take a chance like that?"

"I'm sorry—like what?"

"Why would you borrow fifty thousand dollars to breed a horse so much like one who ended in such a tragedy? Was it for the horse—or the man? Did you really want another racing Thoroughbred, or was this one last desperate attempt to reunite with Brig Chambers?"

Becca's green eyes grew deadly. "I think that's about enough questions. Good day." Refraining from slamming the door in Marian's pleasant face, she

watched the reporter step into her waiting car, make a
full circle and drive down the lane. "And good rid-
dance," Becca mumbled under her breath once she was
assured that the reporter had left the farm. Becca
wanted to make certain that Marian didn't try to snoop
around the barns looking for Gypsy Wind.

"Bravo," a strong male voice asserted from somewhere in the house.

Becca closed the door behind her and noticed Brig
leaning against the staircase, just out of Marian's range
of vision from the front porch. "Have you been lurking
there, listening to the entire conversation?"

Brig's grin wasn't the least bit sheepish. "Most of
it," he admitted.

"Then why didn't you add your two cents?"

"With that vulture? Not on your life."

"Chicken," she accused with a laugh.

He came up to her and put his hands on her waist as
he looked deeply into her mocking green eyes. "You
did an eloquent job," he insisted.

"And you could have helped me out."

He touched her lightly on the nose. "Not true, beautiful lady. I think my presence here would only add
fuel to the rampant fires of gossip."

"I wouldn't worry too much about that. It seems as
if those fires are blazing pretty well with or without
you."

Brig laughed and his eyes twinkled. "It's good to
see you smile again," he whispered. "You handled
yourself very well and I'm proud of you. What brought
about your sudden change of heart?"

"Marian Gordon's holier-than-thou attitude might
have had a lot to do with it. I suddenly realized that I
had to put my life back in order with or without Dean."

"Are you sure you can do that?" he asked, serious concern clouding his sharp features.

"I hope so. I can't believe that he would sell out to a cheap scandal sheet like the *Stateside Review,*" she fumed.

"There were quite a few things you couldn't believe about your brother," he whispered, folding her into his arms. She sighed as she leaned against him.

"The worst is that I was so easily duped. God, what a fool I've been."

"Becca, we've all made mistakes. This whole thing about Sentimental Lady colored everyone's judgment. Besides, it's not stupid to love someone or care about them the way you did with Dean."

"Unless you become blind to their flaws."

Once again he smiled. Dear God, she thought she could die looking at the warmth of his smile. "Are you blind to mine?"

"I don't know," she whispered against his chest. "Do you have any?"

"Why don't you tell me . . ." His finger touched the gentle pout of her lips, forcing them apart so he could run it along the serrated edge of her lower teeth. She touched the tip of it with her tongue and the salty impression started a yearning deep within her.

He groaned and his hand lowered to the neck of her sweater. "You're the one who's perfect, lovely lady," he stated in a rough whisper. His hands gently cupped a breast through the lightly ribbed fabric of her sweater, while he softly kissed her eyelids. Feeling the weight of her breast in his palm, his throat went dry with sudden arousal. "Marry me," he pleaded. "We've run out of excuses and out of time."

His voice was as persuasive as the tips of his fingers

running lightly over her nipples. He gently lifted the sweater over her head and let her naked torso crush him. "Marry me and end this torment," he coaxed.

"You're right," she agreed with an acquiescent sigh. "We have run out of time. I need you." She let her fingers twine in the coarse strands of his dark hair. His gray eyes held her bound. "We've waited much too long . . . let too many things come between us. I was just too stupid to understand that I have to be with you."

"The one thing you're not, Rebecca, is stupid." He cocked his head as if to study her. "Strong-willed and determined, yes. Stupid? Never!"

His lips found hers in a kiss that was savage with passion yet gentle with promise. His hands slid lightly over her body as he undressed her in the unhurried time of a patient lover. His fingers caressed her breasts as if they were new to him. They explored and demanded, creating restless yearnings that made her impatient in her hunger for him.

Warm blood ran in her veins until she could think of nothing but the quiet mastery of his hands on her body and the unyielding desire building within the most feminine depths of her being. She burned for him, ached for his touch.

His movements were slow as he gently pushed her onto the burgundy carpet and savored the sight of her white body stretched against the dark pile. His palms rubbed against her breasts until they tightened in anticipation of the warmth of his mouth covering her nipples. She was not disappointed and gasped in pleasure when she felt the gentle bite of his teeth against her supple breast.

She duplicated his movements. After removing his

shirt, she traced the hard line of his muscles with the tip of her finger, past his shoulders, down his chest to stop at the waistband of his jeans. He encouraged her by moving over her and pressing his abdomen closer to her fingers. "Undress me," he commanded, the ache within him burning to be released.

Deftly she removed his pants and let her fingers and gaze touch all of him, delighting in the feel and the sight of all of his lean, hard length. She quivered at the feel of his firm flesh against hers.

"It's your turn," he announced in a voice thickened with awakened passion. "Make love to me." Quickly he reversed their positions, pulling her over him.

A slow smile crept over her lips as she kicked off the rest of her clothes and lay the length of her body over his. She let him guide her with his hands, while slowly she pressed against him, coaxing the fires within him to burn wildly in his loins.

"I love you," he murmured, letting his impassioned gaze rove restlessly while he watched her eyes glaze with the desire flooding her veins. He watched her stiffen over him and knew the moment she really wanted him, needed the fulfillment. Then he let go, giving into the rising tide of passion roaring in his blood.

Brig arched up to meet Becca, while his hands pushed her tightly against him. They erupted together in a heated flow of molten lava that began in their souls and ran into each other as their combined heartbeats echoed the thrill of spent love. Spent, they collapsed together.

Becca lay quivering in his arms, exhausted and refreshed at the same time. After a few moments of silence broken only by her shuddering sighs, Brig spoke.

"I meant it, Rebecca," he reaffirmed. His grip on her tightened. "I want to marry you and I won't take no for an answer."

"I'm not foolish enough to deny you, my love," she whispered into his ear. "I think I've wanted to marry you from the first moment I met you."

He grinned at the memory. "Then let's not wait. Get up and get going." He gave her a playful slap on the buttocks to reinforce his impatience.

"Today? Right now? Are you crazy? I'm not ready—"

"Idle excuses, woman," he joked with a mock scowl. "We've waited too long to stand on ceremony. Neither one of us has any family to speak of—not close, anyway. Reno is only a few hours' drive. We could be married by this evening."

She held her hands up, palms stretched outward. "Wait. Everything's moving too fast for me. What about the farm? Your business? Gypsy Wind?"

"I've considered everything," he confirmed, tossing her the slightly wrinkled clothes. She caught them along with the satisfied twinkle in Brig's dark eyes. "The first few months will be rough. There's no denying that much. I'll have to spend some of the time in Denver. But I've already decided that I can work just as well from the San Francisco office."

She wasn't convinced. "But that's still a three-hour drive from here—"

"A lot closer than Denver. Anyway, it will have to do until we can fix this place up properly. Then I'll have an office in the house and only make the trip into the city a couple of times a week. If I'm needed in Denver—really needed—I can fly there." He jerked his jeans on and buckled the belt with authority. "Any other questions?"

Becca struggled into her clothes. "Sounds like you have it all worked out," she observed with more than a trace of awe in her voice.

"It's something I've been thinking about for a long time."

"Since when?"

"Since the night I found you on the doorstep to my father's cabin," he admitted roughly and Becca felt a wayward pull on her heart. He seemed so genuinely earnest. "I just didn't think I could convince you."

She had begun to slip into her sweater, but stopped. A wanton smile pulled at the corners of her mouth and she dropped her eyelids suggestively over misty green eyes. "Why don't you try convincing me again?" she suggested smoothly.

His dark eyes sparked at the game. "You *can* be a capricious little thing can't you?" He crossed the room and stood over her, daring her to respond.

She rose to her full height, and then stretched to her toes in order that she could whisper into his ear. "Only with you, love. Only with you."

Chapter 14

The ceremony uniting Brig and Becca as husband and wife was simple and to the point. A dour-faced justice of the peace and his round sister performed the rite in Reno. Rebecca had never been happier than she was that day, holding onto Brig's strong hand and unashamedly letting the tears of joy run down her face. Although she had always envisioned a large church wedding complete with an elegant white lace dress, Becca felt resplendent in her pale pink suit and ivory silk blouse. Brig stood proudly beside her, wearing his crisp navy suit and slightly crooked smile with ease. For the first time in years, Becca knew that everything in her life had finally come together. She had even managed to push aside her lingering doubts about her brother for the time being. These few precious moments belonged to Brig alone. In the glittery town of Reno, Nevada, tucked in a valley rimmed by dusty hills, she had become Brig's wife.

Smiling contentedly to herself, she leaned against Brig's shoulder as he drove westward. A lazy sun had sunk below the horizon and twilight descended as they

headed through the mountains. Aside from the soft
hum of the car engine, the quiet of the oncoming night
remained undisturbed. In the purple sky, shimmering
stars winked in the dusk. Time seemed to have stopped
and Becca was only conscious of the strong man who
was now her husband. For years she had dreamed of
marrying Brig, and determinedly pushed those dreams
into the darkest corners of her mind. Now the marriage
had become reality and she sighed contentedly with
the realization that nothing could ever drive Brig away
from her.

Their time together was much too short. After spend-
ing a carefree week making love to Becca at Starlight
Breeding Farm, Brig was forced to return to Denver.
He couldn't put off his responsibilities as the head of
Chambers Oil.

Days on the farm without Brig seemed long and
empty to Becca. She was restless and the pleasure she
usually derived by immersing herself in work was
missing. She couldn't help but wonder what Brig was
doing or when he would return to her. She lived for the
short telephone conversations that bound them together. Though there was more than enough work to
keep her busy at the farm, she felt a deep loneliness en-
velop her and she impatiently counted the hours until
his return.

For the most part, Brig's time was spent on air-
planes between Denver and San Francisco. The challenge of moving the headquarters of a corporation the
size of Chambers Oil was monumental. Though Brig
had originally hoped that the transfer would take only
a few weeks, he soon discovered that it would take
months to accomplish his goal of resettling Chambers
Oil on the West Coast. His impatience grew each day
he was separated from Becca.

Becca and Ian continued to work daily with Gypsy Wind. Slowly the temperamental filly seemed to be settling into a routine of early morning workouts. When Brig was on the farm, he, too, would add his hand at trying to shape the skittish horse into the finest racing filly ever to set foot on a California racetrack. It was a slow and tedious job as Gypsy Wind had her own opinions about racing. Without Ian O'Riley's patience and love for the filly, Becca would have given up. But the feisty trainer continued to insist that Gypsy Wind was born to run in the sport of kings.

The remodeling of the buildings around the farm had started and Brig insisted that a security guard be posted round the clock to watch the barns. Becca had argued against the need for the guard, but had finally agreed when she was forced to consider Gypsy Wind's welfare. Brig convinced Becca that Gypsy Wind was a celebrity who needed all the protection available. The horse could be an easy target of a malicious attack aimed at anyone involved with Chambers Oil or Sentimental Lady. Ian O'Riley concurred with Brig, and Becca was forced to go along with his decision.

After the first few uneasy days, Becca recognized the worth of the security guard. The press had been hounding Becca day and night, and with the patient but insistent aid of the guard, Becca was able to keep the hungry reporters at bay. It was hard for Becca to retain her composure all of the time, and the press seemed adamant for a story, especially Marian Gordon. The cool reporter for the *Stateside Review* returned to Starlight Breeding Farm in search of a new angle on Gypsy Wind. The perfectly groomed Marian unnerved Becca, but she managed to hide her unease. Becca reminded herself that she was partially to blame for the furor. Not only had Dean's confession brought Sentimental

Lady's tragedy back into the public eye, but the fact that Becca had married Brig Chambers had fanned the already raging fires of gossip concerning Gypsy Wind. Brig Chambers was one of the wealthiest men in the country, his father and a beautiful young model had recently perished in a traumatic plane crash, and Brig had once denounced Becca publicly—or at the very least refused to come to her defense. Everything touching Brig Chambers was hot copy for the scandal sheets and the press was frantic for any insight, real or fabricated, into the relationship between Brig and his wife. Gypsy Wind and her famous owners were suddenly the hottest story of the year. It was no wonder that the eager reporters weren't easily discouraged. Dean had been right when he had predicted that Becca was begging for trouble by breeding Gypsy Wind.

Throughout most of the ordeal, including Dean's trial, Becca had managed to appear outwardly calm and only slightly perturbed. Though she smiled rarely in public, the security of Brig's love had given her the strength to deal with both the reporters and their insensitive questions. It was only when someone would ask too personal a question about her brother that her green eyes would darken dangerously and she would refuse to answer. Dean still refused to see her and it would take years to heal the bitter sting of his rejection.

Gypsy Wind's first race was held in Sequoia Park. Brig had arranged his schedule in order to witness the running. Though the race was a little-publicized maiden, the crowd was expectant, largely due to the well-publicized fact that Gypsy Wind, a full sister to the tragic Sentimental Lady, was entered. If Brig's confidence wavered, it wasn't apparent in his casual stance or the fire of determination in his eyes. He held Becca's trembling hand in the warm strength of his palms as he watched Gypsy Wind being led to the starting gate. Gypsy Wind's moment of truth was at hand and it seemed to Becca that the entire world was watching and holding its breath. Even Ian appeared nervous. His face remained stern and lined with concentration as he shifted a match from one corner of his mouth to the other.

Gypsy Wind entered the gate without too much trouble and Becca sighed in relief when the nervous filly finally settled into the metal enclosure. Within minutes all of the stalls in the gate were filled with anxious fillies. Suddenly the gates clanged open. Gypsy Wind leaped forward and a big chestnut filly slammed into her so hard that Gypsy Wind nearly stumbled. Becca's heart dropped to her stomach as she watched her game horse adjust her stride and rally, only to be bumped at the three-eighths pole by another filly.

"Dear God," Becca murmured, squeezing Brig's hand with her clenched fingers.

Gypsy Wind was now hopelessly behind the leaders, but found it in her heart to make up some of the distance and finish a mediocre fifth in a field of seven. "Thank God it's over," Becca thought aloud, slowly releasing Brig's hand. She couldn't hide her disappointment.

Brig's smile slowly spread across his handsome features. "Well, Mrs. Peters," he announced. "I think you've got yourself a racehorse."

Becca shook her head, but the color was slowly coming back to her face. "Do you?"

Ian O'Riley cracked a pleased grin. "That you do, Missy," he replied, as if the question were directed at him. He took off his cap and rubbed his grizzled chin. "That y'do."

Ian was assured of the filly's potential, and although the press crucified the dark horse for her first run, the wily trainer was eventually proven right.

Gypsy Wind's unfortunate experiences during her first race affected her running style for the remainder of her career. After leaving the gate with the field, the fleet filly would drop back to avoid the heavy traffic and possibility of being bumped. With her new strategy, Gypsy Wind managed to win her next race by two lengths and the next seven starts by an ever-increasing margin over her opponents. She followed in her famous sister's footsteps and won all three jewels of the filly Triple Crown with ease. Reporters began to compare her to some of the fastest horses of the century.

Becca was ecstatic about Gypsy Wind's success. Everything seemed to be going her way. The breeding farm was being expensively remodeled, her career as a Thoroughbred horse breeder was reestablished, Gypsy Wind was winning, effortlessly, and most important, Becca was married to Brig. The only dark spot on her life was her brother, Dean. He had been found guilty of criminally tampering with Sentimental Lady and still refused to see Becca. Even during the trial, Dean had refused to look across the courtroom at Becca or even acknowledge her presence. When she had spoken with Dean's attorney, the man had suggested that she forget about her brother until he was willing to face her again. The attorney had promised to inform Becca the minute that Dean wanted to see her.

* * *

It was when the fans and the press began demanding a match race that Becca balked. Although she had half-expected it, the thought of a match race and reliving the nightmare of Sentimental Lady's death unnerved her. She couldn't find it in her heart to put the additional strain on herself and her horse. Already there were rumors of Gypsy Wind challenging the colts and settling the arguments concerning which horse was the finest three-year-old of the year.

In a normal racing year, one or two of the best horses prove themselves in regularly scheduled stakes races. But this year the Triple Crown races were inconclusive. Three different colts ran away with the separate events. Added to the colt dilemma was Gypsy Wind, the undisputed filly of the year. Several tracks had made offers for a match race, supposedly a race that would settle, once and for all, the arguments surrounding the favored horses.

Rebecca remained adamant. She wasn't about to race Gypsy Wind, though the other owners pressured her and the various race tracks were offering phenomenal amounts of money to field the event. The bidding by the tracks for the race was incredible, and added to that cash were offers from sponsors and television networks. With an attraction such as Gypsy Wind and the notoriety that followed her career, the sky was the limit in the bidding game, and the American public demanded the race!

Lon Jacobs, a prominent California promoter, couldn't be pushed aside. He called Becca Chambers each week, hoping to entice her into entering Gypsy Wind in a match race.

"Neither I nor Gypsy Wind have anything to gain

from the race," Becca explained to Lon Jacobs for what seemed the tenth time in as many days.

"What do you mean?" the California promoter asked incredulously. "What have you been working for all of your life, Mrs. Chambers? All those years of breeding champions certainly add up. You may well have the horse of the century on your hands, but no one's going to buy it until she stands up to the colts."

Becca closed her eyes and her fingers whitened around the receiver. "I'm just not interested."

"What about what the racing public demands? You have a certain obligation to the American people, don't you?"

Becca ran her fingers through her blond hair. "I have a responsibility to my horse and my family."

Lon Jacobs coaxed her. "I realize that the money isn't important to you. Not now. But what about the fame? With this one race you could establish yourself as one of the premier breeders in the country."

"I don't know if the race is necessary for that. The entire world knows the potential of Gypsy Wind."

"Potential, yes," he agreed smoothly. "But she hasn't really proved herself."

"I think she has."

There was an impatient edge to the promoter's voice. "Well, then think about Ian O'Riley, will you? He was the one who really bore the guilt for your brother's crime six years ago. He was the trainer who was brought before the board. His reputation was scarred irreparably when it turned out that Sentimental Lady was drugged while in his care."

Becca was silent and intuitively Lon knew he'd hit a sensitive nerve.

"Look, Mrs. Chambers, I think I can convince the

owners of the other horses to agree to a race nearby. That way you wouldn't have to ship your horse all over the country. You could prove to all those people who watched Sentimental Lady run that you knew what you were doing—that Ian O'Riley is still a damned good trainer. And Gypsy Wind would have the home-court advantage, so to speak."

"She doesn't need any advantage."

Lon laughed jovially. "Of course she doesn't. She's a winner, that filly of yours." Becca wondered if she were being conned. "So what do you say—do we have a horse race?"

"I don't know . . ."

"You would be doing Ian O'Riley a big favor, Mrs. Chambers. I think he's done a few for you."

Becca's decision was quick. "Okay, Mr. Jacobs. I'm willing to race Gypsy Wind one last time, against the colts, as long as it's here, at Sequoia. And after that she'll retire. I don't want to hear anything more about racing my filly."

"Wonderful," Lon cooed as he hung up the phone. Becca was left with the uncanny feeling that she might have made the worst decision of her life.

She couldn't hide her unease when Brig entered the room. "Who was on the phone?" he asked.

"It was Lon Jacobs." She managed to meet Brig's wary gaze squarely. "He wants a match race at Sequoia. I agreed."

"You did what?" Brig was astounded and an angry gleam of fire lighted his eyes. "Becca, love, why?"

"It was a weak moment," she confessed, explaining about Lon's arguments for the race.

Brig's jaw hardened in suppressed anger. "I don't think Ian O'Riley thinks you owe him any favors. You've always stood up for him, and Gypsy Wind's career added luster to his. Dean confessed to drugging Sentimental Lady. Ian was absolved of the crime."

"I suppose you're right," she said wearily.

"You know I am!" He shook his head and looked up at the ceiling as if he could find some way to understand her. When his eyes returned to hers they were as cold as stone. "Why don't you face up to the real reason you're racing Gypsy Wind?"

"The real reason?" she echoed, surprised by his sudden outburst.

"This is what you wanted all along, wasn't it? To prove that your horse could handle the colts. Six years ago, Sentimental Lady was beaten, and you've never gotten over it. You still have some goddamn burning desire to prove yourself!"

"Not true, Brig," she argued. "I told Lon Jacobs that Gypsy Wind would retire."

"Right after she races against the colts," he surmised. "What is it with you, Rebecca? Are you a glutton for punishment? Wasn't once enough"—his eyes narrowed savagely—"or don't you give a damn about that horse of yours?"

His biting words slashed her heart. "You don't think she can do it, do you?"

"I don't care if she can win or not. I'm only concerned about you and Gypsy Wind, and I don't like the fact that you were manipulated by the likes of Lon Jacobs!" Rage blazed in his gray eyes and his jaw clenched. Before she could defend herself, he continued with his tirade. "Why take the chance, Becca? You know that match races are hard on any horse . . . whether she wins or loses." His anger began to ebb and he looked incredibly tired. Becca's heart turned over. "Oh, Becca, why?"

"I told you why," she whispered.

"And I told you that you're not being honest with me . . . or yourself."

He reached for the decanter on the bar and poured himself a stiff shot of bourbon before turning back to his den. Becca felt alone and depressed. The reconstruction of the house and the barns was finished, the grounds were once again well tended, but there was a black void within her because she had disappointed Brig. Was he right? Did she still feel the need to purge herself of Sentimental Lady's unfortunate death, prove to the world that her filly could outdistance the colts? She felt the bitter sting of tears burn in her throat. Why had she been so foolish?

In the month it took to arrange the race, Brig and Becca avoided the subject of the event. Perhaps if they chose to ignore the argument, it would disappear. Brig reluctantly agreed to go with her to the track, but he advised her in no uncertain terms how he felt about the race. He was against it from the start and considered it a monumental risk on her part. Even Ian O'Riley, the trainer who had predicted Gypsy Wind's supremacy over the colts, seemed unusually pensive and out of sorts as the day of the race drew near.

From the moment she arrived at Sequoia Park, Becca was enveloped by an eerie feeling. The doubts she had pushed into the darkest corners of her mind resurfaced. She should never have agreed to the race, or she should have insisted upon another track instead of the very same place where Sentimental Lady had run her last horrifying race. Though Gypsy Wind had raced before at Sequoia, a thousand doubts, plus Brig's fears, came to rest on Becca's slim shoulders. She attempted to tell herself that it was her imagination, that she shouldn't let the feeling of *déjà vu* take hold of her, but the noise of the crowd, the hype of the race, and the poised television cameras added to her overwhelming sense of unease.

Ian O'Riley was concerned. The tension in the air had affected Gypsy Wind. Though she had never been as nervous as Sentimental Lady, in the last two days Gypsy Wind had appeared distressed and off her feed. The veterinarian hadn't found anything physically ailing the horse and yet something wasn't right. Ian O'Riley wrestled with the decision of scratching her from the race. In the end, he decided against it. This was the filly's last chance to flaunt her speed and grace.

The day had dawned muggy, with the promise of rain clinging heavily to the air. It seemed difficult to breathe and Becca felt a light layer of perspiration begin to soak her clothes. Storm clouds threatened in the sky and the shower of light rain started just as the horses were being led to the gate. Becca prayed silently to herself. Gypsy Wind seemed to handle the adverse weather and entered the starting gate without her usual fuss. That fact alone disturbed Becca. The filly wasn't acting normally—not for her. Brig took Becca's sweaty palm in his and for a moment their worried gazes locked. *Dear God, what am I doing,* Becca wondered in silent concern.

The starting gate opened with a clang and the four horses escaped from the metal enclosure. Becca's heart leaped to her throat as she watched Gypsy Wind run gallantly, stride for stride, with the colts. Instead of hanging back as was her usual custom, the blood-bay filly galloped with the colts, meeting the competition head-on. Determination gleamed in her proud dark eyes and her legs propelled her forward as her hooves dug into the turf.

In the back stretch, two of the colts pulled away from her, their thundering strides carrying them away from the filly and the final horse, who was sadly trailing and seemed spent. Becca's concern increased and her stomach knotted painfully, although she knew she was watching Ian O'Riley's strategy at work. The ex-jockey had decided to let the two front runners battle it out, while his horse hugged the rail. Gypsy Wind had plenty of staying power, and Ian knew that she would be able to catch them in the final quarter.

The dark filly ran easily and Becca noticed the slight movement of the jockey's hands as he urged Gypsy Wind forward. Becca's throat tightened as the courageous horse responded, her long strides eating up the turf separating her from the leaders.

As Gypsy Wind made her bid for the lead, the outside colt bumped against the black colt running close to the rail, jostling the ebony horse against the short white fence. Gypsy Wind, caught behind the two colts, stumbled as she pulled up short in order to avoid a collision.

The crowd witnessed the accident and filled the stands with noise, only to quiet as it watched a replay of the tragedy of seven years past. The jockey attempted to rein in Gypsy Wind, but she continued to race, plunging forward as she vainly attempted to catch the colts.

Becca's face drained of color. Seven years of her life rolled backward in time. "No!" she screamed, her voice lost in the noise from the stands and the address system. "Stop her, stop her," Becca begged as she pulled away from Brig's grip. A horrified expression of remorse distorted Becca's even features and tears flooded her eyes. "It can't be . . . it can't be!" she cried, stumbling after her horse.

One horse was disqualified, and Gypsy Wind had finished a courageous third. Becca felt Brig's strong hands on her shoulders as he guided her toward Gypsy Wind. The jockey had dismounted and Ian O'Riley was running practiced hands over the filly's forelegs. Cameras clicked and reporters threw questions toward Rebecca. She ignored the press and was thankful for Brig's strength throughout the ordeal.

Ian nodded toward Becca as she came close enough to touch the filly. "I think we might have a problem here," he admitted in a rough whisper.

"Oh, God, not again . . . not again," Becca prayed.

"Excuse me!" The veterinarian was at the horse's side within a minute after the race was over. Quickly he examined Gypsy Wind's leg and issued terse directives that the horse was to be taken to the nearby veterinary hospital. The horse attempted to prance away from the noise and confusion, but was finally taken away amid the shouts and oaths of racing officials, attendants, and the television crews.

Brig tried to comfort Becca, but was unable to. Guilt, like a dull knife, twisted in her heart. It was her fault that Gypsy Wind had raced. Likewise Becca was to blame for the horse's injury.

The waiting was excruciating, but didn't take long. It was quickly determined that Gypsy Wind would recover.

"It even looks like she'll be able to race again," the veterinarian admitted with a relieved smile. "She pulled a ligament in her left foreleg. It's only a slight injury and she'll be as good as new," the kindly man predicted with a sigh. "But she won't be able to race for the rest of the season."

"Or ever," Becca vowed, tears of gratitude filling her eyes. "She's retiring—for good."

"That's a shame," the veterinarian observed.

"I don't think so." She took the vet's hand and shook it fondly. "Thanks."

Brig put his arm over her shoulders. "Let's get out of here," he suggested. "Ian's staying here and there's no reason for us to stick around. If he needs us, he can call."

"Are you sure?" Becca didn't seem certain.

"Aren't you? You're the one who always had faith in Ian. He'll take care of the Gypsy."

They walked out of the hospital together and were greeted by a throng of reporters.

"Mrs. Chambers . . . how is Gypsy Wind?" a dark-haired man asked as he thrust a microphone in Becca's direction.

"She'll be fine," Becca replied with more conviction than she thought possible.

"But the injury?" the man persisted.

"A pulled ligament—the vet assured me it's nothing too serious."

"Then you do plan to race her again?"

Becca paused and her green eyes looked into Brig's before she turned her self-assured smile back to the reporter. "Not a chance!"

Slowly, Brig was guiding her to the car. The thick crowd of reporters followed closely in their wake, shouting questions at them. When they finally made it to the Mercedes, Brig turned on the crowd, and the irritation in his eyes was only partially hidden. "Perhaps if you asked your questions one at a time," he suggested.

It was a strong female voice that caught Becca's attention and she found herself looking into the knowing eyes of Marian Gordon.

"Mrs. Chambers," Marian greeted coldly. "How do you feel now that you know you almost killed Sentimental Lady's sister the way you killed her?"

Becca bristled, but felt Brig's strong hand on her arm.

"No one killed Sentimental Lady, Ms. Gordon. It was an unfortunate accident."

"Not an accident—your brother drugged that horse," Marian responded. "Was that with or without your knowledge?"

Brig took a step forward, but Becca held him back with the gleam of determination in her eyes. "What happened with my brother is very unfortunate, Ms. Gordon, and has nothing to do with me, or Gypsy Wind. It's also old news. I suggest that you try writing something a little more topical."

"Such as how Gypsy Wind almost went to her grave today?"

"Such as how that brave filly stood up against the colts."

Before Marian could respond, another reporter edged forward and smiled fondly at Becca. "Mrs. Chambers, do you plan on breeding a sibling to Gypsy Wind?"

"No."

"But you still will be breeding Thoroughbreds—for the future?" the young man insisted. Becca cast a speculative glance in Brig's direction. His eyes were riveted to her face.

"I'm not sure—not right now."

"How do you feel about it, Mr. Chambers?" the young reporter asked, turning his attention to Brig. A smile tugged at the corners of Brig's mouth.

"I think my wife will make her own decision. She's a very . . . independent woman," he observed with a twinkle in his eye. "Now, if that's all—"

The reporters realized that they had gotten as much of a story as they could and reluctantly backed away from Brig's car. Once inside the Mercedes, Becca managed a weak laugh. "So you think I'm independent?"

"Not totally, I hope."

"What's that supposed to mean?"

Brig maneuvered the car away from the racetrack and drove toward the hills surrounding Starlight Breeding Farm. "That means that I'd like to think that you depend on me—some of the time."

"You know that I do." She paused slightly. "What about you, Brig? Do you depend on me?"

His smile turned into a frown of disgust. "More than you would ever imagine," he admitted. "I don't know how I got along without you for the last six and a half years. I must have been out of my mind."

The rest of the journey was finished in silence. Becca bathed in the warm glow of Brig's love. When they pulled through the gates guarding Starlight Breeding Farm, Becca felt her heart swell in her chest. The new buildings, freshly painted a gleaming white, stood out against the surrounding green of the hills.

Brig helped Becca out of the car and they walked to the closest paddock. Two mares were grazing peacefully while young colts scampered nearby. The horses raised their inquiring heads at Becca and Brigg, flicked their dark ears and turned their attention back to the grass. The colts ran down the length of the fence, glad for an audience. As ungainly as they appeared, there was a grace in the sweep of the colts' legs.

Becca leaned her head on the top rail of the fence. "I don't know if I can give this up," she sighed, studying the graceful lines of the colts' bodies.

"I haven't asked you to."

"But I can see it in your eyes." She turned to face him and caught the look of tenderness in his eyes. "I do love you," she admitted, throwing her arms around his neck.

"No more than I love you."

"But you want me to quit breeding horses and racing them," she accused, smiling sadly.

"Not at all, Becca. I just want you to slow down. You've proved yourself today and purged yourself of Sentimental Lady's tragedy. Go ahead and breed your horses—race them, if you want. But slow down and enjoy the rest of what life has to offer."

Slowly his words began to sink into her tired mind. She cocked her head coquettishly to the side and her shimmering honey-colored hair fell away from her face. "Just what do you have in mind?" she asked as she observed him with an interested smile.

His eyes darkened mysteriously. "I thought I might be able to convince you to forget about breeding horses long enough to consider having a child."

Her dark brows arched. "Oh you did, did you?" she returned, touching his chin lightly with her fingertips.

"We've waited too long already."

"I might agree . . . but tell me, just how do you propose to convince me?"

"With my incredible powers of persuasion, Mrs. Chambers—" His head lowered and his lips captured hers in a kiss filled with passion and promise. She closed her eyes and sighed as she felt her bones melt with his gentle touch.

"Persuade away, Mr. Chambers," she invited, her eyes filled with her overwhelming love. "Persuade away."

"Dear God, lady, I love you," he whispered as he scooped her into his arms, straightened, and carried her toward the house. "And I'm never going to let you get away from me again."

With his final vow, he opened the door, carried her inside, and turned the lock.

**Please turn the page for an exciting sneak peek of
Lisa Jackson's newest thriller
OUR LITTLE SECRET
now on sale wherever print and e-books are sold!**

Chapter 1

Seattle, Washington
October 2022

"How far would you go?"

Gideon's words stopped Brooke short. She was already late and she felt the seconds ticking by. Turning in the small cabin of his sailboat, she found him where she'd left him, lying on his bed, his tanned body entangled in the sheets, dark hair falling over his forehead.

"What do you mean?"

He pushed himself upward, levering on an elbow, muscles visible beneath his tanned skin, gray eyes assessing. As if he knew. Outside a seagull cried, and she caught its image flying past masts of neighboring sailboats, then skimming over the gray waters of the bay.

Tell him. Get it over with. End this now!

"For something you wanted," he said, and he wasn't smiling. "How far would you go?"

"I don't know." She finger combed her tousled hair, then started for the short flight of stairs leading to the deck. "Pretty far, I guess." She glanced at her watch. "Look, I really have to go."

Tell him.

"Wait." He rolled off the bed, and she noticed his tattoo, a small octopus inked at his nape, barely visible when his hair grew long. He caught her wrist, spinning her back to face him. A little over six feet, he was lean and fit, his skin bronzed from hours in the sun. "Why don't you ask me?" he said and he leaned down to touch his forehead to hers. His fingertips moved against the inside of her wrist and his pupils darkened a bit. *Tell him!* that damned inner voice insisted. *Tell him now!*

"Ask you?"

"How far I'd go."

Her heart started beating a little quicker, his fingers so warm, the boat rocking slightly under her feet. "Okay," she said, and hated the whispery tone of her voice. "Okay. How far would you go?"

"For something I wanted? For the person I was supposed to be with?" His gaze locked with hers and the breath caught in the back of her throat. The walls of the boat's tiny cabin seemed to shrink, and for a heartbeat it was as if they were the only two people on earth. He leaned close and whispered in her ear, "I would do anything." She swallowed hard.

He repeated, "*Any*thing."

"Anything?" She couldn't keep the skepticism from her voice.

His gaze held hers. "If I had to, I would kill."

Seattle traffic was a nightmare.

And she was late.

Of course.

Not only had she chickened out and not told Gideon

that what they'd shared for the past few months was over, she was running late. Again.

"Come on, come on," she said, as much to herself as to the other drivers in the snarl of vehicles clogging the streets. She drove her SUV through the knots of vehicles, slipping from one lane to another, then turning her Explorer onto a steep side street, hoping to avoid the crush heading to the freeway.

"Come on, come on," she muttered as she caught up with a huge red pickup that inched forward. She glanced at the clock on the dash. She was supposed to be at the school in five minutes. At this rate it would take an hour! She pounded on the horn just as they reached a construction site.

The pickup, laden with a load of cordwood, eased past the orange cones guarding a wide hole in the asphalt as a bearded construction worker held up a stop sign. Though his eyes were shielded by aviator sunglasses, he glared at her through the windshield, daring her to try to slip past.

She didn't. Waited. Impatiently drummed her fingers on the steering wheel while a monstrous backhoe, alarm beeping, backed into the street, then moved forward. It was a warm day for October in Seattle, sunlight streaming through her dusty windshield. And the backhoe seemed to inch its way across the street.

"Oh, come on!"

She wouldn't make it.

Especially now.

Great.

"Damn."

She picked up her cell phone and texted her daughter: **Running late. On my way.**

How many times had she typed in those exact words

and sent them to Marilee? At least once a week, often times more. Especially recently.

Marilee, all of fourteen, no, wait, "almost fifteen," would be pissed.

So what else was new?

Spewing exhaust, the backhoe inched forward, a hefty driver working levers to scrape up huge chunks of concrete and asphalt. In what seemed like slow motion, he swung his bucket high into the air, then tilted it to pour his load into the box of a massive, idling dump truck.

The minutes ticked by before the backhoe started moving out of the street and into an alley.

"Finally."

Her cell phone rang. Startling her.

Then she realized it wasn't her cell, not the one registered on her family plan with Neal and Marilee but her other phone. The burner. Not connected to her Bluetooth. The secret phone no one knew about. No one but Gideon. She flipped open the console, scraped out the bottom of the small space, and found the burner. Yanking it from its hiding space, she glanced at the screen.

She didn't recognize the number.

"What the hell?"

She answered abruptly, her foot easing up on the brake. "Hello."

A pause.

Her SUV started rolling forward.

"Hello?" she said sharply again.

The street cleared and the flagger turned his sign from Stop to Slow.

A rough, whispered voice was barely audible over the rumble of engines and shouts of men on the work crew. "He's not who you think he is."

"What?" she said, straining to hear. "Who's not—who is this?"

The call disconnected.

Her heart sank. Someone knew! Oh God, she'd been found out.

She blinked, staving off a panic attack. No one was supposed to know. No one did. Of course no one did. The call had to be a mistake. Someone who had punched in the wrong numbers. That was it. Sweat began to moisten her fingers and she mentally kicked herself for not having the guts to break it off earlier. She hadn't even found the courage to tell him today.

"Chickenshit," she grumbled. "Coward."

The flagger was motioning her through, frantically waving his arm, but her mind was on the message. What if it wasn't a wrong number? What if someone knew? Oh God.

She stepped on the gas, her heart pounding, her pulse pounding in her ears.

This couldn't be happening—From the corner of her eye, she saw a blur of yellow, a sports car speeding around her, cutting her off.

"Jesus!" she cried, nearly standing on the brakes as the disgusted workman kept waving her through, though he gave the yellow car a shake of his head.

But the Porsche was already through the construction zone and caught at the next light. "Idiot!" she muttered under her breath, driving forward, hoping to make the light as it started to turn green.

The burner jangled again.

What the hell?

The same unknown number showed on the screen.

Oh. God.

She answered sharply. "I don't know who you are, but you've got the wrong number!"

A pause, and then the whispered voice: "I don't think so, Brooke."

The caller knew her name?

"Who is this?" she demanded, frantic. Oh no, no, no . . .

"He's not who you think he is." The voice—male? Female? Old? Young? She couldn't tell. "You'd better be careful—"

Bam!

The front end of her Explorer slammed into the back of the sports car with a horrendous crunch of metal and plastic.

Her body jerked.

The seat belt snapped hard.

"Shit!" She hit the brakes, dropped the phone, her pulse shooting to the stratosphere.

The Porsche screeched to a stop.

The car behind her—a white boat of a thing with an elderly man at the wheel, his wife beside him—stopped within an inch of plowing into her. The driver looked up, startled. In front of her, the guy in the damaged Porsche jumped out of his car and strode to her window.

"What the fuck?" he yelled, his face all kinds of red, his jeans and black T-shirt faded and worn over a large, burly frame.

As she rolled down her window a little further, he yanked the hat from his head and threw the Mariners cap onto the pavement. "You fuckin' hit my car!"

Her mind was racing, her breathing shallow. "You started to go, then stopped."

"So what? You're supposed to have control of your vehicle. You hit me, lady!" He jerked a hand toward the curb. "And if you'd been paying attention, you would have noticed, a kid—that kid—was playing with a ball near the curb!" He stabbed a finger at the boy—four or five years old from the looks of him—staring at them with wide, frightened eyes. "The ball rolled into the street," the driver explained and she peeked past his angry body to see a basketball still rolling slowly on the pavement in front of a stopped van in the opposite lane. "I thought the kid might run after it. Jesus, what are you? A fuckin' moron?"

There was no way to deny it. When she looked to the near side of the street, she saw an older woman dragging the kid into an apartment house.

"You're just damned lucky he didn't chase the fuckin' thing!" The driver was still ranting. "Cuz if he did? And I didn't hit him? You sure the hell would have."

Her heart knocked painfully. He was right. She'd been so distracted by the phone call, by Gideon, by all of her messed-up life that she hadn't been paying attention. At least not enough attention.

But it would be fine—just some twisted metal. Nothing more. Nothing life-threatening. Thank God.

She peered up at him. "Are you okay?"

"Do I look okay?" he demanded, his bald head glistening in the sunlight, wraparound sunglasses hiding his eyes. Beneath a two- or three-days' growth of beard, a muscle in his jaw was working overtime.

"I don't know."

"Well, I'm not. Thanks to you. And my car! Shit, I just got the temporary plates removed! Brand-new and now—Now? Fuck!" He stripped off his sunglasses and looked about to throw them as he had the cap, then thought better of it and pushed the mirrored shades back onto the bridge of his nose. "Do you know what this is?" he said, jabbing a finger at his car. "Do you?"

Before she could answer, he filled her in. "It's a fuckin' Nine-eleven! Did you hear me? A fuckin' Nine-eleven."

"Got it!" she shot back, her temper spiking. She gritted her teeth and tried to remain calm, even though this jerkwad was punching all of her buttons and her nerves were frayed to the breaking point.

The man in the white behemoth of a sedan had stepped onto the street. "We saw the whole thing," he shouted from behind the open car door. "If anyone needs a witness. Aggie and I saw it all." He motioned toward his wife, sitting stiffly on the passenger side of his Buick.

"Are you all right?" Brooke asked, yelling out her open window as other cars eased past them. "And your wife?"

"Yeah, yeah, we're both fine," the old guy said, flapping a hand.

Thank God.

To the angry driver, she said, "I think maybe we'd better pull over," noting the crowd that had gathered on the edge of the street. "Get each other's information."

"Fuckin' A," he said. "You're goddamned right we're going to do that! You're fuckin' gonna pay for this!" He motioned to his car before jabbing a finger at her face. "This is on you." Then he yanked his phone from his pocket, snapped a picture of her Explorer's license plate before motioning jerkily to the parking lot of a strip mall across the street. "Over there," he ordered.

He swiped his cap from the street and jammed it onto his head. As he climbed into his car, he shot her a look guaranteed to cut through steel.

"Ass," she said under her breath and watched as he

rammed his sports car into gear before roaring across a lane of traffic to nearly bottom out as he hit a speed bump in the parking lot.

Served him right. Yeah, she was at fault, but the guy was being a jerk about it. She slid her Explorer into a parking slot in front of a FedEx and got out of her vehicle to survey the damage. The front bumper was destroyed, crumpled beyond repair, a headlight cracked, and who knew what else? But the Porsche had fared worse, a huge dent in the back end, paint scraped away, the hood creased.

"Jesus, would you look at that," the driver said, stalking to the back of his car and shaking his head at the dented metal, twisted to the point that she caught a glimpse of the engine. "I'm lucky I can still drive it. The engine's in the back, if you didn't know."

"I do know." From what she could see, the engine didn't appear to be damaged.

"Who taught you how to drive?" he asked.

Her temper flared hotter and her back stiffened. No way would she tell him she learned to drive a tractor at eleven, a truck for the fields of her uncle's farm at thirteen. None of his business. With an effort, she held her tongue. *Don't get into it with him. It's not worth it! You have other problems to deal with, bigger than this ass's car.* "Let's just exchange phone numbers and information," she suggested as evenly as possible.

"But it's all your fault. You rear-ended me."

"I get that," she shot back, her temper snapping. "Okay? I was there!"

"Good." He started back to his car.

"But you don't have to be a prick about it."

He whirled, his face contorted. "What did you say?"

"That you don't have to be a prick." She'd had it

with the jerk. "Yeah, the car's a mess. Mine too, but what's done is done, so let's just get down to business."

"'A mess?' Do you have any idea how much this car costs?"

"A lot. Yeah, I know. But yelling at me about it won't help."

"'Yelling at me won't help,'" he singsonged back at her.

She bit back another hot retort, refused to be baited any further, and took a picture of her insurance card with the camera in her phone. Out of the corner of her eye, she saw people collecting on the curb. "I'll text this to you. What's your number? Oh, and send me yours."

Grudgingly, jaw set, he rattled off his cell number and she, ignoring the curious looks from cars and trucks driving slowly by, typed it in. "I'm Brooke Harmon."

"Jim Gustafson. But James. Legally. It's James."

"Got it."

"Good, so, you know, when you hear from my lawyer."

"Great. Your attorney can contact mine: Neal Harmon."

He stiffened slightly, obviously catching the connection.

She filled him in anyway. "My husband."

He frowned slightly and she felt a second's satisfaction, then she offered Jim—legally James—a cold smile and sent the text before glancing up from her phone again and spying her distorted image in the lenses of his sunglasses. "We'll let the insurance companies sort it out."

"Not much to sort. Remember, I got witnesses. I

took pictures of the license plates of the cars that were nearby. And that old guy and his wife in the Buick? They saw it all." Gustafson's smile was smug. Proud of himself.

"Good. Then we're done here." She only hoped it was true as she caught a glimpse of the flashing blue and red lights of a police cruiser in her mirror.

Visit our website at
KensingtonBooks.com
to sign up for our newsletters, read
more from your favorite authors, see
books by series, view reading group
guides, and more!

Become a Part of Our
Between the Chapters Book Club
Community and Join the Conversation